Manassas Battlefield p. 1
November 13, 8.

A CALL TO HONOR

A CALL TO HONOR

Cynthia Adair Coan

Pentland Press, Inc.
www.pentlandpressusa.com

PUBLISHED BY PENTLAND PRESS, INC.
5122 Bur Oak Circle, Raleigh, NC 27612
United States of America
919-782-0281

ISBN: 1-57197-316-8
Library of Congress Control Number: 2002101608

Printed in the United States of America

This book is dedicated to the memory of Corporal B. H. Campbell, Company C, 52nd Georgia Infantry Regiment, and Lieutenant James A. Adair, Company F, 8th Georgia Regiment, CSA.

It is also dedicated to my husband for his constant encouragement and to my mother, who made *all* of this possible.

FOREWORD

No greater love hath man than that
he lay down his life for a friend.

Heroes. In the world of the twenty-first century they are in short supply for the youth of our country. *A Call to Honor* reminds young adults of the decisions that the people of the past faced. Decisions made at a time of war, when the fate of many—including the nation—hung in the balance.

Jeremiah McCamey represents the "everyman" of the Southern army. He and main characters Cyril Ash and Jeptha Carroll chose patriotism, honor, duty and loyalty in fighting for the Confederacy. Like their real counterparts of 1861, home and family were the main reasons for going to war, and why men fought. Homesickness, camp diseases and death are obstacles the characters must overcome. Though the book is fiction, it is authentic in every sense in capturing the life and times, and emotions, of a typical Confederate soldier of 1861-1865.

Through Jeremiah and his comrades, another message is conveyed which has not lost its significance to present and future generations. The importance of heritage, and a continuity of the book characters' past is an example to our young people. No American should ever feel ashamed of his or her heritage. It is part of what made this country great.

Unfortunately, an ignorance of the American Civil War pervades our society. Public schools shun teaching history. Inaccurate information appears in textbooks at an increasingly common rate. In fact, most Southerners did not own slaves. Contrary to what is presently believed, people in the nineteenth century were very aware of the politics and events shaping their lives. They were as a whole intelligent and thoughtful people, not backward and uncivilized.

A Call to Honor is a story of friendship and how war forged a special bond between friends. Through its heroes, it portrays a story of sacrifice, courage and all the best a human being can offer. Youth needs heroes of the past. What better example can we give our children than characters with such qualities.

Mauriel Joslyn
Sparta, Georgia
2002

ACKNOWLEDGMENTS

I have discovered in writing a book that there is no one person who deserves to be thanked, but a myriad of people.

My husband, Howard W. "Butch" Coan, hails from the beautiful Shenandoah Valley of Virginia. His roots there are tap roots. It is in tribute to him that I chose this setting for *A Call to Honor*. My gratitude to him knows no bounds. He was behind me when the load got heavy and my plate was full; never allowing me to give up or give in. He has been my friend, my love, and partner in life for twenty years.

My mother, Frances Willis Adair, never failed to foster any of my pursuits in life. I owe my achievements to her and my father, who passed away in 1992. Dad, I wish you were here. I hope you are proud.

Thanks must go to my teaching colleagues; the men and women with whom I work every day. I must especially mention Carla Brown, Kim James and Vickie Owens. Not once have they failed to believe in me.

Tribute must also be extended to J. H. Segars and Mauriel Joslyn. Hank, I will always feel that you opened the door, and Mauriel, what a marvelous mentor you are.

I greatly appreciate the blessing of having a friend in Bobby Horton of Birmingham, Alabama. His inspiration and always cheerful encouragement cannot be discounted, for he helped unleash in me the understanding that words and music have an ardent kinship.

Most of all, my sixth grade students at Clayton Elementary School, I must salute you. Without your enthusiasm this never would have come to fruition. You are the ones who truly motivated me in this endeavor. Never let it be said that teachers do all of the teaching!

CHAPTER ONE

Southerners hear your country calling ye
Up least worse than death befall ye
To arms! To arms! To arms in Dixie!

Jeremiah McCamey stared intently into the parlor mirror, his gray eyes reflecting the storm within his soul. The eldest in a family of four children, he was tall at nineteen and admirably filled out. The hard work of helping to manage their Virginia farm saw to that. His muscles strengthened early and his skin was invariably bronzed. The thatch of unruly brown hair that topped his head was the biggest problem in his life until now.

Well, no, he rethought that one. There had been that crush on Permillia Swilley two years ago. The thought made him sigh.

Living with three sisters wasn't too rough on him, and the entire family worked hard at maintaining the farm. Life was exceedingly self-sufficient.

"I have never had to make a truly difficult decision until now," Jeremiah said out loud to his reflection.

"How quickly things can change, North or South; is there really any question about what I should do?"

He fretfully ran a hand through his untamed crown. "Life is about to take on a drastic change," he brooded out loud. "I'm not sure if I can deal with this."

It was May 1861. Virginia had seceded from the Union, casting her lot with ten other Southern states. The North and the South were poised for war.

Thinking of his two boyhood friends already in the Southern Army, Jeremiah knew Cyril Ash and Jeptha Carroll had joined for Virginia and duty to their state. To a Virginian, duty wasn't merely a word. It was allegiance and respect, an obligation that he absolutely understood.

Virginia's rights as a state must be upheld; her soil must be defended, he thought to himself. He'd make a crack Confederate soldier, of that he had no doubt. He felt the very things his forefathers had fought for in the Revolutionary War were now at stake.

Suddenly his fine statesman heritage came to mind, his own blood a part of making and molding the United States. He slammed his fist onto the table before him. "Should not this Union be preserved?" he questioned, groaning at his inner turmoil. His cousin, Geoffrey Adams, thought so, and he, too, would look the dandy in Union blues. Geoffrey had nothing on him there.

Mulling over his thoughts, he remembered how often they had discussed the boiling political climate of the country during the past several years. He and Geoffrey certainly didn't see eye to eye on all things. The issue was more than merely the preservation of a nation, and it had all to do with the very rights of her citizens being threatened; wrested away.

Jeremiah's heart stuck in his throat as his reflection stared back at him. Thinking once more of Geoffrey and the heritage they shared, he suddenly lost all doubt as to what he must do.

There is really only one choice for me, he mused. *Tomorrow I will go sign those enlistment papers.*

The silence was broken by a smile he could almost hear. Turning, he looked upon his sister, Priscilla, standing in the parlor door. With dark curls and fawn colored eyes, she presented a picture of loveliness, even if she was his sister.

"Jeremiah, what are you doing?" she admonished him. "I thought something had fallen, or that Bonniejean was into mischief of some sort!"

Giving her a crooked smile, the boy peered once more at his reflection in the glass. "Would you look at my hair? It's as tousled now as it was when I was thirteen."

Walking up to him, the girl rumpled his wavy thatch. "Nah, it's kind of nice," she said with affection. "I know lots of girls who would give anything for such hair," she teased.

"Now look at what you've done! It's worse than ever!" he declared, making a pretense of smoothing it down.

"Jeremiah, my dear brother," she sighed, placing her arm about him, "the trouble is not your hair. I haven't seen that look on your face since the fine Miss Permillia jilted you last year."

"Two years ago," he corrected her adamantly, staring at the reflection they made.

"Well, whatever," she shook her head. "Jeremiah, I know of the distress in your soul. I can see it there; and I dare say it must be this whole idea of war."

"'Cilla," he laughed nervously, "I could never hide much from you, could I?"

Jeremiah and the eldest of his three sisters had always been close. Barely a year apart in age, a strong bond existed between them. He loved Violet and Bonniejean, but the fondness he felt in his heart for Priscilla was unmatched. Squeezing her shoulders, determination sounded in his voice.

"I know what I must do, 'Cilla. I'm going to volunteer tomorrow; I'm going to enlist to fight in the army. There may be some tears, but I must do what is honorable; what I know is right. I cannot just sit by and watch things happen. I must do my part. Too much is at stake."

Sighing, Priscilla looked up at him. "Jeremiah, you need not tell me what you have decided. We're too much alike. Your desire may be for the Union to be held together; you're like cousin Geoffrey in more ways than one. But your heart is with Virginia, I know. You are too much like me.

"Oh, the abolitionist can talk of the slave issue. I suppose some actually want to believe that to be the root of the problem, and we'll not change their minds. But Jeremiah," she said, crossing her arms to indicate her seriousness, "we've never owned one servant; and we know far more people who have not one slave than who do. I have to choose the South simply on principle. It is not the slave issue; we all know that. It's only that we are not industrialist; our culture depends on the yield of the earth, and we hold fast to our faith in God. No government of men has the right to tell Virginians what is good for Virginia!

"Besides, what are we expected to do? Just sit aside while Abe Lincoln calls for 75,000 troops to invade our land? I think not, Brother! We have declared ourselves as part of a new and independent nation, and it must be defended if necessary." With a shake of her head, she smiled. "But I'm not telling you anything you haven't already thought through yourself . . ."

"Prissy dear," he said, addressing her by his pet name for her, "you ought to be joining up with me!" Hugging her again, he whispered, "You would put many men to shame."

Priscilla threw back her head in a laugh. "I don't know about that, Jeremiah, but you have chosen well." She placed a palm on his cheek. "God be with you, my dear brother. Father will certainly be pleased . . . Mother

. . . well, she has that Adams blood in her . . . but I know deep down her heart is with ours. After all," she murmured, "we are her children."

Turning to walk off, she looked back at him. "Supper will be ready soon, Jeremiah."

"God bless dear Priscilla," he found himself saying into the mirror. "What would I do without her?"

~

Supper proved to be a solemn affair. As plates were filled and grace was said, Jeremiah looked at each face gathered around the table.

"I have something to say," he abruptly announced, standing. All fell silent as eyes turned to him, and he cleared his throat, hesitantly. "Father . . . Father, I know we have talked much about present circumstances in Virginia; in the South. You have told me more than once that you could not advise me as to what I should do; that I should listen to my heart and mind until they speak in one accord . . . well, I don't suppose there has ever been any real doubt as to what is required of me. My heart and my mind both tell me the same thing; they have from the beginning, but I was afraid to listen; afraid of . . . well, I suppose I have been afraid of many things. But I can no longer pretend that I do not know what course I should take. We are Virginians. We are Southerners. I know how each member of this family feels. It is in all of your eyes; in each conversation, and we all feel the same way. I suppose . . . I suppose I kept hanging on to a thread of hope that it would all work out somehow; that the United States would remain united; that the government in Washington would some way strive to put an end to this madness it has caused. I am well aware now that such is not to be. There is only one thing I can do. Virginia has made her stand, and so must I. Tomorrow I am going over to Staunton to enlist. I stand with my state, my new country and her new government. It is not, to be sure, without fault, but it does offer higher hopes than anything Mr. Lincoln can promise.

"To fight in defense of our land, and winning independence for the Confederate States, is the only prospect I have of seeing an end put to unfair taxes and broken political promises. It is the only hope I see for the survival of constitutional government as our forefathers intended. I am for union, but not at any cost; and the price has already become too dear. I, I . . ." Sucking in his breath, he realized he had run out of words. "Well, I suppose that is all I have to say," he finished, sitting back down.

Suddenly clanging her fork against her plate in the ensuing silence, sixteen-year-old Violet turned her sparkling blue eyes to her brother.

"Jeremiah," she announced with excitement, "I will make you the handsomest gray uniform you ever did see!"

Stifling a cry, Mother instantly fled from the table with Father in pursuit. The four left sitting there exchanged wide-eyed glances until Jeremiah rose.

"This is my fault," he said somberly. "I'll go talk this over with them. I reckon I should have done that to start with."

"Jeremiah, no. Leave them be," Priscilla demanded curtly. "They just need some time to take all of this in; mainly Mother."

Sitting back down with trepidation, he knew his sister was right.

"This will create some drastic . . ." she shrugged her shoulders as she looked him in the eyes, "changes in our lives, Brother. Please give them some time to take it all in. I know Father is proud of your decision. Mother will adjust, too. Her tears aren't for your choice, Jeremiah, but simply that she doesn't want her only son off fighting a war on either side."

All at once, Bonniejean began to cry. At eight years of age, the unfolding scene overwhelmed her. Startled, Priscilla jumped up to comfort the child.

"Sweet one, what is wrong with you?"

Hugging her hard, Bonniejean whimpered. "I don't want Jeremiah to be a soldier," the child sniffled. "I don't want him to die. He'll leave and then won't never come back because a Yankee will shoot him!"

Standing and scooping the crying child into his arms, Jeremiah took her from the room as she clung tightly about his neck. Whispering words of comfort to mingle with her sobs, quiet giggles were soon heard.

Smiling at each other, Violet and Priscilla acknowledged the tender side of their brother. "What do you suppose prompted Bonniejean's outburst just now?" Priscilla questioned her sister as they began to clean up the uneaten meal.

"I know exactly, 'Cilla," responded Violet. "It came right from the mouth of Mr. Plessont."

Being employed on and off for several years by the McCamey's as a tutor, the elder Frenchman and ex-professor had several grandsons desiring to join the Confederate Army. It was well known by many that this had been his response to them all.

"Well, I shall speak to Father about this," Priscilla said in agitation. "The very idea that he should be filling a child's head with such nonsense."

With misting eyes, Violet looked at her older sister. "Is it nonsense, 'Cilla? I have a feeling," she whispered dismally, "that life is never again going be the same."

~

No one slept well that night in the McCamey household, least of all Jeremiah. Up long before dawn, he was ready and waiting to ride out by the time the rest of the family stirred. "I should be back by nightfall," he called to them, taking off down the road.

The town of Staunton and the Confederate camp were a good three hours distance, and Jeremiah looked forward to the ride, needing a chance to be alone with his thoughts. Eagerly anticipating a reunion with his friends, he hoped for the opportunity to spend time with them.

Thinking of the scene played out some weeks earlier, Jeremiah grinned. Jeptha and Cyril had bid him a pleading farewell, both boys ready to serve Virginia the minute she seceded.

Joining the call to arms as soon as it was issued, Jep and Cy considered Jeremiah's thinking confused and unfocused. All three boys had hotly discussed the plight of the state, and all shared the same convictions. Yet he felt it best to wait, and hope that the problems would yet be peacefully solved. And although they implored him to come along, they respected his decision.

Anxious to see them, his excitement ran high. He desired to swap tales with them, and give them news of home. Most of all, he was eager for them to know that he, too, could only go the way of Virginia. There was not, and had never really been, any other choice. He was ready to sacrifice his life for his new country if need be.

Shortly after midmorning, his horse's hoofs clattering into town, Jeremiah noticed evidence of the army camp everywhere. Passing throngs of soldiers going and coming, milling about, he felt an excitement in knowing he was soon to be a part of it all. Asking directions to enlistment headquarters, he shortly found himself inside.

The captain on duty looked up from his books with a hearty friendliness. "Come to sign up, have you?" he asked.

"Yes, Sir!"

"Well, Virginia needs all of her men," he stated with conviction, thrusting a paper into Jeremiah's hands. "Sign or put your X-mark here," he tapped the appropriate line.

Jeremiah wrote out his signature with great deliberateness.

The captain grunted. "Can write, can you? Much educated?"

"Studied under Mr. Maurice Plessont, a former professor at Charlottesville," Jeremiah shot back proudly.

"Good," the man smiled broadly, writing something on his enlistment card. "This will fare well for you. Many who sign these papers can only do so by marking their X."

Suddenly a loud "YEE-HA!" sounded from the doorway, and Jeremiah turned to look at a grinning, familiar face. Immediately he was grabbed in a bear hug.

"I knowed it! I knowed it! I says to Cy the other day, I says, ol' Jeremiah will be along . . . he's as fine a Virginian as any. You jus' wait an' see. He'll be along!'" Clapping Jeremiah on the back, the young man's voice grew thick with affection. "Gee, it's good to see you. How is everbody?"

Turning to the captain before Jeremiah had a chance to answer, Jeptha addressed the officer. "Captain Harris, this fellow must be placed in Company G!"

Narrowing his eyes in obvious irritation, the captain replied through clinched teeth, "Company I is the one being formed now, Private!"

Suddenly growing sober, Jeptha saluted the man. "Yes Sir, Captain! But Company G has room and we need this man, Sir!"

Looking from one to the other, the officer sighed as he considered the request. His first impression of Jeremiah was quite favorable. "Humph," he muttered. "It is true that Company G is a mass of young ruffians most in need of extra and capable leadership. Very well, then. You have spoken true, Private. Perhaps your friend here will prove to be more of a soldier than you seem to be. Now, you're late, and there is much work here to see to!"

Gazing at his friend fondly, and the captain respectfully, Jeremiah arched his eyebrows in surprise, addressing them both. "You working here at enlistment headquarters, Jep? This soldier is an aid to you, Sir?"

"Hardly!" grumbled the captain. "I mean to say he is hardly a soldier and certainly of no aid to me!"

Jeremiah threw back his head in laughter. "Too bad I wasn't here first, Sir. I would have warned you!"

"Actually, Private Carroll here is merely fulfilling a sentence." He glared at Jeptha. "A punishment, if you will."

"What have you done now?" Jeremiah turned to his friend with a half amused, yet knowing voice.

Answering for him, Captain Harris growled. "You might ask Sergeant Wilton that question. He's the one Private Carroll punched out!"

Staring at Jeptha, Jeremiah shook his head incredulously, and replied to the captain, "Well, Sir . . . it's not the first time that hot-head of his has gotten him into trouble . . . but now I tell you true. If you'll allow me to have him for the rest of the morning, he will return by the dinner hour and work twice as hard to make up for lost time. And I tell you also, Captain, Sir, that hot-head will get cooled off."

Not able to resist the seriousness in Jeremiah's voice, the officer relinquished Private Carroll to the care of the new enlistee for the remainder of the morning. There was something about this new volunteer that he liked and trusted. "Mr. McCamey, report back here in six days to begin your duty to Virginia and your country."

Jeremiah saluted the officer. "It will indeed be my pleasure, Sir."

Grabbing Jeptha by the arm, he pulled him along as they parted company with the captain. "I can't believe you, Boy! That hot-head of yours is gonna get you killed even before you get a shot at any Yank! Don't you think you can exercise a little self control?"

Jeptha shrugged. "Shucks, Jeremiah. When you ain't around to keep me in line what d'ya expect?" he grinned.

Shaking his head, Jeremiah laughed. "How many scrapes have I saved you from during our lives, Jep? I can't even begin to count.

"Now, where's Cy?" he demanded enthusiastically. "Won't he be a sight for sore eyes!"

"Aw, Jeremiah . . . it's the other way around! Sight o' him is liable to make your eyes sore!"

Jeremiah guffawed, Jeptha looking at him indignantly. "Well, it's the truth I tell you now. He thinks soldierin' a good excuse to be purtied up all the time."

Being as different in temperament as they were in appearance, the three young men were an unlikely trio. Yet not one of them could remember a time when they had not been friends. From their youngest days the boys had hunted together, played together, worked together and shared one another's secrets.

Jeremiah, tall and strong, with his bronzed good looks and unruly brown hair, courted a reputation for seriousness that often belied his personality. Although his steel gray eyes mirrored determination, they frequently twinkled in sly merriment, and his sprightly laugh could often be heard.

Steadfast and committed, Jeremiah's pragmatic thought easily earned him the confidence of others. Friends habitually turned to him when seeking sound advice.

Jeptha Carroll, though not as tall as Jeremiah, was just as strong and handsome. Able to charm anyone with his animated smile, his recently grown thick mustache added an air of maturity to his looks that he, indeed, did not possess. With hair the color of winter chestnuts, his brooding brown eyes gave the only indication that he was impetuous to a flaw.

Jeptha's way of dealing with trouble was to act now, and think about it later. Other's simply called him "hot-headed."

Life, anything but kind to this nineteen-year-old, saw parents, two sisters and a brother, succumb to a smallpox epidemic when he was a child. Remembering little of his family, Jeptha was raised by an elderly uncle with whom he sometimes clashed.

Different from his two friends, Cyril Ash was blond headed, blue eyed and mischievous. Possessing an infectious sense of humor, Cy could always be counted on to find an amusing side to things.

Though not as tall as his two friends, what he lacked in height he made up for with his sublime, good looks. In an effort to appear more the soldier, Cy, like Jeptha, had recently grown a mustache. It only added to his dandy appearance.

People found it difficult not to like Cy. He was an only child, raised by his mother. His father had died before he was born. Such circumstances instilled in him an affectionate nature that included great compassion for others.

Ending all too soon, the day drew to a close. Having thoroughly enjoyed time spent in the company of his friends, Jeremiah's blood thrilled to the thought of soon being part of all he'd seen and heard. Jep and Cy readily assured him that army life looked more exciting that it was.

"You just wait 'til you're told what you can do, what you can't do, when to go to sleep, what to eat, and if you can go out and about. Now that'll cause you to think long and hard 'bout fightin' for some freedom!" Cy laughed to him. "Can't do nothin' without somebody's permission to do so, and the only good thing about these here chaffing uniforms is that they make the lady folk look at you more'n once or twice."

Jep nodded his head in agreement. "Hee, hee," he laughed. "I've 'bout decided that's the only reason Cy joined up in the first place."

Meeting some of the men in Company G caused Jeremiah consterna-tion as he headed for home. Several appeared surprisingly unruly. How was it Captain Harris had referred to them? "A mass of young ruffians," he recalled, sighing.

At least he had extracted a promise from Jep to keep his hot-head under control. Giving his word to Captain Harris, Jep promised them both to serve out the remainder of his punishment dutifully and without event.

It was not quite dusk as he arrived back at the farm. Tired, dusty and hungry, he hoped he wasn't too late to sup with the family, for his days to enjoy such were now numbered.

Putting his few personal affairs in order made the next week pass quickly. Arranging for help on the farm in his absence proved the most difficult task. Jeremiah hoped the young boy he found would be able to shoulder his chores, for much of his eight dollars a month soldier's salary would be sent home to pay the youth.

~

The night before leaving, Jeremiah bid a heavyhearted farewell to his family. Spending time with each member of the household, he shared his dreams for the future of their new country, and his sorrowful thoughts of what he feared real war would bring.

"Mother and Father have worked hard to bring us up on their convictions of faith, freedom and honor," he lamented to Priscilla. I tremble at the thought of how this war bearing down on us will put these principles to test."

Riding off in the wee hours of darkness before dawn broke, he wanted to depart before the rest of the family rose. Saying his good-byes had been difficult, and quite a few tears were shed. He could hardly control his own feelings. He didn't want the added burden of bearing the emotions of those he so loved. Even with no one to witness his departure, he found the task difficult.

Taking a last look at the farm, Jeremiah noted its two-story, clapboard and whitewashed house appeared strangely still at such an early hour. He tried to etch it all in his mind: the green rolling hills, now black silhouettes in the faint moonlight, the barn, the small corral. He loved this valley of his birth, and the rich soil that yielded lavishly of whatever seed one had a mind to sew in it.

Late May always created pleasant smells around the farm, and even now, as he breathed deeply, he could detect the sweet smell of hay coming in; the apple blossoms from the small orchard on the hill; the oil used to tan hides and maintain tools. The thought loomed deep and well in his mind. *It may be a long time before I lay eyes on all of this again. Indeed, it may be never.*

His heart stirred with an odd sort of pride. Yes, it was true he may never see home again; may never kiss his mother's cheek or shake his father's hand. He may never have another chance to comfort his child sister, or stroke the honey-colored hair of the lovely Violet. He may not ever have another long conversation with his beloved Prissy.

But were these not the very things he was riding off to defend and secure? He wiped away a tear with the back of his hand. He had considered these questions well, for they made him aware of what he must do. The thought gave him comfort.

"Giddy-up!" He spurred the horse down the road, thinking of the decision with which he had finally come to terms. He was indeed with cousin Geoffrey in his aversion to the United States being torn asunder. But Union was no longer an option, so he must do his part to achieve Southern independence.

As he put the farm behind him, he mulled over thoughts of his cousin. As much as they were alike, in many ways they were very different. Geoffrey firmly believed that the Union of the states could not be risked, while he felt passionately that the federal government had no right to decide what was and was not best for the citizens of a state.

Then there were those matters of unjust taxes; an unfair burden placed solely on some southern states . . . and land disputes; so many things that infringed upon basic constitutional rights.

Not seeing things the same way, Geoffrey considered it an act of treason when Fort Sumter was fired upon in April. Suddenly leaving his classes at Washington College, he went North, all fire and fury. Going to the home of his mother's relatives, Geoffrey enlisted in a Pennsylvania regiment with the full support of his family.

Jeremiah grimaced as he thought of their last meeting. It had not been a pleasant affair. "You gotta come with me, Jeremiah," Geoffrey insisted. "We cannot allow this country to be divided!"

"Geoff, you know I can't do that. Not yet, not now," he answered. "Surely the leaders in Washington will work out some kind of peaceable solution. I don't think North or South either one wants this war. Not really."

"But Jeremiah, an American fort was attacked by those troops in South Carolina. How can you sit by and let such a thing happen?"

"Well, Abe Lincoln certainly didn't help by sending out troops and heavy arms ships under the guise of provisions. Them soldiers at the fort weren't starvin'. Fresh food and mail was taken out to them everyday. Charleston couldn't help but look on it as a threat. It was either fire upon Fort Sumter or be fired upon. You need to think things through, Geoff, before you go marchin' off. I understand your reasons, but I ain't able to make such a decision."

"Jeremiah," he cried in exasperation, "our own state is harboring thoughts of withdrawing from the Union. Do you really want that?"

"No," Jeremiah shook his head, "but neither do I desire to live under an oppressive, tyrannical government. Lots o' things lately ain't been done accordin' to the Constitution, and that's what worries me some. I can't tell you what my decision on taking sides is, because I have got to think things through. That's what you oughta do, Geoff."

"Cousin," Geoffrey said flatly, "you're a traitor."

"Ah, Geoff. C'mon! You know me better than that!"

"All I know is that you refuse to preserve our Union of States."

"I ain't said that Geoffrey. But at least I ain't so impetuous as to take up arms against my own people. It just rankles me that you're so enthusiastic to do so."

"Then I guess I don't have anything else to say to you, Jeremiah."

"Guess not."

As Geoffrey stuck out his hand for a final shake, Jeremiah was ashamed of the bitter words they had exchanged. He could not help but feel their brother like relationship had been forever altered.

Even as Jep and Cy departed as volunteers for the South, Jeremiah felt there was still much to consider. A smile came to his face as he remembered Cy's parting words: "No time to think things through, Jeremiah. There's plainly nothing to think about. Duty calls! Virginia, ho!"

He would forever remember that moment, Cy heading down the road at full gallop, his straw colored hair whipped back by the wind. He was screaming for all he was worth. "Join us, Jeremiah! Do it for what your people believe in!"

He looked forward to once again being with his friends. He yearned for Cy's sense of humor and missed keeping hot-headed Jeptha out of trouble. "I fervently hope Jep has honored his word to Captain Harris and kept his temper in check these last few days," he muttered to himself. "If I'm gonna fight in a war, I want friends with level heads next to me; not impulsive and unbridled souls."

Sighing, he truly didn't know if Jeptha could ever change.

～

Soon the sun began to peek over the hills, illuminating the mist in the valley to create an eerie, ghost-like phenomenon. Jeremiah thought of his family beginning morning chores back at the house, and felt strange knowing he was no longer a part of it all. A wave of depression washed over him as he realized he might forever be leaving behind the life he'd always known.

Up ahead in the distance, he discerned the flickering light of a carriage lantern, now yellow and unobtrusive in the early morning sun. As the horses' hoofs pounded closer and the wagon began to slow, he immediately recognized the rig. Starting to acknowledge the familiar face behind the reins he stopped short.

The voice called out to him, "Why, Mr. McCamey, what a surprise to see you out and about so early!" Her honey colored curls bounced as she poked her head out from the carriage awning. The movement caused his heart to flip then flop, and he felt his face grow scarlet. This was the last thing he expected or wanted. Intentionally ignoring the lovely face, he hailed the driver.

"Good day, Cubby. And how would you be faring this fine morning?"

"Can't complain, Sir," the man answered with a toothy grin. "Hear you is off to fight. Thought maybe you was gone by now."

Jeremiah glanced unwillingly at the face under the awning, and the eyelashes batted, long and beautiful. He tried to avert his gaze.

"Well, I'm . . . I'm on my way now," he stammered. "Kinda in a hurry." He hoped the man would beg his pardon and let him continue on, but it was not to be. "They be expectin' me over at camp pret' nigh soon," he tried to say with urgency.

Cubby, however, didn't notice his hurry.

"Miss Swilley here, now she say she's got to go see your sister this mornin'. Says it's mighty 'portant. Reckon it must be," he yawned, "her gettin' up and out so early and all."

Jeremiah had yet to recognize the young lady, so finally he tipped his hat. "Miss Swilley," he mumbled curtly.

"Now Jeremiah, don't you go Miss Swilleyin' me! Why . . . you have never called me anything but Permillia," she cried indignantly, "or Millie." She smiled sweetly. "Remember how you used to sometimes call me Millie?"

"Things do change, Ma'am," he replied bluntly.

"Cubby, help me down. I would like to have a word with Mr. McCamey."

The driver nudged the horses to the side of the road while Jeremiah watched the scene in despair. He did not want to talk to Permillia.

Before Cubby could crawl down from his seat, Permillia leaned over, offering her hand to Jeremiah for assistance. "Mr. McCamey, surely you have not forgotten how to be a gentleman already," she said demurely. "I hear that's what happens to men who go soldierin'; that they become perfect barbarians!"

"Thanks, Permillia," he said sarcastically as he was forced to dismount and take the hand offered to him. "I don't reckon I've had quite enough experience to have become one yet."

"Walk this way with me, Jeremiah." Her voice was as smooth as silk when she spoke, and he felt his knees grow weak. Inwardly, he groaned.

He thought he was over all of his feelings for her . . . he could not let them come rushing back. Not now.

She took his elbow and he let his horse's reins drop free. Liking the feel of her hand on his arm, he could smell the sweet, sweet scent of her perfume. "What business could you possibly have with Priscilla today?" he inquired of her.

"Who says it is Priscilla I am going to see?" she answered, looking up at him.

"Well, I know it's not Violet. She doesn't like you, Permillia."

"Jeremiah McCamey! How hateful of you! I shan't tell you who I am on my way to visit!"

Jeremiah shrugged his shoulders. He really didn't care.

"Permillia . . . what is it you want? I really do have a schedule to keep."

Pulling him off to the side of the road, she whispered, "I heard you were leaving today. I wanted to give you something." Reaching into her sleeve, she pulled out an embroidered handkerchief. It was folded around something small and light, and she pushed it into his hand. "This," she sighed with a smile, "so you won't forget me."

Suddenly Jeremiah understood; she wasn't going to visit either of his sisters. It was merely a ruse to catch him before he was gone. Looking into her velvety blue eyes, he felt almost sorry he was leaving. Taking the handkerchief, he placed it into his breast pocket.

"I . . . got . . . I've really got . . . I've really got to go, Permillia," he stumbled over his words. Feeling embarrassed, he shook her hand from his elbow. "Thank you. It was very kind of you to think of me," he finished.

She placed a hand on his arm. "Jeremiah . . . I . . . I . . . I really do wish you well," she stuttered quickly.

Taking her wrist in his fingers, he removed her hand from his arm. He felt determined not to let her sweep him off of his feet. No. Never again. "I've got to go, Permillia," he said, aware of the sarcasm in his voice. "You really are too kind." He bowed deeply at the waist, and rising, looked again into her eyes. Placing his hands gently on her shoulders, he leaned down toward her face. Instead of what Permillia expected, he whispered with scorn, "And how many other soldiers . . . oh! Excuse me . . . you called us barbarians, I believe . . . have you sent off with such a memento?"

Permillia drew up her fists in anger and he heard the crack before he felt it. Hard and sharp her open hand struck his face.

"Jeremiah McCamey," she shrieked through clinched teeth, "how dare you! You should know you're the only one I'd wish to be remembered by!" She stormed off, her breath coming in furious gasps.

Jeremiah placed a hand to his cheek. It smarted. He couldn't resist calling after her, "Permillia! Why don't you enlist? A few whacks like that at some Yankee faces will surely win the war for us in short time!"

Mounting his horse, he turned back down the road, pushing the animal to a gallop. Permillia had already cost him precious time and he wanted to be well ahead of her carriage should she return home by the route she had taken. He refused to look back for some time. Finally doing so, he was satisfied that he had the road to himself again.

He slowed his horse to a walk. After letting several more minutes pass, he couldn't resist pulling the handkerchief from his pocket to peek inside. The sweet scent of Permillia's perfume wafted up to him, and he breathed in the heady scent from the linen. For a moment he was overtaken with sorrow for the scene that had transpired between them. How utterly lovely she was! He was sure there was no more beautiful girl in all of the Shenandoah Valley, perhaps the entire state of Virginia.

Unwrapping the handkerchief, he delicately held up a perfect, golden curl. Quite surprised, he whispered out loud, "A lock of her hair . . . her beautiful, silken, hair." Pangs of regret began to overwhelm him. How often had he dreamed she'd really care? Suddenly he pulled the reins tight on his horse, bringing the animal to a halt. Gently lifting the golden strands, he let them dangle in the soft morning breeze, his heart skipping a beat.

"No. No," he whispered to himself. "I'll not for one moment fall back into her trap. What once could have been between us was over a long time ago."

Before he could change his mind, he delicately blew the golden strands from his fingers, the morning wind snatching the perfect curl piece by piece and scattering it in a hundred different directions. He watched the tendrils dance away.

Balling up the sweet scented handkerchief, he started to throw it to the ground. Instead, he quickly stuffed it into his pocket.

CHAPTER TWO

You sent your sweethearts to the war
But dear girls, never mind!
Your soldier boy will ne'r forget
The girl he left behind.

Jeremiah arrived at camp before morning had waned away. Not sure where to go to report for duty, he headed to enlistment headquarters, encountering Captain Harris as he arrived at his post for the day. Jeremiah saluted him. "Jeremiah McCamey reporting, Sir, to begin my duty to Virginia and my country."

Captain Harris snapped back the salute. "Good to see you, Son. Got a little matter I need to take up with you. These here troops will be mustered into duty nigh two weeks hence and we've got a problem in Company G. Captain Kertlin is a good man . . . ah, he's the cap'n of G . . . but those boys! They need to be whipped into shape real bad . . . been here near a month already and whilst some companies . . . even newer ones, have learned some discipline and are startin' to train well . . ." He hesitated. "Let me be blunt, Son. Company G is the bottom right now . . . the men as rowdy and undisciplined as the day they arrived. Maybe worse.

"Kertlin, now he's a Staunton man, and some of the boys just ain't takin' to that too well." Suddenly stopping, Captain Harris looked Jeremiah in the eyes. "I don't feel right, Son, placin' you there. You're decently educated, and if instinct serves me well . . . and it usually does . . . I believe you possess some self discipline these other fellas just ain't got, and

I'm offerin' you the opportunity to join up in one of the other companies, where maybe you'll have a chance of becomin' a real soldier."

In thought, Jeremiah stared at Captain Harris for a moment. "Thank you for the consideration and kind words, Sir. If you'll just point out where I can find Captain Kertlin, I'm here to learn soldierin'. Now, if you'll just tell me where to go. From what I understand from the ladies of Virginia, Sir, soldierin' makes us barbarians. Perhaps those of us that are already barbarians can be made into soldiers."

Captain Harris could not help but laugh at the boy's revelation. "Well put Mr. McCamey," he said, "well put. Across the way there," he pointed, "three rows back you'll find Company G." Turning to walk away, he abruptly stopped. "Tell Captain Kertlin I send you with my compliments, Soldier."

"Very well, Sir. Thank you, Sir."

Captain Harris's barrage of information assaulted Jeremiah's mind. Wondering for a brief moment if he did not, indeed, need to join another company, he could not help but think of Jeptha. He meant to ask Captain Harris if Jep had been on good behavior as promised. "Well, I'll find out soon enough," he muttered, watching his mount being led away. Arrangements were going to have to be made to see that the fine horse returned home, for the animal was essential to the farm. He sighed, and then turned his attention to the rows of tents.

Third row back, third row down, Jeremiah noticed the company flag fluttering from the ridgepole of a tent. Men were milling about outside the canvas shelter, some drinking morning coffee, others dousing breakfast fires. Captain Kertlin proved to be easy to find, as he noticed a tall, thin, young man not much older than himself standing at the tent entrance. Deep in conversation with a lesser officer, both leaders looked unhappy.

Momentarily glancing up, the captain glimpsed at the newcomer. Jeremiah saluted.

"Something I can do for you, Mister?" the officer asked, not returning the salute.

"Yes Sir, if you are Captain Kertlin."

"That I am," he replied wearily.

"Jeremiah McCamey reporting, Sir. Captain Harris says to tell you I'm here, with his compliments, Sir."

His demeanor changed instantly. Captain Kertlin quickly returned the salute, dismissing the soldier with whom he had been speaking.

"I'm sorry. I wasn't expecting you. Company has been formed for several weeks now and it's highly unusual to receive a new recruit once a company has been completed . . . besides, Harris informed me he was placing you among this bunch of . . . should I say, raw soldiers; and then he told me he changed his mind. That would have been a reprieve for you, Private. Ha!"

Looking at the ground, Captain Kertlin sighed. "We've had quite a bit of trouble this week," he muttered seriously. "Some of my boys, they mean well, but there's a great lack of discipline amongst them. Just mountain boys, mostly—rarin' for a fight—but seein' as we ain't fought any Yankees yet, they've just sorta started fightin' each other." He grew silent for a moment before resuming conversation.

"Did Captain Harris send you here?"

"Yes, Sir, but he did give me the option of joining another company first. Truth is Sir, I'm aimin' to serve with some friends. Friends that are part of this company."

"Well, Harris says you're different from most of my boys . . . at least he expects you are. Hope he's right. I must be frank with you, McCamey. Some of my boys got into such a row the other day over . . . well, it's not important what it was over, I reckon, but in the fight that ensued . . ." Captain Kertlin let out a deep sigh and shook his head before finishing. "Well, anyways, one of my boys is dead and another under arrest for it."

Taking in a sharp breath, Jeremiah was afraid to know, but even more afraid not to ask, and questioned his new captain. "Who were these men involved, Sir, if I might inquire?"

"One's a man from over Beverly way. An Irish gent too fond o' gettin' his dander up. He won't be seein' the light o' day again. The other, the one now in the stockade waitin' trial, he's a local spitfire."

Jeremiah puffed out a sigh of relief before Captain Kertlin spoke again. "Say, you don't know either of these fellas do you? I'd hate to be givin' you such news about a friend.

"I'm ashamed to be in command here . . . I can't seem to enforce the necessary discipline and we cannot fight a war with our own men killin' each other."

"Tell me, Sir," Jeremiah asked pensively, "Private Carroll, Jeptha Carroll, he weren't involved in this foray, were he? Seems awful hard for him to stay out of trouble."

"Oh, he's been in his share all right! Punched out a sergeant in Company B couple o' weeks back, but he wasn't involved in this business," he said with a shake of his head. "He did have to work for Captain Harris to pay his due, though. Actually, he seems to have steered free from most trouble as of late."

"Jeptha . . . Private Carroll is a good man, Captain. He works hard when he's got good reason, but he does . . . how should I say . . . tend to overreact sometimes. It's caused him a bit of trouble back home more than once. But he will be of good service to you, Sir, if he can learn a little of the discipline the army means to instill in us.

"What about Private Ash, Sir, Cyril Ash?"

Throwing back his head, Captain Kertlin laughed. "Now, that's a fella I'm truly fond of. I've never known anyone who can find a comical side to everything like Ash can. Made me laugh plenty o' times when I shoulda been about my business serious like. All the fellas are fond o' him. I never knew a soldier so bent on lookin' the part!"

"Oh, just wait 'til you see what my sister has fashioned for him, Sir. We'll all probably get to where we can't stand the poor soul."

Violet, in her effort to make Jeremiah's handsome uniform, had not forgotten his two friends. To Jeptha she was sending a fine pair of gauntlets cut from white leather, but for Cy she had sewn a linen sash, infantry blue in color, and trimmed with gold fringe. It was sure to make his uniform as fine as any Napoleon had dared wear, and it confirmed for Jeremiah a suspicion recently garnered. Violet was especially fond of the handsome Cyril.

~

Slapping Jeremiah on the back, Captain Kertlin pushed him in the same direction he began walking. "How old are you, Son?"

His fatherly manner amused Jeremiah. "I'm nineteen, Sir." With no thought of propriety, he added, "And you, Captain Kertlin?"

"Son, I'm not much older," he laughed. "I'm afraid I'm only twenty-three."

"If you don't mind my asking, Sir . . . how'd you come to be Captain?"

"I'd just graduated from the Military Institute down in Lexington when the Yankees got so audacious. Seemed like t'weren't no other choice but to join up in the Staunton Militia right away. Staunton's my home. My learning at the institute promoted me directly to the rank of Captain in exchange for drumming up enlistments.

"Where you from, McCamey?"

"Oh, about three hours ride east of here. Family owns a farm in the New Church district, not far from the Albermarle County line."

"Much family?"

"Besides Father and Mother, I have three younger sisters."

Captain Kertlin whistled through his teeth. "That must be tough. Myself, I've got six other brothers, four younger and two older and no sisters. Military seemed a natural choice. Pa's a lawyer here in Staunton. Not much choosin' when you're competin' with six others. Can't all be lawyers. Four of us now wear the gray, but I'm the only one with no formal legal training and schooled for a military career. How long did you sign up for, McCamey? Twelve months?"

"No, Sir! During the war. Once I made my mind up I meant for it to stick!"

"Well, it won't last more than twelve months," Captain Kertlin replied thoughtfully. "We'll have those Yanks on the run after the first fight. Then they'll be ready to make peace."

The two men walked down quite a length of tents before the captain stopped at one. "I like you McCamey. I hope we can be friends."

"Four others bunk here in this tent. You may be more comfortable elsewhere, but I'll leave that to you to work out."

Without warning, Captain Kertlin stuck his head into the opening flap. "Anderson, Carroll, Ash, Parker!" he bellowed. "Out here. On the double!"

One lone head popped out. "Shucks, it's only you, Cap. I thought it was somethin' important!"

Grabbing the man by the collar, Captain Kertlin pulled him out of the tent. "At attention, Soldier!"

The young boy immediately stood rigid, saluting the captain, and eyeing Jeremiah with suspicion.

"Yes, Sir!" he cried.

Kertlin returned the salute. "At ease, Parker. Where are the rest of your renegade friends?"

"Aw Cap'n, I'm no nursemaid! How should I know? Anderson said he was goin' to find someone to write a letter for him before mornin' drill. I dunno where Ash and Carroll are, but you can count on 'em bein' together, that's for sure."

Jeremiah bristled. If this was an example of the men in Company G, he might be forced to rethink his position. He hadn't even been introduced to this man Parker and already he didn't like him.

Captain Kertlin jerked his thumb toward Jeremiah. "This here is Jeremiah McCamey. Count on him bunkin' with you'ns.

"McCamey, I leave you in questionable hands," the captain grunted as he turned to walk away.

Saluting his new leader, Jeremiah watched him move on, and then he found himself facing a scowling Parker. Finally the man broke the silence. "Company G is already formed, Mister. What are you doing here? That namby-pamby Kertlin some friend o' yours?"

"I hope he'll be," Jeremiah answered. "You have a problem with that?"

Parker again eyed him suspiciously. "This tent's already full up. We don't want another man." He gestured to the long row of canvas. "There's others to choose from. Be my guest," he huffed curtly, disappearing back inside.

Without being invited, Jeremiah pushed through the tent flap into the dark interior, depositing his few belongings on the ground by the door. "If it's all the same to you, I choose to stay here," he said to a glaring Parker. "At least, for now."

To Jeremiah's surprise, Parker merely shrugged his shoulders as he continued to down a cup of coffee. Then tossing the remnants out the door, he threw his tin cup down on a blanket, leaving.

Suddenly, the new recruit heard musicians strike up a familiar tune. "The Bonnie Blue Flag" was a favorite song among Southerners, and he stepped outside to listen to the music. Immediately a sergeant approached him.

"You McCamey?" he asked.

"Yes, Sir." he saluted, "I'm McCamey."

"I'm Sergeant Spruill. Cap'n sent me here, that is Captain Kertlin, to take you to the quartermaster. You're to be examined by the surgeon and issued a uniform and arms. Follow me."

Thinking of the fine gray uniform Violet had sewn for him, he hesitated. No, that was special. He'd save it, he decided, for more appropriate wear.

Following Sergeant Spruill, Jeremiah heard the first of many bugle calls that would come to regiment his life in the next few years. Quickly falling into rank, most men began to drill. It was a fascinating sight, and as he tried to keep pace with the sergeant, he couldn't help but be drawn to watching the men execute various commands: Forward, MARCH! To the rear, MARCH! About FACE! Left FACE! Right FACE! March by the FLANK! Left oblique, MARCH! Right oblique, MARCH! SALUTE!

⁓

The surgeon pronounced Jeremiah quite fit for duty and he was issued an infantry gray uniform trimmed in blue, along with a brand new rifled Enfield musket. Starting to feel like a soldier, he wondered if he would be able to learn all the drilling commands he witnessed earlier.

As he returned to the tent, a bugle call announcing the midday meal sounded. Beginning to question if he would ever encounter Jep and Cy, his doubt was short lived when an unseen hand pounded him on the back hard enough to knock the breath out of him. He gasped.

"Ha! And you wanna fight Yankees!" Cy's blue eyes twinkled as Jeremiah turned around to face the familiar voice.

"Cy! You scoundrel! I heard you was off paradin' around for the ladies in town," Jeremiah spoke laughingly.

Cy punched him in the arm. "Well, now, who done told you that? I don't need to go paradin', Jeremiah. The ladies just naturally flock about to see such a purty soldier like me!" he chuckled. "Glad you's here, Jeremiah."

Another voice pierced the ruckus in camp. "Howdy! Jeremiah! Howdy-do! Ha! 'Bout time you got here! I was beginnin' to think maybe you'd changed your mind and weren't comin' . . . or worse yet, that cousin o' yourn had got the best of you and you decided to go blue on us!"

The new enlistee bowed deeply to Jeptha, brandishing the handkerchief he stuffed in his pocket that morning. "Not on your life, Sir! And . . . I must commend you for the noble report I have received on your behavior since we last met. You, Sir, have proven to be a gentleman of your word!

"Speaking of the finer things, I was privileged to meet up with the charming Miss Swilley this morning as I took leave of home; and to you, Mr. Carroll, she pleaded that I give this fine embroidered and sweet smelling handkerchief as a token of her esteemed and undying devotion."

Jeptha's eyes lit up. "From Permillia? For me?" He took the linen square Jeremiah proffered him and held it up to his face. "Ooo boys! What wonderful parfume. Must be some o' that real fancy stuff from Pair-ee I smell here!" He grinned. "I'm deeply touched. You don't mind, Jeremiah?" he asked, inhaling the scent once again and watching his friend out of the corners of his eyes. "Ooo-ee! Smells divine! No finer token can a lady send a lonesome soldier," he announced dramatically, placing the handkerchief in his pocket. "Sure it don't bother you, Jeremiah?"

"Na," he declared, placing a hand to his face where she slapped him that morning. "She gave me something to remember her by, I reckon." He was almost tempted to tell his friends about the encounter.

"Looky-here!" Cy suddenly yelled out, holding up a handkerchief identical to the one just given to Jeptha. "I got one exactly like it. Only I done fared better than you boys," he chuckled, unfolding it to reveal a perfect golden curl.

Jeremiah nearly burst out laughing.

"The day I left," Cy continued, "Miss Permillia gave this to me. Said she wanted me to have a lock of her hair to remember her by." He held it up. "Ain't it purty, boys? I just ain't said nothin' on account o' . . . well, Jeremiah, we all knowed how you felt about her. She done you purty unfair." He folded the curl back into the handkerchief and replaced it among his belongings.

"Oh! I almost forgot," Jeremiah declared, retrieving from his effects the leather satchel that held his finely sewn uniform and the presents for Jep and Cy. "I have something for you.

"Tell me about this man Parker," he commanded, handing out each gift.

"You met him already?" asked Jeptha.

"Yeah. Weren't none too friendly, either, that's for sure," Jeremiah retorted.

"Oh, don't mind him," added Cy. "He ain't so bad when you get to knowin' him. He just has a chip on his shoulder needs to be knocked off now an' then. Jep's got purty good at doin' it, too. Ain't that right, Boy?" he smacked his friend in the head.

"Quit it, Cy!" Jeptha growled, brushing his friend's hand away in irritation.

"Boys, you two ain't changed a bit," Jeremiah voiced in mock disgust. "I had hopes when y'all joined up in this here army that men would be made out of you. I only see before me the two boys who left home!"

"Go ahead, now. Open them packages before you get into a brawl."

Tearing the paper from his, Cy asked, "You met Anderson yet, Jeremiah, the other fella who shares our fine canvas quarters?"

"Nope," his friend remarked. "Parker was the only one here when Captain Kertlin brought me by."

"Well," continued Cy, "let me tell you 'bout him. Short little fella . . . hair's wilder than yours, Jeremiah. He's from up Monterey way and can't read or write a lick. But, boy oh boy! I ain't never heard no one play the banjo like he can. My! My! Wait 'til you hear!"

Suddenly whistling softly, Jeptha cried, "Would you looka here?"

A proud, but sheepish grin crossed Jeremiah's face. "Violet took a notion to sew me a uniform. Said she didn't wanna leave you boys out."

Jeptha looked at the leather gauntlets admiringly. "Jeremiah, these are fine enough for an officer! You tell Violet I'd save her a kiss if she weren't your sister!"

Awestruck, Cy stood with his gift in hand. "Bless my soul, Jeremiah," he whispered in disbelief, "this is fit for a king." He tied the lovely blue and gold sash around his waist. "There ain't an officer on staff got anything finer." Rubbing his fingers gently across the soft, blue material his eyes shone. "Miss Violet really made this for me?" he questioned.

"Yeah. I asked her the same thing; I couldn't believe it either. She assured me it was true."

"I'll send her my personal thanks, Jeremiah. This is mighty fine, mighty fine. It's the finest gift I do believe I've ever done got."

The new volunteer had no doubt this was exactly the response Violet hoped for.

~

The days passed more quickly than the boys could ever imagine, and Jeremiah found camp life to his liking. Each sun up to sun down was strictly regulated by bugle calls that he soon learned to recognize.

The drilling, somewhat difficult at first, finally became routine, although the men of Company G were not nearly as unified in the exercises as most companies proved to be. Jeremiah quickly excelled in the training, sometimes looking on other companies with longing as he admired their precision at stepping and formation. Not all companies drilled in great order, but most had learned to move together. The one exception was Company G.

No unit looked as poor and disorganized on the parade ground. Finding this frustrating, Captain Kertlin and Sergeant Spruill often took turns about in leading drill. Each time the men were worked a little longer, and a little harder, but usually to no avail. When left flank was called, at least a quarter of the men would form right. If a right oblique was the command, at least as many would sway to the left. The saving grace was that Company G had mastered one call quite well. When the order was given, no man in camp could salute any better than the men of Company G.

Learning to handle their firearms was a different story. Most men of the regiment, being mountain boys from a variety of areas surrounding Staunton, had their very livelihood depend upon conquering the outdoors. The European rifled Enfield muskets issued to them was a new breed of firearm, and it took some mastering to handle them well; but learn they did, and Company G was as good as any when it came to shooting.

The handling of arms consisted of nine steps, sometimes referred to as "loading in nine times." A complicated procedure, it was executed in nine different commands:

1. Load: the musket was shifted into position for loading.
2. Handle Cartridge: this meant taking the cartridge from a box attached to the soldier's belt.
3. Tear Cartridge: the paper end of the "bullet" was torn off by placing it between one's teeth. It was then positioned at the gun's muzzle.
4. Charge Cartridge: the powder in the paper end was emptied into the muzzle and the head of the ramrod, located under the barrel of the gun, was seized.
5. Draw Rammer: the ramrod was removed from beneath the barrel and placed against the head of the bullet.
6. Ram Cartridge: the ball was pressed down into the muzzle.

7. Return Ramrod: the rammer was replaced beneath the barrel.
8. Prime: a musket cap was taken from another pouch on the soldier's belt and placed on the end of the hammer.
9. Shoulder Arms: the weapon was placed on the right shoulder and firing was completed by the orders READY; AIM; FIRE!

The real trick in knowing how to load the musket came from the different positions in which the soldier was required to fire it. Standing, even kneeling, was not so difficult to master. It was learning to fire from a prone position, lying on one's belly, that created a problem. To do this meant rolling over in order to ram the shot home.

The men had to practice these steps several times before being allowed to use live ammunition. Upon mastering these demands, they could go a distance from camp to practice their shooting.

It was on such a day that Jeremiah eyed his weapon with doubt. "This is a fine lookin' musket, boys," he quipped, "but I just ain't convinced that such a handsome gun has the ability to get off a shot well."

Taking aim at his target, he promptly squeezed the trigger. The blast was deafening, and suddenly he found himself sitting hard on the ground, several feet away. His shoulder ached fiercely where the rifle kicked back, and he reached up to grab the spot with a rub.

The sound of laughter brought him out of his daze. "This is somethin' to write home about," Cy chortled. "It only sent you reelin' back 'bout fifteen feet!"

"Fellas," he grimaced, rising in embarrassment, "I do believe I take back what I said."

～

Scheduled near the end of June, the official mustering in was to be a great ceremony. Parading for a variety of visitors, the soldiers would be inspected by mustering officials and tender their oath to the Confederate States Army.

Shortly before mustering in, the regiments formed at Staunton received orders that would take them directly to the seat of war. They were commanded to Richmond, the Confederate capital, where trouble had been brewing for quite some time.

After the soldiers were officially received into the service of the Confederate Army, local citizens would present them with colors. As was the custom, ladies had sewn flags for the companies and regiments. Before men departed for the scene of action, the same ladies always presented these flags to them. Called "The Presentation of Colors," such ceremonies usually did not take place on the same day as mustering in, but as the men were to be moved out quickly, there was no choice. One ceremony would follow the other, promising the day to be quite spectacular.

The June morning dawned clear and warm, and beginning earlier than usual, the regimenting bugle calls came in rapid succession. By mid-morning, all companies were organized on the parade ground, and the review began.

Jeremiah held out high hopes for Company G. He felt they had per-formed better in drill the last few days and he was gratified that the orders advancing them to Richmond caused some of the men to begin looking at their duty in a less frivolous light.

Company G was not impressive on the parade ground, but holding formation and moving together, neither did they prove a disgrace. With so many companies on parade, Company G was not as inferior as they usually appeared in camp.

"Loading in Nine" was the last review, before the men took their oath. Repeating the words, Jeremiah heard his own voice proud and strong. He swore to bear true allegiance to the Confederate States of America, to serve them honestly and faithfully against all enemies and oppressors and to observe the orders of the president and officers placed over them.

The oath signified the point of no return, and a grand shout ended the official mustering in. It was now time for the presentation of colors.

One by one, company captains were called forward to receive their company flag. "Captain John Kertlin, will you please step out to receive the colors for Company G?" the official's voice boomed. Jeremiah's mouth dropped open in total surprise.

Captain Kertlin stepped forward to face Violet McCamey rising from a seat. No one was more astonished, or more pleased, than her brother. Obviously volunteering her talents as a seamstress, she had sewn the Confederate Stars and Bars for his company, and as a result, was presenting the banner. It bore two horizontal red bars with a white one in the middle. A field of blue, displaying an array of circled stars, completed the standard.

Violet spoke, but Jeremiah could not catch all of the words uttered in her low, childlike voice. Hearing snatches of her brief speech, he knew she charged the men to bear the standard proudly, fight valiantly and return home safely.

Captain Kertlin, taking the colors from her, could be heard in a clear, resounding voice. Assuring all present that the colors would be defended, protected and returned in honor, he bowed deeply, bringing Violet's small, gloved hand to his lips.

Suddenly Jeremiah heard a sharp, rasping intake of air. Standing next to Cy, he caught a flash of fire in his friend's narrowing eyes. Arching his eyebrows quizzically at Cy, a slight smile crossed his face. *Gotcha!* he thought. *Gotcha! Gotcha! I knew it! I knew you were sweet on Violet!*

The ceremony continued until the last company acquired its colors, then a great hurrah went up from the men as they were given the command that freed them from the ranks. The soldiers could now socialize with family, friends and guests until sundown.

Great tables, laden with food and drink, courtesy of the people of Staunton and other nearby hamlets, provided sumptuous refreshment. It was to be the last time the parade grounds would be filled with such sounds of laughter and delight.

As soon as rank was broken, Jeremiah dashed forward to enjoy the unexpected, but welcome, presence of his family. Although several letters were exchanged during his absence from home, not one had given him any indication of their plans to be present on this day.

As he stuck out his hand to receive the firm grasp of his father's handshake, exuberance turned the handshake into an embrace, instead, and Jeremiah relished such a sign of affection. Next, grabbing his mother and lifting her off her feet, he could not resist twirling her around. She seemed so frail, so small, as she laughed at his antics, and he placed a resounding kiss on her cheek.

Her eyes glistening with tears, she placed his face in her hands. "Jeremiah, just look at you!" she cried proudly. "I was afraid . . . I was afraid we wouldn't find you well. We've heard some dreadful stories about sickness in some of the camps . . . but look at you! You're the picture of health!" she finished, dabbing at her eyes with a handkerchief.

"Don't cry now, Ma! Soldierin' agrees with me!"

Looking around for Priscilla, he finally folded his arms about her. "Prissy, Prissy dear!" he whispered into her ear, "I've missed you most of all!"

Pushing him back to within arms length, she looked at him critically, her soft topaz eyes shining. "Jeremiah . . . you look wonderful!" she exclaimed. "I believe you're right, soldierin' does agree with you!" She knit her eyebrows together. "You . . . you look different somehow," she concluded.

Priscilla wasn't exactly sure what was different about her brother, but he was changed. She thought he seemed older; perhaps more mature than when he left home, and he looked incredibly handsome in the fine gray uniform he was wearing. She recognized it as the one Violet had sewn for him. "I am so proud you are my brother, Jeremiah," she whispered in his ear.

Someone began pulling at his fingers, and turning from Priscilla, Jeremiah found Bonniejean grabbing for his hand. Whirling around, he scooped up the child, giving her a hug as she sat on his arm. "My little sweetheart," he declared, "you get prettier everyday!" Nuzzling against her ear, he whispered to her until she broke out into squeals of childish delight. Suddenly, flinging both arms about his neck, she squeezed hard, pressing her plump, pink cheek tightly to his firm, tan jaw.

"When you comin' home, Jer'miah?" she whined in her tiny voice. "I've missed you."

"Not for a while, Baby. I'm afraid not for a while. Where is our other sister?" he asked, brushing a wisp of tow colored hair out of her eyes.

Suddenly he felt a gentle pressure on his free arm. Violet, squeezing it tenderly with her long, slim, white-gloved fingers, looked up at him with bright blue eyes. Her dark blonde curls framed a flushed, excited face, and she looked exceptionally lovely, he decided.

Standing on tiptoes, she reached up to plant a kiss on her brother's cheek. As he released Bonniejean from her perch, Violet touched his tan face with a sweet, but timid, peck. "The uniform looks good on you huh, Jeremiah?" she whispered in quiet satisfaction.

"Thank you, Violet," he voiced softly. "I am so proud; so pleased that you are the seamstress behind our noble banner. You have truly honored me by . . ."

His sentence was broken off as he suddenly became aware of another soldier standing behind him. Turning, he discovered Cy, Violet's hand tucked demurely into the crook of his arm. She was trying very hard to act the part of a refined lady, and Jeremiah didn't know whether to be amused or embarrassed. He decided to give Cy a pestering about this predicament later.

"So, Violet," he jerked his head in his friend's direction, "what do you think of Cy's fine new growth of hair . . . the one on his upper lip?" Jeremiah teased them both.

Violet turned her eyes toward Cy in a way that took her brother off guard. Without taking her sight from him, she murmured, "I think Mr. Ash looks divine, Jeremiah."

Jeremiah put a hand up to his face, hoping he wouldn't laugh. The scene was too much for him. In a couple of seconds, his composure regained, he reached out to stroke Violet's lovely curls. "Be careful of this one, Pumpkin," he warned with a laugh, "all the girls think him a purty soldier!"

Violet wrinkled her nose, an old, but definitely unladylike, habit. "Save a moment for your dear brother before the day passes, Violet," he chuckled. But she and Cy were already strolling away.

So, he thought. *I wasn't wrong.* His sister did have a definite interest in his friend, and he was almost certain that Cy returned her affection. Yet, the thought of Violet and Cy together seemed so ridiculous. They were so different! How could he be so close to two people and yet be so blind as to what was happening between them? He was completely baffled by his oversight, for it wasn't until she determined to make gifts for his friends that he begin to question her motives.

The boy suggested to his family that they help themselves to the bounty of food and wile away the hours in the shade of the trees. As they heaped plates full of the scrumptious fare, they found themselves behind Captain Kertlin.

Jeremiah was anxious for his family to meet this man whom he had so grown to admire in these last few weeks. Indeed, Captain Kertlin had no idea it was Violet McCamey who had sewn and presented the colors to Company G.

"Captain Kertlin," Jeremiah hailed the officer. "Sir, I'd like to present my family to you. We would be very honored, Sir, to have you join us while we eat."

"Thank you, McCamey," he answered in a pleased manner. "I'd be delighted to join you."

They walked to a shady grove where blankets were already spread upon the ground. Jeremiah made introductions, presenting one family member after the other.

The captain was surprised to learn Violet was his sister, and graciously exclaimed over the fine standard she had sewn.

When introduced to Priscilla, he lingered a moment over her hand. Bringing it to his lips, no one present missed the obvious admiration on his face. It was no surprise when later that afternoon Captain Kertlin invited 'Cilla to accompany him on a stroll.

Jep, melting into the crowd after the last of the ceremonies, was expected to be part of the McCamey gathering. At Jeremiah's bidding, his oldest sister went searching for him.

When Priscilla found Jep, he was being admired and entertained by a bevy of young and animated ladies. It was clear they were spellbound to be in the presence of such a handsome young soldier. Priscilla, unable to resist an opportunity to vex her brother's friend, came upon him from behind. Hugging the boy soundly, she placed a showy kiss on his jaw that caused him to blush.

"Why Jeptha Carroll!" she exclaimed, "Here you are. That entire family of mine is looking for you. How can you keep us waiting! You will, of course, come join us at once!"

The scene embarrassed Jeptha, and the young ladies, mistaking it for what it looked like, fled his company in indignation.

"'Cilla," he finally snapped, trying to hide his agitation, "don't you know you might have just ruined my future? I'm quite certain I could have married any one of those beautiful ladies today if you hadn't run them off!"

"Yeah," she retorted, "and robbed the cradle. They didn't look too much older than Bonniejean." She rolled her eyes in disbelief. "Really, Jeptha. Now, Jeremiah sent me to hunt you down. You should know without being told that you are to join us."

Jeptha didn't reply. He sometimes felt intimidated by Priscilla. Her handsome looks and self-confidence always made him uneasy.

As the excellent day began to wind down, Anderson and his banjo joined the McCamey clan. The youth, short yet lanky and sporting a wild thatch of long, thick, curly hair, could indeed play the instrument like no one else. A fellow of great merriment, he declared the only thing he'd rather do than play the banjo was to fight Yanks for Virginia.

Before long, a nearby fiddle joined the entertainment and the day ended on a grand note. As the sun began to move beyond the western horizon, it was time for good-byes.

For a fleeting moment, Jeremiah felt an overwhelming desire to return home with his family. The tears, the hugs, the nervous laughter all spoke of one thought looming in the back of their minds. Each one was aware they might never again be together.

Not wanting his emotions to crumble in front of his family, he showed great fortitude, withstanding the difficult farewells. As he trekked back to his tent he found himself humming "Kathleen Mavourneen," the last tune Andy had played.

How did those words go? "It may be a long time, it may be forever . . ." he sang quietly through a veil of tears.

CHAPTER THREE

So weep not, dearest, weep not
If in her cause I fall
Oh! Weep not dearest; weep not!
It is my country's call!

The command was given long before dawn. "STRIKE THE TENTS!" The men were ordered to prepare a day's rations, fall into rank and begin marching. Their destination, the train station in Staunton, would see them loaded upon cars for transport to Richmond.

Though it was early, many townspeople were there to send them off in grand fashion. Banners waved wildly, bands played loudly and flowers were thrust into the soldiers' hands randomly as they boarded. Many cars were already filled to capacity by ranks coming aboard at Lexington and Waynesboro. Jeremiah decided that soon all those cars designed to carry passengers would burst at the seams.

As the train rolled out of the station, it was then the men learned of a change in destination. They would not be heading to Richmond at all. The new orders would take them up to the town of Strasburg and across the Shenandoah Valley to a little hamlet called Manassas Junction. They would be situated close to a vast creek called Bull Run. Traveling to Manassas meant a changeover when the settlement of Strasburg was reached. Here they would have to board the smaller, grimier train of the Manassas Gap Railroad.

As Staunton was left behind and the green rolling countryside came into view, many boys were astounded by the speed at which they were moving. A great number had never before traveled by rail.

Several hours later, upon reaching Strasburg, there were hundreds of other soldiers waiting to board the train. By the time the troops from Staunton were able to make the switch to the crowded, dirty Manassas Gap cars, those designed for passenger transportation had long been filled. The only seats available were not really seats at all, but benches fashioned in boxcars designed to carry freight. They soon became intensely hot and unbearably stuffy as the day waxed warm.

With excitement running high, the men's spirits were not well contained. As the atmosphere in the cars grew stale, fervor increased. Many men, wanting to view the passing scenery, began to bang out great holes in the sides of the cars. As the first wall was bashed out, cool air came rushing through, and the men breathed it in with great gulps.

A couple of bold fellows decided to crawl to the top of the boxcar, and soon men from all over the train were clamoring to do so. More than one fell to be crushed under the great weight of the wheels, serving as a deterrent to many others who gave thought to the exercise.

Jeremiah, nodding off in the heat, was suddenly roused by a commotion. "What happened?" he drowsily asked, twisting his head to look around. Several men were gathered around the hole punched in the wall of the car.

"I ain't sure," Cy answered, "but Jep's gone to find out."

Slowly making his way back to his comrades, Jep shook his head in dismay. "You ain't gonna believe this one, boys. We just passed over a ravine. Some poor fool was wantin' to see how high up we was, so leaned out to do so. He either lost his balance or was accidentally pushed by the crush o' men in this car. But whatever, he done fell several hundred feet down to the base of the trestle.

"Scoot back over boys, and let me sit down." He shuddered. "Humph. Makes me certain glad we ain't sittin' no where near that wall."

What promised that morning to be a great adventure had become a wearisome task by day's end. The ride was long, suffocating and tremendously jolting. When they reached Manassas Station, the sun had set and the men were exceedingly weary.

Being unburdened from the cars at the depot, they were told to form rank, and marched four miles to camp. Upon their arrival, the quartermaster was nowhere to be found, so instead of pitching tents, the men simply fell where they were to sleep the night away on the ground.

As Jeremiah wrapped his blanket about him, the darkness well hid the twinkle in his eyes and the grin on his face. *Well,* he thought to himself, *I believe the time has come to tease Cy just a little bit.* The three friends, having stretched out one beside the other, found Cy in the middle. Fighting his own sleepiness until he heard his friend's gentle snore, Jeremiah whispered urgently, "Cy! Cy! Quick, wake up!"

His friend rolled over, answering in groggy confusion. "Huh? What?"

"Somethin's botherin' me. I got to know, Cy. Just when are you and Violet gettin' married?"

For a brief moment Jeremiah thought the boy had fallen back to sleep. Suddenly Cy bolted upright.

"Married? Married!" he shouted into the night. "Jeremiah, what in tarnation are you talking about?"

"I said," he repeated in feigned exasperation, "when are you and Violet getting married?"

"Whoa! Whoa now! What do you mean? I ain't marryin' Violet, or anyone . . . least not now!"

"Aw Cy, 'tis plain to see she's crazy about you. Don't know how I missed it all these years." He shook his head and scratched it in thought. "Don't know what she sees in you either . . . but she done told me you asked her to marry you."

Although the night was cool, Cy started to sweat profusely. His evident nervousness caused Jeremiah to enjoy the scene immensely.

"Jeremiah," Cy spoke up, bewildered, "I don't know what I could have said to make her think that . . . I don't understand . . . I . . . I mean I never said anything . . ." Breathing in deeply, he shook his head several times, perplexed.

Jeremiah could contain himself no longer. Starting to feel sorry for the fellow, he threw back his head and laughed uproariously. "I gotcha this time, Cy! Ha! Ha! You fell for it all! Hee hee." He continued to laugh. "I gotcha good! I wish I coulda seen your face in this darkness!" Jeremiah guffawed again and a voice from the other side of Cy piped up sleepily.

"Jeremiah, would you please shut up!" Jeptha growled. "Some of us are trying to sleep."

Cy reached out his foot and kicked Jeptha roughly in the shin. "Go back to sleep, Jep."

Mumbling something unintelligible, Jeptha got up, moving several feet away from his comrades. Momentarily, he was snoring loud and hard.

"Ha!" exclaimed Cy, "he's one to talk about disturbing folks' sleep."

"Well, Boy?" Jeremiah asked, not willing to let him off the hook just yet. "What's the story? You do like Violet; it's plain . . . you say 'no' and I'm gonna start worryin' about you."

"Oh, I like her all right," Cy answered dreamily. "I've always liked Miss Violet." Suddenly his voice grew loud, and he spoke adamantly, "But I'm married to Virginia 'til this war is over and that's the dad-gone truth, Jeremiah!"

Jeremiah rolled over, sleep becoming too hard to fight. "Cy," he muttered, drifting off, "don't dare go breakin' her heart. You'll have me to answer to if you do." He yawned deeply and was fast asleep.

Slowly opening his eyes, Jeremiah felt strange. He knew it wasn't yet dawn, for the wake up bugle hadn't sounded, but the flickering of a few fires gave evidence that some of the men were up and stirring.

Realizing that he was drenched with sweat, he sat up. His tongue seemed glued to the roof of his mouth, and looking around, things appeared fuzzy and blurred. The flickering fires hurt his eyes. He knew something was not right, and he was shivering in spite of his perspiration.

Water . . . where was his canteen? He felt so odd . . . he needed a drink of water; then he'd feel better . . . but where was that canteen? Not able to locate it, he reached out to shake Cy awake, and reeled at the touch of his skin. "Cy? Cy?" he whispered, trying to nudge him awake. Cy felt burning hot, and wouldn't be roused. Feeling spent of strength, Jeremiah lay back down.

Jep. Where was Jep? He'd get him some water. The next thing he knew he was looking up at a strange face framed in bright sunlight. Jeptha stood next to the man, whose words sounded muffled and distant.

"We got to get this boy to the hospital tent," the stranger said as he leaned over him. "Son? Son? Can you hear me?" Jeremiah squeezed his eyes shut again, the bright sun making them ache. His thirst was raging. Suddenly the familiar voice of Jeptha rang in his ears.

"Jeremiah," his friend called out, "can you sit up? Can you rise up? Try to stand?"

Blinking weakly, Jeremiah tried to bring Jeptha into focus as his friend knelt next to him.

"Here, Jeremiah put your arm around my neck."

He tried to, but the limb would not cooperate, and again he heard Jeptha's voice as he spoke to the stranger.

"Try to get a litter. This boy ain't gettin' up."

The last thing he knew, he was lifted and carried away.

Suddenly opening his eyes, Jeremiah felt a hand flung across his face. "Get this fella off me!" he cried. "I think he's dead."

Jeptha looked up from the stool upon which he sat, fearing his friend was delirious again.

"Move this man, I say!" Jeremiah implored in weak exasperation.

Jeptha walked over to the cot upon which his comrade lay. The man next to him had indeed, expired, a long arm reaching across the berth to fall in Jeremiah's face.

"Orderly!" Jeptha cried out. "This man is dead . . . see that he is removed.

"Jeremiah, am I glad to hear you!" he clapped him on the arm. "Whew! I done thought you was a goner for sure! What you need? How 'bout some water?" he asked excitedly.

"That'd be good," Jeremiah whispered thickly. "Where am I, Jep? What goes on?"

"Hospital tent. Bunch o' boys is plum sick, Jeremiah. Fever. Somethin' called measles. Your skin is awful splotched up. I thought you come close to dyin' on me a couple of times. Quite a number brought in with you's dead now. Reckon close to thirty . . ."

Jeremiah struggled to sit up. Helping to steady him, Jeptha held a canteen to his friend's mouth, allowing him to guzzle in great gulps of water.

"Thanks, Jep," he mumbled, laying back down and closing his eyes. "How long I been here?"

"Goin' on three days now. You ain't had nothin' to keep you alive but a few sips of water and somethin' the doc forced you to swallow. Don't know what it was; didn't want to ask, neither. Feelin' better?"

"I ain't never felt so weak in my life. Even talkin' tires me." There was only silence as Jeptha lingered over his friend. Suddenly, Jeremiah's eyes flew wide open.

"Whats wrong, Jeremiah?" Jeptha demanded anxiously. "You look like you just done seen ghost."

"Cy," he mumbled, "where's Cy? I couldn't wake him up, Jep . . . or did I dream it?" He felt his thoughts were rambling and disjointed.

"No, no. You ain't dreamed it, Jeremiah." Jeptha shook his head from side to side. "He . . . he, well . . ."

Jeremiah gripped the sides of his pallet. "What Jep? What are you trying to say?" he demanded in a hoarse whisper. "What . . . what's wrong?"

Jeptha let out a ragged sigh. "He's bad off, Jeremiah. Real bad off. Worse 'an you, and I done thought you was lost more'n once."

Jeremiah slowly moved his head from side to side, trying to make some sense out of what Jeptha was saying. He felt confused and bewildered. "How come you to be here, Jep? Ain't you got better things to do than hang around a hospital?"

"Sure I do . . . but none as important. I volunteered for this here detail, as long as you two be sick. You know me. Otherwise, I'd be in some kinda trouble for sure."

Jeremiah smiled weakly. "You're a good friend, Jep. Please . . . please, go check on Cy. Find out how he's doin' right now. Don't think I'll be awake . . ." His sentence was punctuated with a deep breath, as sleep overtook him.

Jeptha walked dispiritedly down the length of cots separating his friends. Not much time had passed since he'd last checked on Cy, so he stopped to administer more than one drink of water in answer to cries for it. He wasn't sure how many men were now crowded into the large canvas facility, but there were no more cots. New men were coming in by the hour . . . some only thinking they should be there, others who should have reported days ago. He felt certain that at least one fourth of the entire camp was sick with the disease.

Reaching Cy, he looked down at him. It was hard to believe this was his friend. The blond hair, dirty and matted with sweat, was stuck to his head; the mustache he'd grown and so carefully groomed appeared wild and long. Cy didn't stir as he forced some water between his lips, and his breathing seemed shallow and congested. Jeptha stared at him. The splotches mottling his skin had turned a purplish color, and were starting to peel as though he suffered severe sunburn.

Jeptha turned his head. The sight both sickened and saddened him. He didn't understand why he was spared this terrible fever. It bothered him that he had no answer, and his friends suffered while he did not.

His mind began to wander, and suddenly he was six years old again, hearing the voice: "She's dead." He listened to the weeping of his Pa, and tossed and turned in terrible discomfort and torturous itching. The blister-like sores oozed, crusting his small frame. He called for his Mama, but she never came, and he didn't understand why she would not comfort him . . .

More cries for water roused him from his thoughts, and he shook his head to erase the memory as he went to the aid of yet another man. He didn't like it when this haunting remembrance took hold of him, for he seemed powerless to stop it when it did, yet it was all he could remember of his family. It was his only recollection of a life apart from his Uncle Cal.

He remembered nothing at all of his younger brother and older sisters, and was troubled by the fact.

Of one thing Jeptha was sure. Once he recovered from the dreaded smallpox, he had never again known a truly sick day in his life. The hand of Providence, he thought; but he didn't understand it.

By the next day, Jeremiah was able to sit up long enough to swallow a bowl of diluted broth Jeptha brought to him. Being sick was hard business, he decided. He longed to be up and about, but his body wouldn't allow it.

As Cy's condition remained unchanged, Jeptha told him of the raging fever that wouldn't subside and gently kept him informed as to the failing condition of their friend. "Gads, Jeremiah," he whispered softly with tears in his eyes, "I even tried to spoon some of this here broth down him. He gagged and coughed so I was afraid I'd kill him. But he never, in all that, once opened his eyes. Sometimes I can get him to take in a little water, but the Doc . . . the Doc says he ain't lookin' so good, Jeremiah. He says . . . he says," a big tear rolled down Jeptha's cheek, "he says it ain't gonna do no good to keep expectin' things to change. It's been near four days, and . . . and hardly a boy comes out of it once they've been under this long with a fever and . . ."

"Cy's tough, Jep," Jeremiah blurted out, trying to convince himself. "He's tough, and he'll be all right. He's gotta be, and I gotta believe that."

He thought of his last conversation with the boy. It had been great fun teasing him about Violet. He sighed, glad she was spared this bit of news. She'd be overcome with apprehension. And Cy's Ma, what of her?

"Has anyone told Mrs. Ash that Cy is sick?" Jeremiah unexpectedly questioned.

"I . . . I doubt it," Jeptha stammered. "Too many sick folk to take care of. Reckon there ain't been time to do no informin'. But Cy does write her every week, don't he? She's for sure gonna wonder why no letter don't come."

Jeremiah nodded his head. Cy was all she had and surely this whole idea of war must have her tormented. He must be sure to ask Violet and 'Cilla to keep a check on her and make sure she lacked for nothing.

"Help me, Jep," Jeremiah impatiently commanded. "I wanna see Cy."

Not trying to argue, Jeptha supported his friend as he attempted to rise from his cot.

"Whoa . . ." Jeremiah cried, getting on his feet. The room reeled about him. "Steady me, Boy," he commanded Jep wearily.

"Jeremiah, think you oughta?"

"I'm all right . . . I'm all right . . . I just ain't been on my feet in near a week, remember?"

Unsteadily, but with the firm support of his friend, he walked the length to Cy's sickbed. "My word, Jep!" he puffed out a long breath. "I weren't 'spectin him to look like this."

"You don't look so purty yourself, Jeremiah, but I don't reckon you looked this bad."

Weakly, Jeremiah reached out to touch Cy's arm. "Cy!" he shouted in a whisper, shaking it. "Cy?"

"Ain't no use, Jeremiah. I done ever thing I could 'cept sing him to sleep at night. Reckon all we can do is pray."

"Jep," he said suddenly, "I gotta go lie back down."

The next morning Jeremiah woke to the smell of real food. Jeptha was standing over him with a plate and tin cup.

"If you can sit up, Jeremiah, Doc says you can have this bit o' bacon and boiled taters. Coffee too."

Rubbing a hand over his face to wipe the sleep from his eyes, he blinked. "Real coffee?" he asked.

"Real coffee!" Jep replied.

He sat up and took the cup from Jeptha's hand, gulping half of it down in one long swallow. "Don't know when lukewarm coffee ever tasted so good!" he declared, reaching for the plate. He suddenly felt very hungry.

"How's Cy?"

Jeptha grinned. "I heard tell from one of the boys that he woke up last night for a couple of minutes and asked for water. He asked for it, Jeremiah; actually asked for it."

Jeremiah was silent for a moment. "That's good news," he mumbled at last, afraid to be too hopeful.

Jeptha pulled up a crude, wooden stool and perched himself at the end of his friend's cot. "Got some mail here for you," he said, drawing letters from his shirt. Jeremiah reached for them.

"Ah, ah . . . Doc says no readin', no usin' them eyes at all. I understand these here measles leaves the eyes real delicate like for a while. No readin', no direct light. Doctor's orders." He looked at Jeremiah. "Guess I'll have to read your mail to you . . . hope there's none of them high falutin' words here . . . you know I ain't as fancy educated as you."

Jeremiah felt foolish. It was bad enough to be sick and have to be waited on for everything, but to have your mail read to you as well . . .

He concentrated on the plate before him as Jeptha gave him the news from home. Uneventful as it was, it was good to have it.

His plate clean, Jeremiah was amazed at how much better eating made him feel. Suddenly a cry pierced the muffled sounds of the canvas hospital.

"Crack that bandit's skull, boys!"

Jeptha and Jeremiah looked at each other knowingly . . . those words had long been a joke between the three friends. At once, both were bounding for Cy's side.

The boy thrashed on his cot.

"Draw back the hammer . . ." he shouted.

The recovering soldier next to Cy shook his head.

"Poor boy's outa his mind again. Can't someone put him outa his misery, for goodness sake? He ain't gonna get well."

Abruptly, Cy stopped thrashing and lay deathly still. Jeremiah grabbed Jeptha's arm for support, and suddenly the blue eyes of their friend popped open, sunken and glassy looking. The dry, cracked lips formed a feeble smile as he recognized his comrades.

His thin voice came in a hoarse whisper. "I was dreamin'," he said. "Dreamin' . . ." his words grew difficult to hear and his eyes looked far off. "I was dreamin . . . dreamin' 'bout that time we was coon huntin', 'member that? You, you climbed up in a tree, chasin' the rascal, Jeremiah. Jep went up after you, and I was . . . I was . . ." he stopped for a second as though trying to remember. "I was screamin' at you'ns to smack that coon in the head if'n you couldn't shoot it. Boys . . . it was the biggest bandit we ever did see." He closed his eyes and fell silent.

After a moment the cracked lips moved again, though the eyes didn't open. "Water . . . please . . . won't someone give me some water?"

The fellow next to Cy passed a canteen to Jeremiah.

"Here, Jep. I don't think I have the strength."

Jeptha held the container to Cy's mouth and the water trickled down between his parched lips.

"Good . . . so good," he mumbled.

Jeptha reached out to touch the splotched face, and turned to Jeremiah. "Gone," he said. "The fever's gone."

CHAPTER FOUR

And on the blood red battle plain
We'll conquer or we'll die
It's for our honor and our fame
We'll raise the battle cry!

It was a long recovery period for both. Though Jeremiah began to feel better, his strength didn't readily return and he was forbidden to leave the hospital. He longed to be able to step out into the daylight, but was ordered to rest, something he found hard to do. It was difficult to sit idle all day. He wasn't allowed to read, he wasn't allowed to write, he wasn't allowed to use his eyes at all. He was certain he would have been driven to insanity had not Cy been confined as well.

As the two improved, Jeptha requested to be relieved of his voluntary hospital duty. Neither of his friends blamed him. The dark interior of the hospital tent and being constantly surrounded by sick and dying men tried the stoutest of hearts. Both Cy and Jeremiah encouraged their comrade to return to normal duty, but Jep came by several times a day as he had chance; to talk, bring mail or tell of the latest news.

Captain Kertlin also made rounds, keeping a check on his sick men. He discovered great enjoyment in conversing with Jeremiah and often spent extra time chatting with him. It had not escaped his notice how most of the men shared a fondness for the youth. His objectivity won him great respect within the company, and he was often appealed to when disagreements arose. His sense of duty was ever apparent and the honesty and consideration he demonstrated earned him popularity. Captain Kertlin had no doubt the young man would rise in rank quickly.

Near the end of the second week of the boys' recovery, rumor spread rapidly throughout the camp that fighting was imminent . . . but not at Manassas. Captain Kertlin made his routine visit in order to talk to his confined troops.

"We're movin' out boys," he said. "We're goin' home. That Yankee General, George McClellan, is massing men to make another move in the western hills, toward Beverly. It looks like that skirmish at Philippi last month didn't satisfy him. Reports say he's got some twenty thousand troops and we're needed. Catch is . . . you boys that's been sick, well, you're stayin' behind. You'll be sent to join us soon as you've sufficiently recovered."

The disappointment of the men was evident. Some of the boys begged to the fact that they were well enough to stand the transport back to Staunton.

"Lads, we're not moving by rail this time; we're marchin' back across and not one of you can tell me you're up to that hardship. Part of my job is to see to your welfare. I don't aim on killin' any of you by testin' your endurance. You're stayin' here. That is not an an option, but an order!"

The men knew Captain Kertlin was right, but it did not ease their disappointment. "I can't help but be a little envious of Jep," Cy complained to Jeremiah one day. "At least one of us might finally see some real fightin', but I just wish it was me!"

"Yeah . . . bet Jep wishes it was you, too," Jeremiah retorted.

The first week of July, the regiment moved out, minus the large number of sick and recovering men. The march back across the state proved arduous. After sixty hours on the move, with only five for rest, they crossed the Allegheny Mountains to be thrown directly into the heat of battle.

Every day, those remaining in camp at Manassas waited for news that didn't come. Almost two weeks passed before the rumors became clear. In several stages of fighting, the men in gray had been forced to retreat, and the names of little known places in western Virginia became prevalent: Rich Mountain, Carricks Ford, Laurel Hill and Greenbrier River.

Despite defeat, wild and great tales of heroism circulated. Fanning the flames of Southern pride, such stories gave the boys in gray great reason to be proud in spite of their loss.

No one was certain how heavy the casualties were, who had been wounded or whom had been killed. Those left behind were anxious and eager to know of such news and to be reunited with their force.

Meanwhile, Union General McDowell began massing troops in Alexandria, Virginia, across from Manassas on the other side of Bull Run. Although the Confederates were aware of such movement, the numbers suddenly appeared overwhelming, and headed to press on the Rebels.

July 17 dawned with McDowell on the move, advancing some men of thirty-five thousand in number. The Confederate forces were still divided between Manassas and the western part of the state. The situation looked desperate.

Jeremiah and Cy ceased to question when they would be sent back to Staunton. It was learned that their regiment would be united with the 2nd, 4th, 5th, 27th and 33rd Virginia regiments, now under the command of Lieutenant Colonel T. J. Jackson, and the units would shortly return to Manassas via rail.

"I know one thing for sure," Jeremiah quipped to Cy, "and that's that I don't envy Jep in havin' to ride back this way. Travelin' in them Manassas Gap Rail cars is one experience I don't care to repeat!"

On July 20, the trains began to roll in. Many of the soldiers at Manassas trekked to the station to meet their comrades as they arrived.

Besides the Virginia regiments, the rails carried the 7th and 8th Georgia, and a brigade of Mississippi and Alabama boys. These men were under the leadership of Colonel Bernard Bee, and chugging in with them was the appointed commander of all Confederate forces, General Joseph E. Johnston.

The spirit of the army was excellent in spite of the recent defeats. Waving at the troops and flashing a smile, General Johnston appeared in a grand mood as he disembarked from the train.

A great cheer went up when the boys began to step down from the cars. Slaps on the back and many a loud greeting welcomed the returning warriors. Jeremiah and Cy grew anxious, feeling apprehensive as neither Jeptha nor Captain Kertlin emerged. Exchanging nervous glances, each was afraid to voice what the other was thinking.

Suddenly Cy began jumping up and down, waving his arms wildly. "Over here, Jep, over here!"

Jeptha spotted the friends from his perch in a car, and returned Cy's wild wave. With musket in hand, he jumped down, momentarily disappearing into the crowd. All of a sudden his rifle appeared at their feet and an arm grabbed each around the neck at the same time.

"By jiminy, you boys look almost purty to me! I thought I come very near to never layin' eyes on you again. Gee . . . say, you two sure look better 'n last time I seen you!"

Jeptha didn't fall into rank when the order was given, but chose to walk back to camp with his friends.

"Where's Cap'n?" Jeremiah was first to ask. "I ain't seen him."

"Ah, he's along. Understand he got to ride with some of the big boys . . . reckon he needs to know what the plan is . . . most of us don't have a clue as to what's goin' down. We no sooner get back to Staunton camp after fightin' and we're bein' marched back up to Strasburg to board this here train again. Whatcha hear, boys?"

"Well," Jeremiah answered, "only that ol' McDowell, he's done got pret near thirty-five thousand men over the big creek here, and headin' 'em our way. That's all."

"Huh," Jep only half laughed at the attempted humor. "How many ranks we got here now?" he asked.

"Dunno . . . maybe five, ten thousand," Jeremiah replied.

"Well, with them Georgy, Mississip and Alabamy lads joinin' us, I'd reckon we brought in about ten today."

"I hear there's some comin' from Richmond and Bethel, too," Cy added. "That'll help us out.

"Say, Jep . . . what's it like? How'd you feel?"

"You mean the fightin'? I gotta tell you boys, it ain't a purty sight, and I ain't ashamed to tell you I was considerable scared. Artillery starts blowin' up around you, sprayin' dirt in ever which direction, shells bustin' over your head as they come whistlin' in . . . and you start rammin' them balls down into your musket . . . sometimes can't even remember if you done fired what you rammed last . . . all you can hear is the roar of these here Enfields around you. Then, you start seein' the boys fall, some bloody; some like they's jus' gone to sleep; some blowed to pieces . . . Sometimes it'll be one right in front of you . . . and you think, well now, if he hadn't been there, reckon it'd be me instead. After a while, though . . . you just sorta forget what's happenin' and you do what you gotta do . . . you just don't think about it anymore . . . it's strange . . . because you forget you're scared."

The friends walked along in silence, Jeremiah and Cy mulling over Jeptha's words. "Somethin' else I'm gonna tell you boys," he suddenly voiced softly. "Don't take this the wrong way, you here? But after that battle at Carricks Ford, when the guns finally quit, I couldn't move. I don't know if it was just that we was scared to death or that thankful to be alive, but a few of us just lay there on that field and cried like babies. I don't feel no humiliation in confessin' that to you either."

When the boys reached camp, it was near suppertime and the mood was electrifying. The fighting that occurred in the western part of the state had been hard, but the troops were scattered. There was yet to be a battle on such grand scale as the impending clash at Manassas promised to be.

Orders were being dispatched in a great flurry. During the boys' meal, General G. P. T. Beauregard, commander of all troops at Manassas, made a ride through camp as he surveyed the ground upon which the fight was expected to occur.

Cy nudged his friends. "Looky there! There's the one that got Fort Sumter for us! Don't he look the finest general you could ever see?" He jumped up and saluted, even though General Beauregard was too far away to notice.

"Oh, don't be so beef-headed, Cy!" Jeptha exclaimed, grabbing him by the belt and pulling him down. "You're such an embarrassment sometimes. He can't see you . . . probably wouldn't care if he did. Do you know how often I have to ask myself if you just ain't dead from the neck up?"

Cy ignored his friend's remarks. "Jep," he asked, "what do you know about this Lieutenant Colonel Jackson we've been placed under? Met him? Seen him? I heard tell some crazy stories 'bout him."

Jeptha shrugged.

"Couple of the men over in the hospital with us, when they heard we was to be under him, said we'd be sorry. Said he was an odd sorta fella . . . didn't he teach at the military academy in Lexington where Cap'n went? Let's ask him about it . . . bet he knows him."

As the soldiers finished mess, Captain Kertlin called his company together to issue orders and inform the troops of the morning's plans. All the boys were anxious.

"Lads," he addressed them, "we're to be in reserve now, in the morning; out above the stone bridge 'bout three miles down from here. We'll be called upon when and if needed."

"Ahhh," the groan went up in unison.

"Seems to me we ain't gettin' in none o' the action," Parker spat out. "I signed up to do some fightin'." He paused. "And what about this Jackson we done been assigned to? I hear he ain't nothin' but a lemon-suckin' odd ball!"

A peal of laughter went up from the men, and Parker, seeing he had the center of attention, took advantage of it.

"I tell you what I think," he continued. "I think it's true, all of it . . . I seen him myself this afternoon; he got off that train with one of them yaller fruits in his mouth . . . and a fella from Company B, he done told me a story that ol' Jackson was considered a fool down in Lexington; that a couple of fellas at the institute even tried to kill him . . . threw a brick down on his head, 'cept it missed him . . ." Parker was on a roll, telling every story he'd heard.

"They say his blue eyes get so wild and crazy lookin' sometimes that they nicknamed him Ol' Blue Light. Ha! Ha! But the best one I heard is the one I 'spect we'll be forced to accept . . . Ol' Tom Fool!"

The crowd of men roared with laughter. Even Jeremiah couldn't help himself until he caught the bristling look of Captain Kertlin. He punched Jep and Cy in the arm to get their attention.

"Don't think Cap'n thinks none of this too funny, boys."

"Want me to knock that chip off Parker's shoulder again? I ain't had a chance in a while," Jep said gleefully.

Jeremiah rolled his eyes.

"Well, bully for you," Cy cried out. "Now looky at who's bein' foolish . . . Yeah, Jep, that's just what we need . . . let's not fight the Yanks, let's fight each other," he cajoled sarcastically, but it was too late. Jep had already sprung up and was having his say.

"Parker, that mouth o' yorn ain't big enough, is it? Let me make it a little bigger." WHAP! Jeptha's fist slammed into his face, making Parker reel backwards as blood spurted from his nose.

Shaking his head, Parker came up with a punch to Jeptha's gut that doubled him over. Head down, Jeptha rammed into Parker, bowling him to the ground.

"Whoa! Whoa, boys! Enough!" Jeremiah shouted as he and Cy grabbed Jep and held him back. Jeptha struggled against their hold, as a couple of other fellows grabbed on to Parker, while he stood swinging at the air.

"Jep, I dunno what gets into you sometimes," Jeremiah declared as he let go of him. "Save it . . . save it, save it men. Save it for those boys in blue tomorrow."

The two men's eyes flashed fire at each other, but their fists remained at their sides. "Jep, what in tarnation got your dander up so?" Cy wanted to know.

"Ah, it's plain boys! Parker ain't got no respect for Cap'n and I aimed to learn him some!"

"Well, brawlin' ain't gonna get it done, Jep!" Cy retorted. "Not when we got a Yankee army breathin' down our necks. Now tell me who's dead between the ears!"

The men began to break up and head back to quarters, forgetting that Captain Kertlin called them together for a purpose. "Men!" Jeremiah called out. "Men, we are not dismissed! I for one wanna be well informed before I put myself in the line of fire tomorrow. Where are your good senses? Let Cap'n finish his say!"

Captain Kertlin nodded at Jeremiah. "McCamey's right, fellas. Let's not go into this fight tomorrow ill informed. But first, let me clear up this matter . . . this matter of Lieutenant Colonel Jackson. Boys, when I attended the institute in Lexington I was privileged, privileged, I tell you, not to just know Thomas Jackson, but to study under him. It's true, he has habits that may seem rather odd to some . . . but well now, I been livin' with you boys nigh three months, and I gotta say, that if I was to write home about the habits I've studied in some o' you . . . well, there'd be plenty to have a laugh at. You can't judge a man by his habits alone . . . anyone who does is lame brained. Jackson may not have been the best classroom instructor, but he was a brilliant man on the field. There's not a man at Lexington can hold a candle to his field and artillery instruction. I'm a better soldier for having learned under him and there ain't no man done the same that can dispute me. He served honorably, and with distinction, in the Mexican War. You will learn much from this leader of men . . . and he is also a man of great faith, boys. That can only be to your benefit. What Parker failed to tell you is that he has another nickname: 'Deacon Jackson.'

"Now, it is true we will be in reserve in the morning. I understand our position is likely to be up above the stone bridge on a slope. Here we will support the boys of Colonel Bee. They will be placed below us on the front of the line. We're to keep the enemy in check.

"Now for some of you fellas, fightin's not new anymore, but to those of you that have yet to feel the fire . . . well, obey your officers, you've given an oath. Fight valiantly and the day will be ours.

"Well, I guess that's all what I have to say . . . try to get some rest tonight. One more thing, men. It's sometimes forgotten . . . this is war. Men die." He saluted them. "You are dismissed, soldiers."

Shortly before sundown, a tremendous thunder was heard. Some men, thinking the fight had begun, came charging from their tents, muskets in hand. The smoke that greeted them was not from cannon, however. It was the result of thick dust kicked up by hundreds of horses. The men found it an unbelievable, yet marvelous sight; hundreds of fine, strong horses passing through camp; gray clad soldiers perched proudly upon their backs. The magnificent sight was surpassed only by the appearance of the man who led them. Attired in a splendid gray uniform trimmed with gold, he created an awesome vision. His plumed hat gave him the look of an ancient cavalier, while his cloak, lined with red silk, flapped wildly behind him. A long, auburn beard lent him an almost holy look.

"Ooo-eee boys! Looks like a king leadin' a legion! Who the tarnation is that? I ain't never seen such a glorious sight!" Cy declared in awe.

"That there be J. E. B. Stuart. I seen him when we marched back to Staunton. Got quite a reputation. I hear tell he's 'bout the most daring cavalry leader on both sides!" Jep answered him. "Was servin' out west before Virginia seceded."

The boys watched the sight until the last horse disappeared and the dust died down. "Almost makes me wish I'd joined the cavalry," Jeremiah stated matter-of-factly.

No one could sleep that night. The atmosphere was too charged with excitement and anxiety. The boys were up long before dawn on the morning of the 21st, boiling coffee and speculating about what the day would bring. About 4:30 A.M., a scouting party galloped into camp, incredulous at their own report. The sergeant in charge laughed. "Must be more'n half the citizens of Washington, D.C., leavin' town this mornin'. By golly, by the wagons full they're loaded down with food and women and young'uns as though goin' on a picnic." He laughed again. "They're followin' their boys in blue to help them make a grand day of this battle. They're comin' to watch this fight like goin' to a play. They think this to be a pleasure outin'. Well, it'll pleasure me plenty to make it worth their while!"

The guns started about 5:30 A.M., artillery fire from the Yanks that was answered by the Rebs. The duel continued for more than an hour as the men fell into rank and began moving into position. At 7 A.M., Jackson's men were ordered to place themselves between Generals Cocke and Bonham, but before 8:30 A.M., the order was changed. They were now to move forward to reinforce the defense of the stone bridge that crossed Bull Run.

The fighting was furious. Jeremiah and Cy stuck close to Jeptha, feeling a security in the fact that he had faced battle before.

Balls whirred overhead, making a thwack, thwack, thwack sound as they sailed through the air. Other shells screamed, while some came in whistling. The intense musket fire from the enemy was heard in a rapid staccato of boom-carooom! Boom-carooom! Boom-carooom! One could see the flash of the fire.

For a moment Jeremiah faltered, understanding the fear of which Jeptha had spoken. His mouth felt like cotton and his heart beat wildly as he wondered if one of those shrieking shells had his name on it. He was loading his musket again . . . had he fired the last shot? He couldn't remember . . . and his hands were shaking.

A thick cloud of smoke engulfed them and he glanced to his left at Cy. *Aren't you scared, Cy?* he thought . . . *you're a cool one.* Unruffled, Cy was loading, aiming, firing his musket repeatedly, as though he often encountered such perilous situations.

The smoke became too thick for the men to know at what or whom they were firing. Friend? Foe? Into the air? An officer on horseback came riding down the lines . . . "Keep up the fire boys! Keep up your fire!" he yelled, shouting to be heard above the roar.

On Jeremiah's right, a body fell in front of Jep, the young eyes open, but unseeing in death. The front of the gray uniform was stained scarlet from neck to waist, the soldier holding a lifeless hand across a gaping hole in his chest.

Jeptha grabbed the dead man by the collar, heaving him to the side.

"Sorry, Friend," he panted, "but this is no time to get in my way!"

Jeremiah oddly found himself thinking of Permillia. *Perhaps she is right,* he thought. *Soldiering does turn men into barbarians.* He squeezed off another round.

Suddenly, an artillery shell hit the ground next to him, exploding in a rain of dirt, blood and debris. Jeremiah frantically turned to where Jep had been fighting at his side. Several men lay sprawled out, mangled and dead.

"Jep!" he screamed. "Jeptha!" Jumping up, he whirled around dizzily, searching for his friend. Captain Kertlin's words came back to him: "This is war. Men die."

Quickly a hand grabbed him by the belt, pulling him down. "Jeremiah, don't be foolish! You stand there like that, you become a perfect target!" Jeptha bellowed from behind.

Feeling a wave of relief crash over him, once more he glanced to his left. Cy remained unmoved, loading, aiming and firing like clockwork. *How much time has passed? Must be hours,* he thought, looking up at the sun. It was not yet near overhead. It couldn't be much past 9:30 A.M. Impossible. It seemed as though they had been fighting forever.

Instantly, the ferocity of the battle began to wind down until only a few short pops were heard. Artillery became still. Another officer on horseback galloped by. "Hold your fire, lads! Hold your fire! We're moving back . . . back up to the brow of Henry Hill, right over yonder," he pointed toward his right. "Form rank . . . at the double quick!" The men scrambled into position, and began to move in a run-like march.

Behind a farmhouse, the brushy brow of the hill was soon reached. "Line in position, men!" a voice boomed out with calm confidence, "and take as much cover as this thicket of trees will allow!"

The three boys at once spotted the officer who issued the command. A magnificent looking soldier, he wore an old uniform from the Mexican War and was seated upon a small sorrel horse.

"Jackson," Cy whispered in awe, "just look at him! Ain't he grand?" The stateliness of the officer was marred only by one action: he put his hand to his mouth and began to suck feverishly on a lemon.

Cy stared wide-eyed, while Jeremiah couldn't help but chuckle. "By jingo, lads, 'tis true! Parker were right about that part, weren't he?" Jeptha laughed.

Fighting below the brow of the hill began to heat up again, artillery firing from points unseen. The boys of Colonel Bee at the front of the line were being smashed; cut to ribbons; chewed up and spit out by the enemy.

Jeremiah guessed it was fairly close to noon. The sun was almost overhead and the heat was becoming unbearable.

The Confederates below began to fall back, retreating toward Henry Hill in disorganization. "This position has to be held! It is the key to victory!" the voice of Lieutenant Colonel Jackson thundered.

Colonel Bee tried to rally his boys. General Beauregard, seeing the melee, sent a command for the colors to be carried to the front. He hoped the sight of them might put order to the troops; but they continued to retreat until Colonel Bee reached the brow of the hill. There he spied Jackson and his men standing in an unwavering line of battle that would enable them to sweep any enemy from the knoll. Secure, compacted ranks, and the cool, calm demeanor of Jackson caused Colonel Bee to cry, "Look! There stands Jackson like a stone wall! Rally behind the Virginians, boys! Rally behind the Virginians!" The soldiers heard, saw and were inspired. The ranks began to steady and form a solid line once again.

The fight continued until about one 1 P.M. when a sudden and unexplained lull fell over the battlefield. It was as if someone had suddenly called a lunch break. The heat was stifling and the men, many up all night, had been fighting for over five hours. They were utterly exhausted. Food was scarcely thought of. Wringing with sweat, covered with dirt and black powder, water and rest were their urgent necessities. Many simply stretched out, and cradling their heads in their arms, drifted off to sleep.

Over an hour passed before the rap, tat, tat of musket fire and the enormous boom of cannon could be heard once more. The combat turned brutal, but the men on the hill continued to hold.

Trying to drive the Southerners back, the boys in blue charged again and again. They were forced to retreat each time.

Jeremiah could tell Jeptha was getting up his dander.

"Those Yanks just don't know when to learn a lesson, do they?" he hissed angrily to Cy and Jeremiah. "Much longer, I'm gonna start runnin' out o' ammunition!"

Load, aim, fire. Load, aim, fire. Jeptha fired off another round and started to reload. Jeremiah was busy ramming a ball into his barrel when he heard the cry.

"Cy! Cy!" Jep screamed in desperation.

Struggling with the hammer of his musket, Cy was oblivious to Jeptha's line of vision. It happened so fast . . . the blue uniform, the aim of the gun, another helpless cry from Jep that split the din of battle.

"Cyril!"

Jeremiah leaped to his feet, ditching his weapon to make a dive in Cy's direction; but it was too late. He felt as though he was viewing it all in slow motion, powerless to stop it. Cy's blue eyes looked up and then widened in disbelief as he saw the enemy musket aimed at his head. A brief flinch of fear crossed his face, and it was over. Jeremiah heard the sharp report of the Yankee rifle before he saw the flash of fire spit from its barrel.

Unable to stop, he landed on top of Cy with a thud, bowling him over. Out of the corner of his eye he saw the man in blue fall backward, then suddenly felt a shove to his chest.

"Gads! Jeremiah! You're breaking my ribs! I can't breathe. Get off me!"

Jeremiah sprang to his knees. "Cy? You're all right? You're all right?" he panted.

"Yeah, now that you're off me!" He breathed in a gulp of air. "What happened? I thought I was a dead man . . ."

"Yeah, me too."

Jeremiah looked over at Jeptha, who sank to his knees without finishing the reloading of his gun. He could only point. Jeremiah turned around to see Parker stumble, grabbing a shoulder as he dropped his still smoking musket. It all happened so fast he felt dizzy.

"You saved his life," Jeremiah said to Parker, flatly. The split second timing of the affair left him void of emotion.

Overcome, Cy ran a shaking hand though his dirty, blond hair as he stared at the man. "Thank you, Parker. You saved my life," he murmured.

Jeptha was the first to notice the wound. "Parker, you've been hit. I, I . . . I owe you my gratitude for my friend's life."

Parker smiled a rare, brief, but wry smile. "Just doin' my duty, boys. Just doin' my duty."

"Well, better get help for that shoulder," Jep advised.

"Aw, it'll be all right . . . hurts a mite, but I aim to see this fightin' out."

Nothing more was said, but the magnitude of what occurred would require some thinking about, Jeremiah concluded. No time to think now. Think later.

Load, aim, fire. Load, aim, fire. The boys could not even begin to guess how long the fighting went on, and Jeremiah discovered once more that Jep had been right. His initial fear had long ago melted into sheer action.

The men in blue weren't making it easy. Finally, word went down the line. Jackson was calling for a bayonet charge as a last desperate means to end the contest.

The command traveled along the ranks, given by each successive captain, sergeant, or whoever else was left alive to be in charge of a company. "FIX BAYONETS!" The metal clanked against muskets as they were attached. "CHARGE!" came the cry. Down the brow of the hill the men in gray went running, bayonets out front, a wild yell escaping their throats; "Wha . . . wha . . . whahooo!" It became as much a part of the fighting as the men. Some called it "The Rebel Yell."

It had the desired effect, the blood-curdling shriek and the flashing metal. By the time boys reached the plateau below, the Yanks were on the run in a rout. With no place to go, they retreated hastily in disorder. The first great battle of the war was over. For nearly nine hours, the two armies opposed each other and the cost was high.

When the boys arrived back at camp they could not recall ever feeling so weary. Hungry, tired and coated with dust and black powder, they were emotionally as well as physically exhausted. During the fight there had been no time to think things through; now there was no strength.

By the next morning, the gravity of the situation was known. The costs were terrible. One regiment of Alabama boys lost every officer, so that in the end, General Beauregard had to lead them. Colonel Bee was killed. Seven of Captain Kertlin's men were dead. "Almost eight," Cy stated bluntly, in hearing the figures. "I aim on goin' to check on Parker. See how he's doin'."

Jep and Jeremiah followed him to the hospital, set up in a stone house about a mile from camp. Parker seemed in good spirits, though he was running a fever and the wound was causing him pain.

"Well," Jep said to him, "looks like some Yank knocked that chip off your shoulder. Reckon I tried hard enough . . . but you know Parker, you're a stubborn coot. Took a Yank to do what I couldn't. Now, I call that embarrassin'."

Jeptha hesitated. Expressing his feelings didn't come easily. "Seriously, Parker, you done good. I gotta thank you for . . . well, me an Cy's done been friends most our years . . . I gotta . . . well thank you for savin' his life."

"So, how ya feel?" Cy asked. "I bet pret near better than I'd be a feelin' if you hadn't been behind me yesterday."

"Pains me some, boys. But not as much as listenin' to your sentiment. Did what I had to do, that's all. Did my duty. We all do our duty. Any o' you woulda done the same."

He shifted on his pallet and grimaced in pain. "I'd be obliged if one o' you would get me some water. I'm feelin' mighty feverish like."

"That's little favor in return for a life," Jeremiah said. "My pleasure."

Two days later an order to strike the tents was given. They were heading back to the Shenandoah Valley.

"Fellas," Cy declared, "I feel the need to check on Parker before pullin' out. Maybe he's well enough to not miss the trip back home." He shook his head. "Don't reckon I'll ever be able to repay him for what he done."

He soon returned to camp to face the certain question.

"Well, how's he doin' today? Gonna be able to move out with transportable wounded?" Jeremiah wanted to know.

Cy stared briefly at his friends, fighting a tightness in his chest. "Well, boys," he said, looking down and stumbling for words. "I . . . uh . . . he died." Glancing up, he felt his eyes water. "Some kind of infection. They say he died of fever."

He turned and walked aimlessly away, feeling the tears sting his eyes. He never even liked the man that much and now Parker was dead because he wasn't. It didn't make sense. Cy grappled with his feelings.

Finding an isolated boulder, he backed tightly up against it and began to cry, seeing the war for what it was; for what it was doing to them all, and neither was a pleasant thought. Trying to stop the tears, he felt as if a dam had burst, and he sobbed long and hard.

What had Parker said? "We all do our duty . . ." Good thought to keep. Captain Kertlin's words rang in his ears: ". . . this is war. Men die."

Yeah, men die, he thought. *Can't stop that. Can only do my duty. Duty is to defend Virginia; fight for the South. Might cost my life before it's over. Is this cause something to die for? The rights of my people . . . my country?* "Yes!" he answered out loud. "Not only worth it . . . but something honorable for which to die. Many men have been willing to die for much lesser things . . ."

Suddenly, everything seemed very clear, and his tears subsided.

CHAPTER FIVE

When to the field of fight I rush
And raise my battle shout
A soldier's pride each doubt will hush
'Though bullets fly about.

The boys didn't return to the Shenandoah Valley by rail, but marched their way back. For some of the company, it was a bad experience relived; for others not yet traveling over by foot, it made for a strenuous adventure. The troops met little resistance along the way, encountering only some minor skirmishing.

Before the week passed, Company G arrived in the town of Winchester. Here, the men discovered, camp would be set up temporarily. They were not returning to Staunton just yet.

Winchester, being close to the Maryland border, was a strategic town in keeping the Confederate Army supplied. The citizens welcomed their presence and the soldiers fell into a routine that changed little over the next few weeks. Days were made up of guard duty, picket duty, and an occasional skirmish with Yankee forces trying to break through. On the evening after one such skirmish, Sergeant Spruill showed up as the friends finished their supper.

"McCamey!" he spat out, "Cap'n would like a word with you."

"Me?" Jeremiah questioned, shrugging his shoulders and glancing at his messmates. "See y'all later."

"What's Jeremiah done?" Jeptha whispered, nudging Cy. "I'm usually the one in trouble."

Cy shrugged. "Beats me. He ain't done nothin' I know of. Don't know why Cap'n would send for him. Maybe you done somethin' Jep, and Cap'n's gonna hafta hang you. He probably just wants poor ol' Jeremiah to break the news to you soft like." He chuckled at his ill joke as Jeptha rolled his eyes in disgust.

Andy had settled down around the cook fire, strumming his banjo. Suddenly, to the tune of "Yankee Doodle," he began to sing out:

> *Once was a soldier name Jeremiah*
> *Got summoned by his Cap'n*
> *Never was heard from again*
> *And no one knows what happened!*

Jep plopped down on the ground beside him. "You sure do know how to cheer the heart, Andy," he said sarcastically. "I hear J. E. B. Stuart's lookin' for a new banjo man. Believe I'll recommend you."

"Wouldn't mind at all, boys; not at all! Hear Stuart likes only the best, and that he's one for havin' a roarin' time!"

"Don't know none about that," Jep replied, "but I hear tell he's got his own banjo man that follows him ever-where."

Anderson merely nodded his head in agreement. "Sweeny's his name." He continued to strum.

"Boys, what d'you suppose is up? Cap'n never sends for nobody. You suppose somethin's wrong? S'pose he's gotten some news from home?" Cy paused. "You don't suppose anything's wrong with any of his family?"

"No, Boy," Jep chimed in, slapping him on the back, "I think Violet's just fine. Besides, you got a letter from her only the other day."

"Yeah," Cy agreed, "everything seemed fine."

All became silent and soon Andy began plucking away at a succession of mournful war ballads. Dusk was falling and it would soon be dark.

As Jeremiah arrived at Captain Kertlin's tent, Sergeant Spruill announced him.

"Come in, McCamey," the captain invited amiably. "Come on in."

"You wanted to see me, Sir?" Jeremiah saluted.

A lantern hung on a makeshift post in one corner and another sat on the officer's camp desk, illuminating the canvas interior well. He glanced around. Correspondence was strewn about the desktop, and Jeremiah's eyes opened wide as he recognized the neat and beautiful script of an open letter. Not intending to pry, he averted his gaze, but he'd know that writing anywhere. How many times had he opened letters written in that same lovely script?

It was too late. Captain Kertlin's eyes followed Jeremiah's stare, and upon seeing the letter he'd carelessly left out, he understood the private's gaze. Captain Kertlin shrugged his shoulders, smiling sheepishly.

"Sorry . . . I shouldn't have left personal letters out."

"Excuse me, Sir. I apologize for staring. Didn't mean to pry, Sir. It's just that I'd recognize that handwriting anywhere. Kinda took me off guard, Cap'n."

"Well, I didn't call you here to talk about your sister."

Jeremiah let out an inward sigh of relief and then looked at Captain Kertlin quizzically.

"She's a lovely woman, your sister," the officer suddenly voiced.

Woman! Jeremiah thought. *Woman! She's a girl . . . she's my sister! Violet and Cy are one thing . . . but Captain Kertlin and 'Cilla? Why, they only met that one time! Surely I'm reading too much into this.* He blinked his eyes to clear his thoughts as the captain continued speaking.

"Excuse me, Sir. What were you saying?"

"You realize, of course, we lost a good man in the skirmishing this morning."

"Oh . . . ah, yes, Sir," he focused in on the words. "I liked Corporal Wallace. He was a good man. I'm sorry we've lost him . . . we're all sorry. Has a wife and small child, I know that makes it all the worse."

"Yes, many good men have died. Irreplaceable men."

Jeremiah wondered what all of this had to do with him.

"McCamey, I've recommended that you be promoted to corporal. Colonel Hartshare has approved the recommendation. I do so hope you will honor me by accepting this position."

Stunned, Jeremiah stared at the officer until Captain Kertlin spoke again.

"Well, McCamey . . . what say you?"

Jeremiah saluted him as he tried to find words.

"I . . . uh . . . yes, Sir! I . . . it is with great honor, Sir, that I accept this rank appointed me."

Captain Kertlin held out his hand. "I know you will not let me down, McCamey," he said as Jeremiah shook it.

"I will try not to, Sir."

"I have great confidence in you."

"Thank you, Sir. Thank you for your trust."

Captain Kertlin glanced once more at his desk and the open letter. He looked at Jeremiah as if to say something and then thought the better of it. "You're dismissed, Corporal. You shall have an extra stripe come tomorrow."

Jeremiah turned to go, but stopped, looking back over his shoulder. "Thank you again, Cap'n."

When Jeremiah arrived back among his friends, they were sitting around the fire, faces glum, the silence strange. He dropped down on the ground with them. "Why the long faces, boys? What's the news?"

"Oh, Andy has just been fillin' our heads with mournful song. Guess we're just a touch homesick," Cy answered.

"Where you been, Jeremiah? What'd Cap'n want with you? We done plenty o' speculatin', but can't think of nothin' you done to get on Cap'n's wrong side. So, what's the story?"

Jeremiah looked at the ground and grinned briefly before looking up. "Well boys," he said glumly, "there's bad news; real bad news."

Everyone waited, scarcely daring to breathe. "Well," Jep demanded, "what is it Jeremiah?"

Jeremiah looked at each face, his eyes following the circle. Finally he took in a deep breath. "Men, from now on . . ." he hesitated . . . "from now on . . . the bad news is . . ." They stared at him in silent, baited anticipation. "You will all have to . . ."

"Yeah, yeah, Jeremiah, we'll all what? What now?"

"You'll all have to answer to me. You're lookin' at your new corporal."

Silence reigned for a moment then Cy let out a whoop.

"Honest, Jeremiah? Corporal McCamey? Aw, seems to me we done listen to you good anyway. Now we don't have a choice, huh?" he laughed. "Congratulations, Jeremiah. How 'bout that?"

Jep stood up and looked down at his friend. "Well, you've been good at keepin' me outa trouble for years. Now I reckon you got official permission to be doin' it." He stuck out his hand and shook Jeremiah's firmly, with affection. "Cap'n couldn't done better in choosin'. I'm real proud, Jeremiah."

"Thanks, Jep."

"Does this mean I gotta salute you and call you sir?" Cy questioned disdainfully.

"Don't even think about it, Cy!" he answered forcefully. "The rank don't go that far!"

Andy, quiet up until now, began plunking his banjo again, this time to the tune of "The Bonnie Blue Flag." He sang out:

> *Was a private from Company G*
> *Jeremiah was his name,*
> *Got summoned by his Cap'n*
> *And a corporal he became.*

And when his men all heard it,
They knew they need not fear.
And from the ranks came one great big
Loud and rousing cheer!

They all laughed at the rendition. "Anderson, you may be a man of few words, but that banjo o' yours sure does do some expressin'," Jep quipped. "Reckon it just sorta speaks for you." Andy simply nodded his head.

~

Not until the fire died down and the men retired for the night did Jeremiah again think of the letter he saw on Captain Kertlin's desk. *Priscilla,* he thought, *my lovely sister. Do I detect too much of the protective older brother in me? Why haven't you told me of your friendship with Cap'n?*

He felt almost betrayed. He and Priscilla were so close and had shared so many things. Was it not 'Cilla he had turned to when he imagined his heart broken by Permillia two years ago? And had she not confided in him when Toby McGee asked her to sit next to him in church? Why would Prissy shut him out of her life now?

He couldn't sleep. Groping around in the dark tent for a pencil and paper, he escaped outside to the dying embers of the fire. *I must write 'Cilla now,* he thought. This war was causing so many unforeseen, trivial problems.

He felt utterly shut off from his family, and a longing to see them overwhelmed him.

As August wore on, the weather became unbearably hot. Vermin abound in camp. Fleas, lice and mosquitoes assaulted the men. Army regulations called for bathing once to twice a week, but it took a daily dip in the creek just to get temporary relief from the constant itching. Clothing, bedding, socks and underwear were infested by the little critters daily. Worms and weevils became a customary part of the food supply.

One morning a boy stood shaking his clothes over a blazing fire, in spite of the heat. "What by jingo is he doin', Jeremiah?" Cy wanted to know. "Sounds like he's poppin' corn for breakfast." A rapid succession of small exploding noises greeted their ears.

Jeremiah threw back his head and laughed. "No, he ain't poppin' corn, Cy, he's shakin' lice outa his uniform. I hear tell that's the best way to be rid of the critters. The bigger the rascals the louder they pop!"

Cy cringed, making Jeremiah laugh again. "Don't worry, we'll probably all be doin' the same thing before it's over with. I understand them little beggars don't care who you are or how clean you be. They like us all the same!"

At last, orders were received to pull out of Winchester and move back toward Staunton. The day before departure, Jeremiah received a letter from Priscilla.

> *Dearest Brother,*
>
> *First I want to congratulate you on your promotion to corporal. Of course, it didn't take me by surprise because I know you so well. I also knew you'd be furious with me when you learned of my friendship with John. Jeremiah, I dare say . . . you should understand that I did not want to place you in an awkward situation when you are already in such trying circumstances. I asked John for his silence as well, so do not hold that against him. He likes you Jeremiah, but not because you are my brother. I am very fond of your captain, and that is all I will say on the matter.*
>
> *There is not much news from home. Things are well. Mother heard from Uncle Boyton last week and he says cousin Geoffrey is doing fine; that life in the Yankee army is all right. He asked about you . . . what unit you were in. It is sometimes so hard for me to believe that being from the same family we can look at things so differently. I wish Geoffrey well.*
>
> *Violet and I have been over to see Mrs. Ash twice. She is so lonesome and frets over Cyril. I will also try to see that Jeptha gets more mail. It made me sad to hear that he receives so little. His Uncle Cal is not well. Preacher Foxly asked us to pray for him in church on Sunday.*
>
> *Violet sends her regards to Cyril. Please, Jeremiah. Sometimes this is just too much for me! I cannot see what the two have in common, but she is mad for him. War does strange things. She says to send you a kiss. Bonniejean gives you a hug.*
>
> *I will close now. I do miss you so. Please be careful.*
>
> *Love From,*
> *Prissy*

He smiled. *How like 'Cilla. Straight and to the point! She's certainly right. War does change things,* he thought unhappily.

Tents were struck the next morning and the march to Staunton began. Once more men were left behind as typhoid fever swept the ranks, filling the hospitals again. The number of men lost to disease was greater than that lost in the fighting.

Lieutenant Colonel Jackson had been promoted to Brigadier General after the Battle of Manassas. His strong confidence and the boldness of his men served him well.

The boys in Company G learned that Parker had been correct in some of his knowledge about the man. He did love lemons and ate them by the dozens. Some thought he exhibited rather odd ways, but no one doubted his concern for them as his men. He constantly encouraged his ranks, seeing to their welfare. He ate what his men ate, slept on the ground with them and suffered what they suffered; but none of the soldiers were prepared for the discipline General Jackson expected from them.

Shortly after camp at Staunton was reached, rigorous training began. Cy wrote to Violet, trying to describe their daily routine:

My Sweet Violet,

Life since we have got back to Staunton has been real hectic like. There ain't been no fightin', but Ol' Jack means to learn us somethin'. He's real hard on seein' we get some discipline and sometimes I think it'd have been real good if'n we'd had him over us to start with, when we first joined up. But I gotta tell you, Darlin' . . . sometimes I'm most fit to drop. When we drill, we don't just march, but we do it in the double quick, which is most like runnin'. When the bugle wakes us in the mornin' we fall right into rank and drill. After that, we drill again. Then the bugle calls us to breakfast, and we eat real quick so's we can drill some more. After this drill, we have a little more drill, and in between drills we drill again. Then "roast beef" sounds (Honey, that's the name we done give to the bugle call for dinner) and after we eat (we gets most an hour and half) the bugle calls us back into rank and we drill, drill, and then drill some more. 'Bout 4:00 p.m., we stop . . . that's how I'm writin' you this. If we done good we're over for the day. If'n not, we drill again after our supper. We're quite a purty sight now . . . we mosts work together as a unit. When you get in the heat o' fire, you find out all this discipline done you good. The boys among us have become men now.

One drill we have on Sunday is called "knapsack" and it ain't no pleasure experience! We all hafta line up by company, then one of the Generals inspects us . . . we hafta leave our knapsacks open at our feets, and if'n we have one thing not up to regulation, we gets a real dressin' down, first by the General, and then the Cap'n will get in big trouble cause his mens not fittin' and then we gets it again from Cap'n. Ain't no fun. I ain't been got yet. General Jackson, he done tell us if'n we go to the church service on Sunday mornin' then we gets excused from this infernal drill. Since most of us have learned the value of goin' to service, we done now been excused 'cept for once. General makes the rest of the Sabbath be for restin'. We most look forward to that!

Darlin', you'd be real proud. Your brother's a real good corporal. Me an' Jep is proud o' him, too. You'd also be proud o' your own soldier here . . . Jeremiah says I'm the coolest one under fire he ever did see.

Honey, I'd best be signin' off now. Pret soon I be back at drillin'. Think of me some and know I'm . . .

Affectionately Yours,
Cyril

CHAPTER SIX

I'm a young volunteer
And my heart is true to our flag that woos the wind.
Then three cheers for our flag and our Southland, too,
And the girls we leave behind.

As summer turned to autumn and the days grew cool, the boys settled into camp routine. Time not drilling was filled with the mundane chores of digging latrines, garbage pits and cutting wood.

November turned cold and winter weather set in. As December rolled around, men began to express a longing for Christmas at home.

"What we need in this here camp is a Christmas tree," Cy declared one afternoon. "Who's game that we go and find one?" With Jeremiah and Jeptha, he took to the woods. Dragging a stout fir into camp later that day, the men became cheered with holiday spirit, decorating it with whatever they could find.

The same evening, a light snow began to fall. Huddled in his blanket, Jeremiah lay close to the tent opening, watching white flakes dance to the ground. A hush seemed to have fallen over the world when somewhere in the distance a fiddle tenderly struck up quiet tunes of the season. His eyes misted, for even as a small boy this was his favorite time of the year. His heart felt heavy, convincing him that it was time to speak to Captain Kertlin about some leave. It had been granted several times to men with homes and families close by. His was but a three-hour ride . . .

How could he leave his friends and his men? Surely it was too much to expect that leave would be granted all three of them, even if just for a day's time. *Well, all I can do is be told no,* he thought.

When "roast beef" sounded the next day, Jeremiah ate his dinner quickly and went to seek out the captain. He found him enjoying a hearty meal with several other officers.

"Captain Kertlin, Sir," Jeremiah saluted, "when you are done with your dinner, may I have a word with you, Sir?"

"Something wrong, McCamey?" he questioned.

"No, Sir, just a matter . . . a personal matter that I'd like to take up with you."

"Certainly. Let's go into my tent now. I'm finished eating. Gentlemen," he spoke to the others present, "you will excuse me."

The day was cold and the tent did not offer as much warmth as the fire out front. Directing Jeremiah to pull up a stool, the captain sat at his desk. Lighting a pipe, he took a long draw and looked at Jeremiah.

Jeremiah shivered from the cold. "You all right, McCamey?"

"Yes, Sir. I just rightly don't know how to speak to you on this matter."

"Does it concern your men?"

"Well, some of them. In a way."

"It's your job to help look after them. What's needed?" Captain Kertlin asked matter-of-factly.

"Sir, well, Cap'n, I was wonderin' if you'd grant leave for me and some o' the boys for a couple o' days."

"Let me guess . . ." he took another draw on his pipe. "Carroll and Ash."

"Yes, Sir. Anderson too."

"Wouldn't that look like favoritism?"

"Yes, Sir, it would. And that's what's worrin' me about this whole thing. Only it's that we all live close to each other . . . in the same area."

"Yes, I know," he nodded, "the New Church community."

"Yes, Sir. Except for Anderson. He's from west o' here . . . ain't got a whole lot to go home to. Was aimin' on askin' him to join us. Take him home with me."

"That's kind of you, McCamey. I of course cannot grant this request. The colonel must do it. But I'll see what I can do to convince him. There is only one condition I ask, McCamey."

"Yes, Sir. You name it. I appreciate this, Sir."

Captain Kertlin hesitated. "I . . . I'll allow you any leave granted, under the stipulation that I . . . that I accompany you."

"Accompany me?" Jeremiah questioned wide-eyed, then understood. "You want to see Priscilla?" he asked candidly.

"Yes, I do."

"Well, I reckon I can't fault you none for that. We ain't got a big place, but I'm sure we'll find some room for you, Sir."

Jeremiah was silent for a moment. Priscilla really never mentioned Captain Kertlin in her newsy letters from home. Would this be something she would want?

"Cap'n, I don't really know much about your relationship with my sister. I will respect your word on this. Will 'Cilla be pleased to have you come?"

"I hope. I have no reason to believe otherwise."

"Then I'm sure my folks will be honored to have you."

"Remember, Corporal, I cannot grant this request. It is up to Colonel Hartshare."

"Yes, Sir. I understand that. Thank you, Cap'n." He saluted, then offered Captain Kertlin his hand.

"Thank you for allowing me to invite myself, McCamey," he responded with a firm shake.

"My pleasure, Cap'n. As long as 'twill please 'Cilla."

"Oh, by the way . . . before you go, here's some mail. Mail call will be sounded shortly, but you might as well take these on to your men." He handed Jeremiah a handful of letters.

Taking leave of the captain, Jeremiah looked at the envelopes in his hands. There was one each for several of the men: Killian, Drew, Noah . . . two for Cy—one from his Ma, the other one from Violet. He recognized the handwriting and held the letter to his nose, detecting a faint whiff of perfume. It smelled like Violet . . . the jasmine scent she always wore. He felt a pang of homesickness; he hadn't smelled that pleasing fragrance in a long time, for she certainly never perfumed her letters to him! He shook his head in wonderment. He'd never get used to the thought of Cy and Violet together.

The last letter he held was for Jeptha. Jep got so little mail, and mostly from Jeremiah's own family. He didn't recognize the writing on this one, though, so he held it to his face and sniffed. No, not perfumed . . . he'd love nothing more than to be able to tease Jep about some secret admirer . . .

"Boys! Mail call!" he shouted as he returned to their fire. He began handing out the letters, watching Cy's eyes brighten at the sight of Violet's. Cy took a long whiff of it, then smiled, putting it aside to open last.

"Jep, my man . . . one for you. Dunno who it's from . . . don't recognize the writin'." He tossed it to his friend, who looked at it quizzically. Shrugging his shoulders, Jeptha tore open the envelope.

"Sorry, you and I get left out today," Jeremiah said, turning to Andy.

Suddenly hopping up, Jeptha walked away, the letter he received crumpled in his hand. Quickly, he disappeared among the tents.

Cy looked up from his mail. "What's got in his craw?"

"Dunno, Cy, dunno," Jeremiah answered with concern, his eyes following in Jeptha's direction.

When the bugle sounded a return to drill, Jeptha was present, but silent. Once the day's activities ceased, he again became scarce. When he did not show for supper call, Jeremiah's concern got the best of him, and he decided to find out the cause of the problem. He felt certain it had something to do with that letter he'd received.

After nearly half an hour of searching, he finally found Jeptha back behind camp lines. In the middle of a creek, stretched out on some boulders, his belly rested against the hard, cold rocks, his hand dapping aimlessly in the bright water now frozen along the sides of the giant stones. He had neither blanket nor greatcoat around him, and the sight made Jeremiah shiver. It was so cold.

With each breath Jeremiah exhaled, a cloud of vapor surrounded his head. "Ho, Jep! What are you doin'?" he called. "Cold as blue blazes out here! Mess is over; ain't you hungry none?"

"Leave me be, Jeremiah," he answered angrily, sitting up on his knees. "Don't bother me. Just leave me be."

Jeremiah stood at the edge of the creek, contemplating the situation. "Well, I ain't gonna allow you to stay out here and freeze! Good heavens, Jep. Sun's soon to be down. If you ain't cold now, you sure gonna be then!"

Jeptha said nothing; his mouth was set in a grim line.

"All right Jep. You want it this way? I ain't talkin' to you as your friend now. As your superior in rank, I order you back across this creek!"

Jeptha knew he was outdone.

"Jep, I ain't gonna have you freeze to death or sickness just because you're so dad-blamed stubborn."

Jeptha smiled a lopsided smile and then threw up his hand.

"I'm comin'," he said dismally.

He picked his way back across the rocks, his teeth chattering as he stepped on the ground.

"You can be so foolish sometimes, Jep," Jeremiah exclaimed in annoyance. "Foolish and stubborn! What in tarnation ails you today?"

Jeptha took the letter from his pocket and handed it to his friend. His teeth continued to chatter, so that Jeremiah took off his own great coat and put it around Jeptha's shoulders.

"Here, take this," he said, "'til you warm up. Those chattering teeth make you sound like a woodpecker." Jeremiah shuddered. "Sure is gonna be cold tonight," he stated, folding open the letter.

As he began to read, Jeptha started talking.

"Uncle Cal's dead, Jeremiah," he said matter-of-factly. "Letter's from Preacher Foxly." He pulled the coat closer about him. "Much obliged for the wrapper."

Jeremiah glanced at the missive. "Says here your land has been confiscated? I don't understand. What happened?"

"Oh, just read on. It'll make sense."

Jeremiah continued to read. "He never owned it?" he asked incredulously. "Your Uncle never owned the land?"

"Obviously," Jeptha replied curtly.

"Never had no reason to ever think about that, Jep. I just assumed . . ."

"Yeah, so did I. Look, the old man did the best he could. You know, he wasn't even my Ma's brother, but her Pa's brother. We got along all right, most of the times, though I'm sure I could be pretty ornery . . ."

"You're that way now."

"Yeah, well, maybe sometimes."

Jeremiah gazed at Jeptha. "I always did like your Uncle Cal. I'm mighty sorry 'bout all this."

"Guess me and him made it all right. Had our differences, though. He was against me joinin' up, Jeremiah. I ain't never told that to no one. I just did what I felt like I had to do. What was the right thing in my mind. Uncle Cal was totally against this secession business. Never could quite convince him that we was havin' to fight for our rights, needin' to defend our homes. He didn't rightly understand it all. We didn't part on real great terms, Jeremiah . . . but to not own the land!" Jeptha shook his head from side to side in disbelief, and grew quiet for several moments. "Why didn't he just tell me?" he sighed through gritted teeth.

"Well, reckon all I got now is this here army. Don't know what I'll do when the fightin's done. Once we're independent though; once we've won this war . . . who knows, maybe I'll stick to the army for good . . . make this my life. Ever think about that, Jeremiah?" he questioned.

"Can't say that I have. Guess I've always just thought of runnin' my folks' farm. Findin' me a good gal sometime . . . gettin' married . . . havin' a passel o' young'uns. Guess that's what I always just figured I'd do. Things change, though, huh? Sure never dreamed I'd be off fightin' in any war." The two friends walked on.

"Well, I'm indebted to you for listenin', Jeremiah. I didn't plan on tellin' anyone about all this . . . just workin' my thoughts out and goin' on."

"Talkin' can help sometimes, Jep. Can give a fresh perspective to things."

"Yeah, well . . . reckon' I was just feelin' a mite sorry for myself."

"I know, Jep. I know. And I am truly sorry 'bout things."

"Yeah, well, me too, Jeremiah. Me too," he heaved a sigh. "Kind of a strange feelin', knowin' you ain't really got nothin' out there in this world."

"Reckon there's lots of folks like that, Jep."

"Yeah."

Jeremiah started thinking about the leave time he had requested earlier. *Sure hadn't intended on Jep havin' no place to go,* he thought. *Maybe he won't even wanna take leave . . . no, can't think that; gotta convince him. He can stay with us . . . Jep, Andy, Cap'n . . .* he laughed. *Mother will love me for this.*

As their quarters came into view, Jep broke the silence. "Jeremiah, don't say nothin' to Cy 'bout all this, all right? Let me handle it. Gee, sometimes he gets so motherly I can't stand it. I feel sorry enough for myself. Don't want his sorrowin' too."

The night was bitterly cold and the boys found it warmer to sleep wrapped up in their blankets by the fire instead of sleeping in their tent. Turns were taken to keep the fire burning all night.

When the bugle sounded wake-up, Jeremiah groaned and rubbed his eyes. He felt frozen to the ground. At some point, the fire had burned down to embers and now exuded little warmth. He stood up, and stoking the flames to life, shivered. Wrapping his blanket around him, he nudged his messmates awake. "Reveille, boys! Let's get up!" He took off down the row of tents to be sure all the men he was responsible for were roused and fit after the frigid night.

Morning drill was short so that the men might eat and down plenty of hot coffee to help keep them warm. As they ate their bacon and corn cakes, Captain Kertlin came into view. Quickly the four rose to salute, the captain returning the gesture absent-mindedly.

"McCamey," he said brusquely, "a word with you."

"Certainly, Sir." Jeremiah placed his breakfast down upon the log on which he was sitting. "Coffee, Sir?" he asked.

"Yes, thank you."

Retrieving an extra cup, he filled it with the hot, brown liquid, offering it to Captain Kertlin. The officer took it, holding its warmth to his face for a moment.

"Inside, Sir." Jeremiah held their tent flap open. "Afraid this ain't as warm as the fire," he said, motioning Captain Kertlin to sit on a crude stool, pulling another one up for himself.

"I've spoken to Colonel Hartshare about your request," the captain began.

"I ain't mentioned nothin' to the men, Sir. Didn't wanna let 'em down."

"That was wise, McCamey" the captain interjected, realizing the sergeant was ready to face disappointment.

"Colonel Hartshare has granted us seventy-two hours," he continued, "from the time we leave to the time we arrive back in camp. No more."

"That's three days, Sir!" Jeremiah counted excitedly. "We only live 'bout a three-hour ride."

"I'm going to try to procure some horses. I, of course, have my own, but I'll need to know how many others to arrange for," the captain offered.

"Yeah . . . I dunno if Carroll will go or not, Cap'n. He's just had some bad news from home. Might find it more to his likin' to stay here right now."

"Well, I'm sorry about that. Anything I can do?"

"No, Sir, I don't believe so. He'll work through it."

"Anything else your men need?"

"No, Sir."

"One more thing, McCamey. To go, we go tomorrow. I don't s'pose that gives you much time to warn your folks."

"Well, Sir, no it don't. But I don't look for it to be a problem neither. Some of us may hafta bed down in the barn, but even that's better than sleepin' in a frigid tent!"

"I suggest we leave midmorning so the sun has time to thaw things up a bit. I need to know who's goin' soon as I can, McCamey, to report intentions to Colonel Hartshare and procure any animals."

"Yes, Sir. I sure do thank you, Sir. Looks like we'll be spendin' Christmas Day in camp, but this is truly more than I'd hoped for."

Captain Kertlin rose, Jeremiah jumping up to salute. "Soon, McCamey, soon," he said.

"Right away, Sir!"

Leaving, he placed his tin cup down upon the log on which sat Jeremiah's unfinished breakfast. Glancing at the plate, the captain raised his eyebrows. "Sorry, McCamey. Didn't know I kept you so long." He picked up a frozen corn cake from the dish and thumped it. "Humph. Might have artillery check into this," he laughed.

Jeremiah's breakfast was frozen solid, ruining what he had left of any appetite.

"Boys, gather 'round the fire," he spoke, "I got a piece of news for you."

"What now, Jeremiah?" Cy questioned in frustration.

The boys simply stared at him quizzically. They had become used to spur of the moment orders.

"Boys, startin' tomorrow we got . . ." he paused, trying not to crack the smile wanting to spread across his face, "seventy-two hours leave. Compliments of Captain Kertlin and Colonel Hartshare!" he finished excitedly.

"Whoopee!" Cy jumped up, shouting. "All right! All right! Ma, your boy's comin' home!"

"Andy," Jeremiah looked at him "you're welcome to come home with me. I know it's a far piece for you to make it home and back in that time."

"Thanky, Jeremiah. But my li'l sister lives in Weyer's Cave with her young family. Believe I can catch the train here in Staunton and get there in a few hours time. They'd sure be a sight for sore eyes."

"All right . . . suit yourself. You are welcome."

"And I thank you, too, Jeremiah. But I do believe I'd like to see 'Lizabeth and her young'uns."

Jeptha, staring into the fire, didn't say a word, and Jeremiah joined him upon the log on which he sat. "Jep, I do hope you'll be goin' with us. Cap'n's goin' too."

Jep faced Jeremiah and smiled wryly. *It is, indeed, a sad face,* thought Jeremiah.

"What's he goin' for?" Jeptha echoed his thoughts.

"Now, why do you think?" Jeremiah huffed sarcastically.

Jeptha nodded his head. "Goin' to see 'Cilla, I reckon. Bein' from here in Staunton I reckon he gets to see his own family enough." Jeremiah had told his friends of the relationship between his sister and their captain, extracting a promise from both that it would never be mentioned to anyone.

"You'll stay with us, of course, Jep."

"Naw, Jeremiah," he looked at his friend with a long face.

"C'mon, Jep," Jeremiah laughed, "we might have to sleep in the barn, but that ain't nothin' new to us!"

"No, don't think so . . ." the boy paused, shaking his head. He enjoyed the dismay he knew he was evoking in his friend. "Reckon I'll just stay with Cy and his Ma," he voiced after a solemn silence.

"Atta, boy, Jep! But you know you are welcome . . . you know that without bein' told."

"Yeah . . . Jeremiah, when will you ever quit bein' Mr. Nice Fella?'"

"Well, now . . . seems to me I weren't none too nice yesterday, orderin' you off them rocks . . . ha! That was a good, direct order . . . it got followed, too!"

~

By midmorning, the four men were ready to set out. Andy left for his trek to the train station in Staunton and Captain Kertlin showed up with three fine mounts for the boys use over the next seventy-two hours. "Count your blessings, lads," he said. "I didn't reckon it'd be fair for me to have the only horse for ridin', but I had to beg, borrow and almost steal to procure these animals for the rest of you!"

The journey passed quickly. Though the day was cold, the bright sun warmed them and by noon, Cy and Jep were turning off onto the fork that led to the Ash homeplace.

Shortly thereafter, Jeremiah and Captain Kertlin reached the McCamey farm. It seemed strangely quiet as smoke curled up from both chimnies of the homestead.

"Reckon it's too cold to be out and about unless one has to be," Jeremiah surmised out loud. The two dismounted.

"McCamey," Captain Kertlin declared, "I'll just wait outside here; give you a chance to make your presence known and . . . and, ah, well, tell them you've brung an added burden."

Jeremiah laughed. He knew the captain did not wish to be an intruder at this homecoming.

He fairly leaped onto the porch. Before opening the door he turned, and giving one last look at Captain Kertlin, disappeared inside.

Sitting on the bottom stair in the entranceway playing with a doll, Bonniejean was first to see him. The little girl squealed, jumping into his arms. Grabbing her tightly, he pressed her face to his. "Sweetheart!" he exclaimed, "How does your big brother look to you?"

She said nothing, but continued to hug him, the commotion bringing Mother and Father to the door.

Placing Bonniejean on her feet, Jeremiah quickly and affectionately shook his father's hand and then embraced him.

"I'm mighty proud of you, Son, mighty proud!" the elder man whispered, slapping his corporal stripes.

Hands clasped as though in prayer, Jeremiah's mother stood transfixed as she stared at her son. A linen napkin from dinner still dangled in one hand.

"Jeremiah!" she finally exclaimed, tears sparkling in her eyes. "Just look at you! You're not my boy any longer . . . you . . . why, you look like a man!"

Laughing, he wrapped his arms tightly about her and planted a kiss on her head. "Ma, Mother . . . you might not be so glad to see me when I inform you that I've brought a guest along . . . and invited Cy, his ma and Jep for the day tomorrow. I've only got seventy-two hours."

Suddenly, a door banged from the back of the dwelling where Violet was busy clearing dishes from their meal. Her voice resounded through the house. "Where *is* everybody?" she asked in loud exasperation.

"Violet! Violet! Come see who's here!" Bonniejean screamed as her sister stepped into the entranceway.

"Jeremiah!" she whispered exuberantly. "Jeremiah!" Opening her arms to receive a warm embrace, she kissed his cheek soundly. "Oh Jeremiah! How good you look!" she cried in a breathy voice. "I can't believe you're here!" She hugged him again, and letting go, glanced around, clasping her hands to her heart. Standing directly in front of her brother, as though this somehow shut the others out, she whispered, "How is Cyril, Jeremiah? Is he well? Oh, tell me, please."

"Reckon you're gonna get the chance to find out," he quipped.

Her hand flew to her mouth. "He's here?" she asked in disbelief.

"No Pumpkin, not right now. He and Jep are with his Ma. But he'll be along later tomorrow. That is, if he can stay away from you that long."

Her blue eyes sparkled as she spoke in an excited breath. "I don't know if I can wait 'til tomorrow!"

"All in time, Pumpkin, all in time. Hey, I'm 'round him every day. He ain't nothin' to get so excited over!" Playfully, he stroked her honey colored curls. "Really, Violet, contain yourself!" he teased her. "I still don't get it," he laughed with a shake of his head

Ready to inquire about Priscilla, he spotted her on the upstairs landing. Gathering her skirts, she flew down the stairs two at a time, dashing into his arms.

"Oh Jeremiah!" she whispered in disbelief. "I've missed you! I can't believe you're here," she said, starting to cry.

"Shhh . . . now don't do that. There's someone outside who wants very much to see you."

"Who?" she asked curiously wiping tears from her eyes. "I've had a terrible headache all afternoon. I look so disheveled."

"Well, go see Prissy! Don't let the poor soul freeze. Here," he said taking off his coat, "put this on. It's cold out there." He wrapped his great coat about his sister, pushing her out the door.

"Cap'n's with me for the leave," he informed the rest of his family.

Only their too quick end marred the joy of the seventy-two hours. It proved to be a time of great reflection for all as Christmas was celebrated early and promises were made.

During the long journey back to camp, there were often lengthy periods of silence. Each man brooded over what was being left behind and on the uncertainty of what was to come.

Becoming involved in an animated political discussion, Jeptha and Captain Kertlin, in pursuit of their ideas, rode several yards ahead of the other two. It was then Cy turned to the corporal.

"Jeremiah?"

"Yep," he answered, riding readily along, his eyes staring straight ahead.

"I asked Miss Violet to wait for me."

Jeremiah rode on in silence for a moment. "I thought you weren't marryin' anybody."

"Well now . . . I ain't. Not now. I asked her to wait for me 'til this war is over."

Jeremiah had already come to the conclusion that this was going to be a longer war than anyone was willing to admit, but he kept his thoughts to himself.

"So what'd she say?" he asked, continuing to peer ahead, keeping his horse at a slow, leisurely gait.

"Now what d'ya think?" Cy answered. "You said it yourself. She's crazy about me!"

Jeremiah didn't say anything for several seconds. "Remember Cy," he spoke matter-of-factly. "I've done told you . . . you break her heart, you answer to me."

Cy stopped the easy walk of his horse and looked his friend in the eyes. "Don't worry, Jeremiah. Don't worry," he said softly, suddenly spurring his mount on again. "I love her!" he cried back to his friend.

"So, what do you think of the news about the fine Miss Swilley?" Cy suddenly changed the subject as Jeremiah caught up to him.

"I don't even wanna discuss it, Cy. It makes no never mind to me. We all shoulda had her figured out long before we did. Especially this boy."

"Yeah, but she's so purty . . . kinda won't let you think straight. But I sure never figured on her runnin' off to marry up with some Yank officer," he shook his head. "Even if he was someone she'd always knowed."

"Yeah . . ." Jeremiah chuckled, "reckon she thinks we're all waitin' on her too . . . or eatin' our hearts out. Ha! I don't know that even some Yankee deserves her, Cy. I can't help but laugh. War does strange things, huh?"

CHAPTER SEVEN

With God and right upon our side,
We'll win the day or die.
The foemen's host will shrink this day
Before our battle cry.

Camp was bristling when they reached Staunton. Captain Kertlin recognized it immediately. "Something's afoot, my boys," he said, quickly dismounting and tossing his reins to Cy. "I'm gonna go find Colonel Hartshare. You will be alerted when I know something. Would you please see that these animals get returned to the camp stables? Just ask for Sergeant Baker."

As soon as they were free of the horses, the three made their way to their own quarters. "I'll go check in with Sergeant Spruill," Jeremiah said, "make sure there were no problems while we were gone."

Quickly, he rejoined them. "Spruill reports all fine in our absence. Lots of the boys is homesick, though. Some just live a piece too far to be granted short leave. One thing, Cap'n is right. Somethin's up, but Spruill don't know anymore than we do. Figure Cap'n will come 'round directly. Reckon I'd better go check on the rest of the boys. Let 'em know we've returned. Anybody seen Anderson?"

"From the looks o' things, Jeremiah," Cy answered, "I'd say he ain't come back yet. Tent looks mighty undisturbed. His banjo ain't 'round neither."

"Well, I 'spect he'll be along directly. Leave time's done run out. Maybe he's with some of the other fellas. I'll go ask if anyone's seen him."

By the time Jeremiah returned, Jep and Cy had a roaring fire going and a pot of coffee on to boil. Captain Kertlin was seated around its warmth, chatting with the two.

"Cap'n, Sir," Jeremiah saluted him, "what goes on? Sergeant Spruill says camp's been set with action, but no one knows what the story is."

"I don't know much more than that myself. Colonel Hartshare says he's been given command to be ready to move out any moment. Maybe tonight, maybe not 'til next week, but we must be ready whenever word is received. General Jackson has been dispatched to set up headquarters in Winchester. When we go, we go to join up with him. This here regiment and the 28th are what will be goin'."

Jeremiah was thoughtful as the three listened to the crackle of the fire. "Why just two regiments, Cap'n?" the corporal finally questioned.

"Dunno. Guess one's stayin' here. General Jackson took some men from the 28th with him. Reckon we won't know nothin' 'til he wants us to know . . . 'til it's time.

"Well boys . . . call for afternoon drill will be soundin' soon. Best you'ns get ready to fall into rank. Our fun's officially over."

Seeming to look for words to continue, the captain was silent for a moment. Finally, he spoke for them all, "Corporal McCamey, I do want to thank you for allowing us to enjoy your family's hospitality the last two days. It, ah . . ." he cleared his throat, "it meant a great deal to me."

Jeremiah didn't respond, but gave the captain a look of understanding. Priscilla had, at last, confided in him concerning her feelings for John Kertlin.

"Well, ah, I'll just be goin' now . . ." he looked at each face as he rose to leave, embarrassed by the stares of Jep and Cy. They glared at him as though they knew every thought he ever had about Priscilla. Sometimes he forgot she was almost like a sister to them.

The bugle calling afternoon drill sounded and the men fell into rank. It was easy to return to the routine of things; the soldiers found more warmth in drilling on such a cold afternoon than standing by the fire.

When supper call sounded and the boys began to cook their rations, uneasiness settled in Jeremiah. Where was Anderson? He was due back the same time they were and had yet to return. He knew he'd be forced to put him on report to Captain Kertlin should he not show by time to retire. Something wasn't right. Andy would never fail to return of his own accord. Some of the men he wouldn't put such nonsense past, but certainly not Anderson.

As they ate, Jeptha echoed the same feelings. "Where do you suppose Andy to be? I just can't see him not reportin' back. He didn't even ask for his leave . . . you just got it for him, Jeremiah. Somethin' ain't right here."

"Yeah, I been thinkin' the same thing," Cy voiced, "just didn't wanna say it. I agree Jep . . . somethin' ain't right."

"Well boys, ain't much we can do about it . . . but I aim on takin' a report to Cap'n before the night settles in," Jeremiah declared.

"You ain't gonna tell on him?" Jep asked in disbelief.

"Jep, it ain't tellin' on him. First off, I gotta job required of me. If I can't do what's expected of my rank I don't deserve havin' it. Secondly . . . suppose Andy's run into some kinda trouble gettin' back? Somethin' that ain't his fault?"

"Well, reckon we ain't done thought none about that," Cy reflected.

"Yeah . . . guess you're right . . . you gotta do what you gotta do," Jep said, looking up at the corporal. He still was not convinced it wouldn't be telling on their comrade.

Shortly before the bugle announced quiet for the night, Jeremiah went to report to Captain Kertlin that Andy was, indeed, absent without leave. "Cap'n, Sir," he saluted.

"What is it, McCamey?" the officer sighed, looking up from some papers he was studying.

"It . . . it's Anderson, Sir. He ain't . . . hasn't come back from leave. I reckoned I ought to put him on some kind of report to you."

"Are you harboring thoughts that Anderson is absent without leave, Corporal? Is that what you are suggesting?"

"I . . . I don't know, Sir. I don't know what to think, Cap'n!" He wiped clammy palms on his pants. "It . . . it just ain't like him," he finished nervously.

"Did you report this to Sergeant Spruill?"

Jeremiah shook his head. "No. I reckon I should have, Cap'n, but I asked for this leave. I suppose I feel responsible."

The captain looked back down at the papers before him. "We're waiting on a report now from some of Stuart's cavalry scouts. Hear tell a train comin' down the pike from Strasburg was hijacked just outside Mt. Sidney. Anderson was probably on that train if the story's true."

"Hijacked?" Jeremiah questioned incredulously.

"Yeah . . . hard to believe," the captain replied in frustration.

"Hijacked by whom? What? There was a large enough contingency of Yankees that close by?"

"Don't take many men, Jeremiah, if somethin' like this is planned well. But that's all I can tell you now. It's all I know.

"But see, Anderson ain't the only man due back from leave that didn't show. Several men from other companies who'd have been on that train ain't showed yet."

"Well then, Sir," Jeremiah exhaled, "can't but feel a mite relieved, and can't help but believe the story's true. Let me know, Sir, when and if you learn somethin'."

"Will do, Corporal. Will do." The captain yawned. "It's been a long day."

"Yes, Sir, it has. See you on the morrow, Cap'n."

"Good night, McCamey."

"Good night, Sir," Jeremiah saluted him, but Captain Kertlin merely waved him on.

Sometime after midnight the three friends were roused from a deep sleep as Sergeant Spruill awakened them. "Men! Men! Up and at 'em. We got a job to do. McCamey, report to Cap'n right away to receive some orders!"

Jeremiah scrambled into his clothes and greatcoat. "Let me go see what's up, boys. I suppose Sergeant Spruill will alert the rest of the men."

Other corporals were arriving at Captain Kertlin's quarters as Jeremiah got there.

"Men," the captain said, "Company G has been called upon to render service to its country. Your lads need to be ready to march in two hours time. Have them prepare three days' rations. We're heading north . . . to free an ambushed train full of our men. Then we're to round up those of our regiment and any belonging to the 28th, and move on to join Jackson at Winchester. The rest of the men will follow Colonel Tristan back to camp, and the remainder of our unit will then be sent join us. Don't know what situation we'll find, men, but let's go prepared to do our duty!"

"Out of curiosity, Sir," Jeremiah asked, "how come we get picked for such a mission?"

"I volunteered us, McCamey. Any more questions?"

"No, Sir!" the corporals thundered in unison.

"Then off with you! Assemble yourselves and your boys where your sergeants tell you. We will be moving out at 3 A.M. None present will be considered derelict of duty, understood?"

"Yes, Cap'n," each replied in salute, moving off.

The men focused attentively to Jeremiah as he explained as much as he could of their mission, and the air crackled with their enthusiasm.

They were ready to do what was necessary to achieve their goal, even if it meant a fight.

At the prescribed time, all men were in good order, ready to move out, and listened intently as Captain Kertlin spelled out their objectives. "Take the train back, boys! Take the train back!" he ended his message.

Into the still, dark, cold night the men marched; ready to do their job; ready to die doing it.

As the darkness turned into light, the soldiers discovered what their constant drilling had accomplished. Quietly and secretly, they had moved out into the night. Facing bitter cold, the old snow of several days ago crunched beneath their feet. As the hours passed, they found themselves surprisingly unfatigued, and full of determination. Trekking toward their destination, they learned in full detail what had occurred as the story filtered down the ranks from one man to another.

"The train done come down from Harrisonburg," cited one private, "then stopped at Weyer's Cave and again at Mount Sidney. I heard the lieutenant say it come through Sidney Gap and was overtaken by blue bellies. Then Colonel Tristan said that Stuart's cavalry scouts discovered the engine dislodged from the rest of the cars, disabling the train."

Jeremiah listened as another boy rattled on. "Sergeant Spruill, now he thinks the mistake made by the Yankees was in thinkin' the train carried supplies. It did carry some necessities, but we all know the majority of our replinishin's come into Staunton through Lynchburg on the Alexandria and Orange line.

"Anyway, when the train was stopped at Sidney Gap, a length of track was also destroyed. According to the scouts, it wasn't until then that the enemy discovered what few supplies the train carried." The soldier laughed. "They were caught off guard by the number of us Rebels on board. Didn't have any idea so many would be returning from leave, headin' back to camp at Staunton.

"The force in blue weren't very large, but big enough to guard a captive train well. They ain't allowin' anyone to disembark. Lieutenant believes they've probably sent for reinforcements from the town of Romney because there aren't enough blue troops to take prisoners of the Rebs on board. To remove them Rebels from the cars would mean outnumbering themselves. They ain't got no choice but to guard the train until reinforcements arrive. Like Cap'n says, if we can get there first, it'll mean the end of this fiasco."

By late afternoon, it was obvious the train could not be reached until the following morning. Cold and fatigue began to take a toll on the men, so at sundown, a halt was called for the day.

A quiet, still camp was set up that night. Fires were limited and quickly doused. Rations cooked up for the journey were frozen in the knapsacks and needed to be thawed before eating. Boiled coffee was the real treat this cold evening. As cups of the hot liquid were drained and refilled, the men seemed to lose some of their fatigue and warmth returned to their bodies. Patches of ground were swept clear of old snow and great coats thrown down as beds. Wrapped in blankets, the soldiers settled down for the night to get what little sleep they could. They would be roused long before dawn in order to continue the mission.

The next morning, Sidney Gap closed in quickly as they filed rank and marched on. Captain Kertlin had devised a plan requiring the men to surround the train by cover of darkness.

Hiding away among the mountains, rocks, trees and brush, they would wait until dawn when the men in blue were eating and warming themselves. They would strike at this time, overwhelming the Federals and setting the train free.

Coming over a ridge that followed along the tracks, Sergeant Spruill sighted the engine, alone and abandoned on a stretch of rail with only the wood car behind it. He commanded the men to be instantly silent.

"McCamey," he whispered urgently, "take a small contingency of your men and check out that engine. Secure it if necessary and wait for word. Then, if practicable, it'll be backed up and reunited with the other cars . . . but guard it for now above all else!"

Jeremiah looked quickly around, calling upon several in his command. "Jep, Cy, get Noah and Franklin, and you, Berry, you go too. You fellows follow this ridge down to the right and approach the engine from the front. Move cautiously now; you ain't got no good cover. Killian, you and Brooks . . . Drew, you go with 'em; follow down on the left. You got some trees there, stay hidden best you can." Jeremiah glanced around again. He needed someone bold and calm to help him approach from the center. "Private Samuels," he called, spotting the tall, strong man behind him, "I like your fightin' reputation. You and me, Sam, we'll go down in the middle. The rest of you men, stay with Cap'n and move on. We'll see you again shortly.

"Ready men? Take your post," he whispered. "We'll meet around on the other side so that the engine gets circled. Any questions? All right, let's go." Putting a forefinger to his lips to signal silence, he pointed out each group as they were to descend from the ridge.

Once the first two groups began to move noiselessly down the slope, Jeremiah pushed Private Jonah Samuels down the center with him.

Muskets primed and ready to fire if necessary, each group executed the corporal's orders until the engine was reached. In the pre-dawn light, it rose like a sleeping giant out of the dark, silent cold. Uniting on the other side as planned, the circling of the engine proved it to be deserted from the outside.

"All right, men, now we search the interior. Who's game? Jep, Cy, Sam—come with me. The rest of you boys post yourselves and give warning if need be, but don't fire unless fired upon!"

As they rounded the backside of the engine, Cy was first to speak. "It sure is dark, Jeremiah. How we gonna see anything?"

"Do the best we can. Can't light any light . . . might draw attention. Our eyes'll adjust," he answered authoritatively. "We'll know, I'm sure, if there are any blue bellies aboard. Cy, Jep . . . you two go check out that wood car. Sam, come with me."

Silently, Jeremiah and Sam stepped up to the engineer's compartment. It smelled of cold oil and burned wood.

"Ho! Anybody here?" Sam demanded in a hoarse whisper. The engineer's compartment was small and Jeremiah made his way to the controls.

"Well, what have we here?" he asked in surprise, forgetting to keep his voice low. "Here's our engineer, Sam." He nudged the man with the barrel of his musket. "Dead as a doornail." He pulled the form back into its seat from its slumped over position. "Bulls-eye. Right through the forehead. Ain't even a Reb soldier. Got no uniform on."

"Well," Sam answered, "guess they figure anyone engineerin' a Reb train must be a Reb soldier."

"Yeah . . . poor fella," Jeremiah said, propping up the lifeless form. "Weren't no young fella neither. This here is somebody's grandpa. Must not even had a chance to put up a fight to be shot this way."

Suddenly, from the back of the engine Cy's voice boomed out, "Now looky here, would you! Boys, c'mon . . . got a couple o' fella's in here."

Noisily, the men rounded the back to join Jep and Cy as they turned over a still, cold form dressed in blue.

"Well, this 'un didn't survive his ambuscade, now did he?" Cy reached over and touched the other motionless form. "I'll be! Boys, this here's a Reb and he ain't dead yet!" Something about the mass of wild hair looked strangely familiar. "Help me turn him over, boys. Get this Yank outa the way."

Jep heaved the dead man in blue to the side, staring sadly at the closed eyes and the circle of gold on his finger. "Well, this was sure some lady's husband and some woman's son. Probably somebody's pa, too. What a waste of humanity," he mumbled quietly.

"Well, now," said Sam, "don't seem to me they be too sad wastin' us, now do they?"

Jep smiled ruefully. "Reckon not," he answered. He was tired of the many wasted lives he'd seen in such a short time.

Cy turned over the man in gray, and a moan escaped from the wounded soldier's throat. He didn't open his eyes, and was cold to the touch. Suddenly Cy exclaimed in disbelief, "Oh, man! Boys, would you looka here! I don't believe it! It's Andy. Hardly recognized him. Great day! Let's get him outa here!

"Andy! Andy!" Cy called out to him, "can you hear me? Hang on man, we're gettin' you outa here!"

Jeremiah bent down to help lift the wounded man and they removed him from the train. "Don't lay him in the snow, boys . . . here, Sam, put your coat down."

The order followed, they carefully placed the injured form on the ground. Jeremiah removed his own coat, covering Andy just as Jeptha emerged from the wood car with a battered banjo.

"Found this in among the wood, boys. Don't know if it can be salvaged or not." They turned to look at the instrument he held out. The neck was broken and the hoop punched through.

"Well, let's just save it for Anderson to decide," Jeremiah said. "Jep, give the poor soul some water . . . melted snow if you can manage it. Maybe it'll revive him some. Can't see where he's wounded . . . have to wait 'til the sun's up better."

The boys on the other side of the engine made their way around front to see what was up. "Nothin' out here, Corporal McCamey," the soldier named Noah spoke. "What next?"

"Well, reckon we'll just have to wait here like Cap'n ordered."

"Some coffee sure would be good 'bout now," Noah stated hopefully.

"No fires! No fires built, boys. I agree . . . coffee would be mighty good in fightin' this cold, but we build a fire and we risk bein' seen, so it's an order. No fires!"

Jeremiah posted men on all sides of the engine as a precaution, though he believed none of the enemy would soon be back that way. He then returned to Andy's side.

"How's he doin', Jep?"

"Got some melted snow down him, but all he done is sputtered. Looks like he might be wounded in the side . . . blood's all over his waist and hips . . . feel's like he got bashed pretty good in the head, too. I ain't no doctor, Jeremiah, but it don't look good. What do we do with him?"

"We got to get a wagon to load him on . . . don't know how we'll do that."

Soon the sun began to rise and the men were able to better determine their circumstances. All seemed quiet. Andy had not regained consciousness, but warmth was returning to his body.

As Jeremiah tried to ascertain the wounds, he discovered that Andy had, indeed, been shot through his side.

"Look boys . . . gone clean through," he said, noting the hole in both his front and back. "I have no idea how to assess this thing. Doesn't appear to be bleedin' none now . . . and I dunno if that's good or bad. But he needs help soon."

"Men's gettin' hungry, McCamey," Sam spat out. "Rations is froze . . . what do we do?"

"You got me there, Sam. You got me there. Maybe settin' your food in a patch o' sunlight will make it soft enough to eat. I dunno. I ain't never had to solve a problem like this before."

Sam shrugged his shoulders. "Might be worth a try."

After a while, the rations were palatable, but not very good. Cold bacon and johnnycakes were quickly washed down with melted snow. The food was gobbled hastily to fill stomachs, not to be enjoyed.

The boys felt better after eating, but the wait became monotonous. Some of the men stretched out in the sun, others huddled in their great coats against the engine they guarded. Several were in a doze when the boom of a cannon followed by incessant musket fire fractured the silence.

Jeremiah jumped up immediately. "This don't sound good, boys; this don't sound good at all. Can't be more than a couple o' miles away. Where are Cap'n's orders?" he asked in exasperation. "If the enemy heads this way, we ain't got a chance of holdin' 'em or fighten' 'em!"

No sooner had the words left his mouth than a galloping sound fell on their ears.

"Shh . . . men, " Jeremiah warned, "back up to the engine. Sam, you watch Anderson."

As the pounding came closer, Jeremiah waited with poised musket, ready to fire. Finally, the horse came into view and Jeremiah lowered his aim. "It's all right, men," he called out, recognizing the rider as Lieutenant Moore. "It's all right." Lieutenant Moore often acted as Captain Kertlin's aid-de-camp.

Jeremiah stepped out into the officer's view. "I sure do hope you brung me some orders, Sir," he saluted the man.

"Yes, Corporal. Cap'n dispatched me to check on your situation and to inform you that you're to hold here. We're involved in a skirmish, but it appears to be minor. We sure did surprise them Yanks, but they be expectin' reinforcements soon, so we gotta do the job fast." He gestured toward the engine. "Got an engineer to run this thing?"

"No, Sir. Engineer on board's dead. We got a wounded man here, too . . . one of ours; mine as a matter of fact. His name is Private Anderson. Don't know how bad off he be."

"All right, McCamey. Cap'n will send one of the assistant engineers down here under escort and we'll move this thing when all else is under control. You hold 'til then. When he arrives, you're free to follow up the tracks and join the rest of us."

"Sir, Lieutenant Moore, would you please tell Cap'n we need a wagon to transport this wounded man?"

"I'll see to it, McCamey. I'll also tell Cap'n things is under control here."

"Thank you, Sir," Jeremiah said, saluting the officer a final time.

The sporadic sound of gunfire continued to be heard for the next couple of hours and then all became silent, at last. Shortly afterward, an assistant engineer arrived under escort to get the locomotive fired. With them was a wagon onto which Andy was placed for a grueling trek up the track. He would be attended to at the closest hospital in Harrisonburg.

The two miles separating Jeremiah's boys from the rest of the regiment were covered quickly, and they all felt relief at being back among the other men. Troops from the train had disembarked gratefully, some to join them on the march to Winchester, others to head back to Staunton.

By late afternoon, those moving north reached Harrisonburg. Here they set up camp where they were able, at last, to make fires, eat hot provisions and drink plenty of coffee. For the first time in hours, the boys felt warm again.

It wasn't until the three friends were wrapped in blankets, bedding down in front of the fire, that Cy reminded them: "Hey, boys . . . it's Christmas Eve. Merry Christmas, Jep and Jeremiah. Guess we've done had better ones, huh?

"Yeah . . . but at least we got to go home for a couple o' days," Jeremiah reminded them with a yawn. "Merry Christmas, men."

CHAPTER EIGHT

Virginia to the South is dear,
She holds a sacred trust.
Our fallen braves from near and far
Are covered with her dust.

Christmas Day dawned colder than any other day had been and the sky was a dark, foreboding gray. "I do believe it's gonna snow again, boys," Jep said as he stoked the fire. "In fact, I can smell it!" he sniffed the air.

"Aw, you and your big nose," Cy mumbled, rolling over in his blanket, unwilling to rise and face the cold. "You've said that all your life and I dunno when you was ever right once! Hey, Jep, it's Christmas ... why don't you bring me a cup o' coffee as a present?" Cy closed his eyes again, not wanting to get up. "Where's our dutiful corporal this cold dawn?" he muttered.

"Right here, boys!" Jeremiah answered, appearing before the fire. "Got some news. We don't march today. We get to stay put and have a nice, quiet, cold Christmas in camp. Compliments of General Jackson and Colonel Hartshare."

From his prone position on the ground, Cy opened his eyes, looking straight up at Jeremiah. "Well, aren't that just dandy," he said sarcastically.

"Now Cy, the best news is yet to come," Jeremiah said, sitting down in front of the fire. "We get the whole day ... no drillin', no marchin' ... how was it Cap'n Kertlin put it? 'A whole day of quiet reflection.'"

"Good," mumbled Cy, closing his eyes again and snuggling back down into his blanket. A second later, his eyes were startled open as something hot touched his face.

"Merry Christmas, Cy! Here's the present you asked for."

Jep stood over him, holding out a steaming cup of coffee.

"Well! I'll be!" Cy declared as he rolled over on his side, gratefully reaching up to take the cup from Jeptha's hand. "Thank you, Jep. Sometimes you sure do surprise me!" He propped up on his elbow and greedily gulped the hot liquid. "Believe I'll just spend the day right here by the fire, wrapped up in this blanket."

"Well, then you'll have to go hungry," Jep replied, "because I ain't servin' you breakfast in bed . . . no dinner neither!"

It proved to be a quiet, restful day for the men. The morning after Christmas, they were up well before dawn for snow had begun to fall and there were no tents to offer shelter.

As the men marched northward, the flakes fell harder. Big, wet flakes of snow that made seeing difficult. At times, the wind blew so fiercely that sight was impossible. The frigid blasts penetrated clothing, and in spite of the brisk pace the soldiers kept, they could not stay warm. Icy fingers caused eyes to sting and skin to burn.

The fresh snow packed beneath their feet, yet its depth continued to grow. It was ankle deep, then over their shins. It was grueling and several men stumbled and fell. At late afternoon, they reached Mt. Jackson and were instructed to set up bivouac for the night.

The snow at last ceased falling, but reached almost to their knees. It was impossible to pass the night comfortably, for the wet snow soaked readily through any blanket or greatcoat.

Dawn found them on the move again and as they struggled against the deep snow, the sun finally peeked out, helping to relieve the frigid cold. Another all day march found them at Strasburg and the following day camp at Winchester was reached before dark. It was an exhausted group of men that fell asleep under cover of tent that night. For the first time in three days, the soldiers were allowed a good rest.

By mid-afternoon, the 28th Virginia and the remainder of Company G's regiment began to filter into camp, having the benefit of boarding rails at Mt. Jackson and being brought in by train. No one could ride from Staunton since the length of track at Sidney Gap had yet to be repaired.

Jeremiah, Jep and Cy, anxious about Anderson, sought Lieutenant Moore, for he had remained in Harrisonburg for several days to help with the transporting of the rest of the regiment. He had also been responsible for seeing that any wounded men received needed care. They located him at camp headquarters.

"Lieutenant Moore," Jeremiah saluted.

"I compliment you on a job well done back at Mt. Sidney, McCamey," he said, returning the salute. "I must say, for I didn't have the chance then, that you and your men proved yourselves well. Believe me, it has been taken note of."

"Thank you for your compliments, Sir," Jeremiah shifted his feet, uncomfortable with the praise, "but we've come to find out about Andy Anderson, Sir. Want to know how he's doin' . . . how bad hurt he is."

"Oh, yes, well . . . a ball got him right through the waist, apparently an intense flesh wound; in one side and out the other. I gotta tell you, he was most fortunate. Lost a good bit o' blood, but it didn't hurt his insides none. He did have a cracked skull. Doc says he'll be all right in some time . . . but he can't remember anything about what happened . . . why he was in that wood car. 'Tis a pity, too . . . might have provided us with valuable knowledge."

"Well, Lieutenant Moore, we're obliged to you for the information. Glad to know he's recoverin'. I'm mighty relieved to hear it," Jeremiah voiced the sentiment for all of them.

"McCamey, if you know anything about his family, you might want to let them know somethin' . . . since your boys found him."

"Yes, Sir. I'll do that."

Thirty-six hours later, they were again given the order to prepare several days' rations. New Year's Eve was not a time of revelry, but of quiet preparation. The order to march had been given for New Year's Day.

January 1, 1862 broke cold and snowy. The first flakes began to swirl down long before daylight, and as the men marched out, just as before, the snow fell faster and harder.

Their destination was the town of Bath, to the west. Union troops under General McDowell had massed there and in the hamlet of Romney. General Jackson aimed to free these towns.

"I sure hope this cruel weather ain't a sign of things to come," Jeremiah remarked to his friends as mid-afternoon rolled around.

"Brrr," Cy shivered. "I do believe Jackson plans on us makin' plenty miles today in spite of these conditions."

The snow kept falling, the temperature dropped, and the men continued to march. After twelve hours, the snow was more than knee deep. Weighed down with knapsacks, blankets, ammunition and weapons, the trek was difficult and dangerous for the soldiers. Moving up and down the mountainous terrain was treacherous. As snow became packed solid by ranks in front, it turned into a sheet of ice for those in the rear. Some men would get part way up an embankment after a great struggle, only to suddenly tumble or slide all the way back to the bottom. Some resorted to crawling up the hills, becoming covered in snow that would melt and then refreeze, so that the men resembled great, gray icicles.

The boys survived a bitterly cold night. Trying to sleep in driving snow, most drifted off being overtaken by utter exhaustion, and many woke to find themselves buried under the white powder.

The town of Bath was reached the following afternoon. The Union forces occupying the settlement were so surprised by the arrival of Jackson's men that it took little conflict to send them retreating back across the border into Maryland. Once accomplished, the Rebels turned westward toward the hamlet of Romney.

After several more days fighting the bitter cold and driving snow, the men became resigned to the hardships. There was little complaining and General Jackson was often seen among his ranks, sleeping without the benefit of tent cover or fire. He commanded no fires be made, for doing so would risk exposing their position to the enemy, thus losing the element of surprise that he so liked to employ.

The morning before closing in on Romney, Jeremiah woke his men. The night had been the coldest by far and his concern for their well being was great. He, Cy and Jep had huddled close together for much of the night, trying to draw warmth from each other.

In checking with the boys, he found most of them endured the night in fair order. Approaching Sam, he encountered the soldier wrenching off a shoe.

"What's up, Sam? Got a problem?" Jeremiah asked.

"Dunno, McCamey. Toes feel funny . . . or rather, don't feel at all. Reckon it could be all this marchin' we done been doin'?"

"Could be," he squatted down, "but let's take a look. I ain't no doctor, though."

Sam peeled back his sock, revealing blackened toes. Jeremiah whistled. "Sam, this don't look too good. Reckon what you got is a case of the frostbites. Sergeant needs to see this. Put your sock and shoe back on.

"Jep! Ho!" Jeremiah hollered for his friend. "Sam here has a bit o' problem with his foot . . . take him and see that Sergeant Spruill takes a look at it."

"Aw, McCamey," protested Sam indignantly, "do I gotta show him? He'll be fit to be tied. I can already hear the dressin' down I'm gonna get!"

"Go, Sam. Now. Jep, see to it that he shows Spruill that foot . . . I mean it!"

All other men appeared to be all right and momentarily Jeptha returned.

"How's Sam's foot, Jep? Did he see Spruill?" Jeremiah wanted to know.

"My! Did he ever! Gave him a real piece o' his mind . . . Sergeant used some words I ain't never even heard before! Told him he was ineffectual, that we was now minus man power because he was lame-brained."

"Didn't Sam tell him it happened while he was sleepin'?"

"He tried to Jeremiah, but ol' Spruill sure didn't have much sympathy for him. Sent him to the rear of the line . . . says he might have to have them toes cut off . . . and that he oughta make him eat 'em if'n he does . . . that that'd learn him to be so careless and . . ."

Jeremiah threw up his hand. "Whoa! Wait! I've heard enough! Remind me Jep, to be hard enough on y'all that none of you has to experience Spruill's wrath again. Sam's one of our best . . . we'll be out a lot if we lose him!"

"Well, he ain't the only problem had last night, Jeremiah. Best be thankful all your men is accounted for. Some was dug up outa the snow, froze to death . . . heard tell they was as blue as a Yank's uniform."

"Where'd you hear about this?"

"Oh, some o' the officers was talkin' 'bout it while we was waitin' on Spruill. Didn't sound like a purty sight, neither . . . and it was more'n one or two fellas."

As they carried on their conversation, fresh flakes of snow began to float down. "Jeremiah, I can't remember when it's ever been so cold and snowy any winter in my life. Reckon it's ever gonna stop?"

"Don't look like it anytime soon, Jep, but I guess I'd rather march in it than sleep in it."

Romney was reached by twilight, and the men didn't rest before launching their attack. The enemy was caught off guard and easily surrounded so that little fighting was necessary. Few men on either side were lost and the Yankees quickly retreated northeast. With Romney secured, the boys in gray headed back toward Winchester, and camp.

As they crossed the Cacapon River twenty miles short of their destination, a small, but tough party of Federal scouts was encountered. A violent skirmish broke out and shots volleyed back and forth for several hours. Some casualties were incurred, delaying their return to Winchester.

The men faced another bitterly cold night napping in the snow. Once the exchange of fire had subsided, the sun quickly set, and many boys, too weary to eat, lay down where and how they were, falling into a deep, cold sleep. The constant struggle against the snow, the long hours of marching, the body numbing cold and the fighting had taken their toll.

Jeremiah, Jeptha and Cy once again huddled together in an attempt to stay warm. The last thing Jeremiah heard was Cy's words: "Look . . . I see some stars and the moon's peekin' through. Why, ain't that a purty sight to go to sleep to. Reckon the snow is finally gonna stop!"

The morning did indeed dawn clear, gray clouds giving way to bright blue skies. Jeremiah was the first to wake. Glancing about, he noted Jep lightly snoring in a crouched position, his head propped up by the barrel of his gun. Cy had given way to lying in the snow, curling an arm under his head to keep it out of the white powder.

Jeremiah tried to stretch, but suffered from an aching, stiff back. He'd spent most of the night in a sitting position, head supported by his knees.

Standing uneasily, he felt much older than his soon-to-be twenty years. Carefully, he took stock of the scene around him as men began to stir, and compassion filled his heart. These men had endured great hardship the last several days and it showed. Faces were scraggly, clothes dirty and torn. Eyes were red rimmed from tiredness and cold, while frost had built up heavily in many mustaches and beards.

Prior to rousing his two messmates, Jeremiah studied them closely. How much they had changed these last several months! He wondered if such changes were as obvious in him. He took off a leather glove, running his hand over his face. He felt certain he was as much a sight as everyone else. He could feel the rough stubble across his cheeks and chin, the result of not having shaved for many days. An unplanned mustache crept across his upper lip.

Looking again at Jep and Cy, he chuckled softly. Fuzzy growth covered both faces and each had a mustache full of frost. He wondered what Violet would think of her sweetheart now.

"Up and at 'em boys," he suddenly hollered, startling them from their deep and oblivious sleep. "Up and at 'em or you're liable to miss our glorious march today! Look! Sun's come out and we'll be back in camp by noon!"

Cy pulled himself up from his snowy berth, yawning. "It's amazing how one can sleep when he's tired enough! Never thought lying in the snow could be so comfortable! Remember when we was young'uns, Jeremiah? A good snow like we've had these several days and we'd be makin' snow angels all over your folks' fields. I remember one time your Pa said looked like the farm had been visited by heavenly hosts." He laughed, and yawned again. "Them were fine days, huh? The young and foolish don't know how good they've got it!"

Jep blinked his eyes and closed them again, sitting still as a statue. Cy nudged his knee with a swift, hard kick. "Let's go Carroll; you heard the corporal!"

"Don't, Cy!" he warned in a pathetic, sleepy voice. "I'm frozen here. Too stiff to move." His back ached fiercely from the position in which he'd been sleeping. He started to turn his head and found it strangely bound. "Uh-oh! Got a problem here . . ."

Both friends ignored Jeptha, knowing once he was up and about, he, like they, would be fine.

"Jeremiah, how 'bout a hand?" Jeptha asked.

"What's wrong?" the corporal answered, approaching him.

Jep felt foolish. "Ah . . . I seem to . . . ah . . . be . . . ah . . . slightly frozen to my musket," he answered, embarrassed.

"I'll be! Jep . . . only you could do this! Great day . . . where your face leaned against it while you slept 'tis frozen solid, just like that time when we was young'uns and you stuck your tongue out on the train rail on a dare, it bein' a freezing day!" He laughed at the memory.

"It ain't funny, Jeremiah." Jep closed his eyes and started to give a yank to his gun.

"No, no. Don't do it like that; you'll take the hide clean off your face just like you did your tongue. Here . . ."

Jeremiah began to huff, open-mouthed on the barrel. "See if I can't loosen it some with my breath." He continued to huff several more times before the metal barrel started to give.

"I ain't never felt so ridiculous, Jeremiah, and I don't wanna be hearin' 'bout this for the rest of my life, neither, you hear?"

Jeremiah gave a jerk and freed the barrel from Jep's cheek and jaw.

"Ahhhh!" Jep yelled, "How much hide came with it?"

Jeremiah looked at the gun and laughed. "Not too much . . . but you do got a nice red streak down your jaw . . . Jep, take off your glove and try to warm that spot some with your hand . . . could have a touch of frostbite there . . . I don't want no more of that!"

Jeremiah felt his face grow hot, remembering the harsh words with which Sergeant Spruill had lashed out at him after the incident with Sam's toes. The sergeant had told him in no uncertain terms that he was inefficient and incompetent if he could not take any better care of his men. What had his words been? "I can't be everywhere and with everyone at once, McCamey. That is why we have corporals. That is your job and if you can't see to it, well, then there are those who can!" Even thinking about the scene embarrassed him. He'd felt so humiliated and angry after Spruill's bitter words that he had kept the entire incident to himself, determining that such a thing would never happen again.

Jeremiah's thoughts were broken by the appearance of Killian and Drew. "McCamey," Drew questioned, "have you heard?"

Jeremiah looked at them. "Heard what?" he asked.

"'Bout our losses yesterday. I understand Sergeant Spruill took a hit."

Jeremiah stared at him, thoughts churning. Finally he answered, "No . . . no, I hadn't heard . . . where'd you come by this information?"

Killian shrugged. "Just been passed down the line this mornin' . . . kinda figured you knew."

"How bad's he hurt?" Jeremiah questioned, running his hand through his hair.

"Hurt?" Killian repeated. "He ain't hurt; he's dead."

Shielding his face with his hands, Jeremiah groaned. *How can that be,* he thought. *That's something else I've failed at; I should have made it a point to check on casualties before allowing myself to sleep. I should have never been made a corporal. Spruill certainly was right . . . I am inefficient and incompetent.*

In spite of being raked over the coals by Spruill, he knew that the sergeant was . . . had been, a good man; a good soldier, and Captain Kertlin's words haunted him again; "This is war; men die . . ."

The mood among the men as they prepared to move out was more heartening than it had been in days. With the snow ended, the sun was out and the sky was a deep, cloudless blue. The march back to camp would not take more than a few hours in spite of the deep snow. By late afternoon, they should once again be able to feel the warmth of fires, eat fresh cooked rations and sleep in the shelter of canvas.

Shortly before they pulled out, Lieutenant Moore came seeking Jeremiah. "Corporal McCamey," he called, dismounting from his horse, "a word with you, please."

"Certainly, Sir," Jeremiah saluted. "What can I do for you?"

"Walk this way with me, Corporal, if you would," Lieutenant Moore said, handing the reins of his horse to Jeptha. "Let's move out of the hearing distance of others.

"You know about our loss of Sergeant Spruill yesterday?"

"Yes, Sir. I didn't find out until this morning. I must say it came as a shock. Sergeant Spruill was one truly concerned for his men."

Lieutenant Moore didn't speak for a moment. "Yes, he was," he finally sighed. "We'd been friends for a long time, McCamey. I shall feel his loss greatly, but I'm not here to talk to you about Spruill. In fact, the last good talk I had with him concerned you, Corporal."

"Yes, Sir?" Jeremiah faced the lieutenant, his eyebrows arching in question.

"Yeah . . . I gave him a real chewing out over Private Samuels's frostbite. Samuels is a good soldier, McCamey, and we don't need to be doin' without him. Henry . . . Sergeant Spruill, told me he'd reprimanded you over the matter . . . as he should have." Lieutenant Moore stopped walking and looked Jeremiah in the eyes. "You know Samuels is gonna lose two of those toes?"

"Yes, Sir. I heard."

"McCamey, didn't you warn your men about the hazards of frostbite? How it could happen when being in such severe cold for so long?"

"I have now, Sir, but no Sir, I hadn't at the time." Jeremiah hung his head in regret as the lieutenant continued.

"Being a good leader requires certain things, Corporal. The first and foremost is attending to the welfare of the men under you . . . in all circumstances. You realize you're responsible for a good infantry soldier losing two toes."

"Yes, Sir, " Jeremiah answered, keeping his head hung and drawing in a sharp breath. "Guess I'm not cut out for higher rank, Sir."

Lieutenant Moore ignored the remark. "If you think I came to berate you again for the incident, you're right McCamey. It should never have happened. Oh! I know you're probably thinking the real fault lies with Samuels, but that's not true. A leader becomes a leader because he possesses certain qualifications. One of those skills must be the ability to think for his men in all circumstances. Do you understand this?"

Jeremiah looked up. "Yes, Sir. I do."

"Now, instead of reproaching yourself for lack of leadership McCamey, simply take what I've said and learn from it as a man should . . . as a leader should. Take it to heart and change what needs to be changed. You have some excellent abilities, McCamey. I've watched you serve since you first joined up. You've proven yourself in more than one situation. But there is always room to improve."

"Yes, Sir. I will, Sir."

"Another thing." Locking his hands behind his back, Lieutenant Moore looked long and hard at Jeremiah. "As soon as Samuels has recovered, he will be filling your role as corporal."

"Yes, Sir, " Jeremiah responded in a thick voice, trying hard not to let his dejection show. "I understand," he whispered.

Lieutenant Moore stared at him. "No, Sir, I don't think you do understand. This is not a demotion, Corporal, but a promotion."

Jeremiah looked up, not making sense of the words.

"You've moved up in rank, Sergeant McCamey."

Jeremiah stared, open-mouthed for a moment.

"This is why it is important for you to take the things I've said and learn from them. I could have had your stripes for Samuels' incident, McCamey. Cap'n couldn't have argued me none on that, either. I know he's become somewhat of a friend to you . . . but cold, hard facts speak for themselves and Kertlin's not a man for favoritism. Making you a sergeant to replace the loss of Spruill was my suggestion. Not that he wouldn't have made the recommendation; but I suggested it first to him." Lieutenant Moore laughed lightly, "Of course, he did have to approve it, and take it before the Colonel, but it is my reputation staked on your advancement, McCamey. Mine. I expect you to remember that, Sergeant.

"Now, form your men. You will be part of the advance guard today."

"Yes, Sir!" Jeremiah saluted the officer as the lieutenant moved on to retrieve his horse from Jeptha's care.

Jeptha turned to his friend. "What the tarnation did he want? He was mighty serious."

"Well, Jep, I tell you. It's somethin' I gotta think on some before I can talk about it."

Jeptha shrugged, "Suit yourself, then."

"Men," Jeremiah bellowed, "take your positions! We are to be among those first in line."

CHAPTER NINE

What matter if our shoes are worn?
What matter if our feet are torn?
Quick step! We're with him ere the dawn.
That's Stonewall Jackson's way!

The march back to Winchester was not difficult, but the deep snow made the going slower than the men desired. The bright sun glaring down on the white surface soon made Jeremiah's eyes hurt and his head ache. He tried to think through the scene played out with Lieutenant Moore a short while ago . . . one minute he was questioning his own leadership ability, the next he was accepting a promotion to sergeant and assuring the lieutenant he would not let him down. *I have certainly got my work cut out for me,* he thought. *Take what Lieutenant said and learn . . .*

"What you so quiet about today, Jeremiah? You sure ain't had much to say. Anything wrong?" Cy inquired. "I noticed you had an awful long talk with Lieutenant this mornin'. You ain't been the same since."

"Naw, nothin's exactly wrong . . ." Jeremiah answered, continuing to march in silence between his two friends.

"Says he's gotta think on whatever it is," Jep chimed in, annoyed that his friend didn't seem to wish to confide in them.

The constant crunching of snow underfoot was the only sound that transpired among the boys for several minutes. Finally, Jeremiah decided to tell his secret.

"Boys, Lieutenant Moore gave me a field promotion to sergeant this mornin'."

"Well now, Jeremiah. I'm bound to say, that don't surprise me none!" Jep declared, not breaking stride or looking at his friend.

Cy crunched along in silence for several seconds before throwing an arm about his comrade's shoulders. "I'm real proud, Jeremiah. Real proud." The sincerity in his voice touched the new sergeant.

"You know what bothers me most about it, boys? Both times I've been given rank is because good men have died."

Nothing more was spoken for a long time.

Winchester was reached with great gratitude. None of the men realized how comfortable camp could be until faced with the Bath/Romney campaign. The entire regiment felt itself to be an elitist group of men. Surviving such difficulties had turned them into well-seasoned, resilient soldiers, and the men making up Company G realized they were no longer the same men they had been eight months earlier.

February rolled around quietly, but the end of the month saw a Union force begin to slip slowly into the valley. Jackson's men, numbering only 3,600, were no match for the 38,000 troops in blue commanded by General Nathaniel Banks.

On the night of March 11, Company G's brigade received orders to begin a march southward, up the Shenandoah Valley.

As the boys fell into rank, Cy expressed bewilderment, "I just don't understand what Jackson means for us to do. Why ain't we fightin'? Resistin' these Yankees? Numbers ain't never stopped us before."

"I tell you Cy," Jeremiah answered, "I ain't got it figured out either. But you gotta know as well as I do that Jackson has somethin' up his sleeve. I'll never be convinced we're withdrawin' without makin' some kinda protest. We all know that just ain't Jackson's way!"

General Jackson did indeed have a plan. A few miles outside of Winchester, the men were called to a halt. Holding a council of war with his officers, it was decided a night attack would be launched. It was hoped that the inexperience of the Federal troops under Banks and the element of surprise would lead to victory.

Jackson left his men after this meeting to attend to other business. The officers in charge were to finalize the plans, but something went awry. Upon returning, the general learned that his munitions and supplies, along with the troops, were several miles apart, divided between Kernstown and Newtown. The proposed attack had to be called off. "I shall never hold another council of war!" Jackson thundered, and next day had the men regroup at Strasburg.

Here they learned Union General Shields would be joining Banks with an additional eleven thousand men, so Jackson marched his small force several miles up the valley in hopes of drawing the Federals out of Winchester in pursuit.

Once the Union leaders discovered the small size of Jackson's force, they did not consider him worth contending with. Banks quickly received orders to send two of his divisions eastward to join McClellan's Union forces.

It was the 21st of March, a cold, sleety night, when "Stonewall" Jackson's main cavalry officer in the valley, General Turner Ashby, came galloping into camp. "General!" he exclaimed, "Banks is breaking rank and moving men from Winchester to Strasburg so that they might join McClellan on a march to Richmond!"

"Well, then," Jackson replied, "I believe the fate of our capital could be decided in this valley. We mustn't allow those men to join McClellan, now must we?"

Jeremiah began waking the boys early on the morning of the 22nd. "Let's go men! Let's go!" he cried urgently. "Orders have been given to move out! Quickly, now!"

Cy sat up from his pallet in the back of the tent. "Where we off to Sergeant?" he yawned. "You're wakin' me up from a good dream!"

"Yeah, " Jep said with a laugh. "I'll bet they were sweet dreams . . . dreams of Miss Violet!" He clasped his hands to his heart and looked at Cy, batting his eyes in mock femininity.

Cy stared at his friend for a moment. "Naw," he finally said, "you make it a nightmare."

"C'mon fellas, this is serious. We gotta get movin'."

"Where we goin'?" Jep asked, quickly collecting his belongings.

"I ain't sure. You know the General; likes to keep things quiet. All I know is that we have orders to move.

"Andy?" he shouted, nudging the boy in the leg. "Let's go, Son."

Andy had returned to the command March 1. He was recovering nicely from his wound, though it pained him at times. However, the blow to his head had erased all memory of the incident from his mind, and he often found himself wondering what he had been doing in that wood car.

Andy rolled over, and touching his side, flinched.

"You all right, Anderson?" Jeremiah asked in concern.

"Yeah . . . reckon it's this dampness that does it to me. When it rains, seems to hurt lots . . . otherwise I hardly notice it."

"Yeah, guess this cold and sleet we've had ain't done you no good."

Andy sat up, in obvious discomfort, but assured the others he was well.

The men marched twenty-five miles that day. During the winter months, Jackson trained his troops so they were capable of marching some seventeen hours a day, fifty minutes at the double quick with ten minutes to rest each hour. An hour was given for the mid-day meal. Although the men found it grueling, it instilled in them a great sense of accomplishment and few complained.

The next day dawned cold and blustery, with a hint of sleet remaining in the air. It was a raw day. A Sunday. Jeremiah again set about the task of rousing his boys. He wanted to be sure they were well prepared for the day's mission.

As he returned from checking on the other men, he found his mess-mates up and about, readily gathering their gear. Cy was writing a letter by the light of the fire.

"What in the world you doin', Cy?" Jeremiah questioned.

Cy grinned. "You don't 'member what day this is, Jeremiah, but I do."

Jeremiah thought for a moment and smiled. "Yeah . . . I do. It's March 23 . . . Violet's birthday."

"Yep, and I was just writin' her a real short note to let her know I ain't forgot."

"Would you be so kind as to put in a line for me, Cy, so she won't know that her brother did?"

"Sure thing, Jeremiah." Cy quickly wrote a few more words and then began searching for something.

After a moment of watching his frustration, Jeremiah started to chuckle. "What are you so frantically lookin' for?"

"I had somethin' I was gonna send to Miss Violet and now I can't find it . . . bother!"

"What is it, a birthday present?"

"Sorta . . . you remember them daguerreotypes we done had made last month . . . the three of us . . . you and me and Jep . . . in Winchester? It was right before Andy got back. I was savin' mine to send to Miss Violet for somethin' special . . . reckon her birthday's mighty special, but Jeremiah, I can't find it no where!" He sat down in a huff as Jeremiah disappeared into the tent.

Returning, he handed something to his friend. "Here, Cy . . . take mine . . . send it. You can give me yours when you find it."

"Thanks, Jeremiah," he said quietly, "I only hope this finds its way to her. Not all mail makes it to where it's supposed to go, you know. Sure you don't mind?"

"Na . . . home's the best place for it, anyway. I sure don't need it here. Don't want a picture of myself and I don't need yours. I gotta look at your two ugly faces everyday anyway. Don't need no reminder of 'em!"

"Well . . . if anything ever happens to me, you know . . . I don't want Miss Violet to forget me too easily. If . . . if she has a picture to look at once in a while, well . . ."

Jeremiah placed a hand on his friend's shoulder. "Now, don't go gettin' morbid on me, Boy . . ."

"Naw, just tryin' to be real about things. If it's my time, it's my time. I'm ready, Jeremiah, you know that. I done thought all this through when Parker died. If it's your time . . . or Jep's . . . well, I hope you done thought it through, too."

"Reckon' you can't be in no battle and not think about it, Cy," was all Jeremiah could answer. "Better take that letter up to the courier quickly. See if any other of the men have mail, would you? It'd be a good thing to take 'em all."

After a brief worship service, the boys set out for the hamlet of Newtown, arriving close to noon. Here they set up temporary camp and by 2 P.M. were marching another four miles to Kernstown.

Word passed along the ranks that an attack would be held soon. General Richard Garnett's brigade, which included Company G's regiment, would be held in reserve to hold the line at the end.

The men in Company G had fond feelings toward their brigade commander. General Garnett was a gallant soldier and a kind man. He'd been serving under General Jackson since November, when Jackson had been given command of the Valley Army. Now was a chance for all of them to prove their worth to their country.

The plan was to attack General Banks' Yankee army as they moved out of Winchester and marched through Kernstown on their way to join McClellan. Today, the Confederate troops in the valley would help determine the fate of their capital.

The Rebels watched the Federals at a distance as they began to arrive in the town. The boys in gray were convinced it was but a thin screen of Yankees. It looked simply like a rear guard.

About 4 P.M., the roar of battle began with an exchange of cannon fire. As the artillery dueled, the infantry organized into position. Company G's regiment was placed in the rear to allow them to make the final assault.

~

For a time, Jeremiah watched tensely from the back of the line. The heavy, enemy artillery some distance away was belching fire and smoke right into the ranks of those brave fellows up front. Over and over and over like rage spewed forth from small dragons, the flames shot from the mouths of the cannon. Soon his men would be in the middle of it and they were ready for the fight. He reached out next to him, grabbing an arm each of Cy and Jep.

"Go steady . . . we're startin' to move in. Give it all you've got, boys, and be careful! See you again in a little bit." He moved on down his line of men.

The order was given. "Close up rank, boys!" Jeremiah shouted. "We're to hold this line as we move forward!

"Close up now, I said!" he bellowed again. "Ready men?

"Steady . . . one foot in front of the other . . . no double time . . . slowly now, just hold 'em back and keep the fire comin'! There's more blue bellies up there than we ever dreamed of seein' in a lifetime! This sure ain't no rear guard!" Jeremiah could barely hear himself as he tried shouting above the musket fire. Could his orders be heard?

"Ready lads? Move it! Move it now! Out into the heat of this fight . . . and give 'em all you've got, boys!"

The customary yell escaping their throats, they eagerly rushed forward, a strong, secure line, the colors out front. Jeremiah focused momentarily on those symbols of his country, and his heart swelled with pride. The Stars and Bars waved true, but he particularly liked the banner that had been adopted after the fight at Manassas. The blue cross of stars on a red field was a flag for the soldiers alone to rally around. This flag represented their courage and determination every time they marched out to meet the foe. It was simply referred to as The Battle Flag.

A shell struck close, jarring his attention back to the men. He watched as they loaded, aimed and fired . . . not wavering at all . . . but continuing forward, guns becoming hot. The men in blue faced them, falling one by one, almost as if in slow motion. Here, there, a man in gray went down, but the line closed up best it could and kept advancing.

The air became acrid and heavy with black powder haze. The battle-field fog began to obliterate things. The smoke was too thick for Jeremiah to see what was happening. All of a sudden, it started to clear, and the gray line began to crumble.

The ranks ahead were pulling back quickly, some men at a run. At once, over the hill they came. It was an unbelievable sight. A tremendous surge of blue was overtaking everything!

Jeremiah looked around frantically. The men were retreating, but he had heard no retreat sound. What was happening?

"Men! Men! Reform . . . close up, forward, I tell you! The orders haven't changed!" It was obvious that sheer numbers were overwhelming them, and he knew it was useless to crush onward. His men would, or did not hear, and to press on would mean sure death. *But I have my orders,* he thought. *They were given to be followed!*

Artillery shells continued to burst around them, and some soldiers, as they engaged in the flight, stopped to fire even as they fled. Jeremiah tried to look around, but could not see, for the cloud of smoke had made things invisible again.

"Are we in retreat?" he yelled to a corporal who came fleeing passed him.

"Yes, Sergeant, I am!"

Jeremiah didn't understand. No retreat had been called, but there needed to be one now!

Suddenly, he heard the blaring noise of bugle notes amidst the roar of battle. The retreat at last was sounded, but his men were already moving back, quickly, least they be mowed down by those from the front.

He caught a quick glimpse of Jep and Cy. *Cy, you're so cool under fire,* he thought. Jep frantically loaded, squeezing off each round, but Cy never showed the anxiety he must surely have felt; he never seemed harrowed. *Good boys,* he thought. *Good boys . . . don't make our retreat easy for them. Give 'em all you've got!* This took true courage and he was proud of his friends . . . proud of his men.

As quickly as he spotted his boys, they disappeared. What was General Garnett doing? He felt confused and in the disorder, suddenly found himself face to face with General Jackson. Jeremiah saluted him.

"Get your men to rally, Sergeant!" he yelled, and immediately began to instruct the drummer at his side to beat the same.

But it was of no use. Garnett's call had won. They had been fighting for three hours and dusk was now upon them. The disorganized retreat was headed back toward camp at Newtown, and a slow, cold drizzle began to fall.

After recognizing Jep and Cy in the storm of retreat, Jeremiah lost sight of his men for good. They were scattered like seeds to the wind and he had no way to assess the damage done to their ranks. The only thing he could do now was to wait for them to begin drifting back into camp.

On the road back toward Newtown, Jeremiah fell into conversation with Sergeant Wilton of Company B. He, too, had been parted from his bevy of men and both were anxious.

"Banks sure did a number on us today," Jeremiah voiced dismally. "I can't say as I know what went wrong. Jackson's always mighty deliberate."

"That might be, McCamey," Wilton answered, "but we weren't being kept at bay by Banks, from what I hear."

Jeremiah looked at him questioningly.

"No, Sir!" Wilton continued, "they was Banks' men all right, but I hear tell Banks himself done run up to Harper's Ferry, that's how much he knowed of our plans today . . . and Shields, his second in command, was wounded yesterday in the skirmish with Ashby's cavalry . . . one of Ashby's aide-de-camp is a fair acquaintance o' mine, that's how come I know this."

They walked in silence for several seconds. "Well, if Banks weren't here, and Shields not on the field, then just who in a pig's eye was in command of that tide of blue?" Jeremiah demanded.

"Colonel Nathan Kimball, and he were tough, huh? He commands the 6th Pennsylvania."

Jeremiah stopped abruptly, and stared. "The 6th Pennsylvania? You're sure? We was up against the 6th Pennsylvania?"

"Sure thing. Didn't you see that blue and gold flag? Well, that was them all right."

Jeremiah had seen the banner, but had no idea. His knees grew weak and he could feel the color drain from his face.

"You all right, McCamey?" Wilton asked.

Jeremiah didn't answer. He looked up at the sky. The clouds were gathering, darker. How could any of them ever be all right again?

~

The rain fell increasingly harder as the blackness of night descended. Jeremiah stood in his dimly lit tent, staring out of the front flap, watching, but seeing nothing. The day had ended in a rout, their whole army being greatly outnumbered. Orders had been confusing; so unclear. How many of his boys were down? He didn't know the answer to the question.

General Garnett had finally called the retreat, but Jeremiah also knew they were supposed to hold the line. Jackson was there and wanted them to rally, but Garnett ordered them to withdraw instead. A general didn't just disobey orders, and greatly troubled by this, Jeremiah sighed. He couldn't think of it right now. This was a problem he would save for another day. The awesome sights and terrible sounds he experienced at Kernstown just a little while ago possessed him, and he had to shake off the fear and the bewilderment he now felt. *Where are my men?* he wondered in exasperation.

As Jeremiah waited anxiously for them to straggle back into camp, he was overwhelmed by the fact that they had been up against the 6th Pennsylvania Infantry. Geoffrey Adams, his cousin, was part of the 6th Pennsylvania.

Suddenly, he covered his face with his hands, shaking his head from side to side as if that would erase the reality of it all. It was too horrible to be true and he couldn't bear to believe it. Could his cousin have really been part of that blue tide advancing against them this day? Could they both have been out there taking aim at each other in the kill?

Feeling overwhelmed, Jeremiah wiped away tears with the back of a dirty gray sleeve. Suddenly the tent flap flipped open and Jeptha burst into its shelter. Startled, Jeremiah quickly turned his back to his friend.

At once he felt a gentle squeeze on his elbow.

"Jeremiah?" Jep whispered hoarsely, sounding odd.

Jeremiah wheeled around to face his friend, caught off guard by the strange sound of his voice. The rain streaked down Jeptha's face, clinging to his mustache in droplets. Jeremiah noted the red brimming eyes, and immediately realized it wasn't rain that stained his face. Jeptha, too, was crying, and now choked on his words.

"J . . . J . . . Jer . . . Jeremiah. It . . . it's Cy," he broke into a wrenching sob he couldn't control, "it's Cy!" Trying to continue, tears coursed down his face in rivulets. Jep attempted to wipe them away with a hand, but there were too many. Suddenly doubling over and gasping for air, he dropped to his knees, racked with desperate grief.

Jeremiah looked at him oddly, not understanding, and turned his eyes to Cy's spot in the back corner of their tent. *Where was Cy? What did Jeptha just say?* Jeremiah wondered.

Suddenly, the blood froze in his veins and he dropped his head with a loud, sputtering groan as reality gripped him. He couldn't breath and began shaking his head.

"No . . . no . . . no!" he cried, "not Cy. Not Cy. No," he choked, falling next to his comrade. Jeremiah placed a trembling hand on his friend's back. "Jep . . . Jep . . . tell me it's not true . . . it's not true. It can't be!"

Raising his head, Jeptha looked at his comrade and nodded, grabbing him around the neck in a tight hold. "It's true, Jeremiah," he wept huskily into his friend's shoulder.

Unable to contain his own tears, Jeremiah held Jeptha, not to offer comfort, but to receive it himself. He felt Jep's body shake with each sob and believed they would drown in their sorrow.

"I saw it, Jeremiah," Jeptha cried. "I saw it . . . I was there. We'd done got separated and I was tryin' to find him . . . I tried . . ." His voice broke as he continued to weep. "When I done saw him it was too late. He . . . he . . . he turned around and spotted me the little ways off that I was, and he raised his musket over his head, like he was sayin' 'Here I am' and then . . . then it just happened. Them shells was whistlin' overhead, explodin' everywhere and . . . and . . ." He suddenly stopped, unable to continue, and the two friends clung together in silence, giving in to their grief and tears.

Jeptha finally broke the embrace and the awful quiet. Raising his frame to sit back on his heels, he looked his friend in the face. "Aw heck, Jeremiah," he choked, "he was blowed all to pieces. Never had no chance." Sniffling, he stood, rubbing an arm over his face to make a feeble swipe at his tears.

Suddenly Jeremiah jumped up. "My boys!" he exclaimed. "I gotta go check on the boys! I've been waitin' for 'em to make their way back . . . where's Andy? You seen Andy?" His usual composure was gone.

"He's all right, Jeremiah. He was with me when Cy . . . when . . . well, he seen it too, Jeremiah. He liked Cy real good."

Jeptha followed Jeremiah out into the rain. News wasn't pleasant. Noah was unaccounted for. Berry was wounded and Brooks was dead. Ash was . . . Jeremiah couldn't even think it. His stomach churned and again he couldn't breath.

Returning to their tent, both men sat down wearily, silence once more overtaking them. After a while, Jeremiah spoke, thinking on the thoughts he had tried so hard to push away.

"Jep," his voice shook, "Geoffrey was out there today . . . part of Kimball's Brigade."

It was a moment before Jeptha could speak. "Your cousin Geoff? Geoffrey Adams?" he asked to be sure he understood.

Jeremiah nodded, as rain pelted more fiercely on the canvas roof. Shaking his head, he hoarsely whispered, "You know Jep, I never thought about it really coming to this. Never. When I chose to go with Virginia . . ." His voice broke. Suddenly he clenched a fist and pounded it over his heart. "I could never raise a hand against Virginia, against my home!" He heaved a sorrowful sigh.

"I weren't surprised at all when Geoff chose to go North," Jeptha voiced quietly. "I mean no disrespect, Jeremiah," he said in afterthought.

Jeremiah waved his hand wearily. "Let us not talk of such things anymore," he said despondently. "I can't bear it." He had never felt so empty and so utterly broken.

Stretching out upon his blanket, he immediately fell into a deep, but troubled sleep. His last thoughts were of Cy, Geoffrey and confusing orders, all mixed together.

~

Jeremiah woke to a distant noise. *How long,* he wondered, *has sleep overtaken me?* He listened carefully and for a moment, all that was evident was the heavy sound of Jeptha's breathing. Once, twice, his friend moaned in his slumber, and Jeremiah thought, *Surely he must be haunted by thoughts of Cy as he sleeps.* Mercifully, he could remember nothing of his own dreams. He looked around in the darkness. At some time, Andy had returned. The boy was curled up in his place, silent and still.

He heard it again. A distant stir, a fracas of some sort.

Soon there were loud voices and horses' hoofs clattered by.

Quietly, Jeremiah crawled from his canvas cover and looked about. Only an occasional flicker from a distant campfire broke the darkness. The rain had long ago stopped and the moon was playing hide-and-seek among the clouds. When it next shown unhindered, Jeremiah made out the form of a nearby soldier either involved in the matter or aware of it. As he came close upon him, he recognized Lieutenant Moore, and saluted.

"Sir, what is this clamor? What is happening?" Jeremiah could see the officer's heavy countenance in the dim light as he spoke. "Do I need to rouse the men and have them prepare to march?"

"No, Sergeant. I'm afraid what has disturbed your rest is something disturbing indeed. General Jackson has just placed General Garnett under arrest."

Jeremiah's eyes widened and he ran a shaking hand through his hair. This was too much. First the retreat . . . then learning about Geoffrey . . . and Cy. *Cy's dead,* he thought. *Now my brigade commander has been arrested.*

Jeremiah felt sick; he was sick of it all and for the first time since leaving for Manassas, he had to fight the desire to simply grab his belongings and go home. He turned away from Lieutenant Moore and in agony made his way back to the tent. His gut was in knots and tears again formed to blur his vision. The dark . . . the dark quiet of his tent was all he sought. There was too much to think about, yet think he must, or the temptation to run, to desert, might prove too great.

Safe again in his canvas cover, he wrestled with himself as he felt sure Jacob must have wrestled with the angel. It was too much at one time and

he had never been so tired in all his life. The long, forced march of yesterday; three hours of fierce battle against that tremendous swarm of Yankees
at Kernstown . . . Geoffrey one of those Yankees; General Garnett had
retreated without orders; Cy—oh Cy!

Cherished friend blown to bits for what?

"Join us Jeremiah! Do it for what your people believe in!" Cy's words
rang in his ears over and over and over. Cy's dead; Geoffrey maybe; General
Garnett, his brave and magnificent brigade commander arrested. When
would all of this end? He was sick to death of war.

"I'm so very, very tired," he whispered out loud, bracing an arm across
his forehead and emotion cracking in his voice.

The next thing he knew, Jeptha was nudging his leg with the toe of
his shoe. "Jeremiah, the sun is well up. Old Stonewall had ordered the striking of the tents. We're on our way south. Get up, I tell you."

Jeremiah groaned, "Go away Jep."

"No, Sir! I tell you sergeant, move before you get arrested, too."

Jeremiah rose quickly into a sitting position, the events of the wee
dawn hours coming back to him. He rubbed a hand over his eyes and
blinked at Jeptha.

"So you've found out about Garnett?" he asked his friend.

"Word's all over camp, Jeremiah. I dunno what to think. I'd rather not
think at all," he grumbled. "How'd you know about this? They say it
happened in the middle of the night."

"I heard it happen, Jep. Saw it, almost. Talked to Lieutenant Moore. I
don't know what to think either . . . too much to think about. Jep . . ."
Jeremiah hesitated . . . "feel like you've had enough of this fightin'? Ever
feel like you've just done all you can do?"

Jep stared at his friend. "Are you foolin'? Are you foolin' me,
Jeremiah?" he asked in disgust. "Sometimes I've thought of nothing else!
It's like a torment. You watch lives get snuffed out in the blink of an eye!
Blue, gray, it don't matter, and then, sometimes, you find yourself wonder-
ing what for . . . and it scares you 'cause you're afraid it's all got so easy to
do. But I'm done thinkin' like that. I'll do so no more!"

Jeremiah looked at his friend inquisitively. "What do you mean?"

"Jeremiah, if anybody ever loved that yellow-headed Cy, it was me.
I can't remember when he weren't part of my life . . . you neither, for
that fact. The two of you's been all the real family I ever had. Cy never
questioned his duty. Never had no doubt as to what it was he believed. We
both know that! And if we're all fightin' for the same thing, for our
country's independence and in defense of our homes, then I know every

time I go into battle I'll be reminded of what Cy was always sayin' to me; you heard him, Jeremiah, he was always sayin' '. . . Jep, we just do what we gotta do . . . can't think on how hard it is. We just do what we gotta do . . . don't have to like it none.'

"So I mean to fight 'til the last. No, Sir! I'll not have him dying on us for no reason, and that'll only happen if we give up; don't do our duty!"

His voice trembled and he groaned. "I can't believe he's not here! I'm so mad at him for dyin' . . ." his voice trailed off as he placed his head in his hands.

Jeremiah stood up and grabbed Jeptha's arm. "Stop it now, you hear! It isn't going to bring him back! Talkin' about it will do no good. He was a worthy man; he died a worthy man; he's left us with . . ."

Jeremiah suddenly became silent; for at once he knew that it was all a matter of honor. It had never been so clear as to what must be done.

"Talking about it won't bring him back Jep," he calmed down, "but to want to stop, to flee, to run from it all is a dishonorable thing to consider. I suddenly see what General Jackson has been telling us . . . we must love our country above all earthly things. Cy did! He died for it. I can be willing to do no less!"

The next morning, as the men began a slow march southward, the task fell upon Jeremiah to inform Mrs. Ash of the fate of her son. A job usually reserved for Captain Kertlin or Lieutenant Moore, the captain specifically asked Jeremiah to take care of the matter and he knew it could not be put off.

Camp was pitched early that afternoon, along the west bank of the Shenandoah River. Here the men were to remain for several days of rest.

After supper, Jeremiah retired to his spot in the dimly lit tent. Trying to face the difficult task at hand, he was glad to be alone.

For several long minutes he sat, pen poised above the paper, but at a total loss for words. He decided this chore was harder than any battle in which he'd taken part.

He began writing, but words came with difficulty, and he didn't like how they read. Cy was her only son . . . her only child! Now there was nobody. An order to march, the flash of a cannon and lives were forever changed.

Though he tried to be personal, the words sounded so cold. "Cy's dead; your son is gone; I've lost a devoted friend; no one was braver; Cy was a hero; be proud . . ." *Of what,* he questioned, *a dead child?*

Jeremiah crumpled the pages and started over. As he brought the letter to a close, his hand began to shake and he started to cry. He pulled out the daguerreotype the three of them had posed for. He was in the middle; Jep and Cy on either side. It dawned on him that this was Cy's copy. He'd found the missing picture among Cy's few belongings. Jeremiah thought of yesterday morning . . . was it really just yesterday when Cy looked for the picture and couldn't find it? It seemed a lifetime ago.

He stared at the photograph again. "Violet," he sighed softly. Suddenly he shook his fist angrily at Cy's likeness. "I told you, Cy!" he cried in a muffled voice, "you break her heart . . ." He put his head down on his knees and wept.

Quietly, Jeptha stuck his head into the tent. "Sorry, Jeremiah. You all right?"

Jeptha looked at his friend knowingly, sadly, as Jeremiah turned up his tear stained face. Jep sat down next to him, his own eyes filled with tears.

"Jep . . . I cannot write to Violet. I can't. Would you do it, please?" he begged.

Jep placed an arm about his friend's shoulder. "Sure thing, Jeremiah," he whispered. "Sure thing." The two friends sat drawing silent comfort from each other until long after the sun went down.

CHAPTER TEN

While up the street,
Each girl you meet,
With looks so sly
Will cry, "My eye!"
Oh! Isn't he the darlin',
The bowld sojer boy!

Slowly, the force of Jackson's men made their way back to camp at Staunton, where they would remain for several weeks. On the leisurely trek back south, the fruitful countryside was scoured for food and other provisions. The soldiers were beginning to acquire an even greater respect for the commanding general of their little army, and Company G's brigade began to develop an iron-like will of its own. They enjoyed sometimes being referred to as "Jackson's foot cavalry."

The few weeks of inactivity resulted in a meeting between General Jackson and the military advisor to President Jefferson Davis. This advisor, General Robert E. Lee, worked with Jackson on a daring and audacious plan. This plan called for pinning down the Union forces in the valley, separating them, and destroying them one by one so that they could not join McClellan as he headed toward Richmond.

By mid-April, the lower end of the valley was swarming with Federal troops and Jackson received the only reinforcements he was to get: 8,500 infantrymen, and 500 cavalry. The total troops of the Valley Army numbered 16,000, with 48 cannon.

When the reinforcements arrived, a march of fifty miles was made to secure a major mountain pass. Swift Run Gap was used by the Union troops to gain access to the valley. The victory here for Jackson's men came quickly and by the end of April, they were on the move again, making tracks southward, up the valley.

Jonah Samuels had rejoined Company G the first part of April. Though he was minus two toes, he declared he never missed them and was ready to assume his new role as corporal. The boys were glad to see him back among the ranks, especially Jeremiah. He'd discovered being a good sergeant meant having good, dependable men to delegate authority to, and Sam was among the best. Although Jep and Andy were loyal, they lacked higher rank. Jeremiah came to depend on Sam and the new corporal found he preferred the company of the sergeant and his messmates over any of the other men. Much had changed during his two-month recovery. The absence of Cy Ash was one of them.

After securing Swift Run Gap, the next imminent threat appeared to be in the hamlet of McDowell, to the southwest. The men in blue heavily occupied McDowell.

Jackson's soldiers reached the town on the morning of May 7 and the next day found them in fierce fighting that ended in a rout for the Yankees. General Jackson was so elated over this victory that he wrote to his wife: ". . . God blessed our little army . . ."

With McDowell secured, the men headed northward, down the valley. Behind cover of the Massanutten Mountain Range, they were well hidden from the army in blue.

Friday, May 23, found the little army in gray creeping undetected into the settlement of Front Royal. The day was bright, cloudless and unbearably hot. By late morning, most Federals were seeking relief from the sun when unexpectedly a battle erupted around them. Jackson's boys drove the enemy from their positions as the "foot cavalry" took them on all sides by surprise. Quickly, the Union force deteriorated and the Battle of Front Royal was over in less than an hour. General Banks and his bluecoats were again on the run.

Jackson sensed a crushing victory and his men faced a test of supreme endurance over the next twenty-four hours as he set their course toward Winchester. The Yankees had broken through and were again threatening to occupy the town.

"Jeremiah, I'm just plum tuckered out! I don't think I can put a foot forward one more time," Jep complained.

"Not to mention bein' famished!" Andy declared. "We ain't eat nothin' since dawn."

"I know, boys, I know. I'm 'bout spent too. I ain't never seen a man so doggedly persevering as the General. He don't seem to never get tired! Sometimes I think he forgets some of us ain't as tireless," Jeremiah reflected.

"Yeah. He ain't missin' two toes, neither," Sam threw in.

"Didn't think you missed 'em none, Sam," Jep replied.

"Well, now I don't . . . 'ceptin' when we've fought a battle, engaged in skirmishin', marched twenty miles, and ain't eat all day."

"Naw, Jackson ain't missin' no toes, but he did get that finger blowed off at Manassas," Jeremiah quipped.

"Well now, Sergeant, don't believe he walks on his hands none, now does he?" Jep couldn't resist being sarcastic.

"Reckon I'd not be playin' my banjo none if I was missin' a finger," Andy laughed.

"You see, boys," Jep stated, "even our conversation is absurd . . . I'd say that's a sign we're jaded for sure! C'mon, General . . . let's take a break!"

No sooner were the words out of his mouth than Captain Kertlin came riding down the line. "Break rank, men. We're takin' a much needed breather!"

"Thank goodness!" Jep declared for them all.

No sooner had the men stopped and sat down, a few dozing off immediately, than the call for reassembly was sounded.

"Blame it all, McCamey! What kinda rest is this?" growled Sam. "My feet are killin' me!"

"No rest!" Jep blurted out.

Jeremiah rolled his eyes. "Sorry, men. This can't be. Let me see if I can find out what's goin' down. Follow the assembly. I'll be right back."

Jeremiah sought anyone of higher rank to shed some light on the absurdly short rest period. Quickly he recognized Captain Kertlin not far ahead, and set off to catch up with him. "Cap'n," he shouted, "what goes? My boys is spent . . . is somethin' goin' down?" He saluted vexingly.

"Na, McCamey. We're just bein' pushed is all. I'm so tired I'm gonna walk instead of ride. Afraid I'll fall off my horse otherwise."

"Sorry, lads," he reported back to his troops, exasperated and tired. "Onward we go."

The disgruntled men declared they couldn't. Some cursed, some just sighed, but move on they did, straight through the long night.

Sunrise found them on the southern outskirts of Winchester, aligned and fixed for battle.

A mist rolled over the hills as Jackson's men struck. It was 5 A.M. Initial reaction from the enemy was a swift, intense and wicked volley of musket fire that ripped into the troops in gray. The hard fighting Virginians refused to give ground and for three hours the horrendous sights and sounds of battle consumed men on both sides.

Eventually Banks' blue clad ranks shattered into bits and pieces. Jackson rode up and down among his soldiers, knowing that victory was theirs. "Order the whole line forward!" he yelled. "Order the whole line forward! The battle is won!" As the command was passed down, a triumphant surge ahead was executed. Banks' army was all but decimated. Confused and beaten, the Yankees began a tearing retreat, scampering straight through the town of Winchester, until safe in the northern outskirts.

The boys had long since forgotten their bone-tired weariness and were running on sheer passion, exhilaration and the thrill of victory. Excitement was at a fever pitch as they prepared to march into town. Word had passed down the ranks that the citizens of Winchester were in an absolute frenzy . . . impatiently waiting to welcome their liberators and fellow Virginians.

"Sarge, I don't know when I've ever enjoyed myself more!" Sam exclaimed. "Did you see how we had them blue bellies on the run? Jumpin' Jehosaphat! I can't wait to catch up with 'em and get 'em in our clutches again! Finish this Banks off, by jingo!"

"I'm wonderin' what they've left behind for us," Jeremiah clamored gleefully. "You can betcha they didn't stop none to secure equipment and munitions! Yes siree! I'll bet we'll be outfitted for a while!"

"Hee, hee!" Jep laughed. "I ain't never seen such an undisciplined retreat! Them boys was plum fear crazed . . . panic stricken, I do believe!" He yawned and stretched. "Makes one feel a little bit powerful, don't it? And I'm too tired to be feelin' much of anything right now! It kinda scares me boys. Well Andy . . . ain't you got nothin' to offer up about it?"

Andy, who'd remained quiet until now, suddenly blurted out: "I got it, boys! I got it!" He sang out to one of the popular tunes of the day:

Johnny had them blue clads travelin' at a run
Straight through Winchester town they passed
Shoutin' 'Look out, boys! Here they come!'
They'll soon be right up on you,

Them Johnny Rebs dressed in gray,
So my fellow Billy Yanks
Run for your life this day!

Wish I had my banjo with me now so I could play it!"

The three other boys howled with laughter. "I gotta say, Andy my man, you do got a way with words!" Sam slapped him on the back.

As the Southern army began pouring into the streets of Winchester, the citizens reacted with great shouts of joy. Flags and banners waved wildly from windows and balconies. The women and children ran out to greet the soldiers, thrusting flowers, handkerchiefs, hams, fresh breads, sweet cakes and other confections into their hands.

"Ooo-eee, boys!" Jeptha cried out in exhilaration, "I ain't seen so many beautiful ladies in all my life!"

So excited were the citizens that all propriety was left behind. Jeremiah smiled gratefully and tipped his cap, though thoroughly embarrassed as a pretty young girl pushed a huge chunk of sweet cake into his hands. Thanking him repeatedly, she stood on tiptoe and kissed his cheek. A little girl grabbed Andy around the leg and hugged him so hard that he was forced to take several steps while she clung to him.

Sam, welcomed with a hearty clasp from a beautiful young lass, enthusiastically returned the embrace, but Jeptha won the prize of the day. Out of nowhere, a striking lady clad in gingham and straw flew from the crowd along the street. Unashamedly, she hurled herself at Jeptha, leaping into his arms. As he carried her for several steps trying to overcome the shock, she suddenly threw her arms about his neck and kissed him hard. Jeptha never broke stride, but one could not mistake the grin spread across his face. Carrying her for a little ways, he finally, though unwillingly, placed her back on her feet. She melted once more into the crowd, but Jep held on to his grin.

All too soon they were through the town and the chaotic revelry. They halted briefly as Captain Kertlin rode past in obvious jubilation. "Great day in the mornin', boys!" he laughed, "I ain't never seen such a welcome as this! Ain't it grand! I'm tempted to ride all the way to the rear just so I can come through again!"

"And what does General Jackson think about all this, Sir?" asked Jeremiah, a smile extended across his face.

"Lads, Ol' Jack had tears in his eyes. He's been wonderfully touched by this display. His heart has truly been moved." The captain took off his hat and tipped it to the boys. "Men," he said, "my hat's off to you. That was

some fightin' you did today. Well done, lads, well done! I'm proud of you!"
He galloped away as suddenly as he appeared.

Jep shook his head in wonderment, a gleam in his eyes. "He's a fine
man, that one. Jeremiah . . . reckon he and 'Cilla might get married
sometime?"

"Don't 'spose I know the answer to that, Jep . . . but she couldn't do
no better, and that's a fact!" Suddenly Jeremiah folded his arms across his
chest, and grinning, looked hard at Jeptha. "You sure did seem to enjoy
yourself today," he broke into a laugh.

Slapping an open hand across his heart, Jep looked at his three comrades. "Boys," he declared, "I believe I'm in love!"

Counting up the loot between them, they discovered a bouquet of
flowers, some scented handkerchiefs, two loaves of fresh baked bread, one
pone of corn bread, a large hunk of cake and a stone jug of fresh churned
buttermilk.

"Look out stomach!" Sam exclaimed as they began to take up their
march again. "Almost makes it worth not eatin' in so long to have such de-
lectee-bles." He broke off a chunk of soft, white bread, and stuffed it into
his mouth. Walking slowly, he passed it down the line to his comrades, each
following suit. This was finished by swigs of sweet, cool buttermilk, rich
with yellow nuggets.

Jeremiah was correct in assuming the Federals had discarded much
equipment. After the Yankees' wild flight from Winchester, the
Confederates rounded up 2 cannons, 9,300 new muskets, a lavish supply
of medical necessities and substantial military hardware.

Jackson's little force remained in Winchester for several days, basking
in the aftermath of victory. Company G's brigade was then sent north to
Harper's Ferry while General Jackson remained behind at his headquarters.

Union President Abraham Lincoln was outraged with his generals
and demanded that Jackson be stopped and the valley taken. He sent in
General John Fremont with orders to close in on Strasburg, while Banks
again pushed southward and Shields drew in from the east. It was a
desperate and cunning plan. When Jackson got wind of it, he acted quickly
to move out of Winchester, heading south. Company G was left behind
at Harper's Ferry.

The Federal forces marched seventy miles in eight days, while Jackson's
"foot cavalry" covered forty miles in two days. On May 31, orders were received at Harper's Ferry. The brigade was to fall back toward Strasburg

with as much haste as possible. Realizing they were alone at the valley's north door, the brigade made a mad dash to join the rest of their army.

As Company G marched out in the early morning hours, the men were greeted by torrents of rain that fell incessantly throughout the day and on into the night. The valley floor turned into a pit of mud, yet onward the men pushed. The mire sucked off shoes and spattered uniforms. It oozed down socks and up through toes. In places, men were drawn in up to their knees, making marching near impossible, but they continued to move forward, the endless mud clinging to everything. They did not once stop to rest, or even to eat, and they consumed forty-five miles in thirty-six hours. When they were at last reunited with the rest of their troops, the boys were utterly worn and frazzled. Their weariness was so encompassing, Jep and Sam simply fell in the muck in the road, letting sleep overtake them immediately, though they were covered in the pasty sludge. Jeremiah and Andy were so exhausted and confused they had no idea where they were.

June 1 saw heavy cavalry engagements, and on June 6, Jackson's beloved cavalry leader, Turner Ashby, lay dead.

On June 8, they faced Fremont, and won the Battle of Cross Keys. On June 9, Jackson's army marched into Port Republic. At 5 A.M., they opened battle against Shields' division, resulting in some of the valley's heaviest fighting. By nightfall, both Fremont and Shields were in retreat. Banks, though close to Winchester, dared not disturb the town.

The great campaign of the Shenandoah was over. The valley was securely in the clutches of Virginia.

CHAPTER ELEVEN

I left my dear old mother
To weep and to mourn;
I am a Rebel soldier
And far from my home.

The men stumbled back to camp at Staunton in the following days. Straggling and war weary, they were in desperate need of rest and reoutfitting. They had marched some 676 miles in 48 days.

The first few days brought in much needed supplies via the Orange and Alexandria Railroad. The chore was to see these necessities distributed. Thousands of shoes and articles of clothing made up a large portion of the goods.

The night after their return found the messmates enjoying themselves around the campfire, having a good laugh at Jep's worn out shoes. The sole on one flopped from heel to toe. The mate had a fist size hole through the bottom and his big toe stuck completely out. He pulled them off his feet.

"Boys, these here shoes have flopped their last flip. I can't stand 'em no more." Jeptha looked at them with a sigh. "Reckon I'd rather go barefooted," he announced, suddenly chucking them into the fire. Immediately, Lieutenant Moore strode up, causing the boys to jump to a salute.

"At ease, men. Go about your business. McCamey, I've come to tell you that Cap'n would like a word with you. Says he needs to speak to you on a personal matter."

"Yes, Sir, right away, " Jeremiah answered. "Men," he turned to his friends, "don't wait up on me."

"No danger in that!" Jep shouted good-naturedly as the sergeant and the lieutenant walked away.

No one spoke for a minute. Finally, Anderson voiced what they were all thinking, "What d'ya 'spose is up, boys?"

"Aw, who can say," Sam yawned, "said he wanted to talk to him about a personal matter."

"You don't know, Sam," Jep exclaimed, "Jeremiah's been summoned like this a couple o' times before, and each time the ol' boy came back with a higher rank. What's next . . . lieutenant?"

"Na, he ain't been a sergeant long enough," Sam reflected. "Them lieutenants and cap'ns and on up are usually elected, anyways."

"Yeah . . . besides, nobody's been lost to us that calls for replacin' . . . I mean ever time he's been given rank it's 'cause someone's bitten the dust. I ain't tryin' to sound unfeelin' or cruel, boys, but it's a fact," Jep declared. "Lots o' men have died; lots o' good men, and in my opinion, they was all irreplaceable."

"Nope," Andy voiced quietly, "Lieutenant said it was personal."

Jep grunted a half laugh. "Maybe he wants to ask his permission to marry Priscilla."

"Yeah . . . Cap'n does have a thing for the Sarge's sister, don't he?" Sam questioned.

"Well, he can have her," Jep replied. "Don't get me wrong, boys. I've knowed that gal all my life; she's good as a sister to me, and she and Jeremiah's closer than a tick on a hound dog . . . least it were that way before the war. She's good lookin' and she's smart, and that there's the catch. That combination in a woman is a mite scary, if you ask me. Makes me nervous."

For a moment, Sam pulled on the thick, full beard he'd grown. "Dunno, now . . . a man like Cap'n might find such a gal to his likin' . . ." Suddenly, he slapped Jeptha on the back. "If I didn't know any better, Boy, I'd think . . ." he stopped in mid sentence, deciding to say nothing more.

Lieutenant Moore stuck his head into the captain's tent and announced Jeremiah's presence.

"Jeremiah, come in, come on in."

The use of his first name caught him off guard. The captain never addressed him as anything other than McCamey or Sergeant. He forgot to salute, but Captain Kertlin didn't seem to notice, and puzzled Jeremiah by putting out his hand for a shake, instead.

"Sit down," he gestured to a stool, sinking back into his desk chair.

"Got some news to pass on to your men, McCamey. We're bein' called out, movin' eastward in a couple of days . . . just soon as we get reoutfitted."

"Well . . . what's up, Cap'n?"

"Been a heap of rough fightin' east of here. General Johnston's got himself wounded bad enough as to not be able to continue in command of this army."

Jeremiah pursed his lips in thought. "So, who's takin' his place?"

"It's been official for several days. Jeff Davis's own man . . . that's right, the president's own military advisor."

Jeremiah looked at him wide-eyed. "You mean Robert E. Lee? General Lee is takin' command now?"

"Has taken," the captain corrected him. "It was official last week."

"Ain't he a little bit old, Sir . . . meaning no disrespect. I know he's a good man; that is without question."

"No better, McCamey . . . and no better record. Fact is, Ol' Lincoln himself tried to sign Lee on as head of his Yankee army when we first went to fightin', right before Virginia seceded."

"Well now . . . this done sure come as a surprise to me, Sir."

"Anyway, McCamey, he's sent for us; for Stonewall . . . now that the valley is secure."

"Where exactly will we be goin', Cap'n?"

"You know General Jackson. He says, 'Always mystify, mislead and surprise' . . . so, I don't know where we're goin'. Just that we're goin' east, cause General Lee says to. Anyway, have your men ready."

"Cap'n," Jeremiah looked down before continuing, "I've been meanin' to ask, Sir, wantin' to know . . . well, what of General Garnett? Heard anything lately? He's sure a fine man, Sir; me and the boys miss him right smartly and was wonderin' what you hear. It's been over two months now."

"Well, all I know is that he's appealin' this thing . . . Lee's intervened. Garnett means to fight the charges. Look, we both know he didn't follow orders. We also know that he felt he didn't have a choice. What d'ya do? It was a no win situation, I reckon. Of course, he should have obeyed . . . but . . . well, I think maybe he'll be reinstated to a command at sometime. But that's my personal point of view. Meanwhile, we answer to General Trimble. He's as capable a brigade commander as any."

"Yes . . . well, I agree, Cap'n." Silence hung thick in the air for several seconds. "Lieutenant Moore told me you wanted to speak to me on a personal matter," Jeremiah continued, feeling awkward.

Captain Kertlin drummed his fingers briefly on his desktop. "He's right, Jeremiah. I . . . I aim on asking Priscilla to marry me."

"What have I got to do with that, Cap'n?" he asked sharply, embarrassed.

"Well, if I do, that will make us family. That's plenty to do with it!" the Captain answered in exasperation.

"When you plan on havin' this wedding?"

"McCamey, I ain't even asked her proper yet!" He looked Jeremiah hard in the face. "Talkin' to you about your sister is like pullin' teeth. Why?" He sounded angry.

Jeremiah looked down, rubbing his hand briskly across the top of his head. "Don't reckon I know, Cap'n. Me and Prissy . . . 'Cilla that is, was very close before this war came along, and now things is changed." He looked up at the captain. "Blame it all, Cap'n! She wouldn't even tell me about you, ah, about your special friendship, until I, we, went home on leave. Reckon it hurt me some. If this was a year or so ago . . . well, she sure did confide in me lots more than she does now. This war just changed things and I reckon I ain't too happy about it none."

"Jeremiah . . . things do change. Sometimes it's circumstances like this war that cause the changes . . . sometimes you can even blame them on other people. To be sure, things change regularly as we get older. But just because circumstances differ doesn't mean people's feelings do. Your sister has enormous love and respect for you. I'll testify to that." He looked at Jeremiah.

"Cap'n, I sure do hope she says yes. I'll be mighty proud if you was to be part of the family. You do have my blessings."

"That's what I wanted, Jeremiah. That's what I wanted. That, and a little advice . . ."

"Now, I'll tell you Cap'n, you best write to Father first and ask for her hand proper. My Pa's real big on doin' things the right way . . . says it's a sign of disrespect if things ain't done proper."

"That's what I need the advice on, McCamey!"

"Oh, my Pa's a good man, Sir . . . he just means for respect to be paid where respect is due. We was all raised that way."

"Well, I aim on writin' him . . . guess I just needed to be put at ease."

Silence reigned again and Jeremiah rose to go. "Let me know about things, Cap'n. Just cause 'Cilla keeps me in the dark don't mean you have to. Reckon I'd best be goin' now, if you're done with me."

Captain Kertlin again put out his hand and shook Jeremiah's. "Thanks . . . you have made this easier for me."

"'Cilla couldn't do no better Cap'n, Sir. Good night."

Jeremiah arrived back at his tent to find that the boys, indeed, had not waited up for him. All were fast asleep, Jeptha's snoring the only sound shattering the silence.

He stretched out on his blanket and began to toss and turn. *So, how do I really feel about Priscilla maybe marryin' Cap'n?* he silently asked himself.

Go on to sleep, his mind urged.

Think it through, Boy, his heart countered.

He opted for the easy out—sleep; but it wouldn't come.

His heart was winning this battle, like it or not.

All right, Jerry-miah . . . take one thing at a time, he thought to himself. *You're hurt that Prissy hasn't shared everything with you. No . . . angry. How can she when I'm so far away . . . that was my choice . . . no, my duty. Nobody's fault.*

Cap'n's a good man . . . yeah, I'd be happy for her to have someone like him. He's an honorable man. None better.

Now, what is so bad about this? Things change . . . so, they change anyway. Can't stop that. All right . . . good boy, Jerry-miah; you're makin' some progress. I don't want her heart broken like Violet's . . . that's the key to this, isn't it? Cy . . . Cy's dead . . . have I really accepted that? He sighed out loud, thinking of the heart wrenching, tear stained letter Violet wrote to him when she learned of Cy. *I don't want that to happen to 'Cilla also,* he thought. *All right, Jerry-miah . . . be a man about this. You can't change things. It is not your fault. You just do your duty!*

Suddenly Sam was bent over him, shaking him awake. "You all right, McCamey? Wake-up done sounded and you slept plum through it."

Jeremiah rubbed his face and struggled to sit up. He shook his head to clear it. "Didn't know I was so tired." He blinked and wiped his eyes. "How long since wake-up, Sam?"

"Been most a good half hour, I'd say. Here, let me see to some coffee for you, Sergeant."

"No, no . . . I need to talk with you boys." He rose, shaking his head again. "That was some sleep I was under. Sam, have all the boys gather round outside . . . I'll see to my coffee."

He stepped out into the first light of day. *How calm,* he thought; how peaceful it seemed; the light mist, the rosy sky and the smell of wood smoke . . . it was hard to believe they were in the middle of a raging war.

His coffee tasted good; he was glad supplies had come in. They were starting to run low on it. The warm, brown liquid greatly revived him.

"Men, men . . . gather 'round," he said, as those in his command made their way to the fire outside his tent. "Got a few things I need to share."

"Mornin' Jeremiah . . . you looked a little haggard," Jep quipped. "Had another one of them long talks with Cap'n last night. What'd he want this time?"

"Boys, don't get too comfortable, but rest while you can. Soon's were reoutfitted, a day or two, we're movin' out again."

A chorus of groans greeted him.

"I know you're tired, men. We're all tired, but look at what we've accomplished these last few months. We ain't done nothin' to be ashamed of, I tell you! Besides, we now got a couple of weeks good rest under our belts.

"It's like this . . . in some heavy fightin' 'round Richmond Ol' Joe Johnston's done got hurt real bad, and he ain't fit right now to stay in command of this here army. So, our president, Jeff Davis, has filled the place with someone new."

"With who?" Jep wanted to know.

"With his own military advisor; good Ol' Robert E. Lee."

"Bobby Lee?" someone piped up.

"Old Granny Lee himself?" Drew shot out. "How's an old man gonna lead an army?"

Jeremiah ignored the remarks. "Trouble is, General Lee's done sent for us; for Ol' Jack. We're marchin' off to the east. Another thing . . ." he cleared his throat, looking around at the men. "Before you get too hard on Lee, he's lookin' in on General Garnett's case himself. I just want you to know that. General Garnett's appealin' this thing and Lee's a fair man. General Jackson did what he had to do, what was the right thing, but we all know we're in desperate need of leaders. Good leaders. General Garnett is a good leader. I guarantee he'll not repeat his mistake."

Within the week, the men were on their way. The entire state, with the exception of the valley, was a hotbed of hard fighting. As the men marched eastward, fantastic tales of J. E. B. Stuart began to filter down to them. It was said he'd ridden a circuit around McClellan's whole Yankee army, coming within sight of the General's tent undetected! By the time Stuart and his cavalry were discovered, it was too late for the Federals to make a serious pursuit. He returned to Lee with valuable information and marvelous tales of his exploits circulated between both armies. Jeremiah's men agreed that such actions took unsurpassed courage and great daring. Many envisioned life with the cavalry as being much more glorious and certainly greater fun than marching hundreds of miles in the infantry.

After making a forced march of twelve hours, the night of June 26 found Jackson's men thrust into the heat of battle at a little town called Mechanicsville. The fight had raged most of the afternoon without either side having an advantage. General Lee's directive was to shove McClellan's army across the Chickahominy River. Once Stonewall's men joined the fight, the army in blue began to fall back, retreating from Richmond. Lee aimed to stop this retreat. His order was to cut them off, and destroy the Union Army.

The day of June 27 saw fighting erupt again, a few miles to the south at a place called Gaines Mill. For several hours, the two forces clashed until sunset saw the men in gray make a charge that finally pushed the troops in blue across the river.

An exhausted Company G turned back to Richmond for rest after the two days of hard fighting. Their reprieve was cut short on the 29th as they were called out to again attack McClellan's army at Savage Station.

The morning of June 30 found Stonewall's men on the march once more, in a second attempt to hinder McClellan's retreat. That afternoon combat exploded at a place called Frayser's Farm. Though the battle was won, McClellan's retreat was not thwarted.

July 1 found the brigade at a site called Malvern Hill. The day was quiet until about 5 P.M. Suddenly, a torrent of murderous Yankee artillery was discharged among the Rebel troops. Three times the gray line charged, wavered, and fell back to cover of woods. The hill was awash in flames and the concussion of artillery shook the earth. Nightfall saw the open field occupied by the Confederates, but success ended there. As the sun went down, over four thousand men of the Army of Northern Virginia lay dead.

To hold the captured ground at Malvern Hill, it was necessary for a contingency of men to remain overnight on the field. Among the wounded and dying of both sides, they were to hold the gained position and assure enemy withdrawal. Though retracting, deadly Yankee artillery continued to shell the location.

Details began the long and painstaking task of removing still, lifeless forms from the terrain and aiding those who were too wounded to remove themselves. The constant enemy shelling made the dangerous job deadly. More than once in the process of removing an injured man, a soldier performing the task became one of the casualties.

The sun was long down by the time Jeremiah's men were situated on the field and picket lines formed along the banks of the river. Though tired and hungry from the fierce, bloody work of the day, rest and food seemed unimportant. Surrounded by bodies clad in both blue and gray, the cries and wails were terrible. Pleas for water reverberated like an echo and Jeremiah simply started giving orders.

"Sam, you and Andy start roundin' up as many canteens as can be found. Killian, Drew, as soon as they start bringin' 'em back, you two go down to the river and fill 'em up. Jep and I will start tryin' to answer some of these cries of thirst. When you've got a good many canteens filled, you boys start doin' the same."

The night was unbearably hot and steamy, the air almost too heavy to breath. As Jep and Jeremiah began lifting heads and draining canteens, gratefulness for their aid was apparent, and both boys saw sights they hoped never to see again.

"This is so odd, Jeremiah," Jep's voice broke through the eerie sound of cries. "You can't tell if these fellas are blue or gray unless you look real close. They're all just hurt men out here. Hurt or dead. You know, I don't think of them as bein' the enemy like this . . ."

"Well, Jep," Jeremiah grunted, raising the head of one man in blue and placing a canteen of cool water against his thirsty lips, "a hurt man don't care who his enemy is, and a dead man, well, reckon he ain't got none."

As Jeremiah lowered the head, the man grabbed him gratefully about the wrist. "Thank you, Sir," he mumbled. "Thank you."

The boys continued their mission of mercy and soon Jeremiah heard Jep call from a short distance away. "Need your help, Sergeant," he voiced. "This poor fella's got two busted arms. Pains him too much to lift his head."

Jeremiah arrived at Jeptha's side to help steady the young lad and ease his thirst. One arm was badly mangled from a shell and the other was twisted in several places, evidently broken. The boy thanked them and groaned. His eyes were wide open and glazed with fever. "Sorry men, but I'm somewhat in a little pain," he gasped with a grimace.

"Don't you worry none. Some boys will be along quick now to take you to the hospital. Them arms will be good as new in no time," Jeremiah consoled him.

"Oh, it ain't my arms that's hurtin' me so much. It's my tummy. I got a fierce tummy ache."

The fellow's blanket had come part way unrolled on top of his gray uniform and Jep quickly reached down to throw it back. What he and Jeremiah saw made both of them sick. There was no way the poor lad would survive and the two friends looked at each other.

"It's bad, ain't it?" the boy asked in short breaths. "Tell me the truth. I can die like a man."

"Well now, I ain't no doctor and I don't know that I can tell a mortal wound from one that ain't so bad," Jeremiah lied.

Jep covered back up the ugly flesh and the young soldier grimaced again. " It . . . it's all right . . . it's all right if I die."

Jep felt the urge to scream at the boy, to yell at him, *No! It's not all right! It's not all right for you to die!* He bit his tongue to keep the angry words at bay.

"Would one of you mind too terribly much writin' down some words to send to my Ma and Pa?" the wounded boy whispered. "Would you tell them not too feel too bad . . . would you tell them I died in defense of my country, and not to mourn too sadly? Tell them . . . tell them it was an honorable thing for which they raised a son to do. I'd be very much obliged to you."

Jeremiah searched frantically in his pockets for a bit of paper or nub of pencil, but had none. "Jep?" he questioned his friend hopefully.

"I ain't got none neither," he stammered, tears glistening in his eyes.

"It don't matter now," Jeremiah said flatly. Looking down at the gallant fellow, he pulled the blanket up to shroud the form.

Through the long night, the boys worked diligently to relieve the suffering before them. As the sun's rays finally begin to rise in the east, the field was nearly cleared of dead and wounded.

Jeptha eased down the last head he was to raise and the soldier in blue grabbed him, a slight smile across his face. "Thank you kindly," he whispered, "I don't guess all you Johnny Rebs is so bad."

Jeptha returned the smile with his crooked one. "Naw . . . I don't suppose all you Yanks is so bad neither." The man in blue was immediately lifted to a litter and carted away by a detail for care. Jep sank back on his heels for a moment, then wearily standing, headed back to his own men.

The fight at Malvern Hill broke the chain of victories for the South and the Seven Days Battle drew to a close. Though his attempt to capture Richmond failed, McClellan remained on the move toward the James River.

CHAPTER TWELVE

Ah! Maiden wait, and watch and yearn
For news of Stonewall's band.
Ah! Widow read with eyes that burn
That ring upon thy hand.

After the fight at Malvern Hill, Jackson's men remained part of the Richmond line for several days. Weary and battle worn, camp in the capital city was a welcome reprieve. The men were told they would be held here, in reserve, for perhaps as long as two weeks.

Sometimes Jeremiah felt like he wasn't sure where he was. The last several months had seen them move about and fight in so many different places there was little time to think about anything other than where the next fight would be.

He was surprised when the letters came. He gave little thought to anyone else keeping aware of their location. But they were welcome, newsy letters that had come as a packet; one from his parents, one from 'Cilla, two from Violet, one of them being addressed to Jeptha. Jeremiah read and reread them, hungry for home, hungry for his family.

"Captain wrote to Father," 'Cilla's beautiful script revealed, "and Father agreed to the marriage between her and his captain. She didn't know when they could manage a wedding, but felt excited beyond belief, and, she admitted to her brother, madly in love with John Kertlin.

Jeremiah smiled, reading her lines over and over. He couldn't help but think of the fact that her happiness was, in some part, due to him. After all, he did introduce them and took Cap'n home in December. It was comforting to know any happiness could come out of this terrible war.

Violet's lines revealed her continued mourning for Cy. "Yes, sometimes my spirits are better, but I will take my grief to my grave," she wrote.

Jeremiah vowed that one day he would tell Violet of the morning before Cy died and the photograph he insisted on sending her, just in case something happened . . . just in case . . .

Jeremiah shook his head, hoping to shake the thought away. *Cy, Cy, Cy . . . have you any idea . . .*

"Mrs. Ash is leaving the New Church community," Violet revealed. "She is going to live with an ancient aunt and distant cousin in Luray. My one last living link to my beloved will be gone," Violet lamented. Jeremiah shook his head, and smiled. Violet did have a flair for the dramatic.

Toward the end of the second week in Richmond, word spread of a great gala being sponsored by the Ladies of Chimborazo Hospital. It was to raise money for the treatment and care of the impaired, sick and wounded soldiers of the South. All men at camp were invited to attend.

Many boys were enthusiastic about such an event, but a number declared it was not something to which they were suited to attend. Jeremiah, Jep nor Sam could imagine being the least bit comfortable among hundreds of people in a social situation. Andy simply declared he wasn't comfortable in any social circumstance. None were interested in going.

The morning of the event, Captain Kertlin made rounds to chat with his men.

"Ho, McCamey!" he yelled out, popping his head in to the tent.

Jeremiah was busy, taking a moment of quiet to write some letters.

"You alone?" the Captain asked, surprised.

"Yes, Sir," Jeremiah saluted. "The boys have gone to bathe in the river."

"Good. I haven't had much chance to speak with you as of recent. What do you hear from Priscilla, Jeremiah? Anything lately?"

Jeremiah stared at the captain blankly. "Ain't you got some mail from her yourself?"

"No, as a matter of fact . . . which is why I'm glad to catch you alone. I haven't had any answer from your father. I've about decided maybe he thinks I'm not good enough; he'd be right. Reckon no one's really good enough for her . . . but I want her for my wife in the fiercest way."

Jeremiah rooted around among his letters as he talked. "Well, you know Cap'n, mail doesn't always get to where it's goin'. I'm sure you've had some answers sent." He opened an envelope, the paper crackling as he unfolded his latest letter. Skimming over it, he began to read out loud ". . .

'Father has agreed to the marriage . . . I am excited beyond belief! . . . Jeremiah, I must admit, I am madly in love with your Captain Kertlin . . . I don't know . . .'"

Captain Kertlin held out his hand. "Enough! Enough! That's enough!" His face was flushed with embarrassment.

Jeremiah enjoyed the discomfort of his captain too much to quit. "'He is true and brave . . .'" he continued to read "'. . . just think, he will be your brother-in-law; isn't it marvelous?'"

"McCamey! Don't! Quit!" Captain Kertlin reached out, attempting to grab the letter. Jeremiah snatched it back, laughing hard.

"Wait, there's more, Cap'n . . . she's got it all spelled out here '. . . don't know when we can manage a wedding . . . I'm sure you agree with me that he is wonderful!'" Jeremiah was laughing so hard tears begin to roll down his face.

"Sergeant!" the captain bellowed.

As suddenly as he started, Jeremiah stopped, realizing this was his captain he was talking to. He held the letter out. John Kertlin shook his head no.

"Cap'n . . . I'm sorry. I apologize. I did forget myself," he said soberly.

Looking at him, the captain suddenly smiled. "She really said all that?"

"Here, read for yourself. I didn't make it up." Jeremiah held the letter out to him again, but he still refused it with a shake of his head.

"She makes me sound pretty good, huh?"

"You are a good man, Cap'n. I cannot tell you how thankful I am for the happiness you've brought to 'Cilla in the midst of this war."

Captain Kertlin nodded his head, "And she has to me.

"Well, to change the subject . . . your men ready for the big social tonight?"

"Yes, Sir. We're ready not to go."

"You ain't plannin' on it?"

"Aw, Cap'n . . . none of us is used to this big-wig social stuff. We'd be mighty uncomfortable; feel real outa place. We just ain't interested."

"It's for a good cause, McCamey . . . Chimborazo Hospital gives our hurt and wounded boys the best progressive care available anywhere, North or South. Can't I change your mind none?"

"I don't think so, Sir."

"All right . . . what if I put it this way . . . it happens to be my father's sister that's helped to organize this thing. I'd consider it a personal favor if you'd go."

Jeremiah stared at him for a moment. He really didn't want to do this, but how could he turn down his captain and future brother-in-law?

"I'll see what I can do to convince the boys, Sir."

"I'd appreciate it, McCamey. I'd feel sorta foolish if my own company didn't make a good showing."

"I ain't makin' no promises, Cap'n."

It wasn't long before the other boys returned from their bath in the river. Noticing Jeremiah had his best uniform hanging outside, Jeptha couldn't help making a comment.

"Now, surely, Jeremiah, you don't plan on forsakin' these fine gray duds that's been officially issued to us for that splendid outfit Violet made you last year. You ain't worn it out yet? Didn't even know you still had that thing."

"I ain't had much occasion to wear it, Jep. But truth is, Cap'n come by this mornin'," he looked at his three comrades, "and I sorta promised him we'd go to that shindig this evenin'. Come to find out, his aunt had a hand at organizin' it, and he felt right bad lots o' his own men ain't plannin' to be there. Blame it all, boys, he asked it as a personal favor."

"Well, you can just go by your lonesome, Jeremiah," Sam spat out. "I ain't goin'. I don't care what you promised Cap'n. I don't aim on gettin' the toes I have left stepped on while I try to do some fancy dancin' I ain't never done before."

"Look, I dunno that there will even be any dancin'," Jeremiah said defensively. "I don't want to go. I'm only doin' it out of respect for Cap'n."

"Well," Jep retorted, "seems to me Cap'n ain't marryin' into none of our families. I don't feel a bit obligated to do somethin' I ain't got no pleasure in doin'."

"You know how I feel, Sergeant," Andy quipped quietly, "best count me out no matter."

Jeremiah glared at his three friends. "Well, I'm goin'," he said in a huff. "It's not that I wanna, but I'm doin' it for Cap'n. You fellas do what you wanna do." He turned to leave. "Reckon I'd better go catch me a bath before afternoon drill. Wasn't plannin' on needin' one earlier."

When afternoon drill and evening mess were over, the boys went their separate ways, leaving Jeremiah to ready himself for the social gathering he didn't want to attend. He was angry and unsure at what: his three friends for deserting him, Cap'n for askin' this of him or himself for agreeing to do something he had no desire to do. He simply hoped the evening would be a short one.

Emerging from his tent, he walked smack into Jeptha. "Where you off to, Jep? Thought you fella's had a checker game planned. You're certain dressed too well for an evening around the campfire."

"Aw, Jeremiah . . . I couldn't let you go this alone. We done been through too much in our life. I couldn't let you down over somethin' as silly as a little social gathering. I aim on headin' over there with you. I just couldn't seem to convince Sam and Andy."

Jeremiah looked at his friend and patted him firmly on the shoulder. "Thanks, Jep. I appreciate this. I should have known you'd not let me down."

"I got to thinkin', Jeremiah. Cy'd have gone . . . he'd have found somethin' funny or amusin' about it all, and he'd have gone right along with it."

"So, where've you been this last little bit? Why didn't you tell me you'd changed your mind?"

"Well now, I had to first try to convince the others to go . . . which I obviously failed at; then I had to find somethin' better than my own uniform to wear. Both of 'em's pretty worn and patched; fact is, I borrowed this here nice tunic from one of the other fellas in the company, so I'd look a little less ragged. Pants are still a mite worn, but maybe this tunic spiffs me up enough. Don't look as fine as you, though."

"Hold on, Jep." Jeremiah disappeared into their tent, emerging with something in his hand. He held it out. "This'll do you up some, Jep. Even make you look like an officer."

Jeptha stared at the sergeant's hand. "Oh, Jeremiah . . . I couldn't," he said in a whisper, "uh-uh."

"Go on Jep . . . it ain't mine. Cy'd be proud to have you wear it."

Jep hesitated and then reached out, taking the beautifully made sash. "What d'ya think Violet would say?" he asked, tying it about his waist.

"I think she'd say it becomes you, Jep."

The two soldiers turned many feminine heads as they strolled to the exhibition hall where the gala was being held. There were hundreds of other people headed in the same direction.

Arriving at the hall, both boys were amazed at the size of the building and stood at the bottom of the steps in awe. Jeptha pulled at his buttoned up collar, "I don't know what persuaded me to do this for you, Jeremiah."

"Neither do I," the sergeant answered. "Can't imagine how I let Cap'n talk me into it. It's too late now!"

They climbed the steep steps among the throng of people: soldiers, old men, matrons, young ladies, girls and boys.

Jep looked around. "Well, one thing's for sure, Jeremiah. We done seen about as many beautiful ladies as a body can stand."

"Ha!" Jeremiah laughed. "You said that back at Winchester."

They entered the building and the first thing to greet them was a large display of sketches depicting Chimborazo Hospital. Accompanying the drawings were various dispensations describing some of the new and progressive techniques being used to treat the South's sick and wounded soldiers.

Both boys spent a good deal of time at the display, not only in an effort to avoid socializing with hundreds of strange people, but because they truly found it interesting.

"Jep," Jeremiah said, "if I ever do get hurt or wounded, this is the place I'd like to end up. Might have half a chance to survive it. Look here," he pointed to one sketch, "this report says they can hold up to eight thousand wounded and are addin' a bakery capable of cookin' up to ten thousand loaves of bread a day. Now, that's somethin'!"

Suddenly Captain Kertlin's voice boomed out from behind them. "Gentlemen," he declared, "I'm very glad to see you among those of our company in attendance tonight." Both boys turned, giving him a quick salute.

"Please, men," he returned it, "allow me to introduce you to some . . . ah . . . shall I say, family and acquaintances."

They followed the captain, meeting more people than they could possibly remember. Jep nudged Jeremiah in the ribs with his elbow. "We're only bein' made over so cause he's marryin' 'Cilla, you realize," he whispered.

In order to ease Jep's exasperation, Jeremiah turned to agree. When he looked at his friend, it was obvious he was far from displeased. Jeptha truly seemed to be enjoying himself.

"Jep," Jeremiah asked quietly, "do my eyes deceive me or are you actually havin' a good time?"

"Yeah, I am, as long as I ain't gotta dance or do no fancy talkin'. It's really kinda nice to be smiled at by all these purty ladies! I don't mind bein' intoduced to 'em neither."

Jeremiah rolled his eyes. "Jep," he laughed, "you just need a gal; one who will be willin' to wait this war out for you."

"Naw . . . there's too many purty ladies to settle for just one!"

The captain cleared his throat to get their attention, "Sergeant McCamey, Private Carroll, it gives me great pleasure to introduce to you my aunt, Velmatina Ellicott. Aunt Tina, I present to you two of my men, Sergeant Jeremiah McCamey and Private Jeptha Carroll. They are among the best soldiers Virginia's got to offer!"

The two men bowed politely. "It is indeed, our pleasure, Madam," Jeremiah spoke.

"Nonsense!" said the older, plump, but not unattractive woman. "It is our pleasure to become acquainted with as many of our gallant men as we can . . . for you are the very ones protecting our homeland and putting your lives on the line!"

"Yes, Ma'am," Jeremiah replied, taking the woman's gloved hand as she offered it to him. He bowed again.

Aunt Tina turned to Captain Kertlin. "McCamey? Is this the young man you spoke of? Your fiancée's brother?"

Captain Kertlin looked down, blushing. "Yes Ma'am, it is."

"Well, then, it is twice the pleasure, Sergeant. It's about time my nephew found a bride."

Jeremiah could tell the captain was embarrassed and tried to make him more comfortable. "It has been a real pleasure to meet you, Ma'am. May I get you some punch? I'm mighty thirsty myself."

"No, no. Thank you. There is someone else I'd like for you to meet, but she's stepped away for the moment. Perhaps later . . ."

"Yes, Ma'am. Cap'n, join me?"

Captain Kertlin grabbed Jeremiah's elbow, pulling him away. "Great day in the mornin'! Thanks, McCamey. She's sweet . . . she means well, but . . ." He looked at Jeremiah and rolled his eyes. "Aunts," he huffed. "C'mon, men, let's go to the table up front. There's food up there you ain't never gonna have in camp!"

The cuisine was delicious; platters heaped with ham and tender turkey; biscuits and yeast breads; boiled shrimp and raw oysters, fare the boys had never tasted; and cakes, pies and puddings. All agreed it was fit for royalty and none of soldiers gave heed to the fact that it was a far richer diet than they'd been used to eating. They heaped their plates several times over.

"I reckon it was worth comin', Jeremiah, just for the eatin'," Jep quipped. "Sam and Andy will sure be sorry they missed out on this," he said, polishing off his third plate.

Suddenly a small group of attractive ladies walked by, flirting with the three soldiers as they passed. "Excuse me, men," Jep said animatedly, "but I believe love is calling me!" He put down his plate and slipped off to follow the girls.

Momentarily, an unfamiliar lieutenant struck up a conversation with Captain Kertlin and soon the captain excused himself to walk away with the unknown officer. The sergeant decided it was time to find Jep and get out of there for the evening. He figured they'd done enough time.

Walking over the spacious room, he craned his head in search of his friend. Suddenly, he heard his name.

"Mr. McCamey! Oh, Sergeant McCamey!" the shrill female voice summoned him again.

He whirled around in search of the sound, only to see his captain's Aunt Tina. She was wildly waving a handkerchief to get his attention.

"Over here, Sergeant! Over here."

Jeremiah knew that she knew he'd seen her. There was nothing to do but make his way over to the matron.

"Jep," he mumbled under his breath, "I'm gonna get you for runnin' off on me like this!" Jeremiah forced a smile and bowed once more to the elder woman. "At your service, Ma'am. What can I do for you?"

"Mr. McCamey, Sergeant McCamey," she addressed him in a lilting voice, "I would like to present to you Miss Christie." Aunt Tina stepped out from in front of a lovely young woman. "She is staying with us for several weeks here in Richmond. Her mother is the sister of my dearest friend and her parents have sent her here to Richmond in order that she might . . . how should I say . . . experience some culture in the midst of this war. There was a good bit of fighting in their area of the state this last year and, well, Miss Christie, let me introduce to you Sergeant . . ." Aunt Tina's prattling came to a halt and Jeremiah realized she had forgotten his first name.

"Jeremiah McCamey, Ma'am. Sergeant Jeremiah McCamey." He bowed, lifting the young lady's bare hand to his lips. "It is my pleasure, Miss Christie, my pleasure indeed."

Lowering her head, she blushed, and Jeremiah thought he hadn't seen so lovely a girl since he'd last laid eyes on Permillia. How strikingly different they were.

The girl in front of him bore beautiful, long hair that fell over her shoulders in dark blonde, almost brown, curls. Her eyes, a light green color, sparkled when she looked back up at him, and her lips parted in a smile, revealing teeth as white and even as pearls in a row.

At once, his thoughts were interrupted by Aunt Tina's words. "This is the brother to John's fiancée . . . he, ah, is the Sergeant's captain."

"Please, Miss Christie . . . call me Jeremiah."

"And you, Sir, shall call me by my name, if it pleases you."

"And your name is?"

"Kathleen Melinda, Sir. My friends call me Katie Melinda and I would be honored for you to do so."

"Where might home be, Katie Lin . . . er, Katie Melinda, excuse me . . ."

Her soft voice drawled in his ears. "I'm from over in the valley. My town is called Luray. Ever heard tell of it?"

"Luray, why we just did a heap o' hard fightin' there this spring, Ma'am. We was . . . is, part of the men under General Stonewall Jackson that helped to secure the valley. Besides, I myself am from a little community south end of it; about three hours ride northeast from Staunton. New Church. Ever heard of it?"

"Mmmm . . ." she thought out loud, "can't say as I have, Sergeant . . . I mean, Jeremiah. But I am truly honored to meet one of those who helped make our valley safe from those blue intruders. And I extend my gratitude to you, Sir."

"All part of my . . . our duty, Ma'am."

"Luray . . . mother of a friend of mine just moved to Luray to live with relatives. Martha Ash is her name. Don't rightly know her relatives' names."

"Well, you must tell your friend to call on me when he's there to pay his mother a visit."

"I . . . I can't, Ma'am," Jeremiah looked down. "He died in the fightin' at Kernstown."

"Oh . . . my," she said, a catch in her voice.

Looking up again, he caught fleeting tears fill her eyes. She reached out and touched his arm.

"I am sorry . . ." she said, "so very sorry."

"Afraid lots of good men have died in this war, Ma'am, and others will before it's over. But let not us talk of such things tonight. You have a large family?"

"No, just me and two older, long married sisters. Got several nieces and nephews, but I don't get to see them often. One sister lives in Lexington, the other down in North Carolina near Raleigh. What about you?" she smiled.

Jeremiah felt his heart melt. "I've got sisters too," he laughed. "Three of 'em. They're all younger. Priscilla, she's barely a year apart from me, she's the one gonna marry Captain Kertlin. Violet . . . she, well, ah, reckon she'd have been marryin' my friend Cy . . . he's the one done died at Kernstown . . . and Bonniejean, why she's still just a baby at eight. Parents own a farm which we all help work . . . helped run. Sometimes I miss the farm work. Don't suppose when the time comes I'll be none too sorry to quit soldierin' and go back to farmin'.

"My Ma and Pa own a mill in Luray. A grist mill. It's busy work."

"The Miller's Daughter," Jeremiah quipped, laughing. "Could I perhaps get you a cup of punch? Are you thirsty?" He forgot all about his search for Jeptha.

"Why, yes . . . Jeremiah, I do believe I am, thank you."

Jeremiah fairly flew on his feet to help to quench the thirst of the lovely Kathleen Melinda. He returned shortly, holding a cup filled to the brim with rose colored liquid.

"Here you are, Miss Katie Melinda," he smiled, handing the cup over to her. Suddenly, a slap on his back sloshed the punch from the glass, splashing it over her hand and down the front of her lovely, mint-green muslin gown. A puddle collected at Jeremiah's feet and mortified, he turned, stepping right into the pool. Suddenly the hem of her dress was spattered with the same pink spots decorating the front.

Jeremiah faced a sheepishly grinning Jeptha. "Geewhillikins, Jeremiah! I'm sorry . . . I really am!" he apologized.

Angered by his friend's carelessness, he thought for a split second about stomping down on Jeptha's foot and belting him in the mouth. Deciding that would only make him appear more foolish, he restrained himself.

"Oh dear," the young lady cried, dabbing at the stains on her clothing with a handkerchief.

"I am truly sorry, Miss Katie Lin . . . Katie Melinda. P . . . Please forgive me. I . . . I am so sorry," he stammered.

"Likewise, Ma'am," Jeptha said, "I had no idea . . . "

"No harm done, men. Please. I've ruined nicer clothes in worse ways. Please. It was an accident." She looked at Jeremiah.

"Excuse me, but I don't believe I've had the pleasure of meeting your friend, Jeremiah."

"Excuse me, Miss Christie . . . but I don't see how you can call it a pleasure."

"Please, Jeremiah. It was just an accident."

"This here is . . . was, a good friend of mine. Private Jeptha Carroll."

"Well, Sir, I'd offer you my hand, but it is a mite sticky at the moment, so, please forgive me."

"The pleasure is all mine, Miss. And I do so beg your pardon.

"Ah, I believe we do need to be goin' . . . callin' it a night, Ma'am, if you'll excuse Sergeant McCamey. Again, I'm mighty sorry, Ma'am. Indeed I am."

"Your apologies are more than adequate, gentlemen. I'm sure a good laundering will take care of these stains."

Jeremiah, for all the pleasure he had in meeting the young lady, was ready to depart after this fiasco. "Miss Katie Melinda," he bowed, "this was a true pleasure."

"It was mine, Mr. McCamey; Jeremiah. And please, do not be concerned."

Jep pulled him by the arm in his haste to depart. "C'mon, Jeremiah," he pleaded in a whisper, "I need some fresh air in a bad way."

As they got to the door of the exhibition hall and went outside, Jeremiah suddenly stopped. "Wait a second, Jep. I forgot something." He dashed back inside before his friend could protest.

Making his way back to the scene of the crime, he saw Kathleen Melinda standing with a shawl pulled about her shoulders in an attempt to hide the hideous stains he'd helped create.

"A thousand pardons, Ma'am," he said as he approached her again.

"Jeremiah!" she cried, startled, "I thought you were gone."

"Yes, Ma'am, I have . . . er, I am. I just . . . just . . ." he let it all out in one breath, "I just wondered if you'd allow me to call on you sometime in the very near future. We're not likely to be in the city long, but I'd be much obliged if you'd allow me to . . ."

"Why, yes, Jeremiah. I'd like that," she interrupted him. "I'd like that very much."

"You would? I mean, you would . . . oh, that's mighty fine, Ma'am. Mighty fine. Thank you. I'll be . . . I'll be seein' you soon, then." Stepping backwards, he bumped into another soldier bearing a full glass of punch. *I gotta get outa here,* he thought. "Soon, Katie Lin," he called out, "good night." He was halfway out the door before realizing he called her by the wrong name again.

Jep was waiting on him. "Now I know why I didn't wanna come here tonight, Jep. I ain't good at socializin'!" He glared at his friend. "You ain't neither." They strode down the steps of the hall and turned into the dark, gas lit streets.

"What happened with them gals you was flirtin' after? I looked for you and couldn't find you none."

"Aw, one on 'em was married to an officer, and I ain't lookin' to get sentenced to no extra guard duty. The other two, well their Ma came fetchin' 'em.

"Who was that pretty gal I made such a fool outa you in front of? I do mean to say I'm sorry."

"She's from Luray of all places. A guest of Cap'n's Aunt that we met. She is purty, ain't she? Name's Miss Christie. Kathleen Melinda Christie or Miss Katie Melinda."

Jep wiped his forehead on the back of a sleeve. As they passed under a gas street lamp, Jeremiah could see that he was white as a ghost.

"You all right, Jep? You look mighty peeked."

"Feel mighty peeked . . . started feelin' this way back yonder . . . that's how come I was wantin' to leave. Thought maybe I just needed some fresh air; got mighty warm and stuffy in there. But the air don't seem to be helpin' . . ."

Suddenly his conversation was interrupted as he grabbed hold of a street lamp. Heaving violently, he threw up every last morsel he'd eaten. Spewing out the contents of his stomach, he sank to his knees, arms around the post for support until his retching finally subsided.

Jeremiah stepped back to avoid being spattered. "Great day in the mornin', Jep! You all right?" Looks like half your insides is now out. Whew!" He had to turn his head from the sight and smell to keep from getting sick himself.

Jeptha shook his head. "I'm all right now," he said, short of breath. "I'm all right now. I feel lots better."

"Either you ate somethin' you sure shouldn't have or ate plum too much. Reckon you can make the walk back to camp?"

"Sure thing, " he replied weakly, standing up, "I'm all right now."

He looked down at himself. "Well, so much for promisin' Tom I'd keep his tunic clean." It was spattered with the vile contents his stomach just rid itself of. He picked up a dangling end of Cy's gold-fringed sash. It was soaked where he threw up all over it. "Sorry, Jeremiah . . ."

"Ah, it'll wash out . . . but I ain't doin' the washin'!"

CHAPTER THIRTEEN

Then here's to brave Virginia!
The "Old Dominion" state
With the young Confederacy
At last has linked her fate!

Finding himself very attracted to Katie Melinda, Jeremiah intended to call on her soon. Drifting off to sleep, he felt grateful to Captain Kertlin for talking him into attending the night's event.

He woke long before dawn with his insides feeling twisted. He had never experienced such intense pain. Stomach cramps came in rapid intervals, shaking him with chills and soaking him with sweat.

At least a third of the entire camp was suffering from the "old soldiers' disease," chronic diarrhea, and most had attended the gala the night before. Whether rich food or tainted food was the cause, the result was the same. For three days Jeremiah lay sick, unable to consume anything but water.

Jeptha, as usual, seemed unaffected. He chalked it up to the fact that he "tossed" everything he ate that night. Jeremiah thought there was probably some merit in the idea.

The first couple of days that he was ill, Sam and Andy were totally unsympathetic. They even laughed about it, for Jep and Jeremiah upon returning from the social had both chastised the two boys, telling them of the delicious food they had missed. Sam and Andy were glad to rub in to their friend the result of having attended such an affair.

Before Jeremiah was completely well, the orders to march were received. General Jackson did not reveal their destination; the boys simply knew they were heading northwest.

Most of the men had recovered from their bout with the "old soldiers' disease," but Jeremiah's strength did not readily return. As the troops put miles behind them, Jeremiah was unable to keep up. He straggled badly.

Out of concern for the sergeant, Jep, Sam and Andy lingered behind. Jeremiah felt chagrin at all of them being so far to the rear, but neither did he wish to be left to the back on his own. He felt frustrated at his inabilities and chided his judgment for not demanding that Sam stay with the rest of the boys. Although thankful for the company of his friends, it worried him that no one of rank was ahead to look after his group of soldiers. He could only hope the captain would have Lieutenant Moore stay close to the men.

Sunset of the first night out, his weakness would let him continue no farther. The four messmates consumed their rations and Sam and Jep went to scout the area. Rain was threatening and they hoped some type of shelter could be found.

Jeremiah and Andy began to feel concerned about the length of time the two scouts were gone. Finally, they emerged from the darkness.

"So dark out here can't see my hands in front of my face," Sam huffed. "Looks like we've found an abandoned building of some kind about a half a mile or so from here. These trees is kinda sparse, boys, and I do believe it's gonna rain. 'Bout a quarter a mile out, there's no trees at all, and Jep and I seen some kinda dwelling silhouetted against the sky. No lights, so must be deserted. May be an abandoned barn. You game, Sergeant? Up to walk that little distance?

"Yeah . . . it ain't no big deal." They set out in the direction Sam and Jep indicated. "I'm just weak. I ain't dyin'," Jeremiah continued. "And I sure don't like bein' separated from the rest of the unit like this. Sam, I shoulda had you stay up ahead; them boys ain't got no one in charge now."

"Aw, they're good men. They'll be all right. Sure come a long ways in little over a year. We ain't the same men no more. It's real hard to believe we was such an unruly lot, huh?"

Jeremiah laughed as he thought of the days passed. "Yeah . . . I came near not joinin' up with you'ns, you know that? Cap'n Harris tried to talk me out of it . . . gave me a chance at another company . . . but I couldn't desert Jep and Cy . . . now look where it's got y'all!"

There was a little laughter, then silence as they trudged along. *Sam was right,* Jeremiah reflected, and his thoughts turned to other things. A desperate feeling of homesickness swept over him as thoughts of summer nights on the farm filled his head: the sweet smell of hay, the sound of the crickets. The family would be sitting on the porch about now . . . Mother in her favorite rocker, Father at his crude porch table. 'Cilla, Violet, Bonniejean; many pictures were dim and he wondered if it could ever be the same again. His thoughts gave him little hope that they would. Too much had changed. *This war goes on and on,* he thought . . . *and more men die.* He sighed out loud.

"You all right, Sergeant?" Andy asked.

"Right as rain, Andy. Right as rain. Just thinkin' about some things."

"Yeah, I know what you mean . . . and speaking of rain, here it comes, boys!"

First one drop, then a few spattered to the ground. Suddenly, the sky opened up, dumping a deluge of water on them. They could see the abandoned building up ahead, but could not reach it before becoming soaked.

Jep pushed the rickety door aside and they entered an old and deserted barn. The hay could be smelled; it was old hay—musty, dank and sour. But it was soft and it was dry. Wet as they were, there was no way to dry off, so they threw their bodies down on the straw and in their fatigue, began to drift off to sleep. Jep was the first to fall into a doze as his snoring gave him away.

Jeremiah, Sam and Andy exchanged an occasional word, until at last, their weariness won out. Surrounded by the sound of rain on the roof and sleep filled breathing, Jeremiah felt exceedingly tired, but couldn't shut off his mind.

Little thoughts kept creeping in. He was having strange thoughts from childhood and other thoughts of home. Katie Melinda . . . he never got to call on her. He had truly wanted to. *Suppose it's for the best,* he decided, but he heard her voice and saw her smile in his mind. *Well, after the war; maybe then, Jerry-miah, maybe then.* The next thing he knew, the sun was broiling down through a hole in the roof, causing him to rouse from his hard-to-come-by slumber.

He rose, the others still in deep sleep. His gut twisted. He was extremely hungry, but thoughts of their rations, corn bread and cold, soggy fatback, turned his stomach.

Walking across to the barn door, he swung it open. It was very hot for early morning. Judging by the sun, it had to be near 8 A.M. *Late,* Jeremiah thought. *We'll never catch up this way.* He noticed a house in the distance. It wasn't a small dwelling, but certainly not grand. It reminded him of home.

"Up and at 'em, boys!" he shouted. "It's already late. Need to be movin'."

The other men shuffled about with moans, groans and yawns. "That was some pretty good sleepin', fellas," Jep stretched and joined his sergeant at the door. "Look Jeremiah, there's a house over yonder," he said, rubbing the sleep from his eyes. "D'ya suppose they might be good enough to feed some hungry soldiers a decent breakfast?"

"You read my mind, Jep. C'mon, boys . . . get your gear and let's go see."

A small fence surrounded the home. "Jep, you and Andy wait here; Sam and I will go to the door. Don't wanna scare anybody with us four suddenly fallin' on 'em."

Jeremiah knocked. No answer. He knocked a second time and presently the door was cracked open by a woman with graying hair. She wasn't old . . . but looked weary.

"We don't aim on surprisin' you none, Ma'am," Jeremiah said, "but we're soldiers here . . . all four of us, and we was wonderin' if perhaps you might have a little breakfast you could share with us. We've done been separated from our unit and could sure use a good meal. We'll be happy to pay you for your trouble."

The woman said nothing for a minute. Finally she spoke up, "I'll see what I can do."

"Thank you, Ma'am," Sam tipped his cap, "we're sure obliged."

"Just wait at the fence out yonder," she replied, almost shutting the door in his face as she disappeared.

They waited. And waited. And waited.

"Aw, she ain't comin' back to feed us none," Jep growled along with his stomach, "we're just wastin' our time."

"Yeah, boys," Sam declared, "I believe we've been had. Reckon we best be movin' on, right Sergeant? Even our rations of corn bread and bacon's startin' to sound good."

Suddenly the door swung open and the woman looked at them. "Y'all may come in now," she said flatly, "but I reckon you'd best leave them guns outside the door on the porch."

The four laid down their arms and followed her into the dining room. The table was set with wonderful food: a mountain of fresh biscuits and churned butter; boiled grits, good and hot; slabs of ham and homemade syrup. The coffee was the best the boys had had in many a day.

Each one heaped his plate full, never enjoying plain food so much. One serving wouldn't do, and Jep finished a second round, sopping his biscuit in the syrup when his fork suddenly clanged to his plate. Jeremiah looked up, all at once having plenty to eat. His blood ran icy cold as he stared at the apparition in the doorway. Each of the boys' eyes saw the same.

A somewhat older soldier, in full Yankee uniform, faced them, pistol in hand. Jeremiah's thoughts went back to their own weapons at the door . . . outside.

The blue soldier took several steps forward, making sure his gun could be seen, and all four friends exchanged wide-eyed glances, each unsure of what to do.

Suddenly, the stranger spoke. "Go on with your breakfast, men. Go on, eat hearty." But the four were no longer hungry as the Union man sat in a chair against the wall, watching them.

After a very long silence, Sam spoke first, "What is a Union man doin' here?"

"This is my house. I happened to be home for a little rest. Had a real hard time convincin' my sister here to let you in. She was afeared for me, seein' as I'm outnumbered four to one."

Andy looked nervously at the man's pistol before speaking. "This is your home? Then how come you're wearin' blue? What's a Virginian doin' wearin' blue?"

"Well, I know a few of us . . . we're all fightin' to preserve the Union."

Jeremiah watched Jep seethe at the thought and suddenly his friend burst out, "You mean you'd rather fight against your own home and your own people as part of an aggressor that has invaded these very lands?"

The man toyed with his gun as if in thought. "I reckon if that's what it takes to preserve the Union, then I suppose I'm willin' enough."

"Well, now, that's just real hard for me to understand," Sam grunted. "I can't say as I see how anybody would be willin' to join up with an invader against his own land."

Jeremiah couldn't resist telling the man the feelings they all shared. "I can't say as I condemn you for wantin' to preserve the Union; my own cousin chose to go with the blue, but I gotta tell you, none of us here wanted this war . . . what we really wanted was a peaceable solution to the problems, but you Yankees just couldn't leave us be. Just like ol' King George a hundred years ago, you couldn't leave us alone.

"For years, the South tried to work out our troubles with the North, and in peace. As a Virginian, you surely know that! But the government in Washington just kept right on legislatin' one unfair deal after the other— illegal taxes, illegal land gain, breaking promises. We just had enough! It's that simple. The main government of a people should be the home of the same people. Not some folks hundreds of miles away decidin' what is and ain't good for 'em.

"The United States Constitution don't say nothin' against a state secedin'. If anything, it gives states the right; in fact, back during the War of 1812, some of them New England states wanted to leave the Union; some wanted to when the Louisiana Territory was purchased. No one argued that they couldn't; they just somehow worked the problems out. No one hollered that them states couldn't secede, though. But then, when the South did, we was told we couldn't. So next, Abe Lincoln calls for soldiers to invade what he claims is his own citizens! Now, that just don't make sense to me! To none of us! In fact, that there act is downright illegal if we ain't a separate country. The U.S. Constitution says so! That's how come we all be fightin'!"

Jeremiah felt himself getting angry and his voice rose. "We couldn't turn our backs on our own people. Neither could we fight to preserve a union that cares not one whit for us and the rights we hold dear; that main right being self-government; the very foundation on which American liberty was built, and . . . and . . ." Suddenly he was at a loss for words.

Continuing to hold his pistol, the man appeared to be thinking over the words. Suddenly he spoke out, "You's just boys! What do you know or care about politics and such? Why don't you go home? You ain't gonna win this war and you're wastin' your good, young days."

Sam slammed his fist down on the table, staring straight at the Union soldier. "Tell ya somethin' now," he said, "we'd all rather fight and die before we'd let you talk us into desertin' our country!"

The other three shook their heads in agreement.

"He's right!"

"Absolutely!"

"Yes!" echoed around the table.

"Tell me somethin'," Jeremiah voiced, "you ever own any slaves?"

The man was startled at the question. "Well, yes," he confessed, "how did you know?"

"I didn't," Jeremiah replied, "in fact, I'm kinda surprised at your answer. We ain't seen none about. Where are they now?"

"My sister didn't think she'd be able to handle things by herself when I joined the army, so we sold 'em off. Didn't have many."

"Well, you see us?" Jeremiah questioned. "Not one of us have ever had a slave. Fact is, probably not five men in every one hundred of our army has ever had one, and your Yankee government suddenly seems to be tryin' to shove the idea down everybody's throat that listens that we're fightin' to keep slaves. Good night! If you're any kind of Virginian, you know the truth. If this war's bein' fought over that idea, then why ain't Abe Lincoln set 'em free? Suppose you Yanks was to win this war today? What would be different?

"Now our constitution," Jeremiah continued, "the Confederate States' constitution prohibits the importation of slaves! Can the Constitution of your government claim that? I don't believe it can. All we're fightin' for is the rights of our own states to decide what's best for governin' it's own people . . . and that's what I . . . what we're all puttin' our lives on the line for everyday; that and defendin' our homes from your invaders. We didn't want this war. It was forced on us by the aggressive actions of the government you serve."

The soldier in blue was silent as he tried to take in Jeremiah's angry words. Finally, he rose. "Gentlemen," he said, "I suppose it'd be best if you left now. You'll find your muskets outside by the gate." He stood, his pistol still in his hand.

"Reckon you're right," Jeptha added. "C'mon boys." He rose from the table. "Sergeant, let's not forget to pay for this fine meal."

"What do we owe you, Ma'am? Sir?" Jeremiah nodded politely to the woman and turned to the Yankee.

"Nothing. Nothing at all. I'm a soldier. I know what it is to be hungry."

As the boys began to file out, Jeremiah looked at the man once more. "What outfit you with?" he asked.

"The 6th Pennsylvania," he answered. "I have some folks live up in Pennsylvania. Joined there. I belong to the 6th Pennsylvania Regiment."

Jeremiah stared briefly and then lowered his head, talking to the floor. "You know Geoffrey Adams?" he inquired quietly. "He's my cousin that I told you about."

"Sure thing I do. We're part of the same company, Company H."

Jeremiah looked up hopefully. "He all right?"

"Last time I saw him, a couple of weeks back, he was," the Yankee answered curtly.

"Would you tell him Jeremiah asked about him the next time you see him, Yank? I'd be obliged."

The man said nothing, so the sergeant turned to join the others already outside.

It was two days before they caught up with their command at the small town of Gordonsville. Captain Kertlin, on the verge of sending a scouting party out after them, chided Jeremiah. "If you think you can keep up with us, McCamey, our job is to guard the southern end of the Alexandria and Orange railroad."

CHAPTER FOURTEEN

Avenge the patriotic gore
That flecked the streets of Baltimore
And be the battle queen of Yore
Maryland! My Maryland!

In August, a new Yankee general was sent Jackson's way; a man named John Pope. On August 9, a grand battle broke out between the two armies, just north of Gordonsville at Cedar Mountain. Pope swung around Jackson's left flank and began to crush his army. The situation looked desperate, but for once, the men in gray outnumbered the Union troops. Eventually, Jackson's men were able to rout Pope, resulting in a splendid Confederate victory.

The army in gray approached Thoroughfare Gap and the northern branch of the Alexandria and Orange Railroad. Here they tore up track and destroyed cars carrying supplies to Pope's Union forces.

The end of the month found them again at Manassas, a little more than a year since many of the men had experienced their baptism by fire at the place. The second fight that ensued was as bitter and as fierce as the first, the sound of cannon over the same field taking the men back in time.

For two days the fighting was hard, and on September 1, in driving rain, Jackson drove his men to the hamlet of Chantilly where the Confederates attacked Pope's rear guard. The fight resulted in a standstill with heavy losses on both sides.

Two weeks later found one corps of Jackson's men again at Harper's Ferry attempting to secure the Federal arsenal. Others marched eastward toward the Maryland border and the single bloodiest day of the war.

As they formed rank and moved out, Jackson was seen watching his men in concern, head bowed in prayer for their well being. Company G halted briefly in front of him and Jeptha was struck with admiration. He looked up at his commanding General and saluted the man. "General, where are we headed?" he asked in awe.

General Jackson leaned down from atop his horse. "Soldier, can you keep a secret?" he whispered to Jeptha.

"Yes, Sir!" Jeptha answered in delight.

The general stared at him briefly. "So can I," he said, riding off, "but God go with you, Soldier."

Jeremiah rolled his eyes at his friend. "Jep, you know the General keeps everything a secret . . . right smart idea, too. Never know when important information may find its way about and into the wrong hands. That was a half-witted question to ask."

Jep smiled, nodding his head in agreement. "Yeah . . . but I had to say somethin', just so I can say I talked to the General!"

Jeremiah simply shook his head at his friend.

It rained heavily on the nights of September 15 and 16, the men arriving outside of Sharpsburg, Maryland at Antietam Creek, long after sundown. Captain Kertlin was ordered to take several of his troops into the cornfield by Dunker Church. They were to help ready positions for the next day's fight, expected to begin about sunrise.

Through the night they worked cutting stalks and placing fortifications. Shortly after midnight, as they rustled among the corn, a voice boomed out at them through the dark.

"Who's there?"

"Shhh . . . Federal pickets," Captain Kertlin whispered as the men exchanged glances.

It came again, "Who's there? What goes?"

To the fearful astonishment of his comrades, Jeptha yelled back through the darkness, "Why Yank, it's just us Rebs here gatherin' corn for some hungry soldierin' stomachs . . . you go on back to sleep, now. We'd warn you if we was comin', make no mistake about that!"

Captain Kertlin put a shaking head in his hand.

"Carroll, that was a confoundingly fool thing you just did!" he shouted in an angry whisper. "You better be thankful I didn't give a direct order for quiet or I'd have you up on charges of insubordination so fast your head would spin!"

Jeremiah had never seen the captain so mad and he tried to help remedy his friend's blunder.

"Cap'n, listen. Men, you hear that?"

"What?" Sam asked.

"The quiet!" Jeremiah countered. "That's what they think we're doin' . . . gatherin' corn!"

Unexpectedly, the voice called out again, "Hey Johnny, you still there?"

Jep looked around at Captain Kertlin as if to ask for permission to speak.

"Well, go on! Answer him!" the Captain said. "You got us into this!"

Jep grabbed a green ear of corn and bit into it, filling his mouth with the raw kernels. "Sure thing, Yank! I'm busy eatin'! Either come join me or go back to sleep!"

"Be shootin' at you tomorrow, Reb. Too dark tonight."

"Well, at least you'll not be shootin' at a hungry Reb! Good night, Yank!"

"Good night, Johnny!" the man shouted back.

When silence reigned for several moments, the boys breathed in a sigh of relief. His mouth still full of raw corn, Jep began laughing so hard that he started to choke. Jeremiah slapped him on the back.

"You all right, Jep?"

"Sure . . . sure. I didn't even have to lie, fellas! True to my honor!"

"It was still foolish, Carroll!" snapped the captain, unmoved.

Soon their work was completed, and they lay down among the green stalks to wait for the rest of their men and the coming sun.

On the morning of the 17th, the pre-dawn fog was as thick as a brick wall. The men spending the night in the cornfield could see no better than they had during the hours of darkness. Sleep on the wet ground had been sporadic; the men were edgy and raring to fight. Soon, an order spread throughout the corn field—"Charge!"

Men in gray rose silently to blend with the gray shrouding fog. Obscurely, they moved forward, and as the edge of the cornfield was reached, a piercing cry soared up from the morning haze. "You best wake up, now, Yank! We're comin' your way!" Jeptha cried, and the guns began.

The sun was not yet completely up when the concentrated assault started. Some of Jackson's men were in the cornfield and others on the hill of Dunker Church. Across the open and into the woods musket and artillery fire ripped into the ranks of both sides, shredding them. Men were dying at the rate of two thousand per hour.

A full Federal corps had three-dozen cannon aimed toward the high ground of Dunker Church, but Jackson's men proved a formidable foe. Losses exceeded one half of their number, but the Rebels refused to budge and held the hill against an exploding world.

Victory seesawed back and forth between the two armies. Several times within just a few hours, both sides could have claimed a win.

McClellan sent in a third Federal Corps, only to be smashed by Confederate reinforcements, and the brutal fighting began to die down until it seemed little more than a skirmish. It was only 9 A.M. and a full-scale battle had been waged.

By afternoon, General A. P. Hill's corps of Jackson's army, having secured Harper's Ferry, made a forced march to Antietam Creek. Here they tore into a Federal flank at the last minute, causing the furious fight to pick up again.

Jeremiah watched from his position. Their color bearer went down, yet the flag was caught by another hand. Suddenly, to the ground it floated once more, and Jeremiah saw a man discard his musket onto the field in order to raise the standard anew. Soon this soldier, too, disappeared, and down the colors wafted another time. Immediately they fluttered into full view yet again. He wasn't sure how long the scene took . . . minutes? Seconds? *What bravery,* he thought as the colors continued to march on, *what valor.*

All at once, fire begin grinding into Company G and as he reloaded his weapon, Jeremiah glanced anxiously about, looking at his men, seeing only determination in their faces. Suddenly his heart fluttered and the blood in his veins turned to ice as Captain Kertlin, sword raised in rally, fell to the ground before his eyes.

Jeremiah knew there was nothing he could do. Immediately, men surrounded the captain and it would be an impossible task to try to make his way over to his fallen leader. His duty at the moment was to thunder ahead and help hold the ground. There was nothing he could do for his beloved captain except weep and there was no time for that now as he desperately tried to defend their position.

Back and forth the savage fire continued. Several times Jeremiah caught sight of General Jackson on the hill by Dunker Church. Atop his little sorrel horse, spyglasses in hand, he was a perfect target for the enemy's bullets, yet he never wavered, never flinched and never received an injury. It seemed an absolute miracle and he earned his nickname anew.

A situation that appeared desperate became hopeless as the sun slowly fell from the sky. McClellan, though he had lost some thirteen thousand of his men, still had superior numbers, and the Southerners knew their ability to force the battle was at an end.

Lee began to withdraw his men. They had held for hours to gain nothing more than a lane; a lane now muddied by blood. Ten thousand lives seemed an enormous price to pay for keeping a supply line intact.

By the time the fighting ended and the troops began to withdraw, Jeremiah was numb. Numb from fatigue, numb from the horrors, numb from the ever-assaulting sound of explosion, numb from the vision of Captain Kertlin falling before his eyes.

His little group of men had fared well. All were intact and no one was wounded, except Andy was experiencing a difficult time with his ears. The nonstop concussion of the guns caused them to bleed, a phenomenon not unusual, but commonly restricted to noses. Andy's ears bled profusely and the problem did not come under control though the guns were now silent.

Jeremiah gave orders as they completed their brief retreat and planned to set up camp for the night. "Sam, I'm leavin' you in charge and takin' Jep. We're gonna try to find out what to do for Anderson's ears before he bleeds to death. And Sam . . . see if you can learn some word 'bout Cap'n . . . where . . ." Jeremiah sighed; he was forced to think on something he'd rather push away . . . "see if you can find some word on what's been done to . . . with . . . to Cap'n."

"Don't worry none, Sergeant," Sam reassured him quietly, "things will be fine here and I'll see what I can learn."

"Jep," Jeremiah hailed his friend, "you walk on the other side o' Anderson, case he starts to pass out, and let's get him some help."

Andy, starting to feel light-headed, rose from his position of sitting by a tree. Blood streaked down his neck on both sides, and continued to flow, not heavily, but steadily.

"Andy, can you hear me?" Jep shouted.

The boy shook his head. "I ain't deaf, Jep. But things sound a mite muffled and I've got a fierce ringin' in my ears. But they don't pain me none."

The boys found their way to the makeshift hospital and the sight appalled them. Screams from inside the stone dwelling were heard as men were forced to have arms, legs and other extremities removed. Injured men waiting for attention littered the ground.

"Sergeant," Andy voiced, "I don't need care near as bad as these boys! I don't need to be takin' time away from those that really need help. Look at this!" he gestured, mesmerized by the suffering he saw. "I don't need help near as much as these fellas do. Let's go. I'll cope all right."

"No, Andy, . . . we're here. Let's see if you are bad hurt. Might be worse'n we know."

Jeremiah approached a man sitting at a table outside of the hospital. He appeared to be keeping some kind of records. While Jep and Andy watched in silence from several feet away, the sergeant talked to the soldier for a few moments before motioning the two to join him.

"This here corporal says no doc is available to help out, Anderson, but the next orderly comes by he'll have him take a look and maybe he'll see what needs to be done."

Quickly such a man appeared, and receiving directions from the corporal, bade the boys to follow him.

"This here can be a bad situation," he said after treating Andy. "He's to keep these ears plugged up for a while, even after he removes these bandages. They need to remain in place for a few days. He's to stay out of any fightin' for a couple of weeks, 'less he chooses to be deaf."

"Thanks," Jeremiah spoke as Andy fought dizziness.

The orderly looked down, his gray uniform and white apron stained with dirt and blood.

"Best leave him here for a little while. The dizziness will pass momentarily and I'll send him on his way."

"Appreciate the help for my man," Jeremiah stated. "C'mon, Jep. I wanna talk to that corporal back at the table again before we leave. I asked him if Cap'n had been brought in."

Jeptha looked at him anxiously. "Well, what did he say?"

Jeremiah looked down. "He ain't come in with wounded, " he said flatly, "least that boy says he ain't got no record if he did."

"Well, maybe we can find some of the boys that was with him . . . Jeremiah. Maybe they can tell us . . . can tell us if . . ." he shifted his feet, "if he was wounded or . . ." he couldn't finish his sentence.

"Say it, Jep," Jeremiah commanded, "say it! Dead . . . if he's dead. Face it. Not doin' so won't change nothin'. Sometimes I think we're all gonna die in this war, and we'd better be ready as we'd better be willing, or we don't believe in what we're fighting for; and all of those that have gone before us, we've dishonored. Let's grieve for those we've loved and lost, and take their sacrifice with us every time we meet the foe. The heartache, the heartbreak, the tears, the strife . . . it's all part of the supreme cost we must be willing to pay to preserve those truths we hold dear . . . the very same things our forefathers fought for."

"McCamey!" The call came loud and clear from a short distance away. "McCamey! Carroll!"

Jeremiah whirled about, recognizing the voice and searching for its source. He could not recall ever feeling so thankful to see anyone and waited for the man to catch up with them. Overcome by the moment and emotion, he found himself embracing the captain he'd grown to love. "John," he addressed the officer by his first name, "John . . . I thank the Lord to see you here!" Jeremiah's eyes shown bright with unspilled tears, and suddenly remembering himself, stepped back from the clasp the captain returned. "Cap'n, I ain't never been so glad to see a body! We was sure you'd been hurt . . ."

"Or killed," Jeptha added. They both noticed the hole ripped in the captain's tunic, just above his heart. It was ragged and black, but not bloody.

"I got knocked down good, boys," he said, "but I have two to thank." From his pocket, where the bullet tried to make its mark, came a couple of objects. Captain Kertlin held them up. "Priscilla and the Lord."

In his hands was a daguerreotype of Jeremiah's sister, a hole where her face had been, and beneath the picture, with a ball imbedded in its pages, was a ragged and torn testament. "The impact bruised me up a bit. Hurt like I was dyin' for a while, but I ain't any worse for wear. Thought I was killed at first. Have to say I'm a bit thankful to be here.

"What are y'all doin' at the hospital? Who's hurt?"

"Aw, Andy's havin' some trouble with bleedin' ears from the guns," Jep recounted.

"He'll be all right," Jeremiah spoke. "We're all all right, Cap'n. We done good. None o' my boys is hurt. We're ready for another day."

"I gotta tell you, lads. This fight here at Sharpsburg . . . it's got to be the worse day of this war," the Captain said sadly. "C'mon; walk with me back to camp."

The battle proved to be a draw, but the victory prize went to the Union, the fight at Sharpsburg a strategic defeat for the army in gray. Jackson, always proud of his men in combat, said, ". . . with heroic spirit, our line maintained their position in the face of superior numbers with superior resolution."

McClellan chose not to pursue Lee's crippled army, throwing away his chance for a clear victory. The Confederates withdrew only to regroup and prepare to fight another day. But "Little Mac" assumed they were in full retreat and took a walk over the field upon which the two armies had waged battle. Overcome by the carnage he viewed, his warrior instincts died. President Lincoln was soon to dismiss the man.

~

After Sharpsburg, the war went into a strange lull. Jackson moved his army westward, back toward the Shenandoah Valley, encamping along the Opequon River. It was a time of renewal, a time of refreshment, a time of rest. It was also a time for Captain John Kertlin to be married to Priscilla McCamey.

As September melted into October, and the front remained quiet, letters were exchanged, leaves procured, and a trip to the New Church community made.

Captain Kertlin, Jeremiah and Jeptha were granted time for one week. The train was taken to Staunton, then the journey to New Church made by rented wagon.

It was a poignant homecoming. Jeremiah was not the same son or brother who had left home almost two years ago. He had changed a great deal even in the year almost gone since Christmas.

Jeptha, as always, was welcomed with open arms in the McCamey household, embraced and treated as one of their own. Bonniejean, just turned nine, was infatuated with her brother's friend, and Violet peppered both boys with questions about Cy as she tried coming to terms with what the war had cost her.

Jeremiah told his sister about the final morning he and Cy shared. He told her of his friend's courage and honor in service to his country. Both boys told her of Cy's constant humor under hardship and his total devotion to the cause for which he died. The three laughed and cried together, and as Jeremiah placed Cy's gold-fringed sash back into Violet's hands, she broke into fresh tears.

It was a bittersweet time.

The marriage of Captain John Kertlin to Priscilla McCamey was a simple affair. Held in the farmhouse parlor, Jeremiah stood with his captain as Violet stood with her sister.

The wedding was lovely, though spartan, the house filled with family and friends as Preacher Foxly pronounced them man and wife. All agreed the captain a handsome man, standing in a fresh gray uniform adorned with his sword, white gauntlets, and officer's sash.

'Cilla's shimmering brown waves framed a radiant face. Dressed in a plain gown of ivory colored muslin, she and Violet had trimmed it with lace and tied it around the waist with a satin ribbon. Crowning her head was a wreath of autumn flowers. Intertwined with ribbon, it dropped a filmy layer of net to her elbows.

It was over quickly. *Well, it's done,* Jeremiah thought. *Cap'n is my brother-in-law and Prissy is his wife.* His heart felt full as he thought of the love, encouragement, laughter and tears that had been his under this roof. He knew it was going to be very hard to leave again.

Shortly after the ceremony, the Captain and his new wife set out in the rented wagon for a brief visit to Staunton and his family. Jeremiah and Jeptha were to join him there in a few days, allowing the three to return to their command together.

The remainder of the boys' leave was marked by beautiful October days. Cool afternoons and crisp nights hearkened Jeremiah's heart to the life he'd left behind. He and Jeptha both helped to catch up on lagging farm work, enjoying the respite from endless march and battle. Neither boy knew when they enjoyed such work more, but the time was over quickly.

The morning arrived when the two soldiers climbed into the farm carriage for the ride to Staunton. Jeremiah's father accompanied them to bring Priscilla back to the farm, where John Kertlin felt his new wife would fare better for the duration of the war.

Good-byes were said and tears were shed, only for the scene to be repeated in Staunton. By sundown, the men were in camp once again. Leaving the events of the past week behind, they made ready to settle into the familiar routine.

John Kertlin found it difficult. Leaving a new wife behind did not breed incentive to fall back into rank and file with other men.

Several weeks later, the lull in the war was over. The Union Army had been reorganized. George McClellan was gone and General Ambrose Burnside was in. Men in blue began massing along Virginia's Rappahannock River, directly opposite the town of Fredericksburg. The army in gray was fragmented and spread out. They needed to be united in order to meet this new threat head-on. Robert E. Lee sent for Jackson's men.

CHAPTER FIFTEEN

The Battle Flag of Dixie
Oh! Long triumphant wave!
Where'er the storms of battle roar
Or victory crowns the brave!

The weather had turned cold and wintry by the middle of November and the end of the month found the men on the move, heading toward the town of Fredericksburg. Arriving the first week of December, they encamped along the river at a narrow place, a mile or so above the town proper.

The army in gray was reoutfitted after the Battle of Sharpsburg, but Union blockading of Southern ports began to put a squeeze on supplies. New arms were received only by ships capable of running the blockades, and rations of coffee and sugar could not be met. What the boys once considered necessities were now luxuries.

Several nights after they set in on the Rappahannock, Jeremiah and his men drew picket duty along with Lieutenant Moore. They were to patrol the river's edge. As the moon rose in a cloudless sky, silhouetted forms of the enemy guard could be seen across the water.

Suddenly a voice from the opposite shore split the cold night. "Hey, Johnny . . . you got some of that good southern tobacco?"

Lieutenant Moore took up the game. "What you got to trade for it, Yank?"

"Got some coffee here; tea too."

"Any sugar to go with it?" Lieutenant Moore shouted back.

For a moment all was silent, then came the reply, "Yeah, Johnny, we got some good brown sugar just rationed out today."

Lieutenant Moore once again bargained with the man. "All right; trade you some tobacco for some o' that coffee and sugar."

"Now, hold on, Reb. That don't seem like a fair deal to me," the man in blue replied from the other side.

Jeptha took up the parlay. "Reckon not," he said. "Too bad. A little coffee and sugar would be mighty fine to have, but I suppose this here good, Southern cured tobacco will just have to sit. Some o' us never quite took a likin' to the stuff, but plenty o' the men here do, so it'll not go to waste. Sorry we can't strike up a trade."

There was silence again before another voice spoke up from across the water. It sounded strangely familiar to Jeremiah, but he couldn't place it. "Hold on, Johnny . . . we're rounding up some of both. Gonna float it across now on a little raft. Watch for it. Moon's bright enough to see. Put your tobacco on it and send it back over."

"McCamey, Carroll, Drew, go round up as much tobacco as the men will spare. I ain't got much on me . . . don't think you fellows have none. Go fast, now, I see the raft a comin'!" Lieutenant Moore commanded them.

As the boys moved off, a few pouches were rounded up among those present. Momentarily, the three soldiers returned with a fair supply of the brown leaves.

They watched the little skiff transverse the moon lit waters. Soon it was pounding against the shore, the men readily gathering the generous supply of coffee and sugar aboard.

"Thanks, Yank!" Jeremiah yelled across the river. "Make way now; we're pilin' a heap of tobacco on board this little launch and sendin' it back. Careful, though. It ain't a sturdy raft . . . seein' as it's a Yank outfit. Should have let us Rebs use our engineerin' talents. Woulda been a mite stronger," he teased, gliding the skiff back across the water to the sound of laughter on both sides.

Several moments of silence passed. "Ooo-eee! Johnny! Thankee! This here is beautiful tobacco! We'll sure find a bit o' pleasure in it," the oddly familiar voice called out. "Got anything else to trade?"

"Naw," Jeremiah shot back, "tobacco's 'bout all we got plenty of. Your ships blockadin' our ports been a mite too effective, I reckon. Say, any of you boys know the whereabouts of the 6th Pennsylvania these days?"

A loud round of laughter greeted his question. "Sure, Reb. We *are* the 6th Pennsylvania!"

Jeremiah, stunned, was at a loss for words. Finally he shouted his thoughts, "Anyone know Geoffrey Adams of Company H?"

"We are Company H, Johnny. Adams ain't out here at picket. What you got to do with him?"

"He's my cousin," Jeremiah answered, "and I'd sure like a holler with him!"

"Say," the voice from the other side countered, "you ain't a gray boy that stopped for some breakfast at a farmhouse just 'fore that big fight at Antietam Creek, are you?"

"You mean the fight at Sharpsburg?"

"Yeah," the voice answered.

"Would be me, for sure, Yank; me an a couple o' other boys here . . . say," Jeremiah continued, "you don't happen to be that very same Yank that fed us, pointin' a pistol at us all the while, is you?"

"Ha! I don't believe it! That was me all right. You boys had my poor sister scared half outa her mind!"

"Say, sorry about that . . . I knew I'd heard that voice o' yours somewhere before!"

"Well, hold on. I've sent one of the men for that cousin' o' yours."

Several minutes passed, and all that could be heard was the rippling of the water. Suddenly, from across the lapping sound, Jeremiah recognized the familiar voice he was once so close to.

"Jeremiah?" the voice asked excitedly, "is that really you over there?"

"Geoff?" Jeremiah questioned in excitement, "Geoffrey? How you be, Cousin?"

"Fair as can be expected in the middle of this war, I suppose. Jeremiah . . . I wanna see you. We're pullin' a larger skiff down the bank . . . I'm comin' across! Me an' a friend is comin' across."

Doubtful, Jeremiah looked at Lieutenant Moore. "Sir? What say you? Should I tell him no?"

"Na, McCamey. Let him come."

They could see the form gliding across the water. Jeremiah found himself at once eager and uneasy. It had been so long since that day they last saw each other; so long since each one had made his decision to fight for . . . well, that didn't matter right now. He only wanted to see his cousin.

The raft bumped into the shore and before his eyes stood his cousin, Geoffrey Adams. Unable to contain himself, Jeremiah embraced him for a long silent moment, Geoffrey returning the hug. It didn't matter right now that they wore different colors or that they fought on opposite sides. They were family.

"You're lookin' good, Geoff," Jeremiah broke the silence, "that is, what I can see of you in this moonlight."

"Jeremiah . . . what's this?" Geoffrey asked, rubbing the stripes on his cousin's shoulder. "Sergeant? Sergeant? You for real, Jeremiah? You're a sergeant?"

"Yeah, well . . ." Jeremiah started to explain.

"Sergeant McCamey . . . you Rebs is dumber than I thought!" Geoffrey burst out laughing.

"How come I don't see no stripes on those blue arms of yours?" Jeremiah asked him.

"You ain't lookin' good enough, Cuz. Here, see?" He turned his shoulder to the moonlight. "I got some here . . . got my corporal stripe just after Antietam. I believe you fellas refer to that fight as Sharpsburg."

"Your cousin been a sergeant near a year, now, Geoff," Jeptha's voice made himself known.

"Well I'll be . . ." Geoffrey huffed in his breath. "Jeptha Carroll. I didn't realize you two was fightin' together. O' course, I shoulda realized it, I reckon."

"There's lots o' things you don't seem to be too smart about, Geoffrey. Otherwise you wouldn't be wearin' them blue clothes," Jeptha declared with disdain.

"All right, boys. Let's shake hands and be civil here," Jeremiah said good-naturedly, aware there had always been friction between the two. They tolerated each other through the years out of respect for Jeremiah, a fact known to them all.

Jeptha put out his hand and Geoffrey grabbed it without hesitation. "Say, where's good ol' Cy Ash? Don't tell me he ain't with you . . . what he'd do? Get smart and go blue?" Geoffrey laughed at his own absurdity.

Jeremiah didn't smile. "He's dead, Geoff. Got killed at Kernstown. You know that fight. You was there."

Geoffrey's smile instantly dropped from his face and he looked between the two friends. "Gee, fellas. I'm sorry. I really didn't know," he whispered. "Reckon we've all lost . . . we've all lost lots," he said looking down.

Jeremiah stared at his cousin for a moment. Geoffrey hadn't changed much. His brown hair and gray eyes still favored his own, and he was nearly as tall. He was stockier, though, and fairer in complexion.

Suddenly, Jeremiah remembered his cousin wasn't alone. "Who's your friend, Geoff?"

Geoffrey looked over his shoulder. "Oh. This here is Lucias Brock. A good friend o' mine. He came along for the ride . . . or swim, as the case might have been!" he chuckled.

Jeptha and Jeremiah acknowledged the soldier and Jeremiah put out his hand for a shake. The man refused to offer his own.

Jep leaned over to whisper in his friend's ear. "Now, he seems like a friendly sort, don't he?" he snickered sarcastically.

Lieutenant Moore passed the boys as the others continued their patrol. "Men," he said straight to the point, "remember, there is a war goin' on. I hate to hasten up your visit, but let's not prove ourselves ineffective here."

"Yes, Sir," Jeremiah responded. "I appreciate your permission to visit with my cousin, Sir."

"Just don't be much longer, McCamey."

"No, Sir."

Jeremiah looked at Geoffrey again. "So, how's the folks?" he inquired about his Aunt Mary and Uncle Boyton.

"Fine, last I heard from them. Ma, she's been sick some, but Pa says not to worry; he don't believe it to be anything serious. How 'bout you? Your folks? Uncle Colum and Aunt Fralise and all those pretty sisters?"

"Priscilla got married about six weeks back. You heard?"

"Na . . . I reckon there hasn't been opportunity for the folks to exchange news. Well, well . . . who'd she marry, Jeremiah? Somebody from back home? Anyone I might know? Do give her my love and congratulations."

"Yeah . . . I will. She married Captain John Kertlin. My Cap'n . . . captain of my company. He's a real fine man, Geoff. She done good!"

"Glad to hear that. Know she's always been special to me."

Leaning on his musket, Jeremiah looked down, "Yeah, I know. She was pretty disturbed when you went North, Geoff. I understand what you were thinkin' . . . but Geoffrey, if you'd have let yourself think things through and given it some time, like I did, I can't help but feel you'd have chosen different."

"Aw, Jeremiah . . . we done had this conversation before. I don't care to repeat it. I'm not like you. I didn't need to think on anything."

"I know, I know . . . but listen, Geoff; these Yankee politicians of yours have turned this all around. With Ol' Abe Lincoln's speech after Sharpsburg, or Antietam, whatever you fellas call that fight back in September, it's obvious they're tryin' to make slavin' the issue of this war. You know, Geoff, that's not what this is about! You know it!"

"I'll do whatever I have to do to preserve this Union, Jeremiah."

"Yeah . . ." Jep chimed in, "just like that man o' yours in the White House. First he says that to preserve the Union he'd free all the slaves if that'd do it. Then he says that if freein' none o' them would hold the Union together, he'd not free one . . . can't seem to make up his mind, if you ask me.

"Then he goes and makes this . . . this . . . this Emancipation Proclamation; this little speech after he could claim some sort o' victory at Sharps . . . er, Antietam. What a fine deal that was! So he sets the slaves free, supposedly. But, only in the Confederate States, mind you . . . states he ain't even president of . . . and not only that, he doesn't free those that are under your Federal control; those places you Yankees gained capture of early in this war, like in New Orleans, and even parts of our own state of good ol' Virginia! Suddenly this war is about slaves. Well, it's only because France and England is thinkin' 'bout givin' us recognition, and Ol' Lincoln sure don't want none o' that . . . he knows that if he makes slaves the issue, then Europe ain't gonna come to our aid none. Don't bother that his little speech didn't free any slaves in the Union.

"What I'm fightin' for is the rights o' my state; my rights as a citizen of my state and in defense of her soil. I'm fightin' to defend my country! If what we're really warin' over is slavery, then just tell me why did Mr. Lincoln not set free those slaves in Missouri and Kentucky . . . in Maryland and Delaware? It's because he's afraid to make them states mad. If this war is over that issue, then why didn't he just free them all when we were forced to fire on Fort Sumter!" Angry, Jeptha's words bubbled out in a furious boil, "It seems to me his little Proclamation hasn't really freed anybody! It ain't nothin' more than war politics!"

"Reb, I do believe you done said all I want to hear from some ignorant Southern mouth. The whole world knows we're fightin' to set other men free!" Geoffrey's silent friend suddenly made himself heard.

"I'll show you who's dim-witted!" Jep declared, drawing back his fist. Jeremiah grabbed it, holding him at bay.

"Whoa, Jep! Whoa! Don't do nothin' foolish now . . . you'll only serve to give reason to this man Brock here to think he's right. Geoffrey, get this friend o' yours back on that raft, how 'bout it? Guess we'd best part now."

"Lucias, c'mon. Get back aboard here. We'd better leave the company of these gentlemen," Geoffrey spoke.

"Gentlemen!" Lucias spit into the water, looking back at the boys in gray. "Ain't no gentleman here!"

"Brock, I'm orderin' you!" Geoffrey said fiercely. "Let's go!"

Jep strained against Jeremiah's hold. He was too eager to shut the man's mouth. "Let it go, Jep. Let it go," Jeremiah commanded, easing his hold. "Let me say good-bye to Geoffrey."

As Geoffrey began to push the raft off, Jeremiah stuck out his hand. "Geoff," he said, "I hope you're not leaving in anger."

"Na, Jeremiah." Geoffrey looked at his cousin, grinning at him fondly. "I'm real glad I got to see you. I've thought about you lots."

"Yeah, me too, Geoff. Lots of prayin' been done for an end to this thing . . . lots o' folks prayin' for ya'll, too. Your army and government, I mean. Not that we'd whip you . . . just that your hearts and minds be changed to see what's true . . . just not to hate us so much."

Suddenly a shot crackled into the night. "Go, Geoff! Go!" Jeremiah cried urgently, pushing the skiff across the river. Grabbing his musket he scrambled to his post.

The boys on picket duty up and down the riverbank lay on their bellies, watching the enemy, watching each other. Several minutes passed. The sound was not repeated and they soon rose to their feet, but any more amusement the night promised had come to an end. They had been reminded they were at war and patrol was seriously renewed.

Jeremiah couldn't help but think of the encounter he just had with his cousin, and he could only assume Geoffrey recrossed the water safely. It was good to see him, but the exchange left a feeling of depression to mingle with the excitement of it all. How he wished he and Geoffrey could have seen eye to eye about things. They were family! They were blood! How could their views be so opposed? He sighed deeply, knowing there was no explanation. He was anxious to write home and tell his family about the meeting.

At the end of the second week of December, the town of Fredericksburg was evacuated. The citizens fled in light of the impending fight.

On the 11th of the month, Union General Burnside began to lay out pontoon bridges that his army might cross the Rappahannock and enter the town. Confederate guns signaled this movement and the force in gray began to move.

The morning of December 13 dawned enshrouded by fog. The Southern Army was entrenched on the heights surrounding the town and Jackson's men were posted in the low, marshy woodlands fringing the high places. This lowland, not within easy view of the enemy, made it difficult for the army in blue to aim artillery that could strike the place with accuracy.

General Jackson appeared before his men to be sure all was in good order and according to his plans. When his presence was seen, the men cheered out of respect and admiration. He was clad in a brand new resplendent uniform, complete with gold braiding to signify his rank as Lieutenant General.

"Don't he look a fine, grand man?" Jeptha whispered with reverence and awe. "We done got the finest commanding general ever known. I truly believe that," he finished.

"Look at him! Just look at him!" Sam said with admiration. "We be blessed, boys! We be blessed. He ain't only a fine general but a true Christian man."

"You've got that right," replied Captain Kertlin, standing near the messmates. "I was awed by him at the military institute, but I've learned these past two years that he's an even greater man than I knew. Do you lads realize what he's asked of us?"

"A plum lot," Andy volunteered, laughing.

"Yeah," Jeremiah said, "he's expected a plum lot of us and if you ask me, we've done things I would have never thought possible of any army, let alone ours. He asked, expected, and then believed in us to deliver. And most times we did . . . even when it seemed impossible. There ain't no better leader anywhere, and for all my days I'll be proud to tell folks I served under the great Stonewall Jackson!"

"That's a fine new uniform he got on, ain't it?" Jep asked, changing the subject.

"Yeah," Captain Kertlin replied, "I hear tell J. E. B. Stuart had it made up for him. Gave it to him for a Christmas present."

Jeremiah laughed. "From what I hear, that sounds like somethin' J. E. B. Stuart would do, don't it?"

Soon, the general disappeared from view and the atmosphere crackled with tense anticipation.

As the morning sun rose higher, the fog began to lift, and the sight greeting the Confederates in position was one resembling the end of time. In a magnificent mass of imposing dread, the Federals began to move in. The sight was so powerful that General James Longstreet, as he stood next to Jackson, turned and asked, "General, do not all of these Federals frighten you?"

Stonewall's eyes lit up and he replied with a smile, "We shall soon see if I do not frighten them."

As the curtain of mist rose, three hundred cannon began to echo their thunder; hill-to-hill they wrestled with each other until the battlefield haze was worse than the morning fog had been.

Jackson's men were ordered not to fire; to hold altogether still as the blue hoard approached. By doing this, their position would not be given away. They would receive the order to shoot at the appropriate time.

As round after round of musket fire tore into Jackson's location, the marshy woods remained silent. By the time the Yankees were within eight hundred yards, they were satisfied no Rebels were present. Suddenly the order was given and Confederate guns opened up a hot and intense fire on the unsuspecting bluecoats.

The musketry was fast and intense, drenching the enemy with shot, and soon visible gaps could be seen in the line of blue. Before long they wavered, then began to scatter, breaking rank in retreat. For the next two hours, the battle seemed to become a skirmish between sharpshooters.

At midmorning, Federal infantry emerged from the town, storming Mayre's Heights, the highest point of Confederate entrenchment. The army in gray began to inflict horrendous losses on the boys in blue, wiping out whole lines. As the Yankees charged the hill, they were swiftly mowed down. It was a grisly, awesome sight to behold, and eventually the fighting was forced to a close.

As the guns at last fell silent, "Thank God" was all the prayer Jeremiah could utter. Shaken and dazed by the intensity of the fight, he could not help but think of his cousin, wondering if Geoffrey survived the brutal onslaught. He didn't see how anyone could possibly come out of it alive, and the thoughts of what might be attempted to consume him. He had to push them away.

The other boys could say nothing as they surveyed the sea of casualties before them. In profound sorrow, they looked upon the dastardly, gruesome deed their army had been forced to commit. "General Lee is certain right," Jeremiah uttered in sadness. "War is so terrible."

Jeptha furrowed his brow quizzically at the sergeant. "I hear tell," Jeremiah smiled wryly, "that General Lee watched as some of our boys came marchin' in this mornin'. They presented quite a spectacle with them bayonets flashin' while drums beat and fifes played. The general was heard to say, 'It is good that war is so terrible, or we might become too fond of it.'" Jeremiah shook his head. "Ain't no way any man could ever become fond o' havin' to do somethin' like this," he whispered.

The men of Company G were thoroughly spent as they prepared to bivouac for the night. Little conversation was exchanged.

"Gentlemen," Jeremiah heaved a sigh to his boys, "I feel we've been mighty blessed today. Not one of us, not one in our company, was killed or seriously wounded." He shook his head "We'd best be thankful and give those thanks to the Lord."

"Reckon they'll be back again tomorrow," Jeptha stated matter-of-factly.

Sam nodded in agreement, "Yeah . . . it don't appear they're goin' away."

Andy looked at his comrades. "I don't know 'bout you boys, but I'm plum tuckered out. If they be there tomorrow, we'd best be ready. I agree with the sergeant. Jeremiah's right. We've been protected by Providence today, but how long can it last? I'm goin to sleep now, boys. They're comin' again, so we'd best do our part and be ready; I can better do that by bein' rested."

When the sun came up, the Federals appeared on the field in full order, but as the morning passed, it was evident the only fighting was to be between sharpshooters and artillery. During the following night, the army in blue withdrew from the area, ransacking the town of Fredericksburg and leaving another Confederate victory to be counted. The South was elated and the North was beginning to demand explanations from its president.

The Battle of Fredericksburg marked the end of a short winter campaign and Jackson's army settled into winter quarters, their line stretching from New Guiney Station to Port Royal. The General established headquarters at Moss Neck while the men built fortifications and fashioned little huts to take the place of tents for the season.

CHAPTER SIXTEEN

They've borne him to an honored grave,
The laurel crowns his brow.
By hallowed James's silent wave,
He's sweetly sleeping now.

Several days into winter camp, it was suggested that the boys compete in the felling of trees. Because the number of logs needed for building huts and fortifications was numerous, such a contest would help to get the work done quickly.

Company captains made arrangements for the contest and sergeants were responsible for overseeing their teams. The reward for the winning teams would be two days free of camp duty and routine. Company G would be pitched against a company of Georgia boys that were part of Jackson's command.

"I don't know 'bout you'ns," Jep said, "but I'd be mighty obliged to have the time off. Tell us what to do, Sergeant, and we'll just do it, right men?"

A chorus of enthusiastic "Yeahs!" greeted Jeremiah's ears.

"All right, men," he said, gathering the unit about him, "here's what I figure we oughta do. We'll divide up into crews and rotate every rest period. Three will fell, two will clean and one will cut. Two will split. That's eight of us . . . the other crew that's not doin' these chores, well, their job will be to build on our huts. Any questions?"

"Yeah, Sergeant. Who wins? I mean, how do we know?" Drew asked.

"Well, our two companies, us and them Georgia lads, compete unit by unit. Whatever unit in the two companies comes closest to gettin' its huts built first, a cord o' fire wood cut and has the most number of logs left for fortifications, well, that there'll be the winner. You fellas up to it?"

Sam held his hands over the fire for warmth against the dark cold. Looking around at the group of men, he said, "I don't know 'bout you boys, but I'd a heap rather be sleepin' in some log huts tomorrow night over layin' out here in the cold again. I'm game to take part. I'm like Jep; I sure wouldn't mind a time off."

"Count us in, Sergeant!"

"We'll show 'em how to log some trees!"

"Hurrah! Let's start now!" all echoed around the fire.

"All right, fellas," Jeremiah said, "I'm countin' on you! We begin at sun up, after breakfast. I'll go tell Cap'n we're in for sure."

It was a frigid night, many soldiers forced to sleep out in the open. Tents were severely limited as were other necessities. Each day the ports remained blockaded, things became a little harder, a bit more miserable for the men in gray. Yet few complained and many simply worked harder, their spirit seeming unbeatable.

The next morning dawned cold and bright. After rations of moldy corndodgers and salt pork, the men were eager to begin the chores of the day. Jeremiah and Sam rounded up the needed equipment: axes, rope and wedges for splitting. The corporal helped the sergeant divide the men into crews.

"Jep, you and Drew and I will fell first," Sam explained. "Killian and Andy, you'ns will clean the brush from the trunks. Berry, you'll cut while the Sergeant and Franklin split."

"The rest o' you boys will begin to lay out the huts and assume construction as logs become available," Jeremiah commanded.

Soon, Captain McCormick of the Georgia company fired his pistol into the air, getting the contest underway. Shortly, the woods were filled with the sounds of axe and timber. Chop! Chop! Chop! Crash! The men worked feverishly for three hours in the morning frost, backs bending, arms swinging, axes striking wood.

Drew would shimmy up a tree, tie a length of rope around it and rapelle back to the ground. Then Sam and Jep would begin their task.

"Heave, Jep!" Sam shouted as his axe found its mark.

"Ho, Sam!" Jep yelled as his blade cut into the wood.

Drew and his rope next guided the tree to the ground, resulting in a reverberating crash. Then, Killian and Andy begin cleaning off limbs and leaves. This completed, Berry began chopping the bare trunk into lengths, which Jeremiah and Franklin split. It was hard work, but the men enjoyed it.

Midmorning, a rest was called, and as Jeremiah had earlier dictated, his crews rotated jobs to keep fresh. A good start had been made on the huts and a cord of firewood was beginning to stack up. The rest period did not allow time for checking on the progress of the opponents, so when it was time to resume activity, Jeremiah's boys started up with renewed vigor, afraid they might well be behind in the game.

As Jeremiah, Jep and Andy, Sam, Killian, Drew, Berry and Franklin began work on hut construction, they discovered they favored their previous duties. Though they worked well and diligently at building the small quarters, after the dinner break they were ready to switch jobs once more.

The work continued. Trees came down, were cleaned up and cut up. Logs were split and crude huts rose against the sky as afternoon break came.

Time to switch jobs again. Though the day was cold, sweat rolled from the bodies of the men, soaking through clothing, glistening in hair.

At this point, the boys were impatient to know who was ahead, but there was no way to determine who was winning. All men involved in the contest were hard at work.

The boys favored Jeremiah's idea of rotating jobs, for it did keep them fresh for the work at hand. Tree felling was strenuous, and hut building tedious, so the constant switching kept them in a state of renewal.

But is it enough, Jeremiah found himself wondering. *Will it help us to win?* His men were working so hard and so harmoniously. He felt a mixture of pride and distress. No one could ask more than what his boys were giving.

At supper call, the sound of the axe was to end, and no more effort toward the winning goal could be taken. Colonel Hartshare would decide the victor. He agreed to visit the scene of the competition with several of his aides. Once they judged the outcome, the winner would be announced.

Before twilight, Colonel Hartshare appeared, he and his men making rounds to examine the efforts of the two companies. Clearly pleased by the soldiers' accomplishments, he called the participating boys together.

"Gentlemen!" he addressed the small crowd enthusiastically, "It gives me great pleasure to compliment you on your work of today. In fact, I am so impressed by your contest I am going to encourage other companies to do likewise. I am even going to call it to the attention of General Jackson. Well done, men, well done!"

"I wish he'd get on with the winner!" Sam whispered impatiently to Jeremiah.

"Yeah, me too, Sam"

"But either way, Sergeant, there's gonna be some mighty disappointed boys. All of us in this here contest today worked plum hard. Too bad we can't all get rewarded."

"Seems to me, Corporal," Jeremiah mused, "that doin' that would keep fellas from givin' it their all and meetin' the bottom line to get as much work done as soon as possible. If everyone gets rewarded, then ain't no one gonna give it a hundred percent. We end up with only a fair to good job being accomplished as compared to a great job."

"Well now, I do declare, Sergeant . . . I reckon you've got a point there. Must be how come you're the sergeant and I'm still just a corporal."

Jeremiah gave Sam a slap on the back, accompanied by a hearty laugh. "I appreciate the speculation," he said, "but I don't reckon that's got a thing to do with it. Sometimes I wonder how come I'm a sergeant myself. I'll try to keep your brilliant deduction in mind from now on!"

"Shh! Shh! Fellas!" Jep whispered from behind Jeremiah. "Colonel's fixin' to let us know the good news. By the way . . . I keep askin' myself how come either of you has any rank . . . even private!"

At the comment, they all burst out laughing, just as Colonel Hartshare announced the winner.

"Congratulations to Sergeant Thompson's unit of Captain McCormick's Company C!"

"What'd he say?" Drew nudged Jeptha, "what was he sayin'? I couldn't hear over y'all laughin'!"

"He just congratulated Sergeant Thompson's boys of the Georgia Company," Jep answered in disappointment. "I knew them Georgy boys was goin' at it!"

"I wish I could give a second place award," Colonel Hartshare continued. "Sergeant Thompson, your men outdid everyone by far in either company," he paused . . . "with one exception. Sergeant McCamey's unit of Captain Kertlin's Company G! Men, you did an astounding job! Your work far exceeded anyone's! Even Thompson's, and I was duly impressed by what I saw there. Sergeant McCamey, I salute you! I salute you, and your men! It is with pride I order you free from duty for the next two days!"

"Yahoo!" Jeptha threw his cap into the air. The rest of the boys followed suit. Shouting hurrahs, and congratulating themselves, they pounded Jeremiah on the back.

Soon Captain Kertlin appeared before him. "Cap'n!" Jeremiah saluted with a shout, "Ain't it grand? I am pleased. I am very pleased with our men!"

Captain Kertlin returned the salute with gratification. "Sergeant McCamey . . . I am proud for professional," he paused and looked at the ground, "and personal reasons," he murmured. The Captain looked back up at his recently acquired relative. "You've done your brother-in-law well, Jeremiah.

"Congratulations!" he shouted to all the men. "Boys," he said, looking around at each one, "thank you! This speaks well not only for your cap'n here, and your sergeant, but of yourselves, men. You've done quite a job! Be proud! Be proud of yourselves! I am!"

Jeremiah, looking forward to his two days free from duty, went to sleep quickly that night, intending to sleep all day if he could. Suddenly, he woke with a start, sitting bolt upright on the dirt floor of their little hut. He was wrapped tightly in his blanket and all was quiet except for Jeptha's snoring. It took him a moment to realize what woke him.

Cy. He had dreamed of the tree cutting contest and his blond headed friend. He was splitting logs while Cy chatted with him.

"You see that there log, Jeremiah?" Cy had said, "That log's just like America. It's split into two separate parts now . . . a wedge has been driven between the North and the South, and no matter who wins this war, that log is split. It ain't ever goin' back together again." Cy laughed and continued, "I understand that's how Abe Lincoln got started—splittin' logs. Reckon he's still doin' it. Say, Jeremiah, how's Violet? I wrote her, but I ain't heard nothin' in a long time."

As the dream had persisted, he looked at his friend and suddenly realized he was dead. He started to get angry with Cy for leaving them and then suddenly woke.

It was a while before dawn, but Jeremiah couldn't go back to sleep. The dream haunted him and the familiar ache he thought he'd finally conquered returned. He couldn't get Cy out of his mind. He missed him so much, and it was hard to believe a year had almost passed. Things had been so different then; so different this time two years ago!

He knew no matter what happened in the future, his existence would never again be the same. His decision to enlist changed his life and the lives of his family. It wasn't altogether a pleasing thought, but given the chance again, he would do no differently. He couldn't. Too much was at stake. He smiled to himself, thinking of Priscilla as Mrs. John Kertlin, the one good thing wrought out of all the heartbreak and hardship.

Jeremiah crept outside to make a fire for heating water. He wanted coffee, but there was none. There hadn't been for some time . . . not since that trade across the river with Geoffrey's unit. Parched corn covered with boiling water would have to do. It wasn't appetizing, but it was liquid, and it would be hot.

Sitting on his haunches waiting for the pot to boil, he noticed a shadow in the doorway of their crude cabin.

"Mornin', Jeremiah," Jep spoke in a whisper, careful not to wake their other messmates. "What you doin' up? Thought we was gonna sleep all day."

"Waitin' on water to boil," Jeremiah answered. "What's your excuse?"

"Fixin' some of that good corned coffee, huh? Blame it all! I wish we had the real stuff." Jep rubbed his hands together against the cold.

"Yeah, me too. But we don't," Jeremiah said matter-of-factly. "What got you up? You was snorin' like a train a moment ago."

Jep perched beside his friend, sitting cross-legged on the cold ground. He stared off into space, the fire reflecting a dance in his dark eyes. Suddenly he turned to Jeremiah.

"I dreamed about Cy. It was so strange . . ."

Jeremiah stared at his friend in disbelief. Finally Jeptha asked, "What's wrong? Are you all right?"

"I, I don't know, Jep. I . . . I had a dream about Cy, too. That's what got me awake." Jeremiah shuddered, not so much against the cold as the haunting thought of their dead friend. "We was splittin' logs, Jep," Jeremiah smiled ruefully at the thought, "And Cy was bein' real philosophical like. You know how he would get sometimes . . . he just talked to me about splittin' logs, and about how that was like the country, and about Abe Lincoln . . . how odd, huh? Then he asked about Violet and I realized all over again he was dead, and I started gettin' mad at him for leavin' us . . . then I woke up." A tear threatened to escape from the corner of his eye and Jeremiah swiped at it with the back of his hand.

"We was sittin' under a big shade tree in my dream," Jep began, "fact is, seems like it was that big maple tree back of your farmhouse, Jeremiah. The one that gets so red in the fall."

Jeremiah knew exactly what tree Jeptha meant. The three boys had idled away many a summer day in its shade.

"Anyway," Jep continued, "I don't know how we happened to be there, but Cy was tellin' me how much he missed me, Jeremiah. Then he just suddenly got up and started walkin' away. All at once he stopped, turned around and let those blue eyes stare at me with that twinkle they'd sometimes have. Finally, he says . . . he says, 'Jep, I'll be seein' you soon' and I said, 'Cy, wait. Don't go. I've missed you too much, you scoundrel!' And he says without smilin', kinda sad like, 'I know, Jep. I know.' Then he starts walkin' away, and just disappears, and I think he's been blowed up all over again. That's how come I was to wake up, Jeremiah.

"You know . . . sometimes it still hurts real fierce like. I try not to think about it much; his bein' gone I mean. But sometimes I think I'd give anything . . . anything, to have him back with us," he whispered, filled with emotion.

As his friend grew silent, Jeremiah turned to face him, and Jep wasn't ashamed that his deep brown eyes were filled with tears. "Water's boilin'", Sergeant," he said, brushing them aside.

⁓

The winter, cold and wet, was weathered away in the crude little huts the soldiers built. The line from Port Royal to New Guiney Station was well fortified for defensive action.

The season was quiet, the main event occurring a few miles to the north. Burnside's Union Army broke winter camp in an attempt to attack Lee's line. They got bogged down in the mud instead.

Food for the Confederates had become scarce and often Jeremiah and his men felt as if they would starve to death. Uniforms badly needed replacing, but there were no new ones. Patches on knees and seats kept them from falling off in total rags. It was a miserable, exhausting existence, but most of the men bore it steadfastly. Sagging spirits were replaced by pride in home, pride in self and an intensive faith in God.

Occasionally, General Lee or General Jackson held parades or reviews to keep morale from sinking to the ground. There were church services every Sunday and often during the week. Many men found comfort in attending such, and Lee and Jackson often went together, praying side by side for their troops.

Some soldiers had deserted; those unable or unwilling to withstand what was required of them. General Jackson summed it up by declaring they were men lacking in patriotism. Before the end of winter, the timid and unfaithful had dropped from the ranks, leaving only the bravest behind—those warriors stoutest in heart and unbreakable in spirit. Fortunately, such men were the majority.

In February, another of Lincoln's leaders was replaced. Burnside had fallen out of favor and General Joseph Hooker was now head of the Union troops. "Fighting Joe" was a blond, handsome man, with an evil reputation. General Hooker had some plans for the warmer weather. Plans that included Generals Lee and Jackson.

Once again spring came to Virginia's countryside and with it, the hostilities resumed. By the end of April, Union forces were crossing the Rappahannock once more, massing in colossal numbers near the scene of December's fighting at Fredericksburg.

Masked by heavy, dense woods he filled with sharpshooters, Hooker believed nothing could pry his army from their hiding place and he watched the Rebel troop movements with the aid of hot air balloons.

Jackson knew the Federal position could only be determined by launching an attack. Shortly before midnight on May 1, Jeremiah was given orders to rouse his sleeping men.

"Up and at 'em, fellas!" he bellowed to the boys who hadn't been sleeping long. "Up and at 'em! We're movin' out; being redeployed a little ways south of here."

"Sergeant, in the middle of the night?" Sam questioned in a yawn. "What's up?"

"As if I knew, Sam. I wish General Jackson had enough confidence in me to disclose all of his plans, but I'm afraid I just ain't that important."

Jep, already on his feet gathering his gear, laughed. "That's all right, Jeremiah. You're good enough in my book. What's Cap'n Brother-in-Law had to say tonight? He's filled you sergeants in on some plans, surely. What do you know?"

Jeremiah stood with his arms akimbo, staring at his friend. He despised it when Jep used that term to refer to Captain Kertlin, although he knew it was in jest. "I believe we're gonna get acquainted with Mr. Lincoln's General Hooker. He's only been watchin' us from across the river for this last ten weeks or so. Reckon it's time we met, huh?" He laughed, but then grew serious, "Boys, the report from J. E. B. Stuart is that Hooker's got some ninety thousand men ready and waitin' for us. They're somewhere in the vicinity of the big Chancellor farm . . . Chancellorsville."

Andy drew in a low whistle. "How many men we got now, Sarge?" he asked.

Jeremiah was silent for a moment. "I ain't exactly sure. But I think it's a rather safe bet to say we're hopelessly outnumbered."

"Yeah . . . that's what I figured," Jep stated ruefully.

By 11 A.M. the next morning, the boys were part of a long line stretching innumerable miles. Hooker had made one mistake already. He believed the Rebels to be in retreat as they moved out. Instead, Jackson had an aggressive plan to press the Federals in order to learn of their strength and position.

Lee and Jackson had a better plan for Hooker than he did for them. A small force of Lee's troops kept "Fighting Joe" occupied in the front of the Union line. Jackson took his whole corps around back to put an unsuspecting crush on the Yankees.

Jeremiah and his boys waited, watching, deep in the forest close to Chancellorsville. This wooded area was extremely dense, making it dark and foreboding even during the daylight. It was a wild place. A place referred to simply as The Wilderness.

Boys in blue were not far away, and it was nigh suppertime. Suddenly, an order came down: "Attack! Move out and attack!"

"All right lads," Jeremiah ordered, "keep good formation! These bluecoats is probably eatin' their supper 'bout now. Let's make it their last meal!"

They crept through the cold, dark woods in the twilight hours of May 3. Quietly and defiantly, they were ready to face the overwhelming odds: 45,000 men Lee and Jackson had between them. Hooker commanded 90,000 to 125,000.

Quickly, they were within sight of the Union soldiers at mess; arms stacked and men eating. "The fun begins now, boys!" Jeremiah shouted as they smashed down upon the unsuspecting troops, shattering them in the last rays of day. Cruel fighting prevailed.

As the sun set, a blue coat on a white horse rode straight toward Jeremiah's unit. Unarmed except for a sword, on he came, not intending to quit. As he galloped past, his blade lashed out at Sam.

"Capture him, men!" Captain Kertlin shouted. "Take him captive!"

Jeptha leaped out, grabbing the man by a leg as the enemy sword came crashing down. Jeptha ducked out of the way, and the soldier, losing his balance, dropped his weapon to the ground. Yet he continued his effort to fight, no matter what the risk.

"Hey, fella," Captain Kertlin called to him, "with your bravery and spunk, you must be wearin' the wrong uniform!"

Most of Company G had moved forward, leaving the enemy soldier for Jeremiah and his friends to take prisoner. Pointing a pistol at the man in blue, Captain Kertlin started to march him away, but something in him admired the fortitude the young enemy officer showed; the courage he exemplified. Suddenly, the Captain lowered his pistol and spoke to Jeptha, who was leading the soldier's horse.

"Carroll . . . halt men . . . Carroll, give the Lieutenant here his horse."

The boys stared at their leader.

"But Cap'n . . ." Jeptha started to protest.

"Lieutenant," Captain Kertlin spoke to the enemy in blue, "I'm in favor of setting you free, on account of your valor. I cannot take such courage prisoner. Carroll, the horse . . .

"Men," he addressed the other four, "if you're all in agreement, this man goes free. What say you?"

Jeremiah smiled admiringly, agreeing with the captain. Sam and Andy both shook their heads in the prisoner's favor.

"Carroll?" Captain Kertlin questioned. "We all agree or it's an arrest."

Without a word, Jeptha handed the horse's reins back to the young lieutenant. The soldier in blue mounted his steed quickly and rode off speedily under cover of darkness just as General Jackson appeared on the scene.

"Gentlemen! What goes here? Why was that enemy soldier just allowed to go free?" Jackson demanded.

All five stood at a salute. The general waited for an answer.

"Gen . . . General, Sir . . ." Captain Kertlin stammered, then said nothing.

"Go on, Captain," Jackson fished for an answer.

"General, Sir," Jeremiah spoke out, "the man showed undaunting courage."

"What the sergeant says is true, Sir," Captain Kertlin quickly found his voice. "We released him on account of the bravery he demonstrated."

The other boys shook their heads in agreement.

"Captain, Sergeant, men . . ." General Jackson looked at each one kindly, then addressed them firmly, "he is the enemy. I do not want them brave, sirs." He stared at them with his bright, deep blue eyes. "If you take out the brave men, gentlemen, the cowards will run. And that, sirs, will only lead to victory for us." He paused, looking at them again, "Be about your business."

"Yes, Sir," the five saluted their commander as he rode away.

The Union Army, unable to regain their balance after the surprise attack, created a stunning victory for the boys in gray. After this win and the chaotic manner in which it was made, the Confederates were in great disarray. Confusion reigned among the ranks. On into the darkness of night, Stonewall Jackson rode up and down his lines, in and out among his soldiers, trying to correct the disorder.

Suddenly, a volley of Federal fire ripped into the Rebel lines. The Southern boys returned it in a wild, irregular fashion. In the melee, Jackson was hit twice by fire from his own men—in the left arm and through the right hand.

He was quickly removed from the scene, but not before the litter bearing his wounded form was caught in another lash of enemy fire. The stretcher was dropped accidentally to the ground, causing additional injury to the General.

By the time the fighting at Chancellorsville was over, Federal losses were so heavy that Abraham Lincoln worried about what the country would say.

Once reaching Guiney Station headquarters, General Jackson survived his wound, though his left arm was amputated. Robert E. Lee, on learning of the situation, wondered how he would do without his brilliant leader, even if just for a brief season as he recovered. He sent word to Jackson, saying . . . "You have lost your left arm, but I have lost my right."

Jackson's recovery seemed imminent the first few days following his injuries. But suddenly, respiratory problems developed and began to exhaust his strength. Unconquerable pneumonia set in. On May 12, 1863, he closed his eyes and uttered, "Let us cross over the river and rest in the shade of the trees." They never opened again and the entire South was plunged into a dreadful mourning.

Upon hearing the news of their fallen leader, Jackson's men despaired. Most wept openly, unashamed of the feeling they expressed for their beloved General. Captain Kertlin addressed his troops on the matter. "I am at a loss," he said, his voice cracking with emotion as tears filled his eyes. "I do not know what we will do; what we will become without Ol' Jack."

CHAPTER SEVENTEEN

Staggering and bleeding alone, comrades,
Out-numbered three to one everywhere.
The world coldly watching our fate, comrades,
Without even a sigh or a tear.

The days after Chancellorsville were not happy days for the Army of Northern Virginia. With General Jackson gone, General Lee was forced to do without Stonewall's uncanny intuitiveness and brilliant strategy in planning. He depended on General James Longstreet to help fit the newly missing piece of the puzzle and named two new Lieutenant Generals to help replace his missing one: Richard Ewell and Ambrose Powell Hill.

Captain Kertlin and his company found themselves part of Hill's corps. The men approved of their new commander, knowing Jackson could never be replaced, but A. P. Hill lacked the deliberation that had made Jackson a warrior. He also possessed an aloofness that kept him at a distance from his men.

Despite the stunning victory at Chancellorsville, the Confederacy was steadily being drained of strength. The South was unable to match the North in numbers, provisions and munitions. Soldiers in all parts of the Confederate States were hungry, dressed in rags and shoeless. It was only through their indomitable spirit that the country gained strength.

The defeat of Hooker at Chancellorsville was a blow that dazed the North. Lee knew if one more defeat such as this were dealt the Union, it would demoralize the North and its willingness to prolong the bitter struggle. His plan was to march across the Pennsylvania border, into Harrisburg.

If he could cut the ties of commerce in this city, the North would be crippled, and forced to its knees. The Confederate States of America would then have the victories so desired: peace and independence.

Before the month of May ended, the trek north was underway. The weather had turned very warm, making it difficult for the men to keep up a hard pace of marching. Empty bellies and bare feet made the problem worse.

"No need to make a fire tonight, Jeremiah," Jeptha sighed one evening, soon after they crossed into Pennsylvania. "Too hot and we ain't got nothin' to cook to eat no ways."

Jeremiah stretched out on the ground beneath a tree. "Right Jep, you're so right," he murmured, "and men . . . I'm too tired to care." He rolled over on his side, stuffing his blanket roll under his head. It wasn't yet dark and he felt as though he was ready for a night's sleep.

From his prone position, the sergeant looked around at his men, observing each face and thinking about the man behind it. These were good men. The best there were.

One by one, they begin to drift away, each finding his own diversion for the evening. Jeremiah and Jeptha were soon alone.

"Think I'll just join you, Jeremiah," Jeptha said, placing his blanket roll on top of a fallen log and stretching out at a right angle to his friend. His feet were almost in Jeremiah's face, and the sergeant started to complain about it until he looked at them closely.

Jeptha's shoes, no longer of any use, had been discarded, and Jeremiah was shocked at how battered his comrade's feet were. In spite of the filth that covered their bottoms, he could see dried blood where the brutal ground cut long gashes into them. Fresh blisters and old, oozing ones made them look ghastly.

"Jep," he spoke, "them feet o' your's is in bad shape! Maybe you oughta take my shoes tomorrow for a spell. There ain't much left to 'em, but they'll offer you a little protection! Lord 'a mercy . . . you sure ain't got none now!"

Jeptha sat up, crooking a leg and staring at the bottom of one foot. "Aw, it ain't so bad, Jeremiah. Reckon they toughened up some. They don't hurt much. When they do, I just try not to think about it. The task we gotta do is more important than my feet. I can live without feet. Don't know that I can live without the independence of our country. Beides, my feet is bigger than yours. Don't reckon your shoes would even fit me." He stretched his feet back out, and wiggled them at Jeremiah. "'Course, if I got your sympathy, you could rub 'em some!"

"Ha!" Jeremiah laughed sarcastically, making his blanket more comfortable under his head. "I ain't touchin' them nasty things!"

"Then you ain't as brave as I thought, Sergeant," Jeptha replied, closing his eyes.

Jeremiah stared at his comrade. They didn't often find themselves apart from the other men and he felt a great compassion stir in his heart for this friend he'd known almost forever. He reflected on the tired and weary face. It looked much older than someone twenty-one, with its dark, drooping mustache, and deep tan color. Jeremiah almost wanted to reach out and soothe the weary toes of his companion.

He couldn't help but think of how much Jep had changed the last two years. His temper had greatly cooled down and he showed great courage in the midst of battle more than once. There was a gentleness about Jeptha that was new to Jeremiah.

They had all borne hardships. It made a few men bitter and they had deserted from the ranks. It made many men tougher, finding in themselves courage unknown. Some resigned to their suffering, hearts becoming tender, believing it would all be worth it in the end. This was Jeptha, and Jeremiah felt an overwhelming devotion toward his friend. He was loyal, sacrificial. He couldn't ask more from any of the boys.

"Jep?" Jeremiah heard his own voice shatter the stillness.

"Yeah?" his friend acknowledged him through narrowed eyes.

"Jep," he repeated, "I just wanna tell you that I'm proud to be your friend. Always have been. You and Cy . . . well, you know you was both most like brothers to me. Reckon I just wanna tell you that . . . well . . ." Jeremiah found it hard to voice his affection. "I just never done told Cy, and sometimes . . . sometimes I wish I had . . ." his voice trailed off.

Jeptha gazed at his friend out of half closed eyes, waiting for him to continue.

"Well," Jeremiah drew in his breath, "I reckon I love you some." There, it was said and he didn't feel foolish for it either.

Jeptha stared at him for several seconds before responding. "Yeah Jeremiah, I know," he whispered in a voice thick with emotion, "I know."

The sergeant reached out his hand, giving one wretched foot a sympathetic squeeze.

The next morning, a rumor was in circulation. The men would be making a detour on their way to Harrisburg. About twelve miles southeast of where they were now camped at Carlisle, General Hill had stumbled upon a gold mine. A factory for the making of shoes and a warehouse full of leather footwear was within a days march. General Hill aimed to see that these goods were confiscated for his barefoot army and they turned toward the little settlement of Gettysburg.

The spirit of the men was high as they marched through the state of Pennsylvania. It had rained on and off for several days, but this morning promised clear blue skies. Not only was the prospect of shoes appealing, but also plenty of food had been foraged during the night. Fat, ripe cherries hung from trees along the way and the luscious fruit filled many empty bellies. Though in enemy territory, things seemed far from hostile, and the soldiers in gray marched down the road with purpose and pride.

A grand cheer went up from a portion of Hill's corps when General Richard Garnett rode past them. General Lee had reinstated General Garnett to command several weeks back, but his former men seldom had opportunity to see him.

The boys admired General Garnett and were relieved his troubles seemed to be behind him. Jeremiah never understood exactly what happened that unfortunate March over a year ago, and though deeply affected at the time, other and more consuming thoughts had demanded his focus since then. Still, it was good to see General Garnett. He was respected, and all had been glad on learning he was put in command of a brigade of General George Pickett's division under Longstreet.

Feet kicked up damp dust as the infantry made their way toward the little town of Gettysburg. It was the first day of July and the heat was sweltering, the recent rain adding oppressiveness to the summer misery.

Jeremiah's unit was close to the back of the line, laughing and joking, discussing what a great host the enemy state proved to be. Suddenly, out of nowhere, the roar of musketry and the shriek of shells were heard, followed by the thunder of cannon.

Company G surged along the road, confused and being fired upon. It was believed they faced a few dismounted Union cavalry, and the order to attack was given.

In truth, two brigades of Federal Cavalry belonging to General John Buford faced the army in gray. What started as a skirmish quickly turned into a full-scale engagement. It began on a hill upon which stood a Lutheran Seminary. The mound of earth was simply called "Seminary Ridge."

Combat continued well into the afternoon, both sides sending in reinforcements as quickly as possible. The storm of fire raged through the streets of the town, blasting its way to the higher ground of the village outskirts. General Lee called for all his forces to converge as quickly as possible.

Union General Buford's cavalry had one small hope: that Federal infantry under General John Reynolds would arrive in time to help them beat back the gray foe.

General Reynolds arrived with only a part of his corps, but that part included the dreaded black-hatted men known as the Iron Brigade. Tough and determined, they were among the best infantry men the Union had to offer. They were ordered forward.

Jeremiah watched as one captain in gray led his men straight into a barrage of musket and cannon fire, most of them falling. There was nothing to hide behind except thin fence rail and scattered trees.

Once the Iron Brigade charged, the already frenzied fight became pandemonium. Onward and forward, the men on both sides pushed. Somewhere out of the fury a Rebel sharpshooter's bullet found its mark and handsome General Reynolds lay dead.

By late afternoon, the blue troops began to break and withdraw. With no more than part of General Reynolds' corps joining the fray, there was no other choice for the Yankees. The first day of fighting at Gettysburg ended in Confederate victory, though many Southern boys lay dead and another large number was captured.

Jeremiah had taken shelter in a small grove of trees along with Jeptha and Sam. Though it offered sparse protection from the rain of shell and shot, it provided adequate cover from which to fire. In the constant push of fighting, it had been impossible to remain a cohesive group and Jeremiah wasn't sure where all of his men were. As the roar of battle died down to a simmer, and the explosion of musketry ceased, it was clear the victory belonged to their troops. At last, the three messmates felt no more a target and began to creep from their meager cover. As they stepped out into the clear, a peppering of artillery fire was unleashed, sending shells screaming and bursting overhead. Suddenly, one hit the ground, exploding at the feet of the three soldiers. Dirt and rock spewed into the air as the discharge sent the men reeling. Abruptly, things were quiet again, and three new forms lay spread upon the ground.

Sam was first to stir. Rising to his knees, he shook debris from his back and brushed dirt from his face and hair. Glancing about, he saw one form roll slowly over onto his back, coughing and sputtering. Another, between them, lay ominously still, sprawled out on his belly, musket beneath. Sam could detect no rising and falling of the dirt covered back, indicative to breathing. He shuddered briefly in the heat, knowing that one of them was down.

A knee rose from the other figure, and the man rolled over on his side, blinking, pulling himself up on an elbow. Part of the once drooping mustache was singed off, and black powder residue smeared across his face.

"Sam? You all right?" Jeptha's voice panted out. "You all right?"

Still stunned, Sam managed to nod his head, before gasping, "Jeremiah! Jeremiah! He ain't breathin', Jep!"

Bounding to his knees, Jeptha hastily crawled the short distance between them. "Jeremiah?" he cried, pounding his friend on the back. "Jeremiah? Sam, help me!"

Jeptha felt a panic he had never experienced, and slapped his comrade hard on the back once more. "Jeremiah?" he shouted again, as Sam helped turn the sergeant over.

Blood trickled from the corner of his mouth and the gray eyes remained closed. "Jeremiah!" Jeptha shook his friend's shoulders.

"Sergeant? Sergeant?" Sam pleaded, pounding his chest. "Sergeant?" he struck him again.

Suddenly, Jeremiah heaved a gasp, his eyelids fluttering open. Rising, he doubled over and choked, spitting out a wad of blood and dirt. Gasping for air, his chest and back heaved. Coughing and sputtering, he reached a hand inside of his mouth to clear it of more debris. "Water, I need water," he croaked, his hand searching wildly for his canteen.

Jeptha opened his and held it to Jeremiah's mouth. He gulped the water in, spitting the warm contents on to the ground. He repeated the procedure before allowing the liquid to greedily pour down his throat. "Thanks, Jep, thanks," he stammered, looking at his two comrades. "You boys all right?"

"Yeah; yeah . . . we're fine as can be, considerin'. You done give us quite a scare, Sergeant," Sam said.

"Yes, well, I'm all right, I think." Looking around, he shook his head to clear it. "Reckon we'd best be movin' out."

"You all right, Jeremiah, you're sure?" Jeptha questioned anxiously as the three rose unsteadily to their feet.

Jeremiah spit out a mouth full of blood, his two men viewing the display with apprehension. "I feel a mite disoriented and I got a nasty gash inside my jaw. But reckon I'll live, fellas. Reckon I'm a mite thankful, too." He bent down to retrieve his musket as Sam and Jeptha located theirs.

"C'mon, men, let's head through the trees," Jeremiah suggested. "The fightin' is over for now, but lettin' the Yankees use us for target practice once in a day is enough." Things seemed oddly silent as they trekked through the sparse growth of woods.

Close to emerging into a clearing on the other side, all three boys suddenly became aware of a voice rising out of the undergrowth. "Halt! Halt or I'll shoot now!"

"Hands up, and turn around slowly, Rebs," another voice sounded. "Jimmy-boy, looks like we've captured ourselves some prisoners! Captain?" the voice shouted to someone unseen. "Cap'n Hansen. We've got ourselves some Johnnies here! Three of 'em!"

Brush crackling underfoot revealed three additional men in blue as the Confederates slowly turned around, arms and weapons in the air.

They were out numbered five to three. *There is no question as to who has the upper hand,* Jeremiah mused to himself. He looked at the stripes on each arm. They revealed a captain, a sergeant, a corporal and two privates.

"Sergeant Crill," bellowed the captain, "handle this arrest."

"Yes, Captain Hansen," the man replied gleefully. "Men," he barked to the three boys in gray, "you are under arrest. I order you to throw down your weapons and surrender!"

The boys in gray hesitated. The Union soldiers stepped up, bayonets gleaming. "Your weapons, men!" the Yankee sergeant loudly insisted.

Grudgingly, Sam threw his musket to the ground. Jeptha, no more willing, tossed his down too. Suddenly, to the shock of them all, Jeremiah whirled around, grabbing his musket by the barrel. He bashed it repeatedly against a tree until the butt was smashed, the barrel twisted and the stock split.

"If I can't have it, certainly no Yankee can!" he lashed out vehemently, throwing the shattered gun down.

At once, he felt a hard object jabbed into his back. "Reckon I'm just gonna have to kill you for that, Reb!" said one of the privates in blue, shoving a pistol into his ribs. Jeremiah heard the hammer cock as Sam and Jep exchanged looks of incredible disbelief.

Jeremiah felt remarkably unshaken. *If this is how I am to meet my maker, then I am ready,* he thought. *It isn't so bad.* He felt totally bereft of fear, and heard himself say, "Go on Yank! It'll do nothin' but bring me pleasure to go to my Lord and Savior dying for my country!"

"That's enough, Jimmy-boy!" the Yankee sergeant admonished the private in exasperation. "Put that pistol up before I take it away from you!"

The private didn't budge.

"Now!" the sergeant bellowed.

Jeremiah felt the gun removed, and with his sleeve wiped fat drops of perspiration from his brow. He hadn't even realized he'd broken into a sweat.

"Now men, we're gonna leave these sparse woods," Union Captain Hansen directed, "only we're headin' that way," he jerked his thumb eastward. "In single file, Rebs! Let's go! March out!"

The three Confederates walked single file behind the captain and sergeant, being guarded in the rear by the corporal and overzealous privates.

Jeremiah, in the lead of the three, turned around and whispered to Jeptha, "We ain't gonna let 'em get away with this! By nightfall I plan on us bein' back with our own company of men. I don't know how, but we'll think of somethin'!"

Jeptha nodded in agreement, passing the word back to Sam.

"Silence!" the corporal growled. "Prisoners ain't allowed to talk!"

Before long, they emerged from the wooded area onto extremely rocky ground. "March, Rebs! In the double quick!" Captain Hansen ordered. "Keep 'em movin', men," he commanded his boys in blue.

It wasn't easy to march over the rock-strewn ground even in beat up shoes, and soon Jeptha's bare feet were leaving bloody footprints behind. Jeremiah felt swallowed up by compassion for his friend.

After some time had gone by, the Union soldiers were ready to take a break and eat their supper rations. The boys in gray had no food and nothing was offered. Though well guarded, they were allowed to sit and rest as their captors ate. Sam took off his worn out shoes and rubbed his feet.

"Look-a-here, Sergeant Crill!" the soldier called Jimmy laughed. "This man's got only three toes! Ha!"

The sergeant smiled, his teeth gleaming. "Reckon that makes him a three-toed sloth!"

Jimmy-boy rollicked with laughter.

"Don't see what's so funny about three toes," Sam snapped.

"Do you know what a three-toed sloth is?" asked the other private, laughing.

Sam shook his head. "Nope. Never heard of any such thing."

"A three-toed sloth is a jungle creature, Reb. He hangs from trees with his three toes and he's stupid and lazy. Filthy too. Reckon the description fits well enough. I bet all Rebs only got three toes!" he howled with laughter, seeming to forget his job of guard duty. The men in blue were enjoying their little game.

Jimmy set his pistol down in order to eat. The other private guarding them held his rifle across his knees. The sergeant had walked off, and though the captain and corporal were near, they weren't within sight.

Sam caught the flash in Jeremiah's eyes and quickly put his shoes back on. He knew the sergeant had a plan.

Jeremiah stood, stretching. "I reckon these sloths have gray skin, too," he chuckled, keeping the enemy laughing at their own joke.

"Hee hee hee, ha ha! Now I do believe they have gray fur!" one of the privates offered.

All at once, Jeremiah kicked the pistol into the brush while Jeptha grabbed for the musket. It was not a good escape plan, but it was all they had.

"Run boys! Run for your life!" Jeremiah shouted as he jumped down from the stony ledge upon which they were sitting. They tore off across the rocky terrain they had just marched over. Once in the open, shots rang out as their captors pursued them. Jeremiah heard one bullet whiz right past his head, but didn't stop to look. He simply called out, "You with me boys?" Both answered in unison as they kept up their run. Another round of shot was unleashed.

"No wonder them Yanks have such a hard time winnin' battles! They can't shoot!" Sam panted as the boys put distance between themselves and their captors. Soon, the firing stopped and they found themselves in cover of woods.

"Don't stop now, men," Jeremiah gasped, "Don't stop now! Don't do anything to give them an advantage!"

For another fifteen minutes, the boys continued to run through the woods before being overcome by exhaustion. Finally halting, Jeremiah bent over, pressing his hands to his thighs, huffing. The other two pulled up with him, all three chortling for air. A full minute passed before anyone spoke.

"Reckon we've become escaped prisoners now. Ha!" Sam laughed, finding great amusement in it all.

Jeptha sat down against a tree, examining a foot. "Got something here that pains me a mite," he said out of breath. He drew a large sliver of stone from his big toe. Blood gushed out.

"We gotta do somethin' about them feet o' yours, Boy!" Jeremiah said breathlessly, looking around, trying to sum up their circumstances.

"I have no idea where we are now, men, but this ain't the same woods we was caught in. These here are denser. We'll just have to keep walkin' under their cover 'til we come on somethin' friendly. But one thing's for sure, we'd best move carefully."

The boys slowed their pace and eventually came close to the edge of their cover. Evidence of the day's fighting could be seen as darkness began to fall.

"Well, this was obviously part of the blue line," Jeptha remarked, picking up an abandoned haversack. "Looks like the dead and wounded have done been removed already. Hey! Fellas! Looky here! Coffee! Real Coffee! That's all what's in this here bag!" He threw it over his shoulder.

Other remnants were scattered here and there; another haversack of coffee, with some hardtack; several blue kepis, and an occasional discarded blue woolen jacket. "Here, Jep! Catch!" Sam suddenly called, hurling a black object toward him.

"Well . . . well! Boys . . . I got me a boot," Jeptha declared, pushing his foot into the long cut black leather shoe. "I'll be—it fits! Thanky, Sam. Reckon one's better than none!" He hobbled about, provoking laughter from Jeremiah.

"What's so funny?" he asked his friend indignantly.

"You sure are a sight, Jep! Hobblin' about with one boot on, them couple o' haversacks throwed round your neck and half a mustache gone."

Jeptha reached up and rubbed his upper lip. "Yeah. Reckon I'll have to do somethin' 'bout that, now."

"Boys," Jeremiah declared, "seems to me if a Union line was here, then they best retreated to behind where we are now. If we keep movin' forward, we're bound to come upon our own troops. With darkness closin' in, we'll have to be extra careful, but we'll also be most out of view. So, let's just keep goin'. We'll skirt the woods 'til sunset and then allow ourselves to get out in the open.

As they walked along, Jeptha turned to the sergeant. "Jeremiah," he addressed his friend, "I gotta say . . . you sure had us afeared when you smashed up that musket o' yours. I thought that was the end for you."

"Maybe for us, too," Sam chimed in.

Jeremiah grinned. "Didn't surprise you boys any more than it did me. But suddenly I just couldn't give into them blue bellies. Don't know what possessed me."

"Men, you reckon there really is such a thing as a three-toed sloth?" Sam asked abruptly. Both boys shrugged their shoulders, chuckling.

"You got me there, Sam. You got me there." Jeremiah shrugged again, looking up at the setting sun.

They crossed out into the open after it passed over the horizon. Soon, a hill came into view, a large building sitting on the ridge. Scattered campfires flickered about it. "We're home, boys!" Jeremiah cheered as he recognized the place. "This is where it started; the fight this mornin'. This is where we drove them Union cavalry from. See there?"

In the dancing firelight, several stands of Confederate colors could be seen unfurled in the evening breeze. They were, indeed, back on Seminary Ridge, and Jeremiah inquired as to where A. P. Hill's corps was now located. The boys quickly covered the distance, glad to be back among their own army and their own men.

As they arrived, Jeremiah sought out their unit, locating them quickly. He was anxious to know of their well being since the day's battle, and all three boys were relieved to be greeted enthusiastically by everyone.

They were pounded on the back, grabbed by the arms and peppered with questions.

"What happened?"

"Where have you been?"

"Is anyone hurt?"

Jeptha answered them by breaking out his confiscated coffee. The men cheered and set about the task of grinding and roasting it; eager for the taste and delighted by its aroma . . .

"Men," Jeremiah said quietly to Jep and Sam, "I'm leaving the party to you two. I'd best report to Cap'n."

As Jeremiah approached Captain Kertlin's tent, Lieutenant Moore immediately accosted him. "McCamey?" he questioned sternly, "where have you been? Captain Kertlin has been beside himself not knowin' what happened to you boys!"

Jeremiah saluted the lieutenant. "Well, Sir, seems we ran into a mite of trouble. All ends well, though. Reckon I can see the cap'n?" he asked.

He didn't need to wait, for Captain Kertlin appeared in the door of his tent. "Jeremiah! Thank goodness," he exclaimed in obvious relief. "Where have you been?" He walked toward the sergeant, grasping him in a quick embrace before pushing him to arm's length. "Where have you been?" he repeated. "I've spent the best part of the last hour trying to think of what I was going to say to Priscilla; what I was going to tell your folks."

Sometimes Jeremiah truly forgot his leader was married to his sister. "We're all right, Cap'n. You won't have to write anybody anything. We're all right," he declared again, relating to the officer the adventures of the day, down to Jeptha's confiscated coffee and new boot. The Captain laughed and Jeremiah spent a long time with his brother-in-law that evening.

CHAPTER EIGHTEEN

Advance the flag of Dixie!
Hurrah! Hurrah!
For Dixie's land we'll take our stand
To live or die for Dixie!

The land around Gettysburg was strange land. Elevated terrain south and east of the town formed the shape of a question mark. Along the ridge of this question mark lay the local burying ground, called aptly, Cemetery Ridge. The punctuation mark ended with a small mountain called Big Round Top, the dot below it a little rocky hill, referred to simply as Little Round Top.

With Seminary Ridge being gained by Lee's army on the first day of battle, the high ground of this "question mark" needed to be controlled by them as well. General Lee expected General Ewell to achieve this on the initial day of fighting, but it went undone. Gaining Cemetery Ridge as well as holding Seminary Ridge would give the Confederate Army the advantage it needed to sweep down over the open Union forces, crushing them, and ending the war.

July 2 dawned hot and muggy as General Lee met with his commanders. A plan was discussed. The high ground General Ewell failed to take the day before must be taken today. It would not be an easy task, for seven corps of the Union Army of the Potomac had begun to converge in the small town. All through the night they worked, becoming well entrenched on the heights that needed to be won.

General John Bell Hood of Longstreet's corps was to lead the major assault. Throughout the long day in camp, A. P. Hill's corps listened to the sounds of the fighting. Sometimes there were ominous lulls of silence, only for the guns to begin again.

If Company G was needed as reserve troops, the men were present, but the hard fighting the previous day had cut their brigade to little more than half strength. Today it was their turn to rest, and listen, and wonder what was happening.

Occasional reports came in. The army in gray had taken the Wheat Field and the Peach Orchard! The men cheered and the distant sounds of explosion continued.

The enemy had been repulsed from their position at the rocky setting of Devil's Den, another dispatch claimed. Hill's tattered and ragged corps was jubilant; but the fighting went on and on. Word was received that the Southern troops were having a hard time taking the little rocky hill, the one where the left flank of the Union army stood. If they could get up that hill, and take the Yankees from the rear by surprise, they could roll right over the vast number of Federals, and victory would be won!

By late afternoon, the news was not good. Three times the Confederates charged the hill only to be repulsed in the end by a bayonet charge that sent them running. Union Colonel Joshua L. Chamberlain and his 20th Maine Regiment claimed Little Round Top as theirs.

When July 3 broke, it promised to be another hot and sultry day. Company Sergeants were called at dawn for a meeting with Captain Kertlin.

"Boys," Jeremiah said ruefully on his return to his messmates, "this day might very well make or break our country."

"Well, what's it we got to do, Jeremiah?" Jeptha questioned anxiously.

"Hold on, Jep. Sam, would you please call the men together. What I got to say, I need to say to all."

As Sam took off to do the sergeant's bidding, Jeremiah stared at Jeptha. Something wasn't right.

It wasn't the fact that he'd cleaned up. Both of them had bathed in the creek the day before. It was more than the fact that his ragged uniform was dressed up by two new boots.

"Where'd you get that other boot, Jep?" he asked, though he full well knew.

"Dunno, really. Lieutenant Moore done brought it to me this mornin', right after you left to go meet with Cap'n. Said it was compliments of Cap'n himself. I says, 'Well, Lieutenant, what I need is a boot broken in for a left foot; that or a brand new boot,' and he says 'Carroll, this here is a left footed boot.' Now, what do you think of that?"

Jeremiah looked down to hide the grin on his face. So, Cap'n had come through for him. He said the other night that he'd try to find a spare boot from somewhere. Jeremiah wondered from where it had come, indeed.

"It fits, Jep?" he inquired.

"Yeah . . . and I got me a suspicion that you had somethin' to do with this."

Jeremiah looked up at his friend and smiled. "Honestly, Jep, trust my word. I do not know where it come from." *It is true,* he thought. He didn't know where Cap'n had come by the boot. But he was grateful for his friend's sake.

"It spiffs you up a mite, Jep. With that bath yesterday and them new boots, reckon you'd turn some pretty female heads . . . if there were any around!" He continued to stare at his friend.

"Tarnation, Jeremiah! What are you lookin' at?" Jeptha thundered in exasperation.

"I . . . I don't rightly know, Jep. Somethin' 'bout you don't look right."

His friend smiled. "I can't believe you don't miss it, Jeremiah!" He rubbed his upper lip. "It's gone, I shaved them singed hairs off this mornin'."

Jeremiah laughed. "Of course! How come I didn't notice?"

"Aw, Jeremiah, you just done knowed me too long and most of them years I ain't had no hair on my face. Think I might keep it off for a while." He threw an arm around the sergeant's shoulders.

"Want some coffee, Jeremiah? I saved the last of it for you."

"Yeah, Jep. Thanks! I really appreciate that."

He savored the warm brown liquid as the men began to gather. Sam soon had them all rounded up.

"Boys," the sergeant said grimly, "we got important work to do today. I don't need to remind you that some of us might not be back here tonight . . . or tomorrow. I don't need to tell you how viciously the foe can fight. These are things all of you know, just as you know your duty. You've all risked making the supreme sacrifice." He stopped talking for a moment and looked at each man before continuing.

"General Lee has called on two more corps to help complete the task of today, and boys . . . we're part of one of those corps. We'll be commanded by General Longstreet. Most of his boys executed a hard march yesterday and were sent right into the battle. Their numbers is down, and it's their time to rest. So it's up to us. We'll be joinin' the division led by

General George Pickett, and men . . . we gotta take that hill. That one with the cemetery on it. Cemetery Ridge. Ol' Abe Lincoln might have replaced General Hooker with this here General Meade, but that don't mean he ain't tough just cause he's new at the job. We done seen the last two days how hard he plays this game." He paused.

"Well, what's the plan, Sergeant?" Andy asked.

"How soon we joinin' in?" Jep wanted to know.

"Yeah," Killian asked, "what's the details? We got any time?"

"Boys, our army was beaten in takin' that little rocky hill yesterday, as you know. Our only chance to win here now is to storm Cemetery Ridge. There's a little grove of trees at the top. We're to charge that hill from several angles, converging at those trees. We must knock the Yankees from this position, boys. We must break the Union line here!"

"But Sergeant," Franklin spoke up, "they got a stone wall at the top to hide behind! We ain't got nothin' . . . nothin' but open space!"

"Yeah," mused Drew, "kinda reminds me of Fredericksburg . . . only it was us who got to take cover behind a wall."

"That's right, men," Jeremiah said matter-of-factly, "we got to get over that stone wall."

The men were silent as they thought of the weight of the situation. Finally, Franklin voiced what they all were thinking. "Sergeant, it's a mile or more up that hill, out in the open, and when we hit that road that goes to . . . to . . . er, Emmitsburg, or wherever it leads to, there's a fence on the other side of it we'll have to get over. We'll probably have enfilade fire raining down on us. How? How are we supposed make it up that hill?"

"We'll just do it," Jeptha snapped, "we'll just do it, that's all!"

"The artillery will fire with all they've got," Jeremiah continued, "savin' just enough to support us when we go in. But before we do, they'll try to blow away as much enemy artillery and men from that hill as they can."

"You say General Pickett is leadin' this charge?" Killian asked.

"Mostly. He has his whole division," Jeremiah answered.

"He's good, boys. He's a fine General, George Pickett is," Killian replied thoughtfully. "How many men will we have?"

"Somewhere's around fifteen thousand, I think," Jeremiah answered.

No one spoke for several minutes. "I don't know that even fifteen thousand of us can do this job," Andy piped up pensively.

"Well, men . . . I'm sure we'll be given our orders to move out momentarily. Any questions?" Jeremiah asked.

Everyone was silent and as they sat there, Captain Kertlin came riding through their encampment.

"Men," he stopped to speak, "I'm sure Sergeant McCamey has explained well to you our job of today. I have just received word that we are to start movin' into position. So, get your gear, and form your lines. The order to march will come down directly. Soldiers," he raised a hand to his brow, "I salute you for your devotion to your duty." Lowering his arm, he rode away.

"Well, men, you heard the captain," Jeremiah said with authority.

Jeptha spoke up as though he were in charge, "Boys, say your prayers . . . and let's go take that hill!"

Within moments, the beat of the drum was heard, and the men started falling in line. They had a two-mile march to the base of Cemetery Ridge.

Once their position was reached, the men took cover in a wooded area at the base of the hill. Far in the distance, across the wide-open space, one could see the small grove of trees, fronted by the stone wall on top of Cemetery Ridge. Their brigadier general, Isaac Trimble, commanded the boys to lie in the cover of brush and trees. The idea was to remain out of view of the Yankees.

Jeremiah looked down the long line. Men stretched as far as he could see. Besides his own brigade from Hill's corps, he knew there was also that of General Dorsey Pender, commanded by General James Pettigrew on this day. Pickett's division had three brigades: that of General Jimmy Kemper, the speaker of the House of Virginia; General Richard Garnett, Company G's former brigadier; and General Lewis Armistead, a kindly officer and veteran soldier.

In the distance on his right, Jeremiah spied a man clad in a brightly colored uniform. The unfamiliar soldier was walking to and fro, chatting with some of the officers. The sight amazed him.

"Hey, Cap'n," he called upon seeing the officer, "Who is that fella yonder, down the line, all decked out in them fancy duds? Ain't he makin' a target of himself?"

"Jeremiah," the captain answered in awe, "that there is Colonel Arthur J. Fremantle, of Her Majesty's Cold Stream Guards."

"A Britisher?" Jeremiah asked incredulously. "What's an Englishman doing here?"

"Well, if I understand, he's been sent here to visit our army as an emissary; maybe take a report back to the Queen to help persuade Britain to come in on our side, or at least come to our aid. I hear tell he's quite a character. Most of the officers have developed a real liking for him. It's rumored he has also become fond of our little outfit, The Army of Northern Virginia."

Jeremiah looked at the captain then shook his head in laughter.

The sun rose higher in the sky, its rays becoming insufferable. The men could only lie still and wait. The intenseness of the heat broke when the sky clouded over and a brief shower cooled the air, but soon the sun returned in all its fiery glory, broiling the men where they lay.

Shortly after noon, the guns began. All available artillery had been placed in a line and aimed at the crest of the hill. Napoleons, parrots, howitzers, mortar—all different cannon and all deadly cannon. With Colonel E. Porter Alexander in charge, the results were sure to be deadly.

BOOM! It started. BOOM! BOOM! BOOM! BOOM! BOOM! It was a terrible thunder even nature could not imitate. One round after another was fired successively. The acrid, sulfuric smoke gasped in huge puffs as the mouths of the cannon were emptied.

To the Yankees on Cemetery Ridge, it created an awesome vision; to the Rebels on the ground, it produced a savage, deafening roar. The earth shook, the sky rattled and the earsplitting blasts went on and on.

Enemy fire from the hill began to answer: shrieking shells, solid shot, canister and grape. The world was exploding. The heavens were on fire.

Jeremiah covered his ears after awhile. The constant bombardment caused them to ache, but his hands could not blot out the reverberation. His nose started to pour blood as the fierce concussion of the cannonading got to him. He realized that in two years of battle, it was the first time the noise affected him.

Jeptha rolled over on his back. "Great day in the mornin', Jeremiah! How long do you suppose this will keep up? I'm gonna be deaf if I'm not already!" He looked at the sergeant. "Your nose is bleedin'."

"Yeah, I know." Jeremiah swiped at it with his arm. "Don't seem to be so bad now," he said, noticing only a smear of blood on his sleeve.

The cannon never let up. BOOM! BOOM! BOOM! BOOM! BOOM!

ZING! KER-PLOW! BOOM! BOOM! BOOM! BOOM! BOOM! Every shell from Colonel Alexander was answered with one from General Cushing's Union battery—over, and over, and over, and over.

The boys were becoming restless. It was hard to be still. Often, shots came through the trees, crashing down limbs, shattering trunks, hitting men. Killing men. There was nowhere to go. Nowhere to hide.

"What time is it?" Sam wanted to know.

Franklin pulled a watch from his pocket. "Pret near two-thirty," he replied.

Jeptha rolled on his back again, an arm shielding his face from the sun. "I'm gettin' my dander up, Jeremiah. I hope we get to shoot at these Yankees soon. I'm 'bout tired of this!"

BOOM! BOOM! BOOM! CRASH! A gigantic tree limb splintered from the sky, barely missing Andy as its branches scratched and tore at the faces of other nearby men.

Another quick shower sprang up. It lasted only a moment, and as it died down, so did the cannonading. Shots became less frequent and fewer and far between. BLAM! WHISTLE! BOOM! Suddenly all was quiet. The silence seemed as deafening as the guns.

"What's happenin', Jeremiah?" Sam glanced about in confusion.

"Don't know, Sam. Don't know," he replied, wondering.

In the far away distance, he could see General Pickett riding up and down his lines, speaking to the men. He was much too far away to be heard, but Jeremiah could tell he was talking with animated determination, almost exhilaration. He flashed a smile and threw back his head in a laugh. His horse pranced in anticipation.

Jeremiah scanned his immediate surroundings, looking for Captain Kertlin. He hadn't seen him for some time. He noticed General Pickett again, his sword raised to his face. The sergeant knew this signified the beginning, and suddenly boys began to rise from the ground. He could hear the distant drums beat formation: TRUMP, TRADITRUMP, TRADITRUMP, TRUMP, TRUMP.

Men began to rise from among the brush and trees as the order went on down the line. More drums sounded the roll. Jeremiah watched in awe as they fell in, for there were men as far as the eye could see. It was an astounding sight. It gave him a chill. He knew the line had to be a mile or more long, and how many men deep he couldn't begin to guess.

Suddenly shouting, chanting, cheering could be heard. All the men bristled with emotion, ready to get the job done. The clamor was as deafening as the cannon roar had been, and it inspired the soldiers.

Colonel Hartshare faced them. "Men," he shouted above the roar, "you are all honorable men. You all know your duty today. You could have chosen to run, but you've committed to stay. Up, now. Up and to arms, men! Your country calls on you this hour and you are all worthy of the call. I invoke God's help for you; I invoke God's mercy on you. For the glory of your country, in answer to a call to honor . . . FORWARD!" he bellowed.

The color guard stepped to the front and Jeptha reached out, squeezing Jeremiah's arm in a fierce demonstration of affection and admiration.

"Ain't they purty? Jeremiah. Ain't them banners beautiful?" he whispered with pride. The flags were unfurled and snapped to attention by a breeze. "What a lovely sight for which to be willing to die!"

"MARCH!" came the sudden command as Colonel Hartshare quickly raised and lowered his sword.

First in line, behind the colors, Company G joined the sea of men. Like a tumultuous wave, they surged slowly forward with muskets gleaming, their faces filled with determination.

Unwavering and defiant, out into the open they moved.

Jeremiah turned and faced his men. "Boys," he shouted, marching backwards, "remember, keep the ranks tight. When a break appears, pull together and close it up! Whatever you do, don't leave a hole in the line! Keep it together; keep it tight! And don't forget, no use in firin' until we're about to the fence; it'll be wasted shot!"

The scene unfolding overwhelmed him. He'd never seen so many fine looking soldiers at once and his heart swelled with pride for their ragged, battered army. What a magnificent sight they were, their dignity belying their tattered clothes and bare feet. They presented a vision of grandeur as the tremendous mass of men moved with exactness and order. He knew their undeniable majesty had to prove an imposing sight to the enemy on top of the hill.

It was as though there were no end. The higher on the slope they moved, the more Jeremiah could see. Over the wheat field they flowed; out of the peach orchard they poured. The thrill it produced in him was so great that he could not imagine any soldier, anywhere, viewing this and not burning to be a part.

He turned and fell back in stride with his men. They were passing the artillery position now, and those minding the cannon waved their caps, cheering them on.

Forward they climbed, and soon the shots began again. Yankee artillery burst upon them, shrieking overhead and exploding on the ground. Their own artillery began to answer in support of their charge. The sky overhead was a rain of bursting, exploding, shattering shell and shot.

Holes began to appear in the line, and quickly, methodically, the men closed them up. *Courage!* Jeremiah thought. *Unmatched courage! There are no cowards here!*

On his right a shell hit the ground, sending a shower of dirt over them all. Several men went somersaulting into eternity, but the gap closed up. Another shot burst close by and men fell with a groan; still, the ranks moved in and the space disappeared.

Up ahead, in front of them, the colors fell, but before the flag hit the ground, another hand retrieved the standard to march it onward. Shortly, this man too, was down, and the flag lay in the dirt. A third man of the color guard quickly again held it high and safely it remained a beacon.

Shells begin falling more rapidly, bursting in every direction. Men were reeling, groaning, falling and dying. It became harder to keep the ranks closed. Too many men were down too fast. The fence wasn't much farther ahead; they could soon begin firing.

Another shell burst in their front, putting the remainder of the color guard down. Quick as lightening, Jeptha pulled out of line and grabbing the standard, waved it wildly with one hand, musket in the other. Forward he continued to march, undaunted by what was happening around him. Onward and forward. Jeremiah was overcome by the pride he felt in his friend. *'Atta boy, Jep!* he said to himself. *'Atta boy! Wouldn't Cy be proud of you?*

Suddenly, the men began covering ground at the run-like march. Someone ordered them to move at the double quick. Jeremiah didn't know whom; he hadn't heard the command and didn't even know if it applied to them, but at the double quick they all joined, and soon their order turned into disarray. The ranks weren't closing in as well when shells blew spaces in them. The lines were no longer straight, though the men's urgency to duty seemed more passionate. The fence loomed ahead.

Jeremiah turned around to face his disordered men. "Boys," he shouted, "lads . . . take that fence apart if you have to . . . jump over it . . . crawl over it . . . crawl under it if need be, but get over it swiftly! Make haste! Make haste!"

He turned back around just in time to see Jeptha, with the flag still in hand, slide over the top rail. Jeremiah's heart beat wildly for a moment as he watched Jep drop the banner to the ground and tumble to the earth as a shell sent fence rail splintering. A hole was knocked into the section Jeptha just crossed. Dead men littered the ground beneath the fence on the other side.

"Jep!" he heard himself shout over bursting shells, knowing full well he could not be heard. "Jeptha!"

Suddenly the flag appeared, raised again in full glory. It was peppered with holes and shredded at the edge, but Jeremiah could see his beloved comrade continue to march it forward.

"That's the way to go, Jep!" he shouted with unfettered emotion. "That's the way to go!" He found himself climbing over the fence as a ladder . . . a rung beneath, a rung on top. Many of the men were pouring through the gaps left by exploding shells.

Suddenly, as he straddled the top rail, Jeremiah felt airborne. To his right, artillery found its mark as a section of fence was shattered, pitching men outward. He heard the ominous sound of several groaning in unison, like a strange musical chord. "Ahhhh," they all seemed to moan at once, rocketing into the air and plunging to the ground.

He hit the dirt hard, but unharmed, the fence rail beneath him. He looked back; it was impossible to see most of his men. The acrid smoke from the guns burned his nose and throat and made his eyes water. His chest hurt, and the heat . . . the heat was insufferable.

He found himself close up on Jeptha, still bearing the banner. He was holding the staff clasped tightly in both hands, his musket gone. Jeremiah thought angrily, *How are you going to defend yourself? Wave the flag in the enemy's face and beat them with the staff?* Suddenly he laughed in spite of the chaos and the tumultuous activity around him. He was laughing at his own thought. That was exactly what Jep would do!

At once, Jeremiah was gripped by a terrible fear and he surged forward, groping out for Jeptha's arm. "What are you doin, Jep?" he demanded as his friend turned around and grinned at him.

"Sergeant . . . I'm bearing our colors," he shouted over the incessant noise, waving them with wild abandon. "Ain't they purty?"

"Where's your musket, Jep? Where's your gun?" Shot and shell whizzed past. Jeptha shrugged as the bullets rained about them, unconcerned for his own well being.

Jeremiah saw the grim determination in his face and dropped his hand from his arm. At once he was ashamed; ashamed that for a few seconds he had despised the bravery, the incredible courage demonstrated by his friend; ashamed that his own selfish fear for his comrade's life over-shadowed the magnitude of their immediate situation.

The men had already begun to return the bloody fire inflicted upon them by the troops in blue. Some loaded and fired as they continued to ascend the hill to the stone wall. Others stopped and took deliberate aim . . . some kneeled to squeeze off their rounds, and many simply lay on the ground. There was no good way; no one way was better than another, for they were all in the open with nothing behind which to hide; nothing to protect them.

Jeremiah glanced behind him, spying some of his men at last. He recognized Sam, Andy, Killian . . . he couldn't see all of their faces for the mixture of sweat and black powder residue masked many.

They unleashed a round of musket fire. "That's it, boys!" Jeremiah cried jubilantly. "That's it! Make it good and hot! Let 'em feel the fire! Let 'em feel it! Keep it up, boys! Keep it up!" he shouted. He realized he was shooting, loading, ramming the balls home as he tried to keep pace with Jeptha. The heavy smoke burned his lungs with each breath.

The incessant ripping of musketry and the roar of cannon surrounded them. It engulfed them and threatened to consume them. The dead stretched as far as the eye could see—past the fence and down the hill until the terrain dipped out of sight.

Jeremiah was certain, for one split second, that he could hear music on the wind. It was so eerie, so strange, it made his skin crawl.

They could see the stone wall well now, though there was still a ways to go, and suddenly, as if rising from the dust, a whole legion of boys decked in blue unleashed a round of consecutive fire, the balls exploding from their muskets one right after the other in timed precision.

Suddenly, Jeptha was down. Jeremiah stopped. He saw Jep trying to rise up, and as he did, Jeremiah was at his side.

"I got it in the leg, Jeremiah. Go, now! Go!" He struggled to lift the flag. "I'll be all right, but the colors, Jeremiah, they must go forward! Take them; here," he gasped, straining to hand them over.

Jeremiah could tell Jeptha was in great pain. As he took the banner from his grasp, he realized his friend's gray trouser leg was quickly turning scarlet. Blood pooled rapidly beneath the bent limb.

"Go, I tell you!" Jeptha panted urgently. "Take them colors and get out of here!"

Jeremiah stood, bearing the tattered standard and giving one last look at his friend.

"It's all right, Jeremiah . . . I'm all right. It's only in the leg," he shouted raggedly.

Jeremiah saluted his fallen comrade, the colors fluttering at his side. "I'll see you later, Jep," he grinned, and turning, fled on up the hill.

Jeptha was glad he was gone. He didn't want Jeremiah to know how much pain he was feeling. He bent over his mangled limb, certain it was broken. It was twisted in a freakish and unnatural way, but worse than that was the hole in his knee . . . a gaping, ragged hole from which his life's blood was flowing freely. He rubbed his thigh and heard himself groan. He never knew anything could hurt so much, so terribly much. It was like a fire that licked at him.

His head felt light, his palms cold and sweaty, and he feared he might pass out. Leaning back on the ground, he looked up. The sky overhead was steel gray silver. *Odd color for a sky,* he thought. Quickly, a burst of wind blew the silver away and he could see the sun against the blue. Oh, yeah

. . . yeah . . . the smoke from the guns. He threw an arm across his fore-head to shield his eyes from the burning, yellow glare. Oh! How he hurt! What was all this clamor around him? The shrieking, the exploding, the constant roar?

The guns. The guns . . . yeah, the guns. They were in the middle of a battle . . .

His mouth felt like sawdust and sand. He groped about for his canteen, and finding it, raised it to his mouth. The water was warm, but it eased his thirst. The pain became more intense.

What happened to the flag, he wondered in alarm.

Jeremiah. I remember now . . . Jeremiah took it. Feeling himself sinking uncontrollably into darkness, he wondered if his friend had yet made it to the stone wall.

As Jeremiah left his comrade, he continued to head up the slope. The stone wall was near . . . he could see the blue, smell it almost, and the colors continued to flutter magnificently in his grasp. He felt an exhilaration he had never before known and understood the feeling Jeptha experienced when he had carried them forward. He had no idea what had happened to his musket. The only thing that seemed important was getting those colors over the wall. He was so close now!

Suddenly a gigantic force ripped the flag from its staff and sent Jeremiah tumbling; somersaulting down the hill. He blacked out.

When he opened his eyes, he was confused. Where was he? What had happened?

He sat up. His head hurt fiercely and his tongue was parched. He rubbed a hand over his face in an attempt to revive himself. His nose again had been bleeding and dried blood caked his cheeks and mouth. He groped for his canteen, only to discover it missing.

He noticed men retreating slowly from the crest of the hill; ragged, dirty, exhausted men; some alone, some in groups, some helping wounded comrades. They all had the look of failure in their eyes . . . the horror of defeat on their faces. Jeremiah knew what it meant. He jumped up. Shielding his eyes from the sun, he scanned the ridge. Some of their colors draped the stone wall; others were scattered about the field, some over men as though a shroud. Rising into the sky, behind the ledge, several stands of stars and stripes waved boldly and victoriously. Jeremiah sat back onto the ground, wanting to weep, not just for their defeat, but for the thousands of men scattered upon that hill; men who had made the supreme sacrifice.

He felt dazed and watched a small group wander past him; familiar faces. "Andy! Sam! Franklin!" Jeremiah called to his boys. They turned around slowly, as if afraid to believe they'd heard right. They stared.

Suddenly Andy hollered, "I'll be, boys! It's Jeremiah! It's the sergeant!"

They bound to his side immediately and helped to steady him as he rose. "Is it really you, Jeremiah? Blessed be!" Sam said with tremendous relief, "blessed be!"

"I need some water boys, real bad. Any of you got some?"

Three canteens were at once thrust out to him. None offered a lot, but he drained the first one dry of it's warm contents, and took a second one, splashing the water across his face to rid it of the dried, caked blood.

"You all right, McCamey?" Franklin asked, "You really all right?"

Jeremiah nodded, noticing details were already gathering up wounded men. "Reckon they'd have passed me over for dead. I musta looked a fair bad sight when you boys first see'd me." He placed a hand on the back of his neck, and rubbed it. "My head hurts somethin' awful.

"What about the rest of the boys . . . anybody know anything?"

They all stood silent. "Well?" Jeremiah demanded.

"Killian, Drew . . . a few o' the other fellas . . . they made it over that wall, Jeremiah. It was the awfullest thing I ever did see . . ." Sam declared. "If they ain't dead, they're prisoners for sure. Colonel Hartshare got himself wounded in the shoulder. He'll be all right. Lieutenant Moore, well, we ain't heard nothin' of him. Cap'n . . . he done busted a couple o' fingers . . . he's all right, Jeremiah. Seen him a short while ago. He asked 'bout you; couldn't tell him nothin', though. Jep . . . well, Sergeant, ain't got no clue as to what happened to him . . . I . . . I'm sorry."

"Jep got it in the leg, boys. I was with him. It's pretty busted up, but reckon he'll be all right." He looked about at the detail gathering wounded and surveyed the large number on the field. "Suppose he's probably been taken to the field hospital by now . . . don't reckon we could find him in all this no ways. I'm all confused as to where he fell as opposed to where I am now . . ." He looked at the haggard, defeated faces of his men. "Let's go home, boys. Maybe we'll learn more back at camp."

They began to trudge down the hill and Jeremiah turned around to take one last look at their failed goal. "We came so close, men. We came so close," he whispered through gritted teeth, squeezing his eyes tight to stop the tears.

Jeptha knew nothing else until he opened his eyes, two strange faces swimming before him. One was talking.

"This man's alive. Looks like he got it in the leg good."

"Think he's got a chance?" the other man asked.

"Yeah . . . let's get him up and load him on the wagon."

When they lifted him, the pain was excruciating, and he involuntarily cried out. Suddenly, he noticed the silence surrounding them. As he was being laid into the hospital wagon, he groped for an arm of one of the men.

"Is it over?" Jep asked feebly. "The fightin', is it over?"

"Yeah, Son, it's over," the man answered glumly.

"Well . . . how . . . how'd we do?" he asked through his pain. "Did we take that wall?"

"Not a chance, Son," the man shook his head. "Not a chance."

Jeptha closed his eyes at the answer and let the pain take him mercifully away.

It seemed as though it took the boys forever to reach camp back among Hill's corps, and the defeat weighed heavily on everyone. It showed in their faces and was heard in their words.

Some said General Longstreet didn't want to make the charge in the first place. Others said General Lee placed the blame squarely on himself. "It's all my fault," Lee had said. "I thought we were invincible."

Jeremiah wanted nothing more than to talk with his brother-in-law at the moment. "Men," he said, his heart heavy, "let us hope the enemy does not reform and force us to defend our positions now. I don't think there is much fight left in any of us this tragic day. Be cautious, in case, but do what you will. I am goin' to find the cap'n . . . perhaps he knows of any news there might be."

"Lieutenant Moore!" Jeremiah cried, startled to see the man as he arrived at Captain Kertlin's quarters. He saluted the officer, "Lieutenant . . . no one seemed to know what had become of you. I'm glad to see you all well, Sir."

"Yes, McCamey . . . reckon I can count it nothing more than Providence. So many good men have been lost or wounded this day. It is a sad, sad day for our Confederacy."

"What news do you hear, Sir?"

"Our own brigade commander, General Trimble, has been captured, Jeremiah. Of our other divisions . . . well, General Pettigrew is wounded, maybe dead. Colonel Hartshare is wounded, but it's minor. In Pickett's division, all thirteen of his colonels are down. Seven dead, six wounded. Of his three brigade commanders . . . General Kemper's been mortally hurt . . . least, they think it's mortal. General Armistead is nowhere to be found; it is rumored he's captured or killed, but no one seems to rightly know.

General Garnett," he lowered his head, "well, he's dead now, too. Shot through the head, they say."

Jeremiah groaned and thought, *What a disastrous, grisly day this has been!*

Lieutenant Moore continued to speak, "General Lee says we will move out in the morning if all wounded can be secured and head back across the Potomac; back to Virginia." He heaved a sigh.

"Cap'n Kertlin, Sir . . . is he available to see me now, do you think?"

"He busted up a hand. He's over at the field hospital havin' it seen to."

"I was aimin' on headin' that way if permissible, Sir. Private Carroll took a fair good hit in the leg. I'd like to go find him."

Lieutenant Moore looked at Jeremiah with sympathy. "Don't know that you'll be able to. I don't know how many wounded we've got . . . but I'm fair certain that by the end of today at least fifty thousand boys, some blue, some gray, will have been wounded or died on the fields of this wretched little town."

The lieutenant shrugged his shoulders and smiled wryly. "You know, McCamey," he said, "sometimes people do strange things when in combat. I understand that some North Carolina regiment had its musicians playin' polkas, waltzes and hymns as the rest of their boys were tryin' to take that hill. Don't that beat all! Ever heard o' such a thing?"

Jeremiah nodded his head. "For sure. I mean, I believe I done heard 'em, Sir. 'Twas so odd . . . hearin' snatches o' music like that amidst all them guns. Gave me the willies."

Lieutenant Moore stared at Jeremiah as though he were about to make another comment, but let the words drop. He sighed, "Go ahead, Son. Go ahead. See if you can find your friend."

Jeremiah considered getting Sam or one of the other boys to accompany him. *No,* he decided. *I'd rather see Jep alone in these circumstances.* He headed off to the field hospital by himself.

⁓

Jeremiah entered the abandoned barn being used for a hospital. Though the doors were open and light filtered in, dusk was not far off, and lanterns helped to brighten the interior. He squinted, attempting to adjust his eyes to the darkness. The warm, metallic smell of fresh blood assaulted his senses, and the sound of incessant groaning filled his ears.

Close by, he heard the grate of a saw and tried to ignore the scream of the man the surgeon was attending. Quickly, an arm was lifted from the table and carted outside by an orderly. As the doctor moved to the next patient, Jeremiah heard him shout in exasperation, "I told you! There is no more chloroform with which to knock you out or deaden the pain! Now, bite this stick and bear it like a man!" Jeremiah squeezed his eyes tight to shut it all out. *How sad,* he thought, *that such a scene should leave me so unmoved.* The battlefield carnage he'd witnessed these last two years had numbed his senses to such sights and sounds.

Where was Jeptha? Several crude tables held the pitiful, but live remnants of men who a short while ago were charging up that hill, and almost in front of him, by the door, he recognized his friend on one of them. Slowly tossing his head from side to side, Jeptha flailed his arms back and forth, striking a bizarre thought in Jeremiah: snow angels. It looked like Jeptha was making snow angels on the blood soaked plank upon which he lay. He shook his head in an effort to clear the peculiar image from his mind.

Jep's good leg slid up and down, the heel of his boot scraping against the wood in an obvious effort to bear the pain. A continuous, low moan escaped his throat.

Jeremiah grabbed a flailing arm and gripped it tightly.

Jeptha's eyes flew open, wide and glazed, looking up at his friend.

"Jeremiah . . . Jeremiah, I knew you'd come." A slight smile crossed his face and he grasped Jeremiah's forearm, holding on as tightly as his failing strength would allow.

"Jeremiah, Doc says the leg's gotta go," he spoke through obvious pain. "Don't let 'em cut it off, Jeremiah. Don't let 'em do it," he groaned, and closed his eyes again.

The surgeon, working on a young lad one table over, turned to the scene between friends. "That leg's gotta go, Son," he addressed Jeremiah without sympathy. "Knee is shattered and a primary vessel ripped. It's gotta go or he'll die for sure. Already lost too much blood. Don't know how he's holdin' on as it is."

Jeptha's eyes remained closed, but he squeezed Jeremiah's arm tighter. "It don't matter, Jeremiah. I'm ready," he whispered hoarsely, "you know I'm ready to face eternity."

"Stop it! Stop it!" Jeremiah screamed to his friend.

Jeptha's breathing came in deep, rapid gasps, so ragged that Jeremiah watched his chest rise off the table with each breath and fall back with a thud every time. His cartridge box, attached to his belt, clanked ominously against the wood, counting cadence each time he breathed.

Jeptha's eyes opened again, bright and shimmering. "Jeremiah . . ." He looked straight up as though he couldn't see, and squeezed his friend's arm again. "Jeremiah? Can you hear me? Are you there?"

Jeremiah continued to grip Jeptha's arm in his own. "I'm here, Jep. I'm here," he whispered.

"Jeremiah," a lone tear found its way out of the corner of Jeptha's eye. "Jeremiah . . . I've got no place to go," he struggled, speaking softly through his gasps. "I've got no place to go. Will you see to it that I get buried proper? Will you do that for me, Jeremiah?"

"Yes, Jep. I will, I will. But you're gonna be all right, Jep . . . you can't die on me, you hear?" Jeremiah's mouth felt parched and his heart began to pound wildly.

Jeptha continued to stare straight ahead, but nodded ever so slightly in agreement. He closed his eyes and mumbled incoherently.

Jeremiah leaned closer. "I can't understand you, Jep. What did you say?"

"Thank you, Jer . . . Jeremiah," he whispered with great effort. "God blessed me, for I . . . I couldn't have had a better friend than you." He was silent for a second, then squeezed his friend's arm one last time. "Thank you, Jeremiah." The brown eyes never reopened and suddenly his grip on the sergeant's arm relaxed. He released a final, struggling breath, and was still.

"Doc! Doc!" Jeremiah panicked.

The surgeon took a step toward the makeshift table, looking down at Jeptha's fixed form. He said nothing to Jeremiah, but called for an orderly. "This man is dead. Lost too much blood. Remove him and get another patient up here."

The orderly took a step forward.

"No! No!" Jeremiah cried in anguish, "I'll take care of him!"

Blinded by tears, he lifted the dead weight of his friend in his arms, struggling to carry him through the door. Once outside, he laid him gently on the ground, his hot tears falling on the frozen countenance. "Jep," he shouted, "don't do this to me! Jep? Jep!"

He pounded the lifeless body on the chest with his fist. "Jeptha! You quit it, ya hear?" he hollered madly. "You can't die on me!" he choked through his rage.

His friend didn't flinch, and his breath didn't come. Jeremiah laid an ear to his chest, listening in vain for the beat of a heart. When it couldn't be heard, he unashamedly began to sob.

A wisp of Jeptha's hair blew insipdly in a gentle breeze that brushed the ground; the only movement his still form would yield, and Jeremiah cradled his comrade to his chest. He felt as if his own heart would burst and all semblance of reason had shattered into a thousand tiny shards.

"Jep! Jep! Don't leave me. Please . . . please," he cried, his voice a pathetic wail.

Leaning his head upon the breast of his fallen comrade, he wept long and bitterly until exhaustion set in. Sleep overtook his weary frame as his arms grasped the dead, but most beloved friend he'd ever known.

A shake on the shoulder roused him. Captain Kertlin was at his side.

"You all right, Jeremiah?" He sucked his breath in sharply as he recognized the motionless form beneath the sergeant. "Oh, Jeremiah . . ." He groaned in sorrowful disbelief. "What can I do? What can I possibly do?"

"Help me, John . . ." his voice trembled, "help me get him home . . . to my folks' farm."

CHAPTER NINETEEN

As fall heroes struggling for their homes, comrades
So fell the soldier in gray
Their honor unsullied lives comrades,
For that which enobles brave men.

By the following evening, tents were struck, the few there were, and the weary, decimated Army of Northern Virginia began its move southward. A successful crossing of the Potomac River would once again find them on Virginian soil. The devastation at Gettysburg had been great and the boys in gray desperately needed a time of renewal and restrengthening. The rear guard of the retreat, made up of A. P. Hill's corps and Company G, guarded a wagon train of wounded men that stretched over seven miles.

Captain Kertlin made arrangements, to the best of his ability, to see that Jeptha Hamilton Carroll was returned to the land of the southern Shenandoah. The soldier would be interred on the McCamey farm, and Jeremiah felt an overwhelming gratitude toward his brother-in-law, for such arrangements were not an easy task to accomplish. Most men surviving the charge, only to die hours later, were buried in mass graves. The terrible heat, humidity and sheer number of dead souls left no alternative. The most severely wounded simply had to be left behind at the field hospital.

Jeremiah, feeling the burden of his grief, knew he had two choices. In his pain he could give in to the overwhelming desire to let mourning consume him, or he could face his loss, bearing the deaths of his friends as a badge; a symbol of unsurpassed valor and great commitment to their cause. To give into despair would defame those comrades he'd loved and lost, and that, he knew he could not, would not do.

He marveled at the changes time and events had wrought in him. A year and a half ago, the death of Cy made him want to run. With Jep gone, he could only purpose to fight that much harder.

The trek southward, though not easy, was steady. Heavy rains made the roads muddy and difficult. By the time the Potomac was reached, the waters had started to rise. General Lee could not breathe easily until his army was safely across the swelling river. The only words he uttered as the last man crossed, he did so softly. "Thank God," he said. His fear that the Federal army would pursue them was cut short by the flooding of the stream. The Union Army could not follow them now.

On July 14, camp was set up in the little settlement of Bunker Hill. Here, the Army of Northern Virginia would have time to rest and recover before crossing the Blue Ridge, to head south of the Rappahannock once more.

Recent rains made the night air chilly and firelight flickered next to the boys' makeshift shelter. They mostly slept out in the open, but had rigged up a covering of torn and tattered canvas to ward off the damp elements.

Jeremiah's unit was less than half its original size, and his mind weighed heavily on such thoughts this evening. He sat and stared at the dancing, orange flames.

"Sergeant, you sure are quiet tonight," Sam said, stirring the fire.

Jeremiah looked up from sipping the warm grain beverage he was trying to enjoy. Suddenly he put the cup down. "Ain't no use, lads. I don't care how hard I try to pretend this here stuff is real coffee, my imagination cuts me short."

"Well, surely Jeremiah," Andy speculated, "that ain't what's demandin' so much o' your attention this evenin'."

"I was just thinkin' on our men, boys. Just thinkin' on our men," he sighed. "Wish we coulda learned about Killian and Drew before havin' to withdraw from Pennsylvania."

"Yeah," Franklin said laconically, "if we'd not gotten so separated at that wall I might know the answer."

"Or, be part of the problem!" Sam declared. "Well, no use to talk of all that now."

Jeremiah was contemplating something else, and rose.

"Men, I'm goin' to speak with Cap'n a few minutes."

When he arrived at Captain Kertlin's quarters, all was quiet, but light flickered from within the canvas walls. "Cap'n!" Jeremiah called. "John . . . I'd really like a word with you if you're available."

"C'mon in, McCamey," his voice answered, "c'mon in. I'd like the company."

Jeremiah entered the yellow-lit interior of his brother-in-law's tent. John Kertlin was seated at his camp desk, a stack of correspondence piled in front of him. Next to it all sat a picture of Priscilla.

Without waiting for an invitation, Jeremiah pulled up a stool and sat at the corner of the desk. He had begun to feel a comfortable familiarity with Priscilla's husband that he revealed only when the two were apart from the other men. He had no desire to foster the idea that he had anything but utmost respect for Captain Kertlin, regardless of their kinship.

Jeremiah reached out and gently picked up the picture of his sister, glancing at it fondly for a few seconds before replacing it. "That's the picture you made her sit for right after you was married, ain't it? If I recall her words, she weren't none too happy with it. Said it made her appear stiff and stern."

"The one she took home of me was worse!" the captain chuckled. Picking up the daguerreotype, he gazed at it lovingly.

"She'd sure be a sight for sore eyes, John. I think about home so much sometimes it hurts."

The captain gave him a long, hard stare. "Well, Jeremiah, you ought to try it sometime . . . . go on . . . get married, and then have to leave your wife after less than four days . . . not knowing if you'll ever see her again. Let me tell you, love for my country and strength from God is the only thing that keeps my sense of duty from bein' twisted sometimes. It is agony; it's cruel! Sometimes I'm so miserable . . ." He put his head in his hands, and shook it. "You realize, Jeremiah, next week we'll have been married three-quarters of a year, and I ain't spent but three days with her?" He looked up. "My greatest comfort is in knowing that she is safe at home and waiting for me.

"Now. What's up? Or is this just a little friendly visit?"

"Naw . . ." Jeremiah answered. "Well . . . yes; I mean, John . . . my cousin Geoffrey . . . you know, the Yank . . ."

"Yeah . . . he's a real favorite of Priscilla's . . . least he was."

"Yeah . . . we was all pretty close before this war changed things. Anyway, his folks, Uncle Boyton and Aunt Mary, live fair close to here. I'd say less than half a day's walk, in toward Charlestown, and I'd sure like to go see 'em. I'd sure like to . . . and as 'Cilla's husband, I'd be obliged if you'd join me; they always doted on her as the first girl in the family. Reckon we could get permission for such a visit?"

"Let me talk to the colonel, Jeremiah. See what he says, though I really can't think of nothin' that would make him object. The Yankees can't be much of a threat for a while. And . . . and thanks, Jeremiah. I appreciate your wanting my company."

Jeremiah stared at his captain. "John . . . I joined up with this company two years ago to learn soldierin', to serve a country I love and be with some friends." He smiled ruefully. "I gained me a brother-in-law in the bargain . . . I've lost me my two friends, John; my country is strugglin . . . Sometimes it's hard not to be overwhelmed. Don't misunderstand. I've got some good boys, Cap'n. Men I'm mighty fond of and proud to serve with." He sighed.

"Jeremiah, I know the heartache you have to feel; the pain you've suffered in the breaking of lifelong bonds . . ."

Jeremiah nodded, wiping a tear from the corner of his eye. "I can't even let myself think on it, Cap'n. Sometimes I wake up in the night, rememberin' things we done together, things we laughed over and fights we had. All them years I shared with Jep and Cy—they can't be just wiped away, and it . . . it don't seem fair . . . it don't seem one bit fair that I'm still here and they . . . they . . .

"As Jep died, he thanked me, Cap'n; thanked me for bein' his friend! I shoulda been thankin' him, for givin' his life to his country . . . I shoulda thanked Jep and Cy both, but I didn't Cap'n . . . and if we don't win this war, then who's gonna do it? Who's gonna thank them or any of our boys that's died?"

"It will have to be left for future generations to do, Jeremiah. That can't be changed. Win or lose, none of our lives are ever gonna be the same again. It's hard to understand sometimes, I know. Look at me . . . almost a whole family of brothers in the army, and yet not one of us has been hurt . . . not seriously. It's hard not to question things when you learn stories like about the Gordon brothers in Company A. You know about them?"

Jeremiah shook his head.

"Well, their Mama has sent seven out of nine sons to fight for their country . . . and all seven has died." The captain's eyes misted over as he continued, "She says they all want to fight, and she's willin' her country have 'em, if needed. Now, there's courage, Jeremiah. There's true heart. But if you wanna talk fair . . . what's so fair about that?"

Jeremiah smiled slightly and looked up at the captain. "Reckon one reason I'm so fond of you is because you always help me put things into perspective."

Captain Kertlin reached out and slapped him on the knee. "Jeremiah, I've a mind to go find Colonel Hartshare tonight. Perhaps he'll give us an all right for goin' as soon as tomorrow."

"Oh . . . that'd be good, John," he said excitedly, "real good."

"In the morning, then, perhaps," Captain Kertlin asserted.

Jeremiah rose, turning to go, and suddenly looked back. "Cap'n, I meant to ask about the hand."

The officer looked down at the dirty, ragged bandage. "Ah, it's all right . . . glad it ain't my right hand. Doc says them fingers most likely will be crooked when they're healed up."

"Well, John, good night. See you tomorrow. And John . . . thank you."

"Good night, Jeremiah," the captain nodded.

Jeremiah woke long before dawn, hoping with anticipation that Captain Kertlin had been able to procure permission for them to walk to Charlestown. As he stirred a fire to heat water, he heard the slow easy gait of horses' hoofs. Suddenly a voice cut through the darkness.

"Jeremiah! You're up! Good." Captain Kertlin's face was illuminated as the fire jumped to life.

"John! Cap'n! You took me by surprise. I wasn't 'spectin' to see you this early." Jeremiah eyed the horses. "What's up?" he asked.

"Good news, brother-in-law! Colonel Hartshare heartily gave permission for us to travel to Charlestown today. Not only that . . . I done us one better than walkin'. I got my horse here and Lieutenant Moore was more than obliging when I asked to borrow his mount for the day. So, you see . . . we get to ride!" he grinned, handing reins to Jeremiah.

"Brother-in-law, you do beat all!" Jeremiah laughed good-naturedly. "Let me go tell Sam I'm goin'."

Momentarily, he jumped on to the back of the gray charger that belonged to Lieutenant Moore. "Good night, John! I ain't been on a horse in a while . . . hope I can still ride!" He leaned over and gave the animal a pat on the neck. "Good boy," he cooed soothingly, "good boy. You ready for an adventure today?

"I've been thinkin', John," he said as the two headed out of camp, "Aunt Mary is sure a fine cook. Maybe she'll be glad enough to see us to feed a couple o' hungry kinfolks."

"Just what do these people of yours do, McCamey?"

"Uncle Boyton has a fine mercantile business. At least, it was before all this unpleasantness. Me an' Geoffrey was most like brothers, even though we lived a distance apart. We spent many summer hours idling away time together . . . me, Cy, Jep and Geoff. You know, it was fine when we was young 'uns . . . though Jep and Geoffrey almost always seemed at odds about somethin'." He turned and looked at the captain as they rode steadily along. "If you remember, Jep had a pretty hot temper when he first joined up in this war."

Captain Kertlin nodded, never shifting his gaze, just listening.

Jeremiah continued, "Jep had the temper and Geoff had the stubbornness. Umm, umm. Sometimes when the two would get to goin' on with each other, Cy and me would just kinda find a place to hide. When Geoffrey went off to Washington College he was around more, seein' that Lexington ain't as far from New Church as Charlestown. He was studyin' accounts and stuff like that; wanted to help with his Pa's store. Geoffrey's a good man, John. Always was fiercely patriotic . . . only we didn't quite see eye to eye politically speaking. I didn't want the country dissolved . . . but, well, no use on talkin' 'bout that now. I still can't believe he was willing to compromise the freedom of his state," Jeremiah shook his head, "and not defend his own soil. It's like fightin' against your own people." He sighed, "I blame it on that Adams blood we share. For myself," he laughed, "I reckon the fierce Celtic blood of the McCamey's rule!" He glanced at his brother-in-law.

"I've just rambled on, John. Sorry. Wish we could be seein' our own folks, you and me, but this is almost as good."

"I'd just like to see my wife," the captain mumbled, and no more words were shared for a while.

Soon they were turning off the main road close to Charlestown. "They have a nice place here. Do a little farmin'. It ain't much farther, " Jeremiah said.

Before long, the men approached a nice, but weathered, small frame house. A large front porch made it a welcome sight and Jeremiah dismounted from his horse excitedly. "C'mon, John!" he said full of enthusiasm.

The sergeant bound up the steps and rapped loudly on the door. His expectancy made him impatient and he rapped again.

Soon the door was thrown open and a woman stood in disbelief, hands to her mouth. Jeremiah recognized her at once. "Aunt Mary!" he spoke softly, folding her into his arms.

She placed her hands on his face. "Jeremiah! Is it really you? Oh my! Look at you! I hardly recognize you!"

Suddenly a man appeared behind the woman, and Jeremiah identified the tired, aging frame of his Uncle Boyton. Stepping out onto the porch, the man closed the door behind them.

"Jeremiah, my boy!" he exclaimed, giving his nephew a hearty hand-shake. "How good to see you! How glad we are you're here!"

"Uncle Boyton and Aunt Mary, I've got someone special to introduce to you." He motioned for the captain to step up beside him. "This here is Captain John Kertlin . . . your nephew by marriage. This is 'Cilla's husband."

"Oh, my!" Aunt Mary voiced. "'Cilla was our first niece and she is something special! I do hope she is well."

Uncle Boyton shook the man's hand. "I reckon under other circum-stances I might be sayin' this is a pleasure," he spoke.

Jeremiah and Captain Kertlin exchanged furtive glances. *What an odd comment,* they seemed to say to each other.

Uncle Boyton continued, almost stiffly, "It is good to see you, Jeremiah. And I am certainly glad to be acquainted with Mr. Kertlin here, seein' as he's Pricilla's husband. And boys, you're most welcome to come in if . . . if you'll just take them uniforms off."

Jeremiah and Captain Kertlin stared at each other in astonishment. This certainly wasn't the reception they expected.

Jeremiah spoke first. "Thank you, Uncle, Sir. There's nothin' we'd rather do right now, I 'spose, than to come in and visit a spell. But don't reckon we'll be doin' that. Just come to pay our respects, seein' as we was close by. Figure we best be on our way. It is good to see you folks." He could not hide the disappointment in his voice. "Glad to see you well. Hope Geoffrey's all right. Saw him back in December at Fredericksburg. 'Spose he done told you. It was a good meetin'."

"He told us," Uncle Boyton said curtly. "I'm sorry you can't come in."

"Well, uh, take care of yourselves," Jeremiah said hesitantly. "It's good to see you."

Both men turned, walking off the porch together. After mounting their horses and turning reins back toward Bunker Hill, Captain Kertlin broke the silence.

"Well, well, brother-in-law, they sure were friendly folks," he said sarcastically.

"I'm sorry, John. I'm sorry. I was expectin' a warmer welcome than this." He felt so very sad.

A scraping thud came from the porch behind them, but neither man turned around.

"Jeremiah," the soft sound of a young man's voice called to him hoarsely. "Wait, Jeremiah . . . don't go."

The familiar voice was filled with a hollow emptiness. The sergeant abruptly stopped his horse and stared back over his shoulder. A strange form on the porch greeted his eyes, and when Jeremiah realized at whom he was looking, they filled with tears of compassion.

"John, wait . . ." he cried, whipping his horse around and trotting back up to the house.

A crutch under each arm held up the fellow standing there. One leg was bent and twisted and the side of his neck and face disfigured by frightful scarring.

"Geoffrey?" Jeremiah asked incredulously, "Geoffrey?"

Tears spilled down the scarred cheek.

"Geoffrey . . . what happened? Why didn't your Ma and Pa tell me you were here? What is goin' on?"

Jeremiah leaped off his horse and bound back up to the porch. He held his cousin for a moment in a warm, sympathetic embrace. Geoffrey didn't resist, and when Jeremiah let go, pulled a handkerchief from his blue pants. They were of the uniform of a Federal soldier, but a faded red shirt, not a blue woolen jacket, completed the outfit.

Geoffrey wiped the tears from his face. "Say, Jeremiah . . . sorry. I was just overwhelmed to see you come ridin' up here today."

"Why didn't your Ma and Pa tell me you were home? Geoffrey, what . . ." he let his words drop.

"They didn't want you to see me like this . . . and didn't think I'd want to see you. They truly are glad you came, Cousin . . . but you're the enemy . . . and I'm sorry. Pa ain't lettin' you come in with them uniforms on."

"They ain't comin' off, Geoff," Jeremiah claimed adamantly.

"No, I don't 'spect they would. Give me a hand, Jeremiah. If you'll help me down these here steps, we can sit out yonder under the big hickory and visit for a spell. Who's your friend, Cousin?"

"This here is Captain John Kertlin . . . my company captain and 'Cilla's husband. John, meet cousin Geoffrey Adams."

The captain dismounted and facing Geoffrey, extended his hand. "So we meet at last," he said, shaking Geoffrey's warmly.

"Geoffrey . . . what happened?" Jeremiah inquired as his cousin hobbled on his crutches to the shade of the tree.

"Give me a hand, fellas," Geoffrey requested, needing help to sit down and stretch out his twisted limb.

"Well, it's like this. Right after Fredericksburg, back in December, we was riddin' ourselves of some unused powder . . . to keep your Rebel hands off of it. Somethin' happened and a bit exploded on me. Burned me up real good, all down my left side. Leg don't work no more. Spent near six months at the Federal hospital in Washington. Took real good care of me, but my soldierin' days are done." He shifted painfully, looking up at the stately tree that provided a canopy for them.

"You know, Jeremiah . . . this old tree kinda reminds me of that maple on your farm. Lots o' good hours spent there. I reckon the last time was . . . when would it have been? The summer of '60? Reckon so. Me and Miss Lucille whiled away some pleasant time in its shade. Now, that was some summer!"

He turned to tell the story to John Kertlin. "Me and Jep Carroll had the idea of courtin' the same lady . . . beautiful she was, too. Lucille Moxley. Remember that, Jeremiah?" he started laughing.

"We were both foolish boys, but that hot-headed Jep challenged me to a duel over her. Can you believe that? A duel!" Geoffrey laughed again. "Then," he continued, "she just up and says she don't believe she likes either one of us. Well . . . if that didn't beat all." He suddenly reached up, touching his scarred face and neck. "Reckon I'll not be havin' a problem like that again.

"Say, where is Jep? He didn't follow you fellas along today? Reckon not," he snickered, "if he knew you was comin' here." He turned to Captain Kertlin. "Jep Carroll and I ain't never got along real well."

"Jep is dead," Jeremiah stated bluntly. "Died at Gettysburg. Cy and Jep is both dead."

Geoffrey hung his head. "Is that a fact?" he sighed, looking back up at his cousin. "Well, Jeremiah . . . I am sorry."

Nothing was said for several minutes, as all three men seemed to be lost in separate thoughts.

Suddenly, Mary Adams appeared from the house, carrying a tray. It was loaded down with apple cider and sandwiches made from fresh, warm bread and slabs of ham. It had been a while since the boys in gray had sampled such fare.

The remainder of the afternoon was spent in idle talk. To Jeremiah, merely being close to family was a balm to his soul, and even though Uncle Boyton didn't appear again, at least he didn't object to their stay outside. He felt sure the visit was good for Geoffrey, too.

As the sun began its escape into the western sky, Captain Kertlin looked overhead. "Sergeant," he said, "we'd best be goin'. We've only permission to be gone the day."

Jeremiah knew the captain was right, but today it had been almost easy to forget they were in the middle of a war.

The warm, quiet day, the company of his cousin, the idle conversation, reminiscing, and good food made the fighting seem so far away. Jeremiah felt greatly renewed.

"Well, Geoff," he said rising to leave, "don't know when I'll see you again. Don't know if I'll see you again if this war keeps up much longer. But thanks for today." He helped his cousin to his feet. "Tell your folks so long for me," he said, giving his cousin a quick embrace. "After the war then, huh?"

Captain Kertlin shook his hand and Geoffrey Adams watched sadly as they rode out of sight.

CHAPTER TWENTY

Long ago we were falling fast comrades
Our numbers daily much thinner grew
Our courage the cause could not win, comrades
When the men in the ranks were so few!

The first of August, the Army of Northern Virginia broke camp and continued their journey south. Crossing the Blue Ridge, the men headed for the Rappahannock River and their familiar territory of the previous spring.

Hunger, a constant and prevailing problem, caused most of the men to become quite good at foraging food. It was difficult at first, for to forage meant to take, and some of the men equated such actions with stealing. It was a concept that didn't coincide with their fierce pride in honor, but empty stomachs almost always won out.

Once camp across the Rappahannock was reached, the soldiers fell into a routine that saw little more than an occasional skirmish. Provisions increased and even some new clothing was issued.

General Lee did all he could to see that his weary soldiers were replenished and restrengthened. Much was beyond his control, but he took care of his men to the best of his ability. The troops understood his love for them, his compassion and concern, and openly demonstrated their affection and devotion. For General Lee to be among his troops meant facing a mob of cheering, worshipful men. At times, the General felt over-whelmed by it, often awed by it, but always, he was humbled by it.

Within a week of returning to camp, letters came—stacks of letters, thousands of letters. It had been so long since any postal service had run for the soldiers that there was no one left out of receiving mail.

Jeremiah carried a pile back to his tent for reading. Sifting through them all, he discovered several from his parents, others from Prissy and Violet, even one from Bonniejean.

There were a couple in handwriting he didn't recognize. Too hungry for news from home, he tossed them aside, deciding to read them last. Tearing into the first letter, he devoured its contents, savoring the words, repeating the process with each missive he opened. Some of the news made him laugh, other pieces made him sad. Some stirred his soul, but all made him homesick. The last letter from his family made him weep, for it bore the story of Jeptha's homecoming and how he was laid to rest.

Jeremiah felt glad there had been a mother's tears for his friend, even if they had come from his own mother's eyes. He was grateful to learn that many in the community came to mourn the loss of one of their own. And he was exceedingly thankful to his father for choosing a place not only in their own family plot, but one that overlooked the sweeping hills and beautiful valleys that Jep once called home, too. His comrade had been given the hero's farewell he deserved.

Jeremiah picked up the last letters. With the news from home safely tucked away in his heart, he could concentrate on them, and wondered from whom they came. Opening the first one, he learned from Preacher Foxly of the words spoken over Jeptha, and received thoughts of encouragement for himself. He was grateful for the kind regard.

Scrutinizing the last piece of mail, he could not imagine who sent it. Slipping his finger beneath the flap, the paper crackled as it unfolded.

Dear Jeremiah,

I am being so bold as to write a letter to you because I fondly remember our meeting at the Chimborazo Hospital gala in Richmond almost a year ago. I had looked forward to your calling on me, but I know your valiant army was summoned to duty. I have often wondered how you are.

Jeremiah scanned the top of the letter for a date. It had been written more than ten weeks ago.

I am prompted to write to you because I have met your friend's mother, Martha Ash. We have become quite amiable. As your sister, Violet, keeps in touch with her, I found out how to address a letter to you. I hope you do not mind.

The mill is as busy as ever, and our valley so beautiful this time of year. I often think of our brave men fighting in defense of our home. How I long to support your efforts! There is not much I can do short of praying, and I do that plenty. Deo Vindice. God is our defender, Jeremiah.
I hope this finds you very well.
Respectfully,
Kathleen Melinda Christie

A broad smile spread across his face as he read, and reread the words. He had not allowed himself to think of Katie Melinda for a long time. Her letter made his heart lighter and he immediately set to the task of answering his mail.

As the Army of Northern Virginia continued to rebuild, great battles took place in the deeper south. In September, General Longstreet was dispatched to northern Georgia where his corps helped to win the bloody battle at Chickamauga. Summer started to fade into autumn. The weather turned cooler and the fighting began to heat up.

General Meade moved his army in blue to a place called Culpeper Courthouse. General Lee desired greatly to come between this army and Washington, D.C. The middle of October saw a plan put into action. Lee would flank Meade's army, and General A. P. Hill's corps became the advance guard. On October 14, they met the enemy at a place called Bristoe Station.

A railroad embankment concealed the vastly superior numbers of the Federal army. Hill's corps was repulsed with many men killed and wounded. The Yankees captured over four hundred Southern soldiers.

Jeremiah learned Charlestown was overrun by the Union Army. He thought of the visit he and Captain Kertlin made several weeks back and had no doubt Geoffrey and his family were elated.

The little ragged army in gray kept on the move. Four days after the fiasco at Bristoe Station, Captain Kertlin summoned his brother-in-law.

"Cap'n, what can I do for you?" Jeremiah asked as he approached his quarters.

Captain Kertlin sat thoughtfully on a log in front of a fire outside his tent. Looking up at Jeremiah, he grinned, "Just got a little word I thought'd be fun to pass on to you."

Jeremiah plopped down on another log across from the captain. "What's up, John?" he questioned, staring into the fire.

"Word just come in that General Imboden has run them blue bellies out of Charlestown!"

Jeremiah eyes lit up, and a laugh escaped his throat. "You don't say?" he shook his head. "Oh, how I'd have loved to have been there!"

"Yeah, it's quite a story. The blue boys was in every building in the center o' town . . . all drill holed for muskets and the courtyard was fortified with wooden planks. But Imboden demanded the Yankee colonel surrender, and the Yankee colonel asked for an hour to consider it. Then General Imboden says, 'I'll give you five minutes,' so the Yankee colonel says, 'Well, take me if you can!' so Imboden opened up on the building with his artillery not two hundred yards away. After only 'bout half a dozen shells, the enemy was driven out into the street. When the Yankee cavalry got there, one volley was exchanged, and them blue bellies simply threw down their guns and surrendered unconditionally!"

The Captain and Jeremiah both chortled at the vision of it all. "Where'd you come by this story?" Jeremiah asked as he wiped tears from his eyes. He had laughed until he cried.

"Lieutenant Moore been over with Colonel Tristan and some pals. Word come in with a courier or scout or somethin'."

Suddenly Captain Kertlin grew sober. "Of course, that hoard of Yankees at Harper's Ferry is bound to have gotten word by now and I'm sure they're on their way to push Imboden out. The Yankees have vastly superior numbers to Imboden's boys, so I do suppose they'll be forced to withdraw, but Jeremiah . . . I'd love to have been with your Adams kin while all this was happenin', especially that Uncle o' yours!" John Kertlin laughed again, and he and Jeremiah whiled away the evening in enjoyable, but idle conversation.

The next morning found them on the move once more. Being sent back to the Rappahannock, Hill's corps was to guard the west side of the Alexandria and Orange Railroad. On November 7, a great battle erupted on the river when an overwhelming tide of soldiers in blue advanced across Kelly's Ford and attacked. The sheer number of enemy caused mass confusion. Nearly two thousand boys in gray were captured, and the position on the Rappahannock was lost. There was nothing Lee could do but command a return to the south side of the Rapidan River.

Twenty days later, the tides were turned at Germanna Ford. When Meade's Yankee army tried to spread the Confederate troops and capture their wagon train, they were driven off with a terrible destruction. The blow dealt to Meade's army was so severe the he was forced to retreat into winter quarters. Once more, the goal of capturing the Confederate capital of Richmond was "put off" for another year.

～

The winter of 1864 was cold and wet, and the men settled into a period of inactivity. The battered Army of Northern Virginia needed just such a time for recovery. The horrendous afflictions suffered the previous six months had left the pitiful ranks thin and weary.

The predominate problems were malnutrition and the illnesses caused by such. Foraging details were sent out daily in order to help supplement the scant and bad diet on which the men were forced to rely.

Drill was constant, but the men found other diversions as well to help pass the monotony. Card games, chess and checkers were popular. Reading, for those who could read, was a great way to pass the time. Books and papers were shared until worn out. Singing was another way in which the men found entertainment. Everyday there were large gatherings for a riotous time of song. Jeremiah's men often found themselves in the center of such, Andy being in demand for his talents.

Jeremiah's favorite pastime was writing letters, but ink and paper had become almost scarce, and mail was extremely slow. He waited for an answer from his letter to Katie Melinda. It never came.

By the time the end of March rolled around, the army in gray was equipped with new recruits and rested men. However, the lasting block-ade of Southern ports continued to make necessary supplies scarce. The spirit of the men remained unbroken, nonetheless, and one new recruit remarked, ". . . after a week in the Army of Northern Virginia, I am convinced there is nothing this army cannot do."

April 1 brought welcome mail from postal lines that became sluggish toward the end of winter. Nearly every man in Company G received a letter, and an entire afternoon was spent around a fire built to take the chill off the cool April day, while letters were opened, read and reread. Three times Andy had Sam read to him the mail he received from his sister, and the corporal also enjoyed several pieces of news from home.

Most of the men had looked at their mail many times over before Jeremiah found a quiet chance to open his. Eagerly he scanned the envelopes before him in hopes of finding a letter from Miss Christie. There was not one, so he ripped into a piece that he recognized as 'Cilla's.

"This can't be!" he suddenly declared in disbelief. "I'll not have it! It's utter foolishness!" He threw his remaining letters down, unread, and clutching the one open in his hand, shot up from the log upon which he was sitting.

"Sergeant, is there a problem?" Sam asked in concern.

"I'll say there is! I must go see the captain!" Jeremiah replied angrily, storming off.

"Cap'n!" he began shouting as soon as he was in view of the officer's quarters. "John!" he bellowed, forgetting formality. Lieutenant Moore looked up from his outside post, startled.

"Lieutenant Moore, I must see Captain Kertlin immediately!" Jeremiah demanded.

John Kertlin stood in the doorway of his tent, sleepy-eyed. He obviously had been roused from an afternoon slumber.

"McCamey! Cool down! You're talking to a superior officer here," he charged.

Jeremiah caught himself and saluted the lieutenant.

"My apologies, Sir. I have been overcome by the moment."

Lieutenant Moore returned the salute, but before he could utter a word, Jeremiah turned to the captain.

Shaking the letter in his hand, he asked, "John, ah . . . Cap'n . . . did you hear anything from Priscilla in today's mail?"

John Kertlin held back his tent flap, signaling Jeremiah to enter. "I wondered how long it would take you to come lookin' for me," he said as Jeremiah stepped inside.

"So, you have gotten news?"

Captain Kertlin nodded his head and Jeremiah threw himself down onto a stool as his leader sat at his desk.

"John," Jeremiah started, looking up at his brother-in-law, "what . . . what did 'Cilla tell you? What did she say?"

The captain picked up a letter from his desk and scanned the contents until he found the words he knew Jeremiah sought. He began reading aloud:

. . . John, father has joined the army. I don't quite know how to feel or what to say, but he says he must do his part . . . that this war goes on and on and that all able men must do what is necessary; they must fight for their homes and their families. And John, it is not just the older men; young boys are going too . . . thirteen, fourteen, fifteen-year-olds. Oh! This is so terrible! Mother is beside herself. First her son, now her husband. Violet and I try daily to stoke her patriotic fires, but she is momentarily overcome . . .

Jeremiah shook his head. "Poor mother," he mumbled. "John! My father is too old for this . . . for the kind of hardships required of us!"

"He's patriotic, is he not? Wasn't he proud of your decision to fight for the South?"

"Yeah . . . he never said so; my Pa's a man of few words, as you well know . . . but I always knew . . . always knew he had pride in me."

"It's like this, Jeremiah." John Kertlin hesitated in passing the latest information to his brother-in-law. "This is not well circulated news, but the Yankee army once more has started to invade our little valley. Cavalry . . . maybe under General Sheridan, I'm not really sure . . . is beginning to slowly infiltrate the area with blue bellies."

Groaning, Jeremiah threw back his head and covered his face with a hand. "John, there is no one there to defend our people; our families. No one to protect them but . . ." He paused, suddenly realizing the truth. "No one to look after them but . . . young boys . . . and . . . old men . . ." he punctuated each word slowly. "Young boys and old men." He sighed heavily, and looked at his brother-in-law. "I want to go home, John."

"Well, so do I, Jeremiah! But we can't . . . I do believe, however, that General Lee will soon dispatch General Ewell's or General Early's corps to the valley in order to meet this new threat. In the meantime, we must be of good faith. I believe it is only a local militia unit that's been organized, not an official regiment, which your father has joined. They'll remain at home unless there is an impending threat, an emergency of some sort. If things start lookin' real bad, do you think I'd leave my precious wife in such a situation? I'll send Priscilla and your mother and sisters packing, to stay with my folks in Staunton. But if, and until, such becomes necessary, I think we're concerned needlessly," he finished.

Jeremiah stared at his brother-in-law. "I hope you're right, John. I hope you're right."

The sound of a loud voices and laughter greeted them from outside. Captain Kertlin raised his eyebrows. "Sounds like Lieutenant Moore has some company . . . I know that voice, Jeremiah!" he said, rising excitedly. Jeremiah followed him outside where a fine looking cavalry officer chatted animatedly with Lieutenant Moore. He turned and looked at the captain.

"Johnny-boy!" he said, saluting him with laughter. "I'll be! It's really you!" He grabbed Captain Kertlin's hand and shook it vigorously.

"Gill! What a sight for sore eyes! Where did you come from?" the captain laughed, slapping him on the back.

"Aw . . . I been on a reconnaissance for J. E. B. . . . for General Stuart. Scoutin' out some o' them Yankee positions and seein' if we can't head General Sheridan off."

Jeremiah and Captain Kertlin glanced at each other. "Where is this Sheridan right now? Heard tell he was movin' toward the Shenandoah Valley," Captain Kertlin voiced.

"Aw, he's had some men trickle that way . . . nothin' significant. Ol' Grant has ordered him down toward Richmond, and that, my boys, is where I'm headed. But I heard tell this place was home to you, Johnny-boy, and just couldn't resist stoppin' in to pay my respects. It's been a while!"

"Sure has! Since before the Valley Campaign . . ." John Kertlin grinned at him. "Captain?" he said, noticing the insignia he wore. "Since when did you catch up with me in rank?"

"Sine J. E. B. and I become friends!" he laughed at his own irreverence. "No, seriously . . ." he continued, "it was after Chancellorsville and the loss of General Jackson." He hung his head, "That was a sad fact, now, weren't it? General Stuart was awfully fond of that man."

"Gill," Captain Kertlin spoke, "let me introduce you to Sergeant Jeremiah McCamey. Jeremiah, this here is Gillam Averette . . . a roommate of mine at the Military Institute."

Jeremiah saluted the officer.

"McCamey here . . . now there's somethin' special 'bout him, Gill. So happens he's my brother-in-law."

Captain Averette's mouth dropped open. "You don't say, Johnny-boy! So you done got yourself hitched? I can't believe it!" He pounded him on the back and turned to Jeremiah.

"Your sister must be some fine gal, 'cause this ol' boy here once told us he weren't never gettin' married."

Shaking his head, he again looked at Captain Kertlin. "I still can't believe it!"

Dropping the subject, John Kertlin addressed his friend seriously. "So, Gill . . . tell me the cavalry's philosophy of this war."

"Well, Johnny-boy . . . Sergeant McCamey . . . it's like this. Just the other day, J. E. B. Stuart says to us, says '. . . well, we're all gonna die in this war. I just ask that I do it leadin' a cavalry charge!' and I reckon that 'bout sums it up! General Stuart's a grand officer to serve under, John. I sure do like that man. You, Johnny-boy, should have gone with the cavalry."

Captain Kertlin laughed, "No . . . don't believe so. I never was that fine a horseman, Gill, and you know it."

Jeremiah turned to his captain, "Cap'n . . . don't wanna interrupt your reunion none, so I reckon I'll be goin'. As always, I appreciate your insight on things. S'pose I'm a mite less troubled . . . I still don't like it, though. I'll see you later.

"Captain Averette," he saluted the man, "it has been a pleasure."

CHAPTER TWENTY-ONE

God shield us, boys!
Here breaks the day,
the stars begin to fade
Now steady here, fall in! Fall in!
Forward the old brigade!

By the spring of 1864, Abraham Lincoln had placed General Ulysses S. Grant in command of the entire Union Army. Grant had proven himself the previous summer by taking Vicksburg, the mighty city on the Mississippi River, at the same time Gettysburg was won. President Lincoln liked this man.

The spring campaign of the Army of Northern Virginia opened up with Lincoln's new man fully in charge of the enemy troops. Grant had one goal: ON TO RICHMOND, and he fell on Lee's forces the 5th of May in that frightful, incredible, ominous growth of woods called The Wilderness.

The first day of fighting began with skirmishing about dawn. As the morning advanced, the battle intensified. Thicket and brush would not allow for the use of cannon, so the Federals assailed the Confederates with hot, furious musket fire. Grinding into the gray troops, the Union Army sent them falling back in great disorder.

General John B. Gordon and his brigade of Georgians were ordered to charge the enemy line. They delivered a brilliant, crushing blow, smashing back the boys in blue; routing them with terrible slaughter.

Hill's corps, several miles behind, listened to the soft, distant roar of battle throughout the day. As the skirmishing continued long into the night, they grew tense and anxious, longing to be part of the brawl.

The next morning Jeremiah woke his men. "Up, boys! Up! We've been ordered out," his voice issued forth with authority. "Get your gear; quickly now, men! Quickly! Fall into line. We got a distance to go."

The soldiers scrambled about, excited and ready to join the fray. The more miles they put behind them, the closer they came to the sound of the guns. At nightfall, they stopped and bivouacked out in the open, eager for sunrise. Many men didn't sleep well; some didn't sleep at all. When the order came at dawn to fall in, they did so defiantly, zealously.

As their feet pounded the ground in determination, a brisk round of small arms fire rang out near by. "Sergeant, there's action ahead!" Sam cried. "I'm goin' to the rear of our unit . . . I'll act as file closer to help keep the men in good order."

"Right Sam," Jeremiah replied, "I'll take the front. Let's keep alert."

The cause of the matter soon became evident. Dismounted Union cavalry had been encountered, but the ranks in gray were able to brush them off quickly and their march continued.

By 2 P.M., Company G became part of a front six miles long. They were covered by undergrowth so thick it was impenetrable.

The rapid fire of Union muskets shredded everything in, or out, of sight. Rata, tat, tat, tat, rata tat tat tat tat tat tat tat tat . . . BOOM! A mighty eighteen-inch oak tree splintered and crashed to the ground, cut in two by the extraordinary fierceness of the battle.

The Confederates moved forward spiritedly, in spite of the ripping apart of their ranks.

Jeremiah turned toward his men. "Breathe fire into 'em, boys!" he shouted, choking on the smoke around him. "Let 'em feel it! Let 'em feel it!" He moved up and down the lines, Sam helping him to keep the men in order. "That's it, my boys! That's it! Good and hot!"

They never wavered, though men fell about them like grass to a scythe. The sound of the guns rolled through the woods like incessant thunder.

"McCamey! Sergeant!" came a shout from one of the men, "I can't tell if I'm shootin' at friend or foe! Oh help!" the voice panicked, "this is terrible!"

Jeremiah couldn't see the man. "Just keep it up! Keep the fire up! Just ram them balls home and spit 'em out!" he yelled above the roar.

The smoke was all encompassing, like the death shroud that it was. No one knew at whom, or what, they were shooting. Neither did they know who fell.

The battle raged fiercely, on and on and on. Night began to fall, and suddenly, flames leaped to the sky. The forest was on fire, the brush catching quickly as tongues of red and orange lapped up everything in their way.

The ground was littered with dead and wounded, both being treated alike by the dancing devil fire. It knew not whether one was dead or living; neither did it care. The crackling blaze devoured it all. The screams were dreadful.

"Out, men! Out! Out! Out! Out!" Jeremiah bellowed to his boys. "Away from the flame . . . away from the fire . . . away from the woods! Move it! Move it! Move it, I say!" he raved.

The blaze rolled on as quickly as rushing water. As he ran, Jeremiah tripped over a form on the ground. It moaned in desperate pain. He rolled the body over. "Wilton!" he shouted to the sergeant of Company B, "Can you get up? Let me help you; hurry, man! Hurry!" Jeremiah could feel the searing heat on his skin. "C'mon! C'mon!" he urged his fellow sergeant, frantically trying to pull him to his feet. When the man couldn't stand, Jeremiah began to drag him, the flames leaping closer. The world was bathed in molten orange.

I'm going to die here, Jeremiah thought; and he felt strangely at peace, ready for the forest furnace to become his funeral pyre. He couldn't breathe, and knew he was falling, Sergeant Wilton's wrist still clasped in his hand.

At once he was aware of a great force under his shoulders. "I'm here, Sergeant, I'm here," Sam said, lifting him. "Lean on me." Suddenly they emerged from the blazing inferno.

Jeremiah sank to the ground, choking, gasping in air in great wheezes.

"You all right?" Sam panted.

Jeremiah nodded his head. Terrified, painful, wretched screams rose above the roar of the flames, and he realized that at some point he let go of Sergeant Wilton's arm.

Horrified and stunned, he knew there was no more he could do to help the man as the fire continued to satiate its appetite.

Unable to get his breath, he doubled over in shocked agony. Feeling paralyzed, he wished that he too, might perish, for he thought his heart would burst with grief for those lives being consumed in this furnace called The Wilderness.

Before the night was over, a Confederate win in the wild woods was evident. However, the victory gained had been done so at a terrible, horrendous price.

With darkness cloaking them and not a moment to recover from the fight, the army in gray made an all night forced march southeastward. The soldiers were desperately tired, yet the morning found them being assaulted by the Yankees once more.

As they moved down the road, Jeremiah's unit listened to the sound of the guns. They were in the rear of the line, and it was obvious a hard fight was in progress far ahead . . . perhaps as much as a day's march away.

They bivouacked that night in the open, but morning found them entrenched at a place called Spotsylvania Courthouse, right across Grant's chosen path to Richmond.

As part of Hill's corps, Company G was thrown into the midst of battle, being pushed into the fight by forming on General Ewell's right. Ewell's corps was formed in a crescent shape a mile wide and a mile deep. The Confederates simply called it "the Mule Shoe."

Combat was ferocious. Time and time again the Union forces tried to break the Mule Shoe in the center. The thunder of battle continued into the afternoon, when a tide of blue came crashing across the open ground in front of Ewell's men. Heavy hand to hand fighting ensued, the Yankees able to drive deep into the Mule Shoe's front. The Southerners refused to yield, though many were taken prisoner and several pieces of artillery captured.

Federal General Mott had his men charge through the opening, but they were met with heavy Confederate cannon fire, causing confusion in their lines. The tide of blue broke and retreated.

By dusk, both sides felt utterly spent, and the fighting began to wind down. Jeremiah threw himself onto the ground in his trench, too tired to move and too tired to eat.

It was a good thing. There were no rations.

When he woke, he felt wet and chilled, for a steady rain was falling. Jeremiah didn't know how long he'd slept, but his stomach churned fiercely in hunger. Sitting up, he blinked in the darkness, looking for signs of his men. Several around him were sleeping, so he groped quietly about for something, anything, to eat. There was nothing, so he had to content himself with a long swig of water from his canteen.

Suddenly, a whisper summoned him, "McCamey; Sergeant . . . you hungry, Sergeant?"

"My insides done growed together, I'm so empty, Sam" he replied in a hushed tone.

"I captured some Yankee sheet iron crackers," Sam laughed softly. "Saved a couple of 'em for you."

Jeremiah's stomach growled loudly. "I'm much obliged," he said, taking the hardtack the corporal offered.

"Good thing it's dark, Sergeant," Sam chuckled, "'cause them crackers is full o' worms and weevils. You'll enjoy 'em more if you can't see your food movin'."

"Thanks a lot," Jeremiah responded in a weary, sarcastic voice, but he really didn't care. He was hungry enough to eat the worms and weevils alone.

He bit into a cracker. "Jumpin' jiminy! I think I broke a tooth!" he exaggerated. "The Yanks sure know how to take the pleasure out o' eatin'." He stared at the cracker for a moment as if in thought. "Say . . . we ought to try to capture crates of this stuff . . . they'd make dandy breastworks and fortifications!"

Sam laughed, then suddenly cried, "Shhh . . . Sergeant . . . somethin's up! Listen!"

Jeremiah heard it too. It was a scratching, a scraping and a stumbling through the not far off woods.

At once, a picket appeared along the trenches. "The Yankees is comin'," he reported breathlessly. "They's already formin' for attack and it ain't even yet four o'clock in the mornin'!"

Shortly, Captain Kertlin moved above them, franticly issuing orders. "The Federals are jammed up, boys! We're to take advantage of the situation and move quickly to form up on the right side of the attack. Now, move out! Move out!" he shouted. "No time to waste!"

"Let's go, boys!" Jeremiah urged. "Let's go, let's go!"

Quickly sloughing off their sleepiness, the men grabbed their arms and scrambled out of the ditches,

"At the double quick!" the Captain commanded in frenzy. "Have your men move at the double quick!"

At the run-like march the soldiers hurried to their new position, arriving just in time to pour a drenching round of fire into the enemy forces. It halted their tide and momentarily stopped the advance.

About two hours later, another Union division succeeded in breaking into the gray line. Again, they were repulsed.

"C'mon, my boys!" Jeremiah shouted as he reloaded his musket yet another time. Anxiously he turned to Sam, "If this continues and the

Yankees gain the advantage, our Army of Northern Virginia will be cut in two and destroyed piece by piece!"

Sam wasn't paying any attention to him. "Sergeant, would you looka there!" he exclaimed reverently.

The noble form of Robert E. Lee appeared in the midst of the battle. The sight of their General made the worn army rally, and he continued to move among his troops, though muskets spit fire, and the battle raged on.

Five times Lee urged his men onward in an assault, trying to recover their original position. Each attempt failed, but enough time was bought so that new fortifications were constructed at the Mule Shoe base. This helped to straighten the lines considerably.

Rain continued to fall heavily throughout the day, coming down in torrents. Rivulets red with blood ran across the ground.

A few hundred yards to the west of Company G's formation, the Confederate defense bent slightly, forming an angle. Here, the men in gray under General Ewell became involved in a fight so vicious that muskets were used as clubs and bayonets driven freely across fortifications as the men fought hand to hand. Riddled with shot and torn with shell, many wounded boys were trampled into the mud, left there to die. The place quickly earned its fitting name: The Bloody Angle.

The intense and destructive fire continued even as the sun went down. It was well after midnight before combat began to cease. For over twenty hours, battle had raged in the little hamlet of Spotsylvania Courthouse, and when silence at last fell over the field, it was almost staggering. As furious as the fighting had been, neither side was able to gain an advantage, and the rain continued to fall.

The men spent another night in the trenches, attempting to grab what sleep they could in the harrowing mud.

An eerie lull settled over the battlefield for the next several days, and the men bore out a thoroughly miserable existence in the cramped, foul, wet ditches. The rain would not let up.

The Yankees didn't appear to be going anywhere, either. Unknown to the boys in gray, Grant sent word to his government in Washington, "I plan to fight it out on this line if it takes all summer."

After several wretched days in the muddy trenches, a last effort was made by the men in blue to break the Mule Shoe line. They were blasted away by the firing of thirty cannon.

The following night of May 20, the Federal Army of the Potomac was on the move again, always edging closer to Richmond. Lee was in desperate need of new troops as he shifted his army on the tide with Grant. For twelve days, the two forces had fought a bloody and fruitless battle.

The Army of Northern Virginia withdrew from Spotsylvania under a cloud of gloomy sadness. Many young and hopeful lives were left behind, causing Jeremiah to marvel that his unit remained intact. Not only had many of their comrades fallen for their country, but also J. E. B. Stuart, the gallant Confederate cavalier, lay dead. Outside of Richmond, as he led a calvary charge, the pistol of a dismounted horse soldier in blue found its mark. He died at a place called Yellow Tavern.

That night, the men were at last able to sleep out of trenches and on open ground. There was no rain to drown their fires, and stale salt pork with parched corn was rationed. To the hungry men, it seemed a feast.

As the stars came out, Andy attempted to brighten the mood. For the first time in weeks, his banjo came out, soon followed by a fiddle, harmonica, mandolin, and drum or two. And oh, how the boys did sing!

Suddenly, Andy stood. "This one's for J. E. B. Stuart, boys!" he announced as his fingers began to strum out "Ridin' A Raid." It was a popular tune about Stuart, and soon all the instruments joined in the song. The hearty voices of the men became lively and rowdy as they sang about the bold dandy:

> 'Tis Stonewall the Rebel
> That leans on his sword
> And while we are mounting
> Prays low to the Lord
> Let each cavalier
> That loves honor and right
> Follow the feather of Stuart tonight.
>
> Come tighten your girth
> And slacken your rein
> Come buckle your blanket and holster again
> Try the click of your trigger
> And balance your blade
> For he must ride sure
> That goes ridin' a raid . . .

As all verses were belted out, the bloody, dirty work of war was set aside.

It wasn't until the singing of "Do You Miss Me at Home" that Jeremiah felt heavy pangs of homesickness. He had heard no news from his family since learning of his father's decision to join the army, and was racked with loneliness and worry. He also harbored thoughts of Katie Melinda and fought to push them away. He'd heard from no one; including her. As the chorus of "Yes, 'twould be joy beyond measure to know that they miss me at home . . ." was sung quietly by the men, Jeremiah felt overcome. An attempt to echo the words threatened to bring tears to his eyes, so he moved a distance from the crowd into the darkness of the woods. All he wanted was to be alone with his thoughts.

"McCamey!" a voice startled him. "So it got to you too, huh? I couldn't listen anymore, once they began that song those North Carolinians always sing:

> Sweet eyes are filled with tears, men
> Sweet tears of love and pride
> As our wives and sweethearts bid us
> Go meet what e'er betide.

The captain repeated the popular words with a sigh as he looked up at the stars. "Jeremiah, how much longer can it go on?" he asked in sad reflection.

"What news you hear, John? Anything . . . anything from home? Any news of the valley?" Jeremiah questioned intently.

"I know nothing new . . . except some rumors that Lee is considerin' sendin' in Early's troops to threaten any Union forces breaking through. That's all I can tell you."

The gray troops continued to follow the blue troops off to the left, always inching toward Richmond. June 1 found them clashing at the cross-roads of Cold Harbor, only miles above the Confederate capital.

The Union forces charged the Confederates in a direct frontal assault, and the murderous fire inflicted by the boys in gray cut down over six thousand Union soldiers in less than an hour. Grant was forced to halt the attack and change his strategy. Although he had lost over fifty-five thousand men in a month's time, his goals remained the same: capture Richmond and crush Lee. He decided his best course of action was to strike Petersburg and destroy its railroad hub linking Virginia to the rest of South.

CHAPTER TWENTY-TWO

The South, she needs no ramparts
No lofty towers to shield,
Your bosoms are her bulwarks strong
Breastworks that never yield.

Quietly, Grant's men moved out from Cold Harbor, disappearing from sight. Lee was greatly vexed and telegraphed Richmond in desperation: "I do not know the position of Grant's army!"

Several days later, Captain Kertlin called his sergeants together. "Men," he said, as they sat perched on logs around a fire outside of his tent, "it's been determined that General Grant and his army are movin' south. Petersburg was attacked today . . . the Federals were repulsed, of course, but they ain't left, so we'll be movin' out shortly. I want you to have your men ready and waiting for the command. Any questions?"

The men shook their heads and echoed "No."

"Very well then. The war continues . . ." he said half mockingly. "You are dismissed.

"McCamey, a word with you, please."

Jeremiah lagged behind as the other men rose to go. Looking up at his bother-in-law nonchalantly, he asked, "So, what's up, Cap'n . . . besides Petersburg, I mean. I gotta tell you . . . can't say I haven't enjoyed these last couple o' days of inactivity none." He smiled, but John Kertlin didn't return the gesture. The captain sat down across from his wife's brother, a blank stare on his face.

"Have I done somethin', John . . . Cap'n? If you need to rebuke me in any way, set me straight, please."

The captain sighed, gazing down. He couldn't look Jeremiah in the eyes for this one. His own fear was too great.

"I just learned that several days ago a force under Union General Hunter, or maybe Sheridan . . . ah . . . ah . . . Jeremiah, the south valley has been attacked and Yankee forces battled for over ten hours at Piedmont with . . . "

"John!" Jeremiah exclaimed, interrupting him, "that's just a stone's throw away from home!" He suddenly felt a chill run up his spine and became filled with anxiety.

"I know . . . I know," the captain paused, finding it difficult to continue. "That's not the worst of it, brother-in-law. I . . . I learned that they fought for over ten hours against the little army of 'Grumble' Jones."

Jeremiah shot up off the log. "John!" he shouted in despair, "Jones! John, that's the man under who my Pa joined up . . . how could this have happened? What went on?"

"Sit back down," Captain Kertlin ordered. "There's more. Over one thousand prisoners were taken by the enemy . . . I . . . I don't know who, of course . . . "

"Oh John," Jeremiah groaned. "This is terrible news; terrible!" he sighed, tears glistening in his eyes.

"'Grumble' Jones was killed, Jeremiah. Who knows who else."

"What of my family, John? What of your wife! We must send them all to Staunton. Right away! Well, what say you, John? We must do it! Can you get word . . ."

Captain Kertlin shook his head, cutting off Jeremiah's question. "Staunton's surrounded," he whispered in his own agony.

"Ahhhh!" Jeremiah crushed the kepi he was holding in his hands, tears streaming down his face. Quickly he wiped them away as he noticed the same glistening in his captain's eyes. He sat up straight. "Then there is nothing we can do, John. Nothing! Nothing! Nothing!" He threw his crushed cap to the ground in exasperation.

The captain looked at him. "We can pray, Jeremiah. We can pray . . . for it's certainly out of our hands."

They sat in silence, watching the fire and listening to it crackle. Finally Jeremiah rose, "Well, John . . . you will let me know the minute you hear anything more?"

Captain Kertlin nodded.

"Thank you for being so frank, with me, Cap'n. My . . . ah, well, my men will be ready when we receive the marchin' orders."

Hill's corps arrived in Petersburg by noon the following day. The city was well defended, for the Confederates had seen to this important position early in the war. Massive breastworks with a chain of cannon extended around the city in a semi-circle, ten miles long.

General Lee's men joined the troops of General Beauregard, already manning the town. The Federals attempted another assault that day, but were repulsed by Beauregard's boys.

General Grant made a decision. After losing ten thousand men in four days of fighting, he decided to entrench the army in blue facing the city. Grant would no longer order any frontal attacks, but dig in and wait. The campaign starting in May at The Wilderness now ground to a halt in the middle of June. Petersburg was under siege.

Company G settled once again in camp. After the circumstances of the previous six weeks, they felt it a haven. Things remained quiet for a time as the enemy worked at digging trenches and erecting forts along their lines. Artillery dueled and occasional rifle fire was exchanged, but routine guided daily life once more, and the weather began to grow extremely hot.

The men shared duty in the trenches and the forts. Artillery manned the cannon and infantry helped guard with muskets.

June's warm temperatures transformed into July's insufferable heat and Jeremiah fought a personal war to keep from being overshadowed by depression. Lack of news from home made his melancholy grow deeper each day. Knowing nothing, he decided, was worse than bearing bad news.

Elliot's Salient was the main Confederate fort along the lines overlooking and guarding the city of Petersburg. From its hilltop one could see for miles, helping to keep close check on Yankee movements. Jeremiah liked duty at this post, for it broke the routine of camp and offered the men a diversion. His unit had drawn patrol at this station several times by the middle of July.

"Sure can see a ways off from here," Sam commented one day as he looked out at the view. "It ain't a bad sight with all them purty rollin' hills 'round here and off yonder."

"Yeah," Franklin offered, "only them blue bellies below kinda distract from all the fineness of it."

"Yeah," Andy agreed, "reckon I seen prettier sights at home."

Jeremiah laughed hollowly. "Andy, my boy . . . I can't remember none what home looks like!"

A lull in conversation caused things to grow quiet and suddenly Sam spoke up intently, "Fellas, do you'ns hear a strange noise? Sounded almost like it was comin' from under the ground!"

"Aw Sam . . . your hearin's foolin you. Gone bad I reckon," Andy joked. "Too many shells bustin' 'round us all these years."

"I'm missin' toes, Anderson. I ain't missin' ears. And I tell you . . . I done heard somethin'. Shhh . . . listen! There it goes again!"

The men immediately grew quiet and a very faint, scratching, pounding sound did, indeed, seem to come from beneath the earth on which they stood. It stopped as abruptly as it started.

"You're right, Corporal. I heard it too," Jeremiah said, baffled. "Odd . . ." he shook his head, without completing the thought. "Reckon we just all had too much warrin'."

Franklin laughed. "If I didn't know it to be impossible, I'd not put it past them Yanks to be up to somethin' devious below."

"Yeah . . . like what," Sam snorted, "buildin' a tunnel to bring 'em up on the inside o' this fort here? Maybe try to take us by surprise?" He aimed his musket at the earthen floor. "Well, this ol' Rebel's ready!"

They all howled with laughter, picturing such a scene. Sam shrugged his shoulders. "Probably rats I'd be shootin' at. Ain't no way any man could build a tunnel under so much earth without suffocating. There'd have to be shafts built for ventilation, and that'd sure blame give away any type o' scheme!"

Suddenly Captain Kertlin appeared in their midst. "Glad to see you boys findin' somethin' to laugh about on this relentlessly hot day," he said, returning their salute. "McCamey, I need to speak with you."

"Yes, Cap'n?" he answered.

Captain Kertlin looked around. "I think this demands some privacy, Sergeant," he mumbled quietly, beginning to walk a length down the fortification walls, Jeremiah beside him. Well out of earshot and a distance from the other men, he pulled a paper from his breast pocket.

"Some mail ran, today, Jeremiah . . . wish I could say I had some for you . . . but I did . . . I did receive this letter," he voiced solemnly, handing it to his brother-in-law. "It's from Priscilla."

Jeremiah had already recognized her writing and his hands started to shake as he unfolded the stiff, crackling paper.

Captain Kertlin smiled halfheartedly. "You can skip all her endearments toward me. It's the third paragraph you have need to start at." He pointed to the section of the letter.

Jeremiah's hands continued to shake as he read:

. . . I'm quite certain you must be very much aware of the horrible fight we had up at Piedmont. It was truly terrible in more ways than one. Our poor men and boys didn't have a chance against those well-trained Federals . . . but never did any soldiers fight with more valor. The loss of life to our little area cannot be comprehended. The good General Jones was killed, as well as our Mr. McPherson, Mr. Burns and Charlie Black. (Add to this the loss of others, like Cyril Ash, Jeptha Carroll and Toby McGee . . . one cannot help but wonder WHO will be next . . .)

Several others were taken prisoner, and we do not know where they have been sent. No one seems to be able to tell us anything! We have even appealed to the enemy, and they have been of no help. Our good Preacher Foxly went up to Piedmont yesterday where some Yankee forces remain. He did this in an effort to help us, but it was to no avail. It is as if they have simply disappeared.

John, I tell you this because your own dear father-in-law was among those captured. At least we can count as comfort the fact that he survived the fighting, and that ever gives us hope. It is very hard to think of our men at the hands of the enemy and the affliction they must surely be forced to endure. But do not worry about us; we are strong in heart, Dearest. Our suffering has already been enough to temper our souls, and though we hurt at the absence of our loved ones, it only serves to make us realize that as you fight and bravely meet your fate, so must we stand strong, and do whatever we need to do. We manage, and never let it be said that Virginia's women are not strong; or that Southern women are faint. We do, and will, meet head on whatever is required of us. It is the sacrifice we must make, ever as you make your lives yours. We WILL survive it!

Mother is all right. She is beginning to grow stalwart. The four of us fare well enough and I say again, DO NOT WORRY. As I write you, Violet has taken on the task of writing our beloved brother. But as mail is so unpredictable, I trust you will share with Jeremiah immediately all that I have told you. And tell him not to be concerned. He was truly upset when father felt the need to join up, and I hope he has come to terms with the fact, by now, that he himself would have done no less. Our prayers and love surround you all . . .

The remainder of the letter was directed to her husband, and Jeremiah folded the pages up.

I will bear this like the man that I am, he thought.

"Thank you, John, for sharing this with me. For letting me know first-hand. It is unfortunate information, and my heart is heavy, Cap'n. But knowing something, even if the news is not good news, brings great relief. At least the wait is over.

"I admit to you that I have been consumed by the circumstances at home. Priscilla has just put me to shame."

He handed the letter back to its owner. "There are no more noble women, Cap'n, than those we can claim to be our own."

"You now know why I wanted to make your sister my wife."

"John . . . I knew the why to that all along."

"I'm sorry about your father, Jeremiah. I grieve with you, but we can take comfort in the fact that prisoners are exchanged. And surely even the enemy will have mercy on those souls that are . . . how should I say? Older than the common soldier."

As the days passed, Jeremiah waited for his own letter from Violet. It never came.

The bombardment of Petersburg continued and seemed to grow more furious with each passing day. The Union army completed its entrenchment and erected several small, superficial forts to dot the landscape. The artillery shelling and musket exchange became constant, lasting from dawn until dusk, and often throughout the night.

Nerves were frayed and tension high. The heat of summer was atrocious and bred killer diseases. Malaria and chronic dysentery took a greater toll than the exchange of fire.

By the end of July, Lee was calling out troops to meet Grant at Deep Bottom, several miles below Richmond. On July 28, the two forces clashed.

Though Yankee advancement to Richmond was blocked, many men in gray lost their lives and even more were taken prisoner. The struggle served little purpose and General Lee expressed concern that Grant had used the massing of troops at Deep Bottom as a diversionary tactic, a tactic to enable his Union forces to carry out some other, more sinister plan.

Each time they entered a fray and the boys came out unharmed, Jeremiah felt profound thankfulness; and such was the case at Deep Bottom. A year had passed since Gettysburg and the capture of Killian and Drew. It had been a year since Jeptha gave his life for the country he loved. How long would Providence continue to bless them? How much longer would the war go on? These questions without answers troubled him as they withdrew from Deep Bottom and marched back toward the city under siege.

It was in the pre-dawn hours of July 30 that Company G's ranks began to filter back into Petersburg. With the city almost surrounded, it was impossible to avoid skirmishing, and the men felt great relief at being secure behind their own lines again.

Wearily stumbling to his tent in the dark, Jeremiah threw his gear onto the ground when he felt the chill. Suddenly, though it was very warm for early morning, his teeth began to chatter and he visibly shook.

"McCamey? You all right?" Sam asked with trepidation.

Jeremiah didn't answer. He couldn't.

"Sergeant?" Sam cried again, "Sergeant?" He reached out and touched Jeremiah's shoulder. He could feel him trembling. "Let me get a fire started. That should ease you some."

Sam worked quickly, and by the time wood was crackling, Jeremiah's chill stopped as suddenly as it started. He sank feebly to the ground in front of the blaze, sweat pouring from his body. His shirt was drenching wet.

"My canteen, Sam," he muttered.

Quickly finding the wooden container, the corporal held it out to the sergeant. Uncapping it, Jeremiah swallowed long and hard as Sam knelt next to him, trying to be of aid.

Jeremiah shook his head and looked at Sam.

"You all right, McCamey?" he repeated the question.

Jeremiah nodded, splashing water onto his face. "Yeah . . . yeah. I'm all right. Reckon it's this heat. Too much of it today."

"That don't look like no heat reaction I've ever seen, Sergeant," Sam replied doubtfully.

"I'm all right, Sam. I'm all right," he said, ripping off his shirt, "just wringin' wet. Sam, don't say nothin' 'bout this to nobody. I'm all right."

Sam stared at him, feeling that his friend needed medical attention.

"I mean it, Sam!" Jeremiah stated sternly. "I mean it!"

Franklin and Andy bound into view, dropping their belongings in front of the fire. Laughing about something, neither seemed to notice anything unusual about the sergeant.

"Oh! I almost forgot!" Franklin said, reaching inside of his shirt. "Cap'n asked me to give these letters over to you." He thrust them out.

"Much obliged," Jeremiah said, taking the mail. He recognized the writing on both, and opened the one from Priscilla first, quickly scanning the pages, hoping for good news. It revealed no one had learned anything yet of their father.

The second piece was one for which he had waited a long time. Its lumpiness indicated something enclosed and he began to tear the envelope apart in his impatience.

Suddenly a huge explosion ripped into the dawn, shaking the earth. For a split second, all four boys froze, motionless as they absorbed the shock. Things of the moment were forgotten, Jeremiah tossing aside his letters in favor of his shirt and musket.

As they dashed from their fire, debris hurtled through the air and all they could do was gape in silence. The pre-dawn light revealed a deluge of dirt raining down from the sky, along with bits of cannon, carts, wood and dead soldiers. Where the fort of Elliot's Salient stood, there was now nothing but a gigantic breach in the earth, a huge hole. It was a crater some thirty feet deep, eighty feet wide and one hundred and sixty feet long.

The sight stunned the men. "Great day in the mornin'," uttered Sam in disbelief. "Great day!"

"Sam!" Jeremiah called, pitching his musket to the corporal. "Hold this while I dress. Fellas, grab your guns! Let's check this out!" Buttoning his shirt, he took off at a run, retrieving his musket from Sam.

Before getting halfway to the detonated fort, they stopped in their tracks. A swarm of boys in blue came up over the fortifications where the fort had stood. They too, were mesmerized by its sight, and stopped to stare in disbelief at their creation. Many jumped down into the opening to observe the astonishing destruction up close.

Jeremiah ordered his men to halt as their own mortar fire began to assail the giant pit. A chaotic, disorganized battle was erupting, and Jeremiah knew it best for his men to stop where they were and do what they could to defend.

The four were swept up in the tide. Moving forward and falling back was a motion repeated relentlessly as the boys made progress in keeping the enemy at bay.

The sun began to pour fierce heat down upon the men. They did not even realize it had risen.

General Lee called for General William Mahone's brigade to move in and defend the bloody crater. By 1 P.M., these men controlled its rim. Placing hats on bayonets and taunting them over the edge of the cavern, the Confederates triumphed at deceiving the enemy within. A volley of fire ripped through the false heads, and before the Yankees could reload their rifles, the Rebels jumped down upon them.

Desperate hand-to-hand combat turned the exposition into an appalling spectacle. Rifle butts, bayonets, fists and shot were used with bitter vengeance. Blood flowed in torrents down the edge of the breach, gathering in pools at the bottom to be slowly absorbed into the ground. The carnage was incredible. By 3 P.M., it was obvious to the soldiers in blue that the Confederate positions were not attainable, and over 4,400 Union men lay dead as opposed to some 1,500 Rebels.

As the boys returned to their quarters that afternoon, the cause of the explosion was clear.

"So, we was certain right when we thought we heard them noises beneath us," Sam said thoughtfully. "They was rats, all right. Rats dressed in blue."

"Yeah," Jeremiah answered, " one o' the lieutenants was tellin' me they suspect at least six hundred feet of tunnel was dug out under that fort and charged with about four tons o' black powder. Don't know yet how they got fresh air in there so they could breathe to work. Ain't no ventilation shafts. But it'll be studied. Had to be some smart engineerin' mind . . ."

Suddenly, Jeremiah remembered the letter he'd been on the verge of reading, before the explosion removed all else from his concentration. How could he have forgotten? He'd waited so long for it and then simply tossed it down by the fire! *That was nearly twelve hours ago,* he mused to himself, hoping the letter would still be there.

The men arrived back at their tent dirty, exhausted and extremely hungry. The sergeant eagerly searched around the cold embers of their morning blaze. The letters were gone, both of them, and his heart sank.

Rations were meager. For supper, the men drew a half-pint of corn meal and a thick piece of salt pork.

"This sure ain't much sustenance for a man that's been fightin' all day," Sam grumbled as he and Jeremiah rebuilt the morning fire.

"Reckon not, Sam, reckon not," the sergeant commented without interest. "Least it keeps us alive. And as long as we're alive to fight another day, our country stays alive."

"Well, reckon I never thought of it like that now, McCamey," the corporal reflected, stoking the embers. "Sometimes you sure have a way with words."

The flames leaped to life. "Let me fetch my skillet, Sergeant. If you make the pone, I'll fry up the bacon.

"Where's Andy and Franklin?"

"Took their rations and said they was joinin' some o' the other fellas so's they could all sing a spell. Go on and join 'em, Sam. Don't reckon I'm up to it tonight. I'm a mite tuckered." *And disappointed,* he thought.

"Might do that after I dine on these fine victuals with you." He dropped the fatback into the skillet as Jeremiah mixed the mush for corn-bread. The pork sizzled, creating an appetizing aroma in spite of the fact that they'd eaten this same fare day in and day out for several weeks.

"Know what I was thinkin' about, McCamey?"

"No, Sam, what?" Jeremiah replied nonchalantly, trying not to burn the bread.

"I was rememberin' about that last time I was home . . . you know, after my toes done had to be cut off . . . I was studyin' on that last meal my Ma fixed to feed me. It was all my favorite eatin's. She'd fried up a big fat chicken for me . . . and ain't nobody that makes biscuits like my Grandma. She made 'em up as big as my plate, and they dripped with butter and gravy. Ma'd cooked up a big pot o' green beans she'd put up for the winter, and some roastin' ears. It was topped off with a special cake only my Ma and Grandma makes. It's white, with these raisins in it, and topped with chocolate. Ummmm, ummm. Could drive a man crazy! I done told 'em it was worth gettin' my toes froze off just to be home for some o' that eatin!" he finished.

"Don't do that, Sam," Jeremiah groaned teasingly. "I'm growin' faint thinkin' of it. You shoulda been at Cap'n and Priscilla's marryin, now that were some fine food. The night before the marryin' we had beefsteaks and ham, bread with apple butter, collards with bacon and a mound of fresh fried taters . . . with onions! Then there were these little confections that were filled with cream. It was mighty fine; mighty fine!"

The two men stared at each other and sighed.

"Reckon we'll ever be eatin' like that again, Sergeant?"

Jeremiah shrugged. "Don't know, Sam. Reckon we be blest to be eatin' at all. I think of all them poor souls out there that'll never be eatin' again, 'cept at the Lord's table."

Things were quiet for a moment, and suddenly Sam said, "Sarge, don't reckon I've told you how bad I feel about your Pa."

Jeremiah looked at the corporal. "Me too, Sam. Me too. But, like the Cap'n says, prisoners is always bein' exchanged. I just wish . . . just wish we knew where he was."

"I'm mighty thankful my Ma's closed up the house and taken Grandma and gone to live with Grandma's brother. I sleep a mite better for it."

"Reckon so. Here, this pone is ready. Let's eat up," Jeremiah said.

The simple meal was finished quickly. "Sure you don't mind I join the other boys?"

"Sam . . . be my guest. I just ain't in the mood. We marched all night and fought all day. Don't know where you'ns come by the energy. I'm just too tired."

"McCamey . . . you're sure you're all right? You ain't had another one of them shakin' spells?"

"Na. I told you it was just on account o' the heat. But I am tired. A good night's sleep will do me good."

"All right, Sergeant. Good night." Sam rose, and started to stoke the fire.

"Never mind, Sam. I'm goin' to sleep now . . . even if the sun ain't hardly down."

As he watched Sam walk off to join the other boys, he chided himself for losing his precious mail of the day. It wasn't just because of whom the letters were from, but also because mail was so unpredictable. He didn't know when he might receive any again.

He stood up, stretching his tall frame. He truly felt weary. Gathering the gear he deposited on the ground that morning, he tossed it into the tent. The interior was dark as he threw his blanket onto the earthen floor and lay down upon it. Closing his eyes, he tried to get comfortable, but a small lump under his back would not allow him. Rolling on his side to smooth things out, he heard the crackle of paper. Reaching beneath the woolen spread, he pulled out his letters.

"Well! I'll be!" he cried in elation, his weariness quickly forgotten. He scrambled out to the dying fire. For a fleeting second he wondered how the letters came to be there. He was certain of leaving them outside. Perhaps some well-meaning soul had simply thrown them into the tent for safekeeping. Whatever, it didn't matter, for they were in his possession again. He stoked the fire that he might read the precious words.

He slid the unread letter out of the already open envelope, and gingerly unfolded the sheet of paper. Out dropped a tiny packet. Jeremiah held it in his palm, curious as to what it could be. Eagerly, he began to read the script that made him tingle.

Dear Jeremiah,

It took forever for your letter to find it's way into my hands. Even the mail suffers in this war!

I am wanting to tell you that everything is fine, but it is not. The mill production has declined a great deal recently, thanks to our intruders in blue. I'm sure you have, by now, become aware that the Yankees have once again begun to amass in our valley. They have destroyed much and sometimes I do fear they will endeavor to torch our mill.

Several weeks ago there was a terrible fight just across the mountain at New Market. To make up for lack of our own soldiers in the valley, the boys at the Military Institute in Lexington were called into battle. Jeremiah . . . these were young men . . . very young . . . some only fourteen and fifteen years old. Oh! Those poor cadets! Life cut down at so callow an age! Never has there been such courage demonstrated by our Southerners! Their bravery checked the enemy, and I dare say that many a life in the valley is owed to these young soldiers. They saved the day for us, and I understand that President Davis has or will hold a personal review of these troops in recognition of their valor.

Jeremiah, it makes me so angry that the invader's foot has once again been pressed upon our soil. Oh! But that the magnificent Stonewall were here again! Never did our valley seem so secure as when he secured it! I'm proud that you were part of that campaign.

I so often wish that I myself could take up a musket and rush at the foe! I wish that I could be part of the fight! Jeremiah . . . I am asking you to do something for me. I hope you do not think me too bold. I am enclosing a locket of mine. It is a special locket because my blessed Grandmother gave it to me on my twelfth birthday. I have never taken it off until this moment. I have placed a lock of my hair inside, Jeremiah, and I am asking that you would wear this locket for me when you go into each battle, for then my presence will be on the battlefield.

Please do not think me too presumptuous, but I know of no other whom I wish to ask this of. I also realize that mail, being as it is, may cause me to lose this locket for good. But it is a small risk when I consider the passion I have to be part of the fight and no loss at all when compared to the lives that are given for our cause each day. I do thank you, Jeremiah, and should this be something that makes you uncomfortable, for whatever reason, perhaps you will be kind enough to simply put it in your pocket when you are called to arms. I just wish it possible that I could be in the position to offer up my life for our country as each of you brave soldiers do every day . . . for I am willing, Jeremiah.

I do so pray this finds you well and safe. When this terrible war is over, then perhaps you will be so kind as to return my locket, and until such a time, I look forward to hearing from you, as you are able.

Deo Vindice, Jeremiah. Deo Vindice.

Truly Yours,

"Katie-Lin"

Looking at her signature, he smiled, remembering all too well how he mistakenly called her by that name at their meeting. His heart felt cheered for the first time in weeks.

He looked at the tiny, odd shaped packet held in his hand. It had been wrapped in a piece of muslin cloth, and suddenly, he recognized it to be the same green muslin of the dress she'd worn that night. He couldn't help but wonder if she did this on purpose, and hoped that she had. He smiled again.

Breaking the thread that kept the packet safely bound, he unwrapped it. From a long silver chain dangled a beautiful, oval, silver locket, engraved with flowers and angels. He turned it over, and on the back were etched the initials KMC. He slipped his thumbnail beneath the catch, and it sprang open. In the small hollow where one might find a picture was a lock of curled, dark blonde hair. Staring at the strands, he reached a finger out to touch them and then gently clasped the oval back together.

He looked at the fastener with dismay, unsure of how it worked. After a moment of study, he placed the chain about his neck, and clasped it together with ease. It felt odd, he thought. A good kind of odd. "Deo Vindice." He whispered his country's motto out loud. "Deo Vindice indeed."

Returning to his pallet in the tent, Jeremiah stretched out and slept long and hard through the night.

The city remained under siege. Two weeks after the Battle of the Crater, Hill's Corps was called out to recover the railroad depot at the settlement of Globe Tavern. The Union forces had captured it.

As the men formed their part of the line, waiting for the command to charge forward, Jeremiah reached up and touched the locket. "This one is for you, Katie-Lin," he whispered.

The guns opened up and the order was given. The men in gray inflicted serious damage to the troops in blue, taking many prisoners. As they pushed them back, however, they were unable to recover the railroad. There were just too many Yankees and the vital supply link to the Army of Northern Virginia was now cut off. Lee's lines could be stretched no farther.

The fight at Globe Tavern was hard, the men facing bitter disappointment at their inability to regain the train line. They knew it meant starvation was imminent and their stomachs were empty enough.

Heavy-hearted soldiers bedded down that night to sleep in the open. Weariness from the fight and exhaustion from the heat was felt by all. Slumber came readily and quickly for the boys.

Jeremiah looked up at the moon. It was fuzzy and he wasn't sure how long he'd been sleeping. He was shivering and shaking, but the night was warm. Once again perspiration poured from his body.

Water, he thought. *A drink of water will help.* He rolled over, groping for his canteen. Finding it quickly, he tried to uncap it, but was shaking too hard. Sweat rolled into his eyes.

All right, Boy . . . he thought. *Lie still. Just lie still for a few minutes. You'll be all right . . .* He looked up at the moon again and thought of the locket he wore. *Well, Katie-Lin,* he mused, *you made it onto the battlefield today . . . and we couldn't achieve our objective. I'm sorry, but there will be other fights, other days, for you to help win.*

He waited for the chill to end, the trembling to cease and the sweating to stop, but it didn't. He began to feel sick to his stomach.

His clothes were drenched, soaking through onto his blanket. How long had this gone on? He wasn't sure, but knew it had lasted too long this time.

All right, Jerry-miah. Help. It's time for a little help. He opened his eyes, trying to remember where Sam was sleeping. *Oh, yeah. Right next to me; he's only a few feet away.* Things looked fuzzy again as he rolled over onto his side. *Nope, don't reckon I'd best get up . . . just crawl a little ways.*

Short distance it was, Jeremiah wasn't sure he'd make it. The chill seemed worse; his teeth chattered as before.

"Sam! Sam!" he croaked, shaking the corporal's arm to wake him. "Sam!"

"Huh?" he answered groggily, then sat bolt upright, eyes wide open. "Oh! Sergeant. It's you! Scared me half to death," he growled indignantly, "wakin' me outa a sound sleep like that.

"McCamey. Your teeth's chatterin' again. You all right?"

"No Sam, I'm not." Sweat dripped from his brow. "This time I'm afeared I need a little help," he said as his body shook.

Sam jumped up, grabbing Jeremiah's blanket. "Dad-blame, Sergeant! Your blanket's soakin' wet!" He pulled his own off the ground. "Here," he said, wrapping it around his friend's shoulders. "Can you stand up?"

"I don't know, Sam. Don't think so."

Sam reached out to touch him. You ain't only soaked, but you're burnin' up with fever. You're hot as blazes. I'm goin' to get Cap'n."

Jeremiah pulled Sam's blanket tighter about him, and crawled dizzily back to his own. Laying down upon the drenched piece of wool, he closed his eyes and lost consciousness.

He woke, staring at wooden slats above him. Where was he? He looked around. Sunlight streamed through a window, falling across his form. He blinked several times and tried to rise up.

"Whoa now, Whoa!" the voice seemed to call from out of nowhere, and suddenly a firm hand was on his back, helping him to rise. He was offered a cup of water and drank it greedily, turning to focus on the face in front of him.

"Where am I?" he asked feebly.

"Hospital," came the abrupt answer.

"Where?" Jeremiah asked.

"Petersburg, of course. You came in with some wounded and sick fellas this mornin' in an ambulance wagon. I helped lift you off the wagon and tucked you into this nice pallet. Name's Willie. Willie Porter."

Jeremiah noticed a patch on the young man's eye and saw that he hobbled as he moved.

"Willie," Jeremiah stated, staring at the young boy.

"That be me, Sergeant . . ." the boy fished for his name.

"McCamey. Jeremiah McCamey," he introduced himself.

"Pleased to know you, Sergeant McCamey. Reckon you gonna be answerin' to me for a while."

Jeremiah continued to stare at him, feeling uncertain and unsure of what had happened.

"Well, Willie . . . what . . . what happened?"

The young soldier placed a hand to the patch over his eye. "An explodin' shell got a little too acquainted with me." He held up his leg. "Put my eye out and blowed off half my foot. I can't be in the fightin' no more," he said lowering his leg, "but I sure can help you fellas that is!" He made a sweeping gesture of the room. "All these pallets in here be under my care. I'm in charge of lookin' after you boys."

"That's fine, Willie," Jeremiah mumbled, "but I mean how come me to be here."

"Oh, well, Sergeant McCamey . . . Doc seems to think you got a real good case o' that malaria that hits so many of us. You ain't gonna be doin' no fightin' for a while."

"Like how long, Willie?" he asked with anxious indignation.

"Depends."

"On what?" Jeremiah demanded to know.

"On how many shakin' spells you have and how long they last."

Jeremiah stared at the wooden slats in the ceiling. *Malaria,* he thought. He knew some boys that had been sick with the disease. He looked at Willie again. "You don't recover from malaria," Jeremiah stated flatly.

"Naw, you don't," Willie said, "but after a few weeks, you usually get well enough. Problem is . . . you never know when it might come back on you. Some people have a bout every few weeks, some every few months. Some goes years without being troubled. Some never have a spell again." He shrugged his shoulders. "Don't know how you'll be, Sergeant . . . but you'll be here a few weeks no matter. At least 'til your shakin' spells quit comin' so often. You was pretty sick when they brung you in. Now no need to worry, though. This quinine I got to give you will sooner or later help things."

252 ~ A CALL TO HONOR

"My boys, though. I got boys to take care of. To see to."

"Well, now . . . I can't do nothin' 'bout that, but I'm sure your cap'n or whoever will see things is took care of."

Jeremiah didn't say anything. He knew Willie was right.

"You just concentrate on gettin' well, Sergeant. You'll be back out there with 'em soon. Maybe."

Jeremiah stared at the crippled young soldier. "Sorry 'bout your accident," he said.

"Aw, coulda been worse. I'm just sorry the fightin' is over for me. I was fair handy with a musket.

"Now . . . you got to take this here powder, Sergeant, if'n we wants to start gettin' you well."

Jeremiah wrinkled his nose. He never was one to like taking medicine.

"Now, just put it on your tongue and swallow the water real fast."

Jeremiah did as he was told and almost choked. The white powder was extremely bitter and hard to gag down.

"That ain't so bad, now," Willie said. "We may be a starvin' army, but quinine's one thing we have a little bit of; at the moment, anyway. You be blessed, Sergeant, cause we ain't had none in quite a while. What you just swallowed was confiscated medicines. When it's gone, who knows if we'll ever have any again."

Jeremiah closed his eyes. *Reckon I'd just better get used to this,* he thought. Sleep soon took him far away, to dreams of other places and other times.

The first few days were the worst. The shaking spells would suddenly hit and sometimes last for hours. By the end of the second week of his confinement, they began to slow down considerably and by the third week, his chills came only every two or three days.

Once he began to recover, he found great monotony in his hospital stay. He was itching to return to duty, and had heard little news of his company. He did know they still held the line at Globe Tavern, but the vital link in supplies had not been restored. With so much idle time on his hands, Jeremiah for once allowed himself to think of the possibility that the South might lose the war. Cold hard facts could not be ignored. They could not be written off in letters to his family or Katie Melinda. Their soldiers were starving and the army in blue had far superior numbers. It was depressing to think about.

Jeremiah missed his old comrades. Lieutenant Moore stopped by one day, up from Globe Tavern as a courier; but he'd been experiencing one of his sick spells, and had to send the lieutenant away.

He longed for a familiar face and to be among his men. He wanted to fight again. It was as if it had all become a part of his blood and he could not rid himself of it.

Willie was good company and Jeremiah had grown immensely fond of him, but the boy had a job to attend to; demands of much sicker men had to be met.

One day Willie shook him from a hot afternoon slumber. "McCamey! Sergeant!" he nudged his shoulder.

"Willie?" he opened his eyes, startled. "What's wrong?"

"Nothin', Sergeant, 'cept you got a visitor. I hear tell," he looked down before continuing, "I hear tell the cause at Globe Tavern has been abandoned, and Hill's corps is movin' back up in the line. Closer to the city."

Jeremiah sighed, but remained motionless.

"Anyways, somebody wants to see you."

"Well, who is it? Where is he?" Jeremiah looked about, but saw no one besides the other sick men in the room.

"I'll go fetch him. He's outside. Said not to disturb you if you wasn't well today."

Jeremiah sat up on the side of his cot. "I'm all right, Willie. I ain't had a shakin' spell now for . . . well, this be five days. Bring him in. I'm hungry for company!"

Before he knew it, his brother-in-law pulled up a crude wooden stool and propped himself next to his pallet. John Kertlin pounded him on the back.

"Cap'n! Dad-blame! Great day in the mornin', if you ain't a sight for sore eyes!" Jeremiah cried excitedly. "I ain't seen none o' you in near a month and was wonderin' if I'd ever see your faces again!"

"You've been missed, Sergeant. Missed fiercely. None o' us can hardly wait for you to join in again."

"How's the boys, Cap'n? Everyone all right? I understand the railroad can't be taken back and we've abandoned that line."

"Yeah . . . well, we win some and we lose some, Jeremiah," he said ruefully. "But the boys is all fine. Everybody all right. Company A took a good hit in some skirmishin' the other day. Lost a good many of their men. But we're doin' all right. I'm thankful."

"John . . . heard any news from home? I've had plenty of time to write . . . not always had plenty o' paper or ink, nor my wits about me, but plenty o' time. I ain't heard nothin'. Have you?"

The Captain looked into his eyes. "They still ain't located your Pa, Jeremiah, though some of 'em, those who were with your Pa . . . some of 'em, anyway, have turned up at Camp Chase, in Ohio."

"That's a prison camp, right?" Jeremiah asked thoughtfully.

"Yeah," the Captain answered pensively, "but I now hear tell that Grant has been tryin' for the stop of prisoner exchanges. Seems to feel that the more of our men they keep locked up, the harder it will be on us. Keep our numbers from bein' replenished." He shook his head with a sigh.

Jeremiah didn't flinch. He had already heard that story and had no doubt it was true.

"And the rest of the family, John? Mother . . . the girls?"

"They're fine, Jeremiah. It ain't been easy for 'em, but they do well enough."

The sergeant let out a sigh of relief. "I'm proud of 'em, John.

"So, you say things have been in good order with the men."

"Tolerable. Sam . . . he's done a real good job while you've been laid up, McCamey. Fact is . . . I've tried to have him promoted to sergeant. Wanted him to act in your place 'til you get back, then put him over another group of men."

"Sam's a good man, Cap'n. He's turned out to be a good leader. Always was a good fighter. I'll sure miss him."

"Oh, he ain't goin' nowhere, Jeremiah. Refused. Said he was obliged and he'd take great care to be as good an officer as he could in your stead, but he reckoned he'd rather stay a corporal and serve under you as to take a higher rank."

"Well . . . I'll be, John. Cap'n, try to change his mind for me. I'll sure miss him, but he deserves the promotion."

"Did you hear what happened just last night?" Captain Kertlin changed the subject.

"Well, now, don't reckon." He stared at his brother-in-law.

"We be eatin' beefsteaks soon, Jeremiah! Beefsteaks!"

"Huh? Cap'n, are you cracked? You just told me we lost our last line of supply."

"Well, listen to this! This is as good as anything J. E. B. Stuart ever did! General Hampton, Wade Hampton, took his cavalry, about four thousand men, and went around the whole rear of Grant's army. He rounded up and returned with some two thousand head o' Union cattle and 'bout three hundred prisoners. Took 'em right out from under their noses, McCamey! Right out in front of 'em!"

Jeremiah laughed. "It's been a long time since we done had any fresh beef, John, a long time . . . I'll be lookin' forward to my share!"

The captain rose to go. "Can't stay, Jeremiah, much as I'd like to. Duty calls . . . got several matters to take care of. You are a sight for sore eyes, though, and you'll be back with us before long. Anything you need?"

"Yeah . . . John . . . Cap'n . . . Could you see if maybe I can be put on some kind of detail in this here place? Orderly, or whatever. Lyin' around here is drivin' me crazy. There's got to be somthin' they'll let me do. I ain't had a chill in five days now. I get a little quinine regular and . . . do you know how hard it is to just lie around waitin' to have a sick spell?" he asked with exasperation.

Captain Kertlin patted him on the shoulder. "See what I can do, Jeremiah."

"Cap'n, tell the boys . . . tell the boys I sure miss 'em and aim on bein' back soon as the Doc will let me. And to enjoy their beef!"

When another week's time had passed, Jeremiah had only one other bad spell. His quinine dose was decreased and he was elated to be put on orderly duty for four hours a day. The work helped him regain his strength, and by the middle of October, the chills had subsided completely. He was allowed to return to his unit, having put six weeks into his hospital stay.

The men welcomed the sergeant's return with great excitement and cheer. Jeremiah never thought it would feel so good to be back with the men on the field and in the trenches again.

"Great day in the mornin', boys! I gotta say, I missed every one o' you fellas!" he remarked as they raised their tin cups of boiled sassafras bark to his honor.

"Where'd you come by the sassafras tea?"

"Scraped some bark from trees down at Globe Tavern. Been holdin' on to this last bit to share with you, Sarge," Sam answered.

"Sam, if you don't mind, I'd like to have a chat with you." Finishing his tea, he motioned for the corporal to take a stroll with him. "You'll excuse us for a few moments, boys."

"What's this I hear about you turnin' down a promotion to sergeant, Sam? I wouldn't be fair none if I didn't encourage you to take it on. It's due you. You go tell Cap'n you done thought it over some more."

"McCamey, I don't reckon so. I'm not lookin' to be in charge none. I'd rather serve with you as to have my own boys. I do believe I'll do my best job that way. If I thought I could be a good sergeant without lookin' to you for a little leadership, then that's how I could best serve my country. But it just ain't so. Besides, what would you do without me?"

Jeremiah laughed. "Got a point there, Sam. S'pose somebody needs to look out for me. Cap'n's got his hands full enough." He turned and looked at the corporal. "I can't change your mind none?"

"Not unless you was to give me a direct order to do it, Sergeant. But you won't do that now, will you?" he asked.

Jeremiah stared at the man sternly and then a grin broke across his face. "Na, reckon not," he slapped him on the back affectionately.

Jeremiah returned to duty in time for the last major action of the year. Though Hill's corps was not part of the fight, the Confederates met the Federals at a creek called Hatcher's Run. In spite of their half starved and exhausted condition, the troops in gray managed to force the Yankees into a withdrawal, keeping them from taking a vital road they desired.

The Army of Northern Virginia settled in for the winter, manning the disease-ridden trenches in defense of Petersburg. Starvation, freezing weather and death began to cast a shadow of despair upon the ranks.

Disconsolation became worse as Union General Sherman, busy in the deeper south, destroyed the city of Atlanta and captured the vital port of Savannah.

One of the worst blows came when General Early's Confederate troops met with defeat in the Shenandoah Valley. Sheridan, the victorious general in blue, began a campaign of great devastation to the area.

It was January 1865.

Men who called the valley home found themselves torn, torn between duty to their country and a desire to go protect their families and lands. For the first time, Lee's army was forced to acknowledge great discouragement. The woe of desertion, an act brought on by desperation, began to demoralize the soldiers. Yet the majority of troops held true.

Jeremiah and Captain Kertlin waited everyday for news they knew wouldn't come. Mail had almost ceased to run. Rumors made them all sick at heart and they could almost understand the motivation causing those who had run off to do so.

During the vicious winter weather, Grant, with his infinite forces, wouldn't let the decimated Confederates rest. On February 5, he again attacked Hatcher's Run. This time it took little effort for the forces in blue to gain control of the vital road sought several months earlier.

General Lee believed there was only one defense left. With his troops numbering barely thirty-five thousand and stretched for over thirty-seven miles, he set up plans to evacuate Petersburg and Richmond. He hoped to march his forces southwestward, uniting the Army of Northern Virginia with the Army of Tennessee, now in North Carolina under the leadership of General Joe Johnston.

It was with trepidation Jeremiah learned of the situation. Sitting in the trenches during the long, cold, February nights, he thought constantly of the last four years. The men had endured incredible hardships, enough to demoralize any army. Yet a spark in them, the spark that sent them to arms in the first place, refused to go out. He thought of the words to a song the men often sang:

> . . . *While right is strong*
> *And God has power*
> *The South shall rise up free* . . .

This thought surely was what held them together.

He listened in the darkness of night to the noises in the cold, dirty ditches where they lay. All he could hear was one repeated sound: the constant, croupy, hacking cough of the men. They were all sick. He had come to a conclusion several days earlier. They would never be well again. There was no medicine, no coats, few blankets, no shoes, no food and wretched winter weather that all worked against them.

This sounds like a hospital ward, he thought glumly. *How can sick men continue to defend their country?*

CHAPTER TWENTY-THREE

The Battle Flag of Dixie
With crimson field shall flame
Her azure cross and silver stars
Shall lead her sons to fame

General Lee decided to launch an attack to cover their withdrawal. He discussed the plan with Georgia's General Gordon and left the details in his hands. After much consideration, General Gordon decided the target should be Fort Stedman, a Yankee stronghold on the northern outskirts of Petersburg.

As the strategy was designed, Captain Kertlin took great care to keep his men informed of all that unfolded. On March 23, he called for a meeting of his officers. Hill's corps was taken from duty in the trenches, getting an unusual reprieve spending the night in camp. The reason soon became evident.

Captain Kertlin looked at the men gathered before him. A small number of aides, lieutenants, all sergeants and corporals surrounded him, anxious for information. They knew they were called together for an important reason.

"Men," he looked at the faces before him, "I cannot mince words with you. You know our situation is desperate. Every day the number in our company dwindles, whether by death or illness; the hospitals are full . . . we're half starved; most of us is sick . . ." he paused, going into a spasm of coughing; an uncontrollable hacking that rose up from deep in his chest.

It was relieved only when Lieutenant Moore handed him a cup of hot water, which he readily downed.

"There, that's better," he cleared his throat. "Thank you, Lieutenant. As I was saying . . ." He looked at the tired, weary faces before him. Discouraged, yes. Sad, absolutely. Exhausted, beyond reason. Hungry, without measure. But these were men not defeated in spirit. These were men who believed wholly in what they were fighting for, determined to see it through to the end.

"Never mind what I was saying, soldiers. Every one of you, everyone in this company . . . are men of great honor. It is my privilege to be your captain.

"Here's what we're up against. Tomorrow we're bein' pulled out at General Lee's request."

"Where in the world are we goin', Cap'n?" Sam asked in surprise.

"Our corps is joinin' the three divisions of General Gordon. Boys, three hundred men have been picked special, some from our own corps. In darkness of the early mornin', they will rush Fort Stedman, silencing the pickets and moving swiftly to the rear. General Gordon believes there to be another fort or two behind Stedman, which they will capture as the rest of us charge, fanning out to the left and to the right. You will be given more specific details directly before the assault is made."

"Is it just Gordon and us?" one of the sergeants asked incredulously.

"General Anderson's corps will be part of the action, too," Captain Kertlin replied.

There were obvious sighs of relief until the captain spoke again. "Men, you realize this is almost one half of our entire force."

"Our numbers have gotten real low, ain't they?" another asked pensively. The question needed no answer.

"Well, men . . . your boys need to be advised. We move out sometime in the mornin'. Enjoy the night spent away from the trenches. No tellin' where we'll find ourselves tomorrow or thereafter. Unless anyone's got somethin' else to say, you're dismissed." Another round of deeply congested coughing followed the captain's words as he watched the men disperse.

"Sam," Jeremiah addressed the corporal, "gather the boys together. I'll be along directly. Go on and start fillin' 'em in on what we know."

"Right, Sergeant," he replied, eager do his duty.

When Sam moved out of earshot, Jeremiah looked at their leader. "Cap'n," he said, "this sounds like one great gamble to me."

Captain Kertlin returned the somber gaze. "It is, Jeremiah. Reckon we ain't got many options left."

"The boy's will put up a hard fight, Cap'n. General Lee can count on it."

"They always do, McCamey." Another fit of coughing racked his body.

"John, that cough don't sound good. You really oughta do somethin' about it."

"I notice lots of the men coughin'. Seems like we're all sick."

"Yeah, reckon so," Jeremiah answered, "still . . ."

"Still what?" the captain replied in exasperation. "Ain't nothin' to be done. Even if there was, we'd just be sick again. As long as we're surrounded in this place, cut off from most lines of supply, we'll be hungry and in need of medicine. We'll still be coatless, and shoeless, as long as there ain't anyway to ship anything in. General Grant ain't movin' out. It's one of the cold, hard facts of this war, Jeremiah. Just like I told y'all in the beginning . . ."

"Yeah," the sergeant reminisced softly, "this is war . . . men die."

Captain Kertlin softened his tone. "Yeah, well . . . I guess you of all people don't need to be reminded of that."

"Cap'n, reckon I'd best go speak with my men. Do try to help that cough ease up some."

"Yeah, Jeremiah. Good night."

The men were up when the bugle sounded, anxious for their change in routine. By midmorning, they were filing into rank to advance to the city's northwest portion, where they would wait for orders to carry out their mission. The soldiers were instructed to rest, for they would move into position at 3:30 A.M. General Gordon wanted the attack underway by 4 A.M.

At 2 A.M., Jeremiah roused his sleeping men, instructing them to gather their arms and any rations they had. At 3:15 A.M., they slipped out into the open, between the two lines of defense. At the base of Hare's Hill, they waited in secret, eyes wrested on its crest and their objective, Fort Stedman.

At precisely 4 A.M., screened by darkness, the three hundred chosen men advanced on the Yankee stronghold. The other troops waited below. Not a sound was heard as the Confederates moved swiftly into the fort, taking its Federal occupants by surprise.

Shortly, the command came down. "All right, boys, steady goes it!" said Jeremiah. "We're sweeping up and fanning out to the left. Fall in, fall in quickly! Now, boys . . . Forward! And take that fort!"

His men moved, executing the order. "It's lookin' good, Sergeant!" Sam exclaimed. "Things must have surely gone as planned!"

Abruptly, musket fire and a shower of shell began to rain down upon the massed Confederates. "Steady, boys, steady!" Jeremiah shouted above the roar. "Move out! Move up! Fire back, my boys! Lay it into 'em!"

Up ahead, the colors lay in the dirt. In the faint light of dawn, men were being downed like chaff to the wind. The banner remained where it had fallen, for enfilade fire was being poured out in torrents, shattering ranks, ripping into units like brimstone from heaven.

"Retrieve the colors! Retrieve the colors! C'mon, men!" Jeremiah bellowed as he scrambled toward the fallen standard.

"Somethin's wrong, Sam!" he panted over the tumultuous din. "These Yankees ain't fightin' like an army taken by surprise! Somethin' has gone wrong, I tell you!"

A shell burst overhead just as Jeremiah dove for the flag. Grasping the staff in his hands, he jumped up and waved the banner wildly. "Forward, boys! Follow me!" he yelled, but the ranks were crumbling around him, unable to withstand the barrage of shot and shell. There was confusion as the lethal fire continued to consume the soldiers in gray. Jeremiah didn't waver. "Let's go, lads! Let's go! Let's go! Let's go! Let's go!" he screamed madly.

The colors continued to flutter miraculously in his hands. Undaunted, he surged ahead against the oncoming, unending tide of blue as though he were oblivious to the bedlam around him.

Jeremiah felt an obsession, an unbridled passion for the life of his homeland. It was as though if he could just get those colors to the fort, it would staunch the flow of his country's life's blood.

"McCamey! Sergeant!" Sam shouted.

Jeremiah didn't respond. He heard the voice, heard his name called, yet felt powerless to stop as the bullets whizzed overhead and down around him.

"Sergeant!" the voice entreated. "We're in retreat, Sergeant! A retreat has been called! General Lee done ordered it himself! Our boys is caught in a murderous crossfire between the lines! We'll all die if we stay here, McCamey!"

Jeremiah wanted to scream, to say, "Then let's all die that our country might live!" but suddenly remembered words he knew General Lee to have spoken, "Life is our duty." It stopped him short. *I'm losing all sense of reason,* he thought.

He paused long enough to look around, and sum up the situation. Vast numbers of men were down on the field, as many were retreating, and others, unwilling to face the slaughterous crossfire, were surrendering.

Jeremiah turned to his men. "Boys, we'll not surrender or be taken captive, and our proud flag will remain aloft as long as I'm alive! I'll die if I must, but being taken prisoner once in this war was enough for me!"

He knew Union forces would soon surround them and to turn his men into the retreat would be signing their death warrants. He was not willing that they or their banner perish. The toll was already too great.

A small stand of trees was not far off and he began to lead his men toward the sparse cover. Reaching up, he ripped the flag from its staff, tossing the naked wooden stick aside.

"What are you doin', Sergeant?" Franklin huffed in bewilderment as Jeremiah handed him the standard.

"Savin' our colors, in case we do get caught," he gasped.

As they reached the trees, he suddenly tore his soiled, worn, gray shirt from his body. He knew they did not have long before being closed in upon, and some other Confederates had retreated to the same refuge. Firing from their cover, they watched the scene in amazement.

Breathing hard from exertion, Jeremiah handed his shirt to Franklin in exchange for the flag.

"Heaven help us, Sam!" Franklin despaired. "The sergeant's done lost his mind! Whatever he's doin', stop him!"

All at once, Jeremiah folded the colors lengthwise, wrapping them about his frame. Grabbing his shirt from Franklin, he donned it hurriedly, buttoning it tightly up against his neck to conceal the flag. "Too many boys has died for these colors, men. They deserve the honor of protection!"

Sam looked at his sergeant admirably and shook his head, grinning in spite of their desperate situation. "McCamey, you do beat all. I gotta say. You do beat all!"

"Well, let's not just stand here, boys! Join back in the fray! We've got some cover now, and unfinished work to do!"

Immediately, Jeremiah realized he no longer had his musket and the soldiers in blue were just yards from descending upon their hiding place. The Confederates were totally overwhelmed by sheer numbers, being easily surrounded and captured despite heroic fighting.

"I mean it, boys!" Jeremiah said, "I ain't about to be captured again if I can help it!" The small copse of trees was hastily being surrounded by the foe. He looked up. "Doff those muskets, men, or secure them, and save yourselves!" he yelled out, leaping from the ground and grabbing for the branch of a tree. With effort, he swung himself aloft and scrambled as high as he could get. His men climbed likewise, knowing it was a desperate move because spring had not come to fill out the foliage. Bare branches and brown remnants of last year's leaves offered little cover, yet other men taking shelter in the grove followed suit and not too soon. The paltry growth of woods was swelling with blue.

Jeremiah held his breath, hoping the furiousness of the fight would keep eyes from looking skyward. Suddenly, an artillery shell hit the tree next to him, splintering it and crashing it to the ground. Incredibly, it avoided falling on any of the enemy in its path.

No one looked up. It seemed to be an accepted fact of combat that sometimes trees fell. The blue horde continued to swarm through the wooded area, and suddenly, they were gone. The smoke started to clear and the guns tapered off. The battle was over.

Jeremiah looked at the sun. It couldn't be much past 8 A.M. He took in the panorama provided from his perch. Bodies lay scattered everywhere. Some were blue, some were gray, but there was more gray than blue and he knew at once the attack he'd looked on as a gamble had been one indeed.

The boys waited on the sergeant's lead before clambering to the ground. When Jeremiah felt it safe enough, he began to alight from his tree. It was a grim group of men that descended to the earth from their hiding places against the sky. The magnitude of the failed attack weighed heavily upon them, for they had all viewed the scene below.

Quietly, without a word spoken, the men followed the sergeant's footsteps. Things were strangely deserted; wounded and dead from neither side being collected, and the large number of Union soldiers that had passed beneath them such a short time ago seemed to have vanished into thin air.

Heading back in the direction from which they had moved that morning, it was the voice of Andy that broke the stillness hanging over them like a cloud.

"Sergeant," he asked in a small, hushed voice, "how long do you think we got?"

Jeremiah didn't say anything for several minutes, all the men unwilling to express what each fearfully felt.

"We still got spirit, boys. We got determination and our army is built on raw courage. You well enough know that. But I don't know how long these things will be sufficient in face of the odds against us. The Yankee army is endless. They got more men to keep drawin' soldiers from. Their numbers ain't gonna dwindle. For every one that dies, or is sick, that deserts, or is captured, there's two more to take his place. We ain't got that option, boys. The manpower of the South, I reckon, is pretty near depleted."

He sighed. "Add to this the fact that they're better equipped and well fed . . . well, this is the only way I know to answer your question, Andy."

They continued to trudge the distance in silence, coming upon a number of other troops straggling to the Confederate line of retreat.

Suddenly, one of their own voices startled them. "I ain't givin' up, McCamey! No sir, Sergeant. I don't care what the odds against us might be. I ain't givin' up!" Franklin cried with vengeance.

"Franklin," Sam broke in, "reckon that's how we all be or we'd have been long gone. Most of us here mean to see this through to the end, whatever it brings. We ain't got much o' nothin' else, but tenacity we abound in!"

Jeremiah was silent. *True, good men,* he thought. *We're blessed with real patriots!*

As soon as they were secure within their own lines, they sought the remainder of their company. It wasn't hard to locate Captain Kertlin, Jeremiah surmised as he came upon him. All one needed to do was listen for that deplorable cough. "Cap'n!" he cried, grateful they both had survived another fray.

The captain turned and looked at the sergeant. Jeremiah was taken aback. It had only been a matter of hours since last seeing him, but John Kertlin looked unexpectedly thin and haggard. Black powder residue was smeared across his face. He was glistening with sweat in the cool morning air, his eyes sunken and glazed and his uniform filthy. He was a haunting and pitiful sight. No doubt his part of the fight had been particularly bitter.

"Jeremiah," he grimaced in a daze, taking long, almost frantic strides to cover the space between them. The captain reached out and pulled his brother-in-law's head down to his shoulder in a brief, almost desperate display of affection.

"We've been hit hard, Jeremiah," his voice shook in anguish. The sergeant caught the captain's body trembling slightly in despair. "Many of our remaining good men are down—dead or captured. I . . . I am filled with distress, McCamey. I cannot tell you when my heart has been so grieved." He went into another fit of coughing. Jeremiah said nothing.

"I'm glad to see you well, Brother-in-law," the captain continued when his coughing was under control. "It surely is the only thing that lightens my heart this sorrowful day. But I had been told you were quite preserving this morning! In fact . . ." he laughed a feeble, wistful laugh, "there's a tale circulatin' already that you resolved to protect our flag at all costs and you resorted to . . . to wearing the colors?" his eyebrows arched, as if begging to be told the story was true.

266 ~ A Call to Honor

Jeremiah reached up, unbuttoning the high gray collar, working his fingers nimbly down the front of his shirt. Pulling it open, he revealed the standard he momentarily forgot he wore. "Yeah . . . reckon it might be true, Cap'n."

John Kertlin laughed, a deep, almost maniacal laugh born out of the despair of the day. "Bully for you, Jeremiah! Bully for you! Now, won't this be a story to tell our children and grandchildren for generations to come!"

"Yeah," Jeremiah said gravely, "providing we live through it all." He peeled the banner from around his midsection, folding it, and handing it to the captain.

John Kertlin took the flag, looking at the colors long and hard. "Jeremiah," he murmured, "if I've never told you before, I'm mighty proud I can say you're my brother-in-law. Mighty proud. Don't reckon there's a finer soldier left in all our little army."

The sergeant smiled as he buttoned up his shirt. "John, I don't rightly believe you speak the truth. All these men are soldiers to be proud of, Cap'n. Ain't none that I can claim to be better than. Truth is, all of us here be loyal to the end, Sir. Ain't no better soldier than one who does his duty with honor. Let us be proud and grateful that we serve with such men."

"Well spoken, Sergeant McCamey," he whispered. "Well spoken."

"What do we do Cap'n? Where do we go from here?"

"Dunno." His answer was punctuated with more coughing.

"Things are a mite confusing at the moment. We can't stay here in this position. I hear that General Lee may be calling for a withdrawal southward, abandoning all defenses at Petersburg. In my opinion, there is no other choice. We will soon be surrounded. But for now," he sighed, "we'll gather our dead and wounded and move back to camp to await orders."

Five days later, the command to march was received. The Army of Northern Virginia had done all it possibly could in defense of Petersburg. During the months of siege, General Lee directed the fortification of a line moving southward and several forts had been erected. The little army in gray would now move along this line of defenses in an effort to unite with General Joe Johnston and his Confederate Army of Tennessee.

As was his wont, Captain Kertlin met with his officers in order that the men might be well informed. It was a council of forlorn faces. Several attending the last meeting before the attack on Fort Stedman were absent. The cost to Company G had been high indeed.

Jeremiah felt extremely contrite as he headed back to his men. The price seemed to get greater each day and they were all so hungry. There was no relief.

Sam was waiting in anticipation, knowing when the sergeant was called to council he would return with news, or directions, or both. He had the men prepared to listen.

"Boys," Jeremiah sighed, "tomorrow we will begin moving out along the Southside Railroad line. It's the only line Grant has not secured, as you know, and there is a good chance we can avail ourselves of this line to meet up with General Johnston. Our force will then be increased enough in numbers to meet Grant head-on."

"How do we know Grant won't take the line first, Sergeant? His army is big enough now to deploy men wherever he so desires. What's to keep him away?" Andy wanted to know.

"Our best protection will be our line of fortifications that we've built to the southwest. Beyond that, well, General Lee has ordered General Pickett's division and Fitzhugh Lee's cavalry down past our defenses to Five Forks Road. Pickett has been ordered to hold the Yankees back at this junction; to hold them back at all cost. We're bein' all spread out, boys . . . once we pass the Southside line. We'll be stretched about forty miles—all our divisions, all our corps. On April 4, we will try and all converge, come together, at Amelia Courthouse. There, my friends, Lee has ordered a train-load of provisions from the storehouses in Richmond to be waitin' for us. We'll have food to eat, lads, real food!"

The men cheered. Just the thought of something to put into their bellies lifted their spirits. As the excitement died down, horses' hoofs were heard approaching the gathering. Soon, Lieutenant Moore reined up his scruffy mount. Even the poor horses were lean and in need of good fodder.

The men saluted the officer; a salute he promptly returned before dismounting from his animal.

"I am here compliments of Captain Kertlin and Colonel Hartshare, Sergeant McCamey.

"We'd held council with the colonel earlier this evening, before meeting with you sergeants, but no sooner were all of you dismissed from that meeting, than Colonel Hartshare showed up. Still there, as a matter of fact; otherwise the Cap'n would be seein' to this matter himself."

Lieutenant Moore reached for something he carried under his arm. "Colonel Hartshare has a special command for you, Sergeant McCamey. A special mission . . . if you'll just accept what I'm about to hand over to you, I'm certain you will understand."

Jeremiah reached out to have the flag placed in his hands.

"McCamey, this banner you protected at the Battle of Fort Stedman is stained with the blood of men whom have borne it before. Because of the valor and dedication you've shown toward guarding it, Colonel Hartshare requests that you and your men be given the honor of bearing the colors from this day forward . . ."

Jeremiah looked at the flag, feeling humbled. His men were silent. All knew this honor was reserved for only the most courageous, the bravest of the brave.

He stared at Lieutenant Moore. "It has no staff, Sir. I shall see that my men fashion one so it might be held high o'er our heads again."

"Remember, Sergeant, we do our duty with honor above all."

Jeremiah said nothing, but returned the salute Lieutenant Moore now gave him. He watched the officer ride off and turned to face his men. "Lads," he said, unfolding the banner, "we are now the color guard. I ripped this flag from its staff. It must be repaired and another staff fashioned. I know it's dark and late, but we've a job to do! When we march out in the mornin', this flag will be aloft! Let's get to it!"

Quickly they worked, mending the ripped edge with the aid of a knife, cutting a new staff from a sturdy, but thin branch of wood, stripping it smooth. It wasn't hard to locate a sewing needle, for the men often carried such to help patch and repair their clothes, but there was no thread and Jeremiah sent Andy to Captain Kertlin, seeking permission to pull hair from the tail of his horse.

Carefully wrapping the standard around its new staff, needle and horsehair were used to sew it tightly and securely. It was a group of satisfied soldiers, bearers of the colors, who lay their heads down for a brief rest that night.

CHAPTER TWENTY-FOUR

'Twas midnight when we built our fires.
We march at half past three.
We know not when our march shall end.
Nor care, we follow lead.

Rising when the bugle sounded, the men fell into rank quickly. They knew the days ahead promised strength—strength in number, strength in body. They moved out, aware that by nightfall Petersburg would lay in the hands of the enemy. The desperate siege of eleven months was at an end. They'd fought a hard fight; had stood steadfast, but now they could do no more. It was over.

The going was slow. The men desired to move more quickly, but hunger, weariness and illness prevented them. By late afternoon, they were forced to stop, having covered only twelve miles. The night was filled with the sounds of bombardment as the last of the Rebel forces in the city answered Yankee shells.

The following two days saw desperate action along the southwest defenses of Lee's army. April 2 found Hill's corps facing the enemy across that much-defended creek, Hatcher's Run. The fighting was hard, the musketry intense. Artillery crashed across the water and men fell.

The color guard of Company G proudly carried the flag forward, acrid smoke filling Jeremiah's lungs. Suddenly, the staff of the newly repaired banner shattered in his hands, the colors falling to the ground. He was amazed that he could hear anything above the din of battle, but from the other side of the creek came a shout of glee: "We've gotten the color bearer! He's down!"

Quick on his feet, the sergeant retrieved the fallen standard. Jumping upon the breastworks, he waved it wildly. "By gads, you've not," he bellowed, "it still flies!"

Their blood-stained battle flag whipped in the wind, snapping at will. It was tattered and it was torn, but as Jeremiah looked up at it, never had he felt such pride in making the decision he had four years earlier. *Even if it costs my life,* he thought, *just as it has Jep and Cy. It would be a good day to die.*

Battling for Virginia, protecting her soil, was his duty. Fighting for her rights was his mandate. The desire to defend true American liberty was a righteous conviction to have, and bearing the standard that stood for these freedoms was something for which he was truly prepared to make the supreme sacrifice.

The sergeant's boldness in waving their flag in the face of the enemy sparked the troops around him, causing them to rally and fight for the impossible all the harder. His own men riveted their eyes to him as they loaded, fired and reloaded their arms. They watched partly in awe, partly in fear, but all in pride. This was their sergeant and they now made up the guard of the colors! These were true sons of the South!

Soon the rush of the foe could not be contained. The stand at Hatcher's Run ended in the way of Petersburg. The last attempt to save the noble city was over, and with it, the life of their corps's commander. Heads fell and eyes filled with tears when the men learned that their general, "Little Powell," A. P. Hill, had fallen, his life given in defense of his country. Many deemed it one more nail driven into the coffin of the proud and valiant Army of Northern Virginia.

As they withdrew from their loss at Hatcher's Run, another blow jolted the men in gray. It was confirmed that the previous night, in a very confused battle, General Pickett failed in holding the Five Forks Road; the one sure route to the Southside Railroad, the only road that guaranteed them success in meeting up with General Johnston.

Now the enemy was not only behind them, but in front of them as well. The Southern men were more than tired and hungry. They were weighed down with the stark possibility of complete and utter defeat.

Hill's decimated corps tried to reorganize and continue toward Amelia Courthouse and food. No one could talk; it was as though their mouths were sealed. When the disorderly columns passed him, Captain Kertlin bore his eyes straight into Jeremiah's, and Jeremiah understood without words being said that hope was all but destroyed. The sergeant kept the unspoken words to himself, trudging next to his men, and all found it difficult to place one foot in front of the other.

Stopping at dusk to rest, some men foraged the countryside. The already stripped land yielded short and pitiful rations.

Franklin bagged a rabbit and the men shared it greedily. One was not enough to satisfy their deep, consuming hunger, and they remained silent, each afraid of his own words.

As eventide crept in, sleep was fitful. Several times Jeremiah dozed off, only to wake up again. In the deep of night, he heard a distant clamor . . . and it reminded him of that night so long ago . . . the Battle of Kernstown, the death of Cy, the arrest of General Garnett and his own foolish fears and desire to run. The memories came back to him in a flood he had to quell. The voices of the present were animated and full of emotion. He listened intently, trying to catch the far away words.

"Richmond is gone," one moaned in disbelief. "Citizens are fleeing in fear of Grant's army and portions of the city are on fire!"

"Well, the Yankees have their long sought-after prize," another spoke up in despair. "They occupy our capital!"

Jeremiah wondered if he heard right. *Could it be true our capital has fallen? If so, what could be left?* The thought was too incredible to entertain; yet deep down, he realized it was likely and felt too disturbed to sleep anymore.

He rose and stirred the embers of the evening's cook fire. There was a chill in the air of this early April morn.

Jeremiah sat down close to the warmth the flames offered. His country was dying, and there was nothing he could do; nothing that he'd not already done to keep it alive. His heart was bitterly sore and ached for his Southland.

Suddenly, Sam appeared at his side. "What's wrong, can't sleep?" asked Jeremiah.

"Somethin' disturbed me. I ain't rightly sure what. Thought I heard some noises."

"Reckon you did, Corporal," Jeremiah voiced hollowly. "I just woke up to hear some far off conversation sayin' that Richmond fell tonight."

"Is that a fact?" Sam asked without surprise. "Guess it was to be expected. McCamey . . . what do you think? Is the end so near?"

Jeremiah turned his somber gray eyes to the face of his comrade. "Don't know that I can answer that question. Facts may speak for themselves, but I'm not willin' to quit yet, Sam; I've still got fight in me! I do know that victory or defeat, no army could have fought a better fight and no country is more loved by her people. The South's sons have bled lavishly, Sam. It's our duty to just keep on keepin' on!"

Sam stroked his beard thoughtfully. "Don't know what I'll do when it's over with, McCamey. Win or lose, all this has become so much a part of me. All these boys here, you, Cap'n and Lieutenant Moore; it's like you all be my family now."

Jeremiah shook his head in understanding. "Well, Sam . . . at least tomorrow . . . tomorrow we'll be fed and perhaps things won't look so grim. And maybe . . . just maybe, those voices I heard a little while ago was wrong."

Dawn began to kiss the sky with faint colors of gold and ruby. Taking in a deep breath, Sam looked around. "You know, sometimes it's been hard seein' any beauty about us in this war, but look at this sunrise, Sergeant. S'pose it could be a hint for things to come?"

"Yeah, maybe, Sam," but his heart was not in his words.

As the men fell into rank later that morning, the news was confirmed. Richmond, that long sought-after jewel, had indeed been captured. They took it in good stride, for their minds were on one thing: reaching Amelia Courthouse and food.

In spite of their weary, hungry and decimated state, Lee's army made excellent time. The retreat was being carried off in remarkably good order as one division after another crossed the Appomattox River, the last group burning the bridge behind them.

April 4 dawned with spirits renewed and excitement once again on the faces of the boys. Not only would they be fed this day, but at last their army would be concentrated. Nearly thirty thousand men, even if they were starving men, were about to converge on Amelia Courthouse.

Rarely was Jeremiah's unit near General Lee, but with a lack of cohesiveness in the retreat, Company G became, as other units, split from their main corps. Today they were almost part of the general's movements and watched in awe as a scene unfolded before them.

Coming within easy distance of the general, the boys observed Lee mildly scolding a young officer who had donned his uniform that morning in haste. The stalwart soldier took the reprimand in silence, embarrassed by having displeased his leader. As the young man turned to go, General Lee beckoned him back. "Son, I only meant to caution you as to the duty of an officer; especially one near high commanders." He looked the boy in the eyes with a slight smile. "You must avoid anything that might look like demoralization, especially while we are retreating."

Good advice, Jeremiah decided. *I must remember those words.*

By early morning, gray troops began to pour into the little railroad town. A train had arrived with large ordnance stores and plenty of ammunition, but no provisions. Lee wearily paced up and down the line, panic-stricken at the thought of his army with no food.

"I ordered 350,000 rations to be sent from Richmond! Where are they?" he thundered in dismay to one of his officers. "The boys cannot eat bullets and gunpowder! If we're forced to wait here too long, the enemy will have a chance to gain upon us," he despaired, "and reach the Southside line before we do. That cannot be allowed to happen!"

Late that afternoon, Jeremiah sought Captain Kertlin. His men were in agony from hunger and he knew not what to tell them. He found his brother-in-law wondering aimlessly among the company, trying to rally their breaking spirits.

Starting to hail him, Jeremiah noticed he was in the throes of a violent coughing spell. He sounded wretched and looked enormously tired, almost haggard. *I'm glad 'Cilla can't see him now,* he thought dismally. *She wouldn't even know him.*

Fleeting thoughts of home and family crossed his mind. Weeks had gone by without any news. They had heard terrible stories about devastation in the valley . . . sometimes desperate thoughts made him wonder if he had a home or family left. He shook his head to erase such ideas.

"Cap'n," he called to his sister's husband.

"Jeremiah," he coughed, "well, how hungry are you today?"

The sergeant shrugged. "I'll live a bit longer . . . but John, you . . . I'm sorry, but you look terrible."

"I feel terrible," the captain replied. "Can't seem to rid myself of this obstinate cough. It's what's sappin' my energy. Hunger ain't had a chance against it. Don't think I'd feel like eatin' even if there were somethin' to eat."

Jeremiah fell in stride with him. "So, what d'ya think, Cap'n? The men is terrible disappointed. You reckon that trainload of provisions is gonna make it?"

The captain looked at the sergeant. "I was on my way to talk to you. It ain't comin', Jeremiah. Somethin' got all miscommunicated at Richmond. I reckon as things started to fall down around them there, they had their hands full. But reasons, good or bad, ain't gonna fill bellies."

"The boys is a mite dismayed, John. They'd be eatin' them ordnances if they could."

"General Lee has called on the people of Amelia County, askin' them to give what they can. He's sent out forage wagons to help feed us tonight, but tomorrow we'll head down to Danville. There's two hundred thousand rations stored there. That ain't a maybe, that's a fact. But we've wasted a day here. Let's hope Ol' Grant don't beat us to the depot."

With an intensely heavy heart, Jeremiah took the news back to his boys. Night was falling, and with it, rain. He had to confront not only hungry men, but now wet men as well.

"Sam, call 'em all together. I ain't got any news too good," he said. Plopping down on a log, he waited for the men to gather, wondering how he could again tell them there was nothing to eat. As he waited and wondered, he also thought of Captain Kertlin. Jeremiah knew he was a very sick man.

A few at a time, the boys joined him, each sitting wearily, looking as if they already knew what he had to say. Jeremiah hung his head and put his face in his hands for a few minutes before speaking.

"Boys," he addressed them, looking up in despair, "there ain't no food and no food's comin' . . . not today, leastways."

"All right, Sergeant," Andy said, "where do we go from here? What's the next thing?"

"What's another day?" Franklin sighed in fatigue.

No one smiled, but neither did they complain. The sergeant looked at their faces. "Well, ain't anybody got anything to say?" Jeremiah demanded. It was too much to expect that none of his men would grumble.

"Yeah," said Sam, "we're hungry. We're all hungry. And tired. But that ain't gonna make things happen. So we just do what we gotta do. Maybe that train will come in tonight after all; but let me remind you'ns of some advice a man once in this unit used to give us. Cy Ash was always sayin' '. . . we just do what we gotta do. Don't have to like it none.' Nobody's tellin' us to be happy about this Sergeant, but we'll just do what we gotta do."

Jeremiah smiled and nodded his head. What true words to rally 'round! *Cy*, he thought, *you may be dead all these years, but you certainly ain't gone!* "Well said, Corporal. Well said. Don't think no train's comin', but tomorrow General Lee will have us movin' down the line toward Danville. Cap'n says there is two hundred thousand rations there in the storehouses for sure." *If Grant don't get there first,* he started to add, then stopped short. The men were trying so hard to keep up their morale. No use in him destroying it with random thoughts.

After a few moments of silence, one of the boys spoke up, changing the subject. "McCamey," he said, "Cap'n don't look so good these days. He's your brother-in-law. He all right?"

Jeremiah stood, and in thought, ran a hand through his wet hair. He stared at the men. "Any of you'ns looked in a mirror lately? Don't reckon none of us look too good."

Later that night as the men tried to sleep, many hoped to indeed hear the sound of a train. The only thing that could be heard was the falling rain.

When they woke the next morning, the sky had cleared and the day promised to be good for marching. Soon the captain made an appearance.

"Men," he said, "I've come to tell you there has been a change in plans." He coughed deeply and Jeremiah could hear his chest rattle with each breath. "General Lee has ordered a train down from Danville to meet up with us at Farmville and he sent some couriers over to Lynchburg with instructions for additional provisions to be sent to Farmville. That will be our destination today, boys. But first, our job is to destroy everything here at Amelia Courthouse that the army can't take with it."

He turned to Jeremiah, coughing. "Sergeant, organize your men. The quicker we destroy all the supplies we can't take, the sooner we can move out."

"Yes, Sir, Cap'n," he saluted. "Cap'n, you said yesterday evenin' that General Lee ordered forage wagons out. My men ain't seen nothin' to eat in several days now. I was wonderin' if there was any forage . . ."

"McCamey," Captain Kertlin cut him short, "the land had nothing to give. The wagons returned with deplorably small amounts. No one's eaten." He turned and rode off.

"He mad at you 'bout somethin', Sergeant?" asked Sam.

"No, Corporal. He's just tired, sick and frustrated. C'mon. Let's help divvy the men up into units and see if we can't help ourselves. The sooner we can start movin' to Farmville, the sooner we can eat."

Before long, flames leaped to the sky as the train and all unneeded ordnances were burned. It was well into the afternoon before Lee was able to order the army off to Farmville.

"Sergeant, I sure hope we don't run into any of the enemy today. I can't think of nothin' riskier than to send our boys into battle in the state they're in; least not 'til we've eaten."

"Sam, I was thinkin' the same thing." Jeremiah glanced up at the colors he was charged with protecting. "If somethin' don't give soon, we're gonna be fallin' out by the wayside. I ain't sure just how much fortitude I got, but I reckon I'm gonna find out."

The sun went down and the men continued to move. Slowly, boys began to melt out of the ranks; some mumbling as though perhaps they'd lost their minds, others dropping in sheer exhaustion.

"McCamey!" Andy suddenly cried out in dismay. "Sergeant! One of the boys is stopped in the road; done sunk to his knees—and we can't get him up! Me and Franklin done tried!"

Jeremiah flashed his eyes at Sam. "Keep on movin', Corporal . . . I'll take care of this." Turning, he moved against the ranks, banner in hand.

Several yards to the rear was a huddled form in the road, being walked around and stumbled into by other soldiers. On his knees, supported by his rifle, the boy trembled as he cried out of control.

Kneeling next to him, Jeremiah touched him on the shoulder. "Woody," he called. "Woody. It's Sergeant McCamey. You gotta get up, Son. You'll be trampled to death if you don't."

The soldier didn't move. "Aw, c'mon, Woody . . . get up!" Jeremiah ordered in exasperation. The boy's red-rimmed and tear-filled eyes looked up at the sergeant, but he continued to cry out of control.

"Woody! I order you to get up from here!" Jeremiah lashed out at the lad. His heart ached for the boy, but he couldn't allow him to be trampled to death. "Let's go, Woody!"

Suddenly the soldier lost the support of his musket and crumpled to the ground. "Andy! Franklin! Help me!" Jeremiah cried.

The two boys were immediately at his side, fighting against the tide of men on the march. "He ain't gettin' up, fellas. We gotta move him. I can't do it by myself."

The three were able to lift the fallen soldier, placing him gingerly on the side of the road. He'd stopped shaking and was no longer crying, but his breath came in irregular gasps.

"Well, what we gonna do, Sergeant? Can't just leave him here."

"We ain't got no choice, Franklin," Jeremiah looked around, gesturing to the many men whose strength at last had failed them. The roadside was littered with tattered, broken forms unable to continue. "He . . . he ain't alone," the sergeant choked.

Making his way back to Sam in front of the line, Jeremiah suddenly heard sporadic firing from the rear. The men, jumpy in their exhausted state, fearfully shot at shadows, some at each other. Jeremiah felt their whole army was coming unraveled.

Through the long night, they marched on. Federal cavalry, in small units, began to harass them, causing a rift in the ranks.

Company G was among the last of the cohesive units. Behind them, as they crossed over Saylers Creek, the gap widened.

By late afternoon, as the first of the troops came within an hour or two of at last being fed, those to the rear became involved in a fray. As the units behind the gap crossed Saylers Creek, a complete force of enemy cavalry cornered them.

The cannon and musket fire came in furious rounds. A full third of the Army of Northern Virginia was under attack.

The men gathered, their march slowed, waiting for news of the fighting. General Lee rode his horse to the rear, waiting with the men of Company G. He appeared haggard and anxious, but always composed as he trotted up and down the lines.

By twilight, stragglers from the bloody combat began to find their way back to their army. Whipped and reeling from the blow, the bedraggled warriors were in a panic and General Lee's composure nearly broke.

Suddenly he reined up next to Sam and Jeremiah. The boys could see tears glistening in his eyes and heard the words he uttered as if in prayer: "My God! Has this army been dissolved?" The compassion for his beaten men was great.

Unexpectedly, General Lee turned and looked at Jeremiah. Quickly reaching down, he grabbed the colors from his hands and riding to and fro among the disheartened soldiers, held the battle flag aloft. His composure regained, he rallied the men and soothed them with gentle words.

Jeremiah knew he would remember the moment for the rest of his life.

There was little sleep that night, but the next morning the first food the Confederates had seen in a week was found in Farmville as promised. At dawn, an initial group of men began to get fed, and midmorning found Company G drawing rations, cooking up corn pone and bacon, even boiling a handful of dried beans.

"I don't know when I've felt so much like I'm feastin' as a king," Jeremiah remarked between mouthfuls of cornbread and pork. "Them beans smell fine cookin', too!"

"I guarantee no king ever set his plate with pone and bacon," joked Sam, "but then, reckon I ain't no king, so this here food is fine with me!"

"Any food is fine with me," Andy declared, "fit for a king or a fool or anyone else! Fellas, I hope never to be this hungry again!"

"I truly thought we were going to die from starvation," Franklin summed up for them all.

As they began to dish out their beans and scoop them into their mouths, there was a great commotion behind them. Suddenly, the rail cars closed up and began to chug down the tracks.

"Hey!" Franklin cried out in rage, "some o' the boys ain't got their rations! I mean those who ain't made it into Farmville. What in tarnation these people think they're doin'?"

Captain Kertlin appeared among his company, walking his mount at a brisk gait. "Cap'n!" Franklin called out indignantly, "what about those men ain't been fed yet? What's goin' on?"

"Franklin, my boy," he said, "there's real trouble. We gotta get out o' here! High Bridge over the Appomattox River failed to get burned after General Gordon's boys crossed it last night." He coughed long and hard, finally catching his breath. "So, guess who's crossing now? That's right," he said sarcastically, "Mr. Grant's army. His well fed and much larger army, I might add.

"General Lee is orderin' the cars on down the track. We'll try to meet up with 'em again so we can finish feedin' all the boys.

"Sergeant McCamey," he ordered, "get your men ready to move out." He headed on down the ranks.

"All right boys, you got the captain's orders. Count yourselves blessed that you've been among those able to eat.

"Cap'n," he called after his brother-in-law, "hold up."

Captain Kertlin reined in his horse, looking down at Jeremiah.

"You eat somethin' yet?" the sergeant asked.

The captain shook his head. "I was plannin' on eatin' after all you boys was fed." He looked over at the now empty track. "But I can wait." He took a deep breath and rattled off another spell of coughing.

Jeremiah reached out, taking a piece of loose harness in his hands. "Please, John," he spoke quietly, "please, eat somethin'. Let me share my portion with you. We got some rations cooked up."

John Kertlin stared at his brother-in-law. "Will that make you so happy, Jeremiah?"

"Yes, Cap'n, it would."

"Will you lay off my case, then?"

"Probably not . . ."

"That's what I figured. If it will please you so much, bring 'em on. I'll eat as soon as I get a chance."

The men began to move out quickly, heading west. General U. S. Grant entered Farmville that afternoon.

The ragged, tattered, worn-out column of Confederates marched on into the night. More rations for them had arrived at Appomattox Station, twenty-two miles away. Lee was determined his men should reach them before the enemy.

Suddenly, out of the blackness surrounding them, a white flag of truce appeared, borne by a small entourage of boys in blue. Quickly galloping by, it was learned they carried a message for General Lee. A message sent from U. S. Grant.

Hearts stood fearful and still, but the soldiers' feet bore on as the sun rose and the day dawned bright and warm. Soon they would reach Appomattox Station and more food.

"What do you suppose that message sent to General Lee was about?" Andy questioned as their feet plodded along.

"I'm sure," said Sam, "he must be wantin' a surrender . . . General Grant, I mean, and surely to goodness, if General Lee proffered one, we'd know by now. I ain't ready to give up, boys! I ain't ready!" he said with determination and grief.

"I ain't neither!" Jeremiah voiced. "As long as we got any kind o' chance, we gotta see things through!" But he was uneasy.

By nightfall, the men were closing in on Appomattox Station. It was now but a few miles away. Suddenly, the sound of cannon was heard and the men looked at each other with anxious eyes. It didn't last long and there was a question as to whether it was enemy fire or their own artillery, which had been sent up ahead.

"Now, what do you suppose that was?" Sam asked in apprehension. A flurry of activity began to take place among the officers.

Jeremiah's ears were alerted to the sound of a horse's hoofs coming up from behind. "Reckon we're about to find out," he said disquietingly, craning his neck to look down the long line behind them.

Captain Kertlin pulled up next to the color guard. "McCamey," he said, his horse skittish in anticipation, "I'm not sure what it was we just heard, but reports are being passed that the enemy is extremely close. Be prepared, in case there is need of a night attack."

"Yes, Sir, Cap'n," the address barely left his lips.

"My word," the Captain suddenly gulped in alarm, "would you look at that?"

Jeremiah didn't have the visual advantage the captain did from his horse, but in seconds, the cause of his alarm appalled and paralyzed them all.

On the horizon, the sky was lit up as though hundreds of fireworks had exploded. Thousands of twinkling orange lights indicated campfires ahead . . . and all the men knew it was no Confederate camp.

The reports came in quickly. General Sheridan and his Yankee cavalry had beaten Lee to the punch. The Union Army now stood between the Southern men and their life sustaining provisions, between the Army of Northern Virginia and their last hope of heading southward to meet up with General Johnston.

The gray columns suddenly stopped and stood stock still as the command to halt filtered down the line.

Captain Kertlin returned to the head of his company. "We'll rest here tonight and wait for the sun to rise. We'll then better be able to ascertain our position." He turned to Jeremiah, "There may yet be a fight that we can win . . ." he paused, ". . . or lose."

When the sun next rose on the Army of Northern Virginia, it was April 9, 1865. Palm Sunday. About 5 A.M., Georgia's General Gordon was to lead an assault against Sheridan's Union cavalry. If it was only cavalry, the Confederates might stand a chance of breaking through and the rest of the men would be called on to join the offensive. If infantry supported Sheridan, there would be little left that the troops in gray could do.

Captain Kertlin's men listened to the sound of the guns from their position along the road on which they'd slept. They waited for word, in the cool of the dawn, to join the attack, fearful the command wouldn't come, dreading that it would.

"The firin' don't sound too furious, Sergeant," Andy whispered in the early light as though to speak up might break some unknown spell.

"Yeah . . . dunno if that's good or bad," Jeremiah commented. "We get ordered to move in, it means we got a chance to break through . . . get our rations and move on to meet Johnston."

"And if we don't," Sam added, "it means there's nowhere left to go."

"But if we do get the command to join the attack," Franklin reminded them, "how much can we stand? Some of us still ain't had much to eat, we've been marchin' for near a week with little rest and we're outnumbered . . . greatly outnumbered . . ." he shook his head, "but I'd rather go down fightin', boys!"

No one else spoke for the sound of combat began to diminish, and the four boys looked at each other, wide-eyed with trepidation. Things were quiet now and a deathly pall hung in the early morning air.

They turned around at the sound of deep coughing. Captain Kertlin sauntered up, crouching among the tense and anxious boys. Glancing at him, Jeremiah rested his head upon the staff of the flag he carried. His brother-in-law reached out and slapped him on the back a couple of times, an unusual display of affection in front of the other men, but he wasn't smiling.

"You seem to be feelin' a mite better this mornin', Cap'n" he said.

"Reckon I might be if I weren't so pained in spirit," he responded grimly. "General Lee sent forth a communiqué to General Grant this mornin'. Colonel Hartshare says Lee desires to arrange a meeting to discuss peace . . . come to some terms without surrender . . . but that was before we tested the Yankee position this mornin'. Don't reckon we'll be goin' in, boys. Sheridan's got a whole corps of infantry behind him."

Suddenly, Lieutenant Moore appeared among them. "Cap'n," he cried excitedly, "we've been ordered to fall into rank and form our brigade on the field! No one seems to understand what's happenin', but General Lee just left, all decked out in his finest of uniforms. He's goin' to meet with Ol' Grant. I reckon he plans to try to talk peace, but we're to be ready if terms cannot be reached."

"What time is it, Lieutenant?" Captain Kertlin wanted to know.

Lieutenant Moore pulled a watch from his pocket. "A little after eight-thirty, Cap'n."

Captain Kertlin jumped to his feet. "All right boys . . . forward the colors! Organize your men, and forward the colors, McCamey! It ain't over 'til it's over!" he cried.

On the field, they waited. And waited. And waited. Sporadic shooting took place and a flag of truce, having been directed by Lee, was sent out to tell his men to halt any firing. Soon, General Lee returned to his quarters. Grant declined the requested meeting and Lee learned that he left orders for one of his corps to attack the Confederates.

The men in gray withdrew slowly. There seemed to be an unspoken joint effort with the enemy to control the shedding of blood. Another Union courier arrived with a note for General Lee. It agreed that an hour-long truce be recognized. Lee, now knowing full well that his army was completely surrounded, sent another note to Grant, requesting a second meeting.

It was nearly 12 P.M. General Lee headed for the settlement of Appomattox Courthouse once again. On the field, his men continued to wait. The color guard of Company G huddled together, but few words were exchanged during the long passage of time. An agony, a pall, seemed to have settled over the ranks. It was so oppressive the boys felt it bearing down upon them.

It was close to 5 P.M. before an agonized Lee returned to his faithful and courageous little army. Jeremiah could see his face well and knew from the lines etched on it, from the glaze in his eyes, that it was over. Even before he heard the words, his vision dimmed with tears.

Great anxiety caused many men to call out and Jeremiah heard his own voice among them. "General Lee, are we surrendered?"

Lee fought to maintain self control as he addressed his men telling them the news they both feared and yet knew. The Army of Northern Virginia had yielded. The soldiers would soon be heading home. Their war was over.

Many began weeping. They gathered around their white crowned leader, clasping his hands, crying out their devotion, their willingness to fight on. They reached out to touch their general, to assure him of their undying loyalty.

General Lee's eyes watered with tears as he watched the despairing bedlam about him.

"Blow, Gabriel, blow!" one soldier cried in utter grief. "My God . . . I'm ready to die."

Jeremiah was unashamed as tears filled his eyes and streamed down his face. They'd fought so hard, so long and had overcome so much. But there was nothing more they could do. He gazed at the banner he'd tried so faithfully to protect and gripped it tightly, his knuckles turning white as he tried to control his trembling; an effect of unrendered sobs.

Glancing at his men, he saw others crying. Sam, always an emotional bulwark, was unable to keep a tear from etching down each cheek. Andy, dry eyed, appeared dazed, as if in shock. Franklin kneeled on the ground, head in hands. "No, no, no, no," he uttered over and over.

Jeremiah watched as Captain Kertlin drove his sword bitterly into the ground and broke off the blade. Falling to his knees, seeming lost, the captain wept. It was the first time, Jeremiah believed, that he'd seen John Kertlin break down and cry. It made his own tears come all the harder.

Some men embraced each other for comfort. Others bashed their muskets against nearby trees. They had hoped . . . they had all hoped.

General Lee fought to maintain his own composure as he once again addressed the men. "You should all be paroled within two days; as soon as arrangements can be made for a formal surrender," he said. "Until then, we are all prisoners of 'those people.' Grant is giving us twenty-five thousand rations, so you will all eat." The white headed general hung his head. "I wish there had been any other way," he sighed.

Looking back up, he continued. "Break rank, soldiers. We will all be encamped here until our capitulation is complete." He took one last look at the devoted men. "I would have rather died a thousand deaths," his voice cracked in emotion.

As General Lee turned to take leave of them, Jeremiah was besieged by memories. He thought of the day four years earlier, when he realized he could only go the way of Virginia; only fight for the South, defending the wellspring of American Liberty. He remembered Cy's words on the day of his parting: "Do it, Jeremiah; do it for what your people believe in!" Cy had been right; there was "plainly nothing to think through."

"How wise, my friend," he sighed in a whisper, "how wise."

Jep . . . oh, hot-headed Jeptha! The years of war certainly changed him before he was required to make the supreme sacrifice. He could again hear his comrade's words as he viewed their colors before making that final charge at Gettysburg: "What a lovely sight for which to be willing to die!" *Oh, I am glad that he was willing,* thought Jeremiah. *It made the pain so much easier to bear.*

Killian and Drew; what had become of them? Poor Woody left lingering at the side of the road?

Sam, Franklin, Andy; the other men he'd had the privilege of serving with . . . well, they'd all be going home now. And Cap'n. *'Cilla, your husband is finally returning to you.*

Suddenly he reached up and felt the locket about his neck. "Well, Katie Melinda . . ." he whispered, "I've no right to wear this any longer." Jeremiah undid the clasp. Popping open the silver oval, he touched her lock of hair. "But I did promise to return it to you or die with it on." He snapped it closed and placed the chain gently in his pocket.

His family. How were they? Were the terrible stories they had heard true? Oh, surely not! Did his father ever make his way home? Or was there at least some word of him? He'd know before much longer. The questions created a storm in his mind.

"McCamey!" Sam admonished him, "Where are you? This is the third time I've called to you! I see you standin' there, but you sure ain't hearin' me!"

"Oh . . . sorry; sorry Sam. I was kinda lost in thought," he said sadly.

"Let's get a fire built, Sergeant, before it gets dark. With the sun goin' down, it's a mite chilly, especially for a Palm Sunday."

"Yeah, Sam. Good idea," he responded, unsure the chill they felt was caused by the evening air.

"From what General Lee said," Sam continued, "we oughta be havin' some fresh rations doled out for to cook fair soon."

Sam was right. The rations came and now no one would be hungry. As they ate their food, Captain Kertlin joined the men around the fire.

Military formality seemed suspended and the camp was quiet except for the sound of a harmonica playing mournfully in the distance. Conversation was hushed, laughter sporadic.

"I've brought my rations to cook and eat with you boys. Does that not please you, McCamey?" the captain asked with fond sarcasm.

"It sure does, Cap'n. You sound a mite . . ."

Jeremiah's statement was interrupted by the captain's hacking cough.

"Never mind. You don't sound no better at all."

"But I do feel better, McCamey. Havin' a little food in my belly has made me feel better, if not sound better. I humbly admit you were right."

"What you wanna reckon these here vittles is probably some of our own rations what was captured this mornin'?" Sam speculated absent-mindedly, not knowing he spoke the truth.

Captain Kertlin looked around at his men as he prepared his food. "Well, Corporal," he asked Sam, "what you reckon you'll be doin' now this unpleasantness is over?"

Sam shrugged his shoulders. "Guess I'll go to my Uncle's place in Charlottesville. Take my Ma back to our own home. It's hard to think about."

"Franklin?" the captain directed the question to him.

"Dunno, Cap'n," he sighed heavily. "I ain't been able to get passed today."

"Anderson?"

"Get my banjo restrung," Andy replied, thinking of how it had been stringless for some time, an insignificant victim of the war.

Captain Kertlin put his head back and sighed, erupting in another fit of hacking. All were silent, each reluctant to speak of the bitter, heart wrenching events of the day.

Finally, Jeremiah broke the solemn spell. "You know, it's like wakin' from a nightmare to find yourself involved in another nightmare. The nightmare of war may be over for us, but will the nightmare of defeat prove greater?"

No one could answer the question.

The captain rubbed his forehead, deep in thought. "Don't know what kind of life we'll go back to, boys. One thing is for sure. None of our lives will ever be the same and I reckon it depends on what Mr. Lincoln has in mind for us."

"Hear, hear," Franklin retorted, "there's the trick!"

"You're more right than you know," the captain replied. "I was just rememberin' about some things. Back at the Military Institute, we had to take all kinds o' classes on things. One year we studied governments— political matters and such. We had to learn and memorize recent speeches of those in the political arena." He laughed. "You know what one of those speeches was? Some talk Mr. Lincoln gave to the state convention of his party back in 1857. Can you believe that? I like what parts of it said, though. I found complete truth in a few sentences. S'pose the best of us can be deceived, huh? Let's if I can remember them.

"'. . . the government, with its institutions, belongs to the people who inhabit it. Whenever they shall grow weary of the existing government, they can exercise their constitutional right of amending it, or their revolutionary right to dismember and overthrow it . . .'"

"Seems to me we done spent the last four years tryin' to exercise some o' the very rights he claimed we had, now don't it?" Franklin spat out. "Well, he sure done changed his mind on us."

"Yeah," the captain agreed, "except we haven't been tryin' to overthrow the United States government, just tryin' to throw its yoke off us, off the South. That's why I feel so much uncertainty about the future, boys. This ain't gonna be easy. A man that changes his mind so don't really know what he believes to start with, now does he? And those of us that's fought for our rights, well, I reckon we'll be considered offensive traitors. Villainous usurpers; and we ain't the ones who've done the usurpin'! Any you boys hear tell of General Cleburne?"

"Patrick Cleburne? Didn't he get killed in the fightin' 'round Franklin, Tennessee?" Sam wanted to know. "Or was it Nashville?"

"Franklin, Sam. Yeah, that's him all right. Well, he was no fool, boys. He was a fine courageous leader . . . and I hear tell he offered some advice a while back. Irving Buck, his adjutant, is from the valley. Front Royal to be exact. He's been an acquaintance of mine for quite a while and not too long after the tragic death of the general, passed a very wise thought of Cleburne's on to me. Reckon we'd all do best to take it to heart, now things is over; or gonna be."

"Well, what did he say, Cap'n?" Jeremiah demanded. "What did General Cleburne have to say?"

"He said, 'Surrender means that the history of this heroic struggle will be written by the enemy; that our youth will be trained by Northern school teachers; will learn from Northern books their version of this war; will be impressed by all the influences of history and education to regard our gallant dead as traitors, our maimed veterans as fit subjects for derision.' Well, we're those veterans now. Remember those words, boys. Our very honor, the very heritage we leave behind, will depend on it."

Two days later, April 12, 1865, the surrender of the Army of Northern Virginia was made complete.

General Lee, too distraught to attend the last rites of his noble army, addressed the men. They stood, listening, hanging on to his every word:

"After four years of arduous service, marked by unsurpassed courage and fortitude, the Army of Northern Virginia has been compelled to yield to overwhelming numbers and resources. I had no choice but to surrender, or else waste more lives that are more precious to me than my own. The terms have been generous and I pray that a merciful God will show you the same generosity in days to come. With an unceasing admiration of your constancy and devotion to your country, and a grateful remembrance of your kind and generous consideration of myself, I bid you an affectionate farewell."

He then retreated into his tent for the remainder of the day.

The boys plodded slowly, with feet made of lead, to attend to the actual motions of surrender: stacking arms and relinquishing flags. General Gordon headed the long gray column in silence. There was no sound but the sound of their feet, for they knew it was the funeral of their once great army they were attending.

"Ain't that Colonel Joshua Chamberlain?" Sam whispered to Jeremiah as they came upon the ranks in blue. "The one who beat our troops at the Battle of Little Round Top, way back yonder in Gettysburg?"

Jeremiah squinted in the sunlight, searching the face. "Reckon it is," he said, "'cept it appears he's a general now."

As the gray ranks drew up along the blue, gasps were audible. The Confederates' former foe were not prepared for the sight that greeted them; wretched, ragged, emaciated men; brigades thinned to the size of companies. Yet flags were held high as defiance, tempered with submission, flashed in their Southern eyes.

General Gordon was weighed down with sorrow as he led the men forward. Suddenly, a bugle sounded, ordering the Union men to rigid attention. The call commanded them to shift their muskets from order arms to carry arms. It was a soldier's salute.

At the sound of altering arms, General Gordon understood the meaning. Veneration. The Yankees were saluting them with honor. He raised his head higher, sitting straighter and prouder as he veered his mount about. Eloquently, he dropped his sword to the toe of his boot, signaling complete surrender. He then ordered the Confederates to pass their former foe in like manner, that honor might speak to honor as the proud men in gray stacked arms, relinquished cartridge boxes and laid their flags enmasse.

As Jeremiah stepped up to heap his banner on the pile, he hesitated. He'd been charged with protecting that standard. It was stained with the blood of his comrades. How could he set it down and walk away?

He caught the sob in his throat before it escaped, but he couldn't stop the flow of tears. They were for everyone who had given a life that their country might live.

Unfurling the edge of the banner, he buried his face in the flag he loved. *Now,* he thought, *it is stained with my tears as well.* Finally, he dropped it on the red mound and moved on. Looking about, he realized there were few dry eyes among any of the men gathered, including their former enemy in blue.

At some point, it was over. No one knew how long it took, but over twenty-six thousand paroles were issued. The men were free to go and they would all be heading in different directions.

Sam shook his sergeant's hand, but it turned into a quick embrace instead. "Well, Sergeant . . . I'll be seein' you in the future. You can count on that, like it or not. Reckon you've been 'bout the best friend I ever had."

"Take care, Sam. I'll look forward to the day."

Sam shuffled his feet hesitantly. "Well . . . good-bye, then," he said at last, turning to leave.

"God bless you, Sam," Jeremiah whispered to his comrade.

The corporal turned briefly, threw out his hand in a final wave and was gone.

As Captain Kertlin made rounds among the company, Jeremiah exchanged last thoughts and farewells with his own men.

Suddenly, he was clapped on the back. Turning, he looked into the Captain's flushed face and fevered eyes. Coughing, he held his war weary horse by the reins.

"C'mon, Jeremiah. Let's go," he said quietly. "I want to see my wife."

"Yeah, John, let's go. Maybe my Pa has come home by now."

The Confederate Army had one last march to make. Through the pages of history and down the annals of time, they marched into legend and immortality.

EPILOGUE

And 'though we weep 'tis for those braves
Who stood in proud array,
Beneath our flag and boldly died
While wearing of the gray.

The old man stood on the knoll, looking out at the sweeping view before him. The hills continued to roll gently, and as always, hues of green and blue dappled the panorama. Its magnificence had not changed.

A breeze blew wisps of white hair into his eyes and true to custom when deep in thought, he ran a hand through it. Though white, it still abound, and he wondered if his own father would have had such thick, unruly hair in very old age.

His father. No one had seen or heard from him again after that clash at Piedmont and the man often pondered on it, for surely the older soldier lay in some plot of earth *Sine Nomine* . . . name unknown.

The scenery had changed, even if the view had not. A small scattering of houses, even some town dwellings, now dotted what once had been pure farmland. His own earth.

He felt profoundly grateful to his grandchildren for catering to his whim. Just one last time . . . one last time, he wanted . . . needed . . . to see his beloved old homestead.

Lost in thought, echoes from the past hammered at him, assaulting his mind. It had been difficult after the war; so very hard. Nothing had been left of their land, the valley utterly destroyed; every house, every dwelling ashes on the ground; all crops consumed by fire and each animal confis-

290 ~ A Call to Honor

cated or killed. Even farm implements and fences had been removed. The men returning to such loss had their citizenship stripped as well.

Suddenly, a small hand grabbed his old gnarled one, jolting him back to reality. "Great-Grandpa, can we go now?" the wee voice whined.

With the aid of his cane, he stooped and looked into the child's bright eyes.

"Are you telling me I'm a *great* grandpa or calling me your Great-Grandpa?" his face cracked in a smile.

She laughed; a small, tinkling, familiar laugh. "You're silly, Great-Grandpa," she giggled again.

"Oooo, what's this?" she asked, staring at a granite slab covered with brush and weed. "It's old!"

Still stooping, he turned and faced the marker, reaching out to pull the vine and scrub from it. His legs ached, so he settled on his knees and her small hand reached out to help him, pulling vigorously at the growth.

"Why are people buried up here, Great-Grandpa?" she demanded. "There's no church around."

He didn't answer, but stared at the stone they cleared, remembering an ancient promise to a friend.

"JEP-THA HAM-IL-TON CAR-ROLL," the little girl's voice pronounced each syllable of the name carefully. "See, I can read real good, Great-Grandpa!"

But he couldn't hear. His eyes were closed and he was on Cemetery Ridge again. He saw Jep's determined grin as he carried the colors forward, intense pride on the young face. What was that wonderful poem written after the war? It had always made him think of his beloved comrade. He couldn't remember all of the words . . .

> *Furl that banner for 'tis weary*
> *Round its staff 'tis drooping dreary . . .*
> *Furl it, fold it, it is best*
> *. . . Furl it, hide it, let it rest*
>
> *Take that banner down, 'tis tattered*
> *Broken is its staff, and shattered . . .*
>
> *Furl it for the hands that grasped it*
> *And the hearts that fondly clasped it*
> *Cold and dead are lying low . . .*

For though conquered, they adore it
Love the cold dead hands that bore it
Weep for those who fell before it.

Furl that banner softly, slowly
Treat it gently, it is holy
For it droops above the dead . . .

He thought of Kernstown and the death of Cy, of Malvern Hill, when aiding the enemy as well as their own. He remembered Chancellorsville and the tragic loss of General Jackson. He vividly recalled Gettysburg and the inferno of The Wilderness, Spotsylvania and their starving forms at Amelia Courthouse. He sighed, thinking of the death of their country at Appomattox. How courageous the men in gray had been; how duty and honor bound. And how pitiful those remaining in the service of their Southland at the end.

"Great-Grandpa, don't cry!" the child suddenly voiced in alarm. Her small fingers gingerly wiped the tears from his eyes . . . tears he was unaware were falling. Throwing her arms about his neck and nuzzling her head on his shoulder, she hugged him tightly, but gently. "I love you Great-Grandpa Jeremiah," she whispered.

Smiling, he placed his arms around her, drawing her close, then slowly stood. She grasped his hand again, tucking her fingers into his. Turning, he looked at her. How much she looked like her namesake, her Great-Grandma. The world had changed so much in the past sixty-five years. He could never make her understand that history was slowly painting a different picture from what he knew to be the truth. He had tried to be a good citizen of the reunited nation . . . whole, but not healed; yet one thing bothered him.

He looked the young girl again in the eyes. "Katie-Lin," he said, "don't ever let anyone tell you there is shame in being Southern. There is nothing disgraceful about hailing from the South. And you must pass this down to your own children and grandchildren one day. Your heritage is righteous and honorable. Stand firm, and *never* let anyone tell you different!"

The child nodded her head. *Perhaps too young to really understand,* he decided.

They turned, hand in hand, to walk back down the knoll and she took her breath in quickly. "Oh, Great-Grandpa Jeremiah!" she whispered in awe. "Isn't the sunset beautiful? I love this land."

He grinned. Maybe she isn't too young, after all.

"Deo Vindice" he whispered. "Deo Vindice."

CHAPTER VERSE CREDITS

Prologue: "The Bonnie Blue Flag," words by Harry McCarthy

Chapter 1: "Everybody's Dixie," words by General Albert Pike

Chapter 2: "The Homespun Dress," words by Carrie Sinclair, 1862

Chapter 3: "The Soldiers' Farewell" (aka "It Is My Country's Call"), words by Harry McCarthy

Chapter 4: "The Soldiers Farewell" (aka "It is My Country's Call"), words by Harry McCarthy

Chapter 5: "The South Shall Rise Up Free," words by John Hill Hewitt

Chapter 6: "The Young Volunteer," words by John Hill Hewitt

Chapter 7: "The Soldiers' Farewell" (aka "It Is My Country's Call"), words by Harry McCarthy

Chapter 8: "Stonewall's Requiem," words by M. Deeves

Chapter 9: "Stonewall Jackson's Way," words by John W. Palmer

Chapter 10: "The Bowld Sojer Boy," words by Samuel Lover

Cahpter 11: "The Rebel Soldier," traditional

Chapter 12: "Stonewall's Requiem," words by M. Deeves

Chapter 13: "The Bonnie Blue Flag," words by Harry McCarthy

Chapter 14: "Maryland, My Maryland," words by James Ryder Randolph

Chapter 15: "Ye Cavaliers of Dixie," words by Benjamin Porter

Chapter 16: "Stonewall's Requiem," words by M. Deeves

Chapter 17: "Long Ago," words by J. M. Carmichael

Chapter 18: "The Bonnie Blue Flag," words by Harry McCarthy

Chapter 19: "Long Ago," words by J. M. Carmichael

Chapter 20: "Long Ago," words by J. M. Carmichael

Chapter 21: "Hood's Old Brigade," words by Mollie E. Moore

"Ridin' A Raid"

"Do They Miss Me At Home," words by Catherine Mason, 1851

"The North Carolina War Song"

Chapter 22: "Ye Cavaliers of Dixie," words by Benjamin Porter

Chapter 23: "Ye Cavaliers of Dixie," words by Benjamin Porter

Chapter 24: "Hood's Old Brigade," words by Mollie E. Moore

Epilogue: "Wearing of the Gray"

"The Conquered Banner," words by Father A. Ryan, 1866

Thank you, Bobby Horton